THE LIVES BEFORE US

THE
LIVES BEFORE
US

Juliet Conlin

BLACK & WHITE PUBLISHING

First published 2019
by Black & White Publishing Ltd
Nautical House, 104 Commercial Street
Edinburgh, EH6 6NF

1 3 5 7 9 10 8 6 4 2   19 20 21 22

ISBN: 978 1 78530 230 5

A CIP catalogue record for this book is available from the British Library.

Typeset by Iolaire Typesetting, Newtonmore
Printed and bound by CPI Group (UK) Ltd, Croydon, CR0 4YY

The Exile's trade is: hoping.
  – Bertolt Brecht, 1943

April 1939

ESTHER

Late in the evening, Esther Niermann sits on the bed in her parents' spare room, trying to read a book, vaguely aware of the sound of an argument the upstairs neighbours are having. Her daughter Anneliese lies asleep in her cot; two brown leather suitcases are by the door, packed and ready for the journey.

For the hundredth time, Esther puts her book aside and checks the travel documents: train tickets, exit visas, passport, tickets for the ship. She is half-fearing, half-hoping the documents aren't complete; that somewhere between here and Genoa, where she and Anni will board the ship, her journey will be interrupted due to a smudged stamp or a missing form, and that she will be able to come home again and say to her parents, 'See, I did try, but they wouldn't let me leave.' And if she didn't have the responsibility for Anneliese – for Anneliese's future – that is exactly what she would do.

She gets up and crosses to the window. Outside, a young girl carrying a coal scuttle walks across the courtyard. Esther recognises her – Lotte Kühnel, who lives with her family two floors below. Lotte glances up, holds Esther's look for a moment and then drops her head with a scowl. Esther steps back and tries to calm herself. She closes her eyes but that only brings a sickening sense of vertigo. She wants this evening to pass quickly. She wants it never to end.

There is a quiet knock at the door and her mother Leah comes in, bringing with her the lingering dark aroma of the cholent stew they had for dinner. Made with non-kosher rabbit – beef or mutton can only be obtained on the black market at exorbitant prices – although her parents pretend otherwise. Leah nods, smiles and goes over to where Anneliese sleeps. She looks at her silently for a long time and then says, her voice breaking slightly, '*Mayn kleyn malekh.*' My little angel.

Esther's heart thumps so irregularly she is afraid she might be sick. She sits back down on the bed and waits for her pulse to settle. 'I'll send for you, Mutti,' she says. 'You and Papa. As soon as Anni and I get there, I'll –'

Leah shakes her head. 'Papa and I aren't going anywhere. Our home is here, on Wittelsbacherstraße, for better or worse.'

Her face betrays her attempt at lightness. She looks to have aged ten years over the recent months. Her hair, long since grey, has thinned alarmingly, hinting at patches of dull pink scalp. In an unconscious gesture, Esther lifts her hand to her own head, then lets it drop back onto her lap. 'They'll come for him, Mutti. Sooner or later.' It comes out as a low, desperate growl.

Leah waves her hand dismissively. 'No. He's a war hero. He fought for his country and they will leave him alone. We just have to keep our wits about us and wait.'

'It'll only get worse. You know that. Otherwise you wouldn't be sending us away.'

There is the sound of a shout, followed by a cry, from the flat above. They both look up at the ceiling.

'Please, let's not argue,' Leah says. She sits down beside Esther. 'Here.' She takes a folded piece of paper from her pocket and presses it into Esther's palm. 'He is there. In Shanghai.'

'Who?' Esther begins to unfold the paper, but her mother lays her hand over Esther's.

'It's Aaron's address. I spoke to his aunt Sara; she gave it to me.' She looks up at Esther. 'See if you can find him there.'

At the mention of Aaron's name, Esther's earlier sense of vertigo crashes over her in a fresh wave of dizziness. How much more will she have to bear tonight? She bites down on her lip. 'Mutti, I . . .'

'Shhh, don't say anything. It doesn't matter now.' Leah taps Esther's hand gently. 'It would make me happy to know that you will not be completely alone. Out there.'

Esther swallows. She forces herself to nod.

'And you will write to us as soon as you arrive.'

'Of course, Mutti.'

Leah gets to her feet. 'Now I must let you sleep. You have an early start tomorrow.' She bends over the cot and kisses Anneliese softly on the forehead. The child stirs but doesn't wake. 'Well, goodnight,' she says quietly and leaves the room.

Esther stares down at the folded-up paper in her hand, her eyes thick with tears. Above her, a voice shouts, a door slams shut.

KITTY

Kitty Blume uses the nail scissors to cut a small opening in the pad. Carefully, she teases out a small wad of cotton wool and places it to the side. The two thin gold chains fit in nicely; the string of pearls – her mother's – is trickier. She works the pearls along the inside of the towel with the tips of her fingers until they are positioned more or less evenly. When the cotton wool is back in place and the opening stitched up, she adds a few drops of red ink to the surface of the towel and hooks it onto the sanitary belt. It will be uncomfortable, but best not to take any chances. She places it on top of the clothes she will wear tomorrow for the journey and slips into bed.

The flat is eerily quiet. Resi, the girl with whom she shares the grubby lodgings in the Naschmarkt, is at work and won't be back before dawn. Kitty plans to be long gone from Vienna by then. She switches off her bedside lamp and the room falls into darkness. The heavy, moth-eaten velvet drapes, bought second-hand, are designed to keep the daylight out and absorb any noises from the street below. But now, at night, they give the low-ceilinged room a funereal feel, hanging there like oversized bat wings. Although she can barely see them in the dark, Kitty turns away to face the wall. If she manages to fall asleep now, she will get five hours. Her train leaves from Vienna Südbahnhof at six fifteen in the morning, and then it will be another gruelling twelve hours before the train arrives in Genoa. She closes her eyes, but despite her tiredness, it is as though her eyelids are on a spring, and it costs her more effort to hold them closed than to let them slide open.

As she lies there, the faint ticking of steam in the pipes the only sound in the room, the last few days' excitement drops away in the musty dark and is replaced – very suddenly – by a gripping anxiety. She has never been further than Salzburg in her life, and now she is about to embark on a journey halfway across the world. Her breathing quickens and she feels slightly sick. She's never coming back. She draws her hands up beneath her face. Her nails are freshly painted and the sharp smell of polish still lingers on them. She tries to pull back her thoughts. There's nothing here to mourn for, she tells herself firmly.

She thinks of the telegram from Vitali, informing her he'd secured passage on the SS *Conte Biancamano*. It's happening, it's really happening. She'd expected to have to wait another month, at least. But there it was, in black and white. And a first-class cabin! She smiles in the dark, and her heart takes on a different beat, quick and light and excited. But she has to sleep!

She turns in bed and a hairpin slips out of place and digs into her scalp. She pulls it out and throws it across the room. It's no use. Her eyes just refuse to stay shut. She gets out of bed and opens the curtains a crack. A glint of moonlight catches the nail scissors on the bedside table. She picks them up and briefly toys with the idea of going into Resi's room and cutting the girl's clothes to shreds. The thought of Resi's face when she returns to find the silk, feathers and fur of her clothes in tatters is wickedly seductive ... But no, Kitty isn't going to sink to that level.

She flicks open her suitcase and drops in the scissors. By now, she is fully awake. Quickly and quietly, she dresses and heads out.

The streets are empty but she walks briskly. It is only a thirty-minute walk from Naschmarkt to her parents' house on Czerningasse, but she cannot remember when she was last here. Six years, seven?

She stops on the pavement outside number 18. A coil of smoke spirals from the chimney on the roof, startlingly white against the black night sky. In a small window on the first floor, she sees the yellow flicker of a yahrzeit candle. This morning, Kitty considered paying a visit to her sister Elli's grave at the Jewish cemetery in the Zentralfriedhof. A morose and sentimental thing to do, and not at all like her, yet it would have been a final goodbye of sorts. But she knew her father would be there, with his *tefillah* and *tallit*, the drone of psalms and *E-l malei rachamim*, and that was more than she could bear.

There are voices at the far end of the road. A couple, a man and a woman, appear in the pool of light from the lamp post and then disappear around a corner. Kitty crosses to the other side of the road. It would only take one policeman to stop, ask for her papers and discover she's broken the curfew, and all her plans will have been for nothing.

In the dark, she stumbles over a loose cobblestone but manages to catch herself before she falls. She straightens up and feels a wild, juvenile urge to pick up the stone and toss it through the window glass on the first floor of number 18. A sound – scraping, rattling – from further down the street stops her. She backs into a doorway and stands very still. The sound stops. Probably rats, or a disoriented fox. She casts a final glance at the building across the street. A stone through their window is trivial compared to what is facing them here in Austria. Feeling something as close to pity as she has ever felt for her parents, Kitty turns and heads home.

She is never coming back. Never.

ESTHER

The sun hangs in a pale-blue sky and shoots a spike of light through the porthole into the cabin. The ship's engines drone, and although the carpet under Esther's shoes is soft and thick, the vibrations travel up through her feet, legs, hips to settle somewhere in the pit of her stomach. She hopes it isn't a portent of seasickness.

'Then I suppose we'd better unpack.' She speaks to herself as much as to Anneliese, something she has done increasingly over the past year. 'Give the creases a chance to unfurl.' Since her husband Carl died.

'Furl,' Anneliese says.

'Yes, *liebling*.'

She sometimes worries that she might miss that crucial tipping point, bound to come soon, at which Anni will begin to understand everything she says, rather than pluck out and echo such words that the two-year-old seems to like the sound of – as though the words leave a pleasant flavour on her tongue.

She snaps open the first of two suitcases. The smell

of damp leather rises up from the inside. The suitcases, along with those of her fellow Jewish passengers on the train from Berlin to Genoa, were taken from the train at the Brenner Pass on the Italian border, where they were inspected by the German customs officials – all and any items of value confiscated – and then left to stand outside on the platform, in the rain, for hours. When one of the passengers got off to complain, an SS officer struck him hard on the side of his head with the butt of his gun. The man climbed back on board the train, dazed and bleeding. There were no more complaints.

Anneliese coughs. Esther lays her palm across the girl's forehead, a reflex. Anneliese had a cold a week earlier; nothing serious, but you can't be too careful. Her forehead is warmish, or perhaps Esther's hands are just cold. She takes a quick look at Anni's tongue – pink and moist – and then kisses her on the cheek. It's a sniffle. Nothing more.

She turns back to the suitcase and riffles through the clothes her mother packed for her and Anni – underwear, nightgowns, blouses, her best dress, now hopelessly creased. Who knows what the weather will be like there? Who knows what anything will be like there?

There is a knock at the door. Esther gets to her feet, but before she has taken two steps across the cabin, the door opens. A steward in a gold-braided white uniform – bleached white, dazzling against the Mediterranean brown of his skin – pushes the door further open and beckons in a young woman.

'Looks like we'll be sharing,' the woman says. Her accent is broad and slightly nasal; Viennese, Esther guesses. The woman smiles at Esther and then looks around the cabin, inspecting it: the two large beds, the mahogany panelling along the walls, the narrow door that opens onto a tiny bathroom, the art deco lamps on the small side tables next to the beds, a bowl of fresh fruit on one. Esther's gaze follows the woman's, and she notices for the first time how luxurious it is.

'Lovely,' the woman murmurs. She is twenty-five perhaps, artificially blonde, with painted lips and perfectly arched eyebrows on a wide pale face. She nods at the steward, who is carrying a suitcase in one hand and a large hatbox in the other, and then turns to Esther. 'You were here first – have you bagged the bed next to the window?' She laughs.

Esther frowns. This is wrong. 'I'm sorry,' she says. 'There's been a misunderstanding. This is my – our – cabin.'

The woman opens her eyes wide, looks at the steward, shrugs, and turns back to Esther. 'This is cabin 201?'

'Yes, but –'

'Signorina?' It is the steward, addressing the woman. '*La valigia*?' He indicates the suitcase he is holding, which looks heavy.

'*Si, si*,' she responds. 'Just pop it here. We'll sort ourselves out.'

'I'm sorry,' Esther says again, more forcefully. 'This is my cabin.'

The steward just places the suitcase and hatbox next to the bed nearest the door – with obvious relief.

'*Due*,' Esther says to him, pointing at herself and then at Anneliese, who has climbed onto a chair to look out of the porthole. '*No tre*. A cabin for two. Myself and my daughter.'

The man answers in a rush of Italian.

'I don't understand,' she says, finding herself glancing at the woman for help. But the woman just looks at the steward, eyebrows slightly raised, as though she finds this all very amusing.

'This is a cabin for two,' Esther urges again. The man spreads his hands out and shrugs. Was this because she hadn't given him a tip earlier? She tried to explain that she had very little money on her, that she was waiting for the ship to depart before she could claim her *bordgeld* from the purser – the money her parents transferred to the shipping line weeks earlier to grant her a little comfort on the boat before her arrival at the other end of the world.

Then the woman speaks. 'Kitty Blume,' she says, offering her gloved hand to Esther. 'And I'm sorry if there's been a mix-up, but –'

Esther doesn't let her finish. She turns to scoop up Anneliese from the chair and props her onto her hip. 'I shall go and speak with one of the ship's officers. This is a mistake. I'm not sharing a cabin.'

She is still feeling so angry when she returns to her cabin that she has to pause for a moment outside the door.

'Mama? Mama?'

Anneliese is pulling at her hand.

'Not now, Anni!' she snaps. One thousand Reichsmarks, that's what Esther's parents paid for passage on the *Conte Biancamano*, their entire savings and more. The silver, her mother's jewellery, her father's Military Merit Cross. The medal he received for services during the war that have so far kept him out of Dachau, or any of the other forced labour camps to which they've been sending so many Jewish men. All for two tickets for her and Anneliese. And a first-class fare was all that was available.

Esther opens the cabin door. A sweet and sticky perfume

hangs in the air. The woman – the intruder, Esther can't help but think – has removed her hat and gloves and is standing at the porthole with her back to Esther. A dark green coat with a fox-fur collar is draped across one of the beds. She turns as Esther and Anneliese enter, and opens her mouth to speak.

But Esther gets in first, saying sharply, 'My daughter takes a nap between one and two. That's' – she looks at her watch – 'in about an hour's time.' She says this, although she knows Anneliese is far too wound up to take a nap today. 'She goes to bed at seven. I think it best if we set down some rules, if we're to share the cabin.'

If we're to share . . . She doesn't have a choice – the second officer made that quite clear when she went to complain. The cabin is large enough for two adults, he said, and this other passenger had paid for a first-class ticket, and that was what she would get, and if she, Signora Niermann, didn't like it, well, the ship hadn't left the port yet and she was more than welcome to disembark and try her luck with another shipping line. Besides, Signorina Blume is also a Jewess – *un'ebrea* – and he refused to discuss it any further. Esther felt like screaming at him, but she knew it would be pointless. She was in no position to argue.

Now, she stands facing this woman, and it is all she can do not to start crying out of sheer frustration.

'I understand,' the woman says, her eyes calm and steady on Esther. Then she looks at Anneliese, who is half-hiding behind her mother's legs, and back at Esther. 'This is all very awkward,' she adds. 'I'm sorry. I didn't mean to cause any trouble. But the ship appears to be overbooked.'

'Kitty,' Anneliese says suddenly. 'Kitty.'

The woman crouches down in front of her and smiles. 'Yes. My name's Kitty. You've got a good memory.'

Anneliese thrusts out her doll. 'Kitty.'

'It's the name of her doll,' Esther says, and Kitty laughs.

'Your dolly has a lovely name. And what's yours?'

But instead of answering, Anneliese crosses the cabin and climbs onto the bed closest to the window. 'Ki-tty, Ki-tty,' she sings quietly.

Just then, the drone and throb of the engines take on a different, more insistent quality, and scraps of calls and laughter can be heard from the deck outside.

'Sounds like we're off,' the woman says.

Esther casts a quick look at Anneliese. It's too late to do anything about it now. They will be sharing the cabin for the next five or six weeks, and that is a long time to be spending with a stranger, even on good terms. She takes a step forward and holds out her hand. 'Niermann. Esther Niermann. And this is my daughter Anneliese.'

The woman shakes her hand. 'Please call me Kitty. And again, I'm sorry for the inconvenience, but –'

She is interrupted by the blare of the ship's horns and more shouting and whooping; passengers calling out their final farewells.

'Are you not joining the crowds?' she asks Esther.

Esther sits down on the bed, reaching across to stroke her daughter's fluff of blonde curls. 'No,' she says. 'We've said our goodbyes.'

Kitty shrugs and goes over to the round window to look out at the sea. 'Shanghai,' she says then, her voice small. 'Who would've thought?'

Until four months ago, Shanghai – the 'Paris of the East' or the 'Whore of the Orient', depending on one's point of view – might well have been on the moon for all Esther

13

cared. Or perhaps an imagined place recreated as a film set, with a lascivious Marlene Dietrich smoking Turkish cigarettes and frequenting seedy, lustful bars and opium dens. But then, overnight it seemed, this far-flung city was on everyone's lips. The lips of Jews, that is. It was rumoured – first as an incredulous whisper, then an urgent cry – that Shanghai was a free port, that anybody, rich or poor, old or young, Jew or Gentile, could step off a boat and enter the city without a visa or passport. Esther heard how people began desperately bargaining life savings, properties, family silver, works of art, all for an elusive ticket on a boat to the other side of the world.

And now she is one of them, circling the upper decks of the *Conte Biancamano* for hours on end, her hand tightly wrapped around Anneliese's. There are plenty of leisure activities on offer for first-class passengers – shuffleboard, an open-air swimming pool, champagne bars, ballroom-dancing classes – but it never occurred to Esther to pack a swimming costume, and ballroom dancing and champagne are out of the question, of course. There must be several thousand passengers on board, she thinks as she glances over the railing to look at the lifeboats, and how many of them would fit in those if the ship went down?

Every morning, she watches as one of the stewards pushes a red pin into a map posted on a board outside the dining room to indicate the ship's position. On the map, the Mediterranean is nothing more than a thin ragged strip of blue, tiny compared to the vastness of the oceans that lie ahead of them. She traces the upcoming route with a finger, through the Suez Canal, the Red Sea, through the Gulf of Aden into the Arabian Sea, past

Bombay, Colombo, Singapore, northwards through the South China Sea, Hong Kong, finally landing with a click of her fingernail on Shanghai – and suddenly she knows it is real. This unknown city will become her home. She pushes down a wave of panic.

She becomes aware of a group of children behind her, jostling to look at the map. She picks up Anneliese and steps aside. Anni stretches out a hand to touch the pigtails of one of the children, a sandy-haired girl of eight or thereabouts. The girl turns and smiles at her, reaches out and tickles her under the chin, and Esther wonders if she might ask if they'd like to play together. It can't be good for Anneliese to spend all day with only her mother for company. But as she opens her mouth to speak, a woman darts forward and grabs the girl by the wrist.

'Don't touch her!' she hisses. 'How many times must I tell you that you are to stay away from Jews?'

The girl pulls the corners of her mouth down and glares at Esther and Anneliese as though they have somehow duped her and that's why she's getting told off. Despite herself, Esther blushes. She clutches Anni closer to her chest and hurries away, stumbling against the titlting motion of the ship. She makes her way along the promenade deck, puts Anneliese down when her arms begin to ache, and sits on a long wooden slatted bench, shaded from the Mediterranean sun. A few metres to her left, a group of passengers sit in a small huddle, talking quietly.

'There is only dirt and disease,' one of them is saying. 'People sleeping and dying on the streets.'

Esther looks across. The man who is speaking has a thin grey face and very short white hair. He holds a cap between his hands, which he twists as he speaks. 'Do you really think they would've let us escape if they knew Shanghai wasn't just another room in hell?'

'That's not what I've heard,' a well-dressed woman sitting beside him says. 'My neighbour's nephew has been there for months. He wrote that there's a committee of Jews to help the refugees with housing and food. Help them find jobs.'

'Committee? Pah!' The man shoves his cap on and gets to his feet.

Esther watches him walk away. She can tell the other Jews at a glance. Not because they are all swarthy and hook-nosed, as the newspaper cartoons would have you believe. No, it is the unmistakeable aura of anxiety and uncertainty they carry around like a heavy shameful cloak, an aura that distinguishes them from the wealthy German passengers: the ones taking extended holidays to more exotic climes, or the young couples on their honeymoon, or the businessmen and their stylish wives en route to money-making opportunities in the east. Only that woman she has been forced to share the cabin with, Fräulein Blume – she is different, somehow. Indeed, if the officer hadn't told Esther the woman was also a Jewess, she wouldn't have believed it.

Esther considers the long weeks ahead on the ship and wishes Anneliese had some other children to keep her company. When she became engaged to Carl, he talked about having lots of children – four at least – but Anneliese's birth left her in a clouded funk for a long time. And just as Carl began to nudge her with suggestions of another child, he had his accident.

She married him because he proposed to her; it was as simple as that. He was her supervisor at work, twelve years her senior, a strait-laced and punctilious man, but with a kind-hearted side he took great pains to conceal for fear of being thought soft. The other girls at work made fun of him behind his back, mocking the way he used a ruler to draw even the shortest pencil line and his habit of sorting the paper clips on his desk according to size. Initially, she also thought him an odd and decidedly unattractive sort of man. But then Aaron left, leaving her bruised and angry and betrayed. When Carl began courting her – very, very tentatively – she didn't resist, and then surprised herself by saying yes when he asked if she would marry him. She told herself that even if she wasn't in love, she would surely grow to love him in time; that the feelings she'd had for Aaron were no more than an adolescent fancy and would sooner or later have burned themselves out with the short-lived flash and excitement of a Roman candle. Now, she knows she was nothing more than a selfish fool, blinded as much by the promise of comfort as by the fire Aaron ignited in her.

She leans back and closes her eyes, trying to conjure up an image of Carl's face, but all she can visualise are individual features – his eyebrows, a curved line to the left of his mouth when he smiled, a small mole near his temple – which come into focus for a second and then fade just as quickly, merging now into a different face, a face she has tried so hard to forget. She swallows hard and opens her eyes again. It is her and Anni now, just the two of them.

She scans the deck. Anneliese is nowhere to be seen. She jumps up, suppressing the image of a small body tumbling from the side of the ship, and spots a middle-aged couple standing close to the railing some twenty metres away, with Anneliese between them, all three looking out to sea.

'Anni!' Esther calls. 'Anneliese! Come here right now.'

Anneliese snaps her head around at the sound of her name, and then runs towards her mother, flinging her arms around her legs.

'You mustn't just run off like that,' Esther says. 'Anything could happen.'

'She is your little girl?' the woman asks, following Anneliese over. She has a stout, round figure and wears a worsted wool jacket and skirt that fall in a way that suggests expensive tailoring. Her nose is red from the sun.

Esther nods. 'Anneliese, yes. I couldn't find her. I was worried.'

'I'm sorry, she was wandering about alone,' the woman says, 'so I thought it best if we keep an eye on her until we found her parents.' She winks at Anneliese and looks at Esther with a smile. 'I think you have a little adventuress on your hands.'

'Baum,' Anneliese pipes.

The woman seems delighted. She beams and takes Anneliese's hand in hers. 'Yes, Rosenbaum, that's my name. What a clever girl you are for remembering!' And to Esther, she says, 'Lieselotte Rosenbaum. Pleased to meet you.' She extends a plump hand.

'Esther Niermann.' They shake hands.

The woman glances towards the man at the railing. 'And that's my husband, Fritz.'

The man nods a greeting but doesn't smile.

'Thank you for watching Anneliese,' Esther says. 'She gets restless, on the ship.'

Frau Rosenbaum nods. 'I understand. Well, it was nice meeting you.'

She gives Anneliese one last smile and turns to join her

husband, who has gone to study the map of their route. A gust of wind blows across the deck, flattening the left side of her silhouette and tossing her hair this way and that.

Watching them walk away, Esther feels a little sick. Her parents should be here, she thinks, with her and Anni, not sitting in their flat hoping the next news bulletin on the radio doesn't announce yet another ration cut for Jews; praying the next knock on the door comes from the last remaining Jewish neighbour Frau Schüler, asking to borrow a cup of flour, and not from a bunch of uniformed thugs. But how could she expect her parents, over seventy now, to leave everything behind? Perhaps she should have stayed with them; perhaps her mother was right – it was just a matter of keeping your wits about you and waiting. But waiting for what?

KITTY

——————

The temperature rises with every mile they travel south; by the time they arrive at Port Said, the chilly Austrian spring is forgotten. There is to be a four-hour stop before the ship begins its squeeze through the Suez Canal, during which the passengers may disembark. The eight days since they set sail from Genoa have passed quickly; even so, Kitty looks forward to leaving the ship for a few hours to feel firm ground beneath her feet. She decides to wear her best dress for the occasion – for who knows whom she might meet? – in emerald-green rayon crepe, with puffed sleeves and a calf-length skirt that widens gradually from the waist down. The only hat she has packed – made of brown felt – not only mismatches the dress, but is also entirely unsuitable for the heat. Instead she fashions a headscarf to protect her from the sun.

Out on the deck, in dazzling bright sunshine, she finds a group of passengers clustered around one of the ship's officers. It appears as though a few of them are arguing with him, their voices tense and sharp, but the others stand silent, heads bowed, as though receiving a judge's sentence. Whatever they are discussing, it isn't amicable. Kitty approaches a couple standing at the fringes of the group.

'Excuse me,' she says.

The woman turns to her. Her nose is reddened and the skin has begun to peel. 'Yes?'

'What's going on?'

'They're not letting the Jews off the ship,' the woman says. The clothes she is wearing look far too warm for comfort; indeed, her forehead and upper lip are covered in beads of perspiration.

On the pier, a dozen or so people have already disembarked and are handing their papers over to the awaiting British officials.

'Well, they're letting us get *off*,' the man says in a low voice, 'but they' – he points towards the British officials – 'are not letting us into the country. We might as well have stayed in Germany.' His voice is trembling as he holds up his open passport to reveal the big red J stamped across the page.

Kitty's hand tightens on the grip of her handbag. Her passport, of course, is also stamped. She didn't register as a Jew when the Anschluss came. It was an oversight, that was all – she'd renounced her religion years earlier. But they found out anyway. 'Are you sure?' she asks.

The man gives her a fierce look. 'Of course I'm sure. And for all the good this will do me' – he lifts his passport into the air, ready to throw it – 'I might as well get rid of it.'

But before he can fling it overboard, his wife catches hold of his arm. 'Don't be stupid, Fritz,' she says. 'That won't solve anything.'

He lets his arm drop heavily. He screws up his face, and for a disconcerting moment, Kitty thinks he might cry. But instead, he leans over the railing and spits in the direction of the officials far below. When he straightens up, a trail of saliva clings to his chin. His wife shoots him a nervous glance and then hands him a handkerchief.

'It's no use getting upset,' she says quietly.

'Upset?' he says in a flat voice, wiping his chin. 'I'm not upset, Lieselotte. I'm not upset.' He turns and walks slowly away. The woman gives her head a little shake and smiles awkwardly at Kitty. Then she follows her husband away.

At that moment, someone behind Kitty clears his throat, and she turns to face a steward. Without a word, he cups her elbow with his hand and steers her towards the stream of people disembarking.

'Signorina,' he says, grinning broadly. 'Beautiful weather today for a trip to the shore. You go and see the market, no?'

Kitty extracts her arm. 'I, um –'

A sudden breeze sweeps along the deck, bringing with it the smell of salt and rotten fish.

'Actually,' she says, reaching up and adjusting her head-scarf, from which the breeze has teased a strand of hair, 'I think it's a little hot today. I wouldn't want to get heatstroke.'

She frees her arm from his grip and hurries away before he can say anything else. Her throat is tight. She feels the heat of the sun beating down and looks around for some shade. Almost as soon as she sits down on a wooden steamer chair, a waiter approaches her to ask whether she'd like a drink or a snack. She orders a lemonade, and after a moment's hesitation, tells him to add a large splash of gin. She places her hand across her eyes to block out the bleaching brightness of the sun. Tears prick her eyes regardless.

She is out of her normal rhythm, she tells herself. That's all. In Vienna, she was used to rising in the afternoon, spending a few hours with Resi, shopping for milk and bread, drinking copious cups of coffee and perhaps a schnapps or two before they got ready for work at the Nachtfalter nightclub. They seldom got into bed before six in the morning, giggling and gossiping and laughing. In her recollection, of course, things are rosy and gay. It was a ball – nights of dancing and drinking and other things, too. The filth, the exhaustion, the revulsion could easily be anaesthetised with a few strong cocktails or a slow, sweet drag on a laced cigarette.

Here on board, there is no need for such things. The cocktails are sublime, and although she feels a little self-conscious among the haughty women in the ballroom who wear a different designer gown each night (she makes do with alternating her two good evening dresses), she will milk this luxury for all it's worth. There will, of course, be more of this to come in Shanghai, but she knows it is best to take one moment at a time.

'Frau Blume?' A woman's voice, to her left. 'Kitty?'

She looks up. It is the woman from her cabin, Esther whatever-her-name-is. She wears a floppy straw hat tied down at the sides with a chiffon scarf, accentuating her cheekbones.

'Is everything all right? You look a little peaky.'

Kitty nods a fraction. 'The heat,' she says. 'I haven't quite got used to it.'

'Do you mind?' Esther nods at the steamer chair next to Kitty's. 'Anni's playing over there, and I need to keep an eye on her.' She points towards the little girl playing hopscotch a few metres away.

'No, please join me,' Kitty replies.

Esther sits down and begins to fan herself, ineffectually, with her hand. 'It *is* hot,' she says with a smile.

Kitty's dress is sticking to her thighs. She plucks at the fabric to let some cool air graze her skin. 'But nothing compared to what we have in store, I suppose.'

'No, I suppose not.'

Esther sits back, eyes closed to the sun. Kitty finds herself assessing her, imagining who this woman was before she boarded this ship. She is pretty, with soft, girlish features and a tidy figure, although she could perhaps accentuate her waist with something a little more tailored than that loose-fitting sundress. She wears a wedding ring, which she twists around her finger almost compulsively, and yet she and her daughter are apparently alone. Kitty looks down at her own bare finger and feels a twitch of excitement.

Then Esther lets out a little gasp. 'Listen!' she says, suddenly stock-still.

Kitty listens, but aside from a sporadic squeal of laughter coming from some children, and one or two screeching gulls circling the sky, she doesn't hear much. 'What?'

'The engines,' Esther says. 'They've switched them off. Oh, isn't that a relief!'

And indeed, now that Esther has mentioned it, Kitty realises that the ever-present hum and vibrations of the ship's engines are gone.

They sit in silence for a while.

Then Esther says, 'Do you have any idea what's waiting for us? I mean, I've heard talk of committees and such, but nobody seems to know anything definite.'

'To be honest, I haven't a clue,' Kitty replies. She picks up her glass of lemonade and drains it, enjoying the kick of the gin.

'But what'll you do, once we arrive?' Esther asks.

'Oh!' Kitty lets out a bright laugh. 'My fiancé is there. Vitali. I'm not' – she waves her hand in the air with as much nonchalance as she can muster – 'a refugee or anything.'

Beside her, Esther stiffens.

'I'm sorry. I didn't mean it like that.' She gives Esther an apologetic smile. 'I'm just lucky, that's all. Vitali and I met a couple of months ago in Vienna, and it was, as they say, love at first sight. He's a businessman. Turns out he works for a tobacco company in Shanghai. So he popped the question, I accepted, *et voilà* – she spreads out her hands – 'here I am.' She drops her hands back onto her lap. Her gaze flicks to the steady stream of embarking passengers.

'Will he be meeting you off the boat?' Esther asks.

'I'd bloody hope so,' Kitty answers, taking her sunglasses out of her bag and sliding them on. 'I certainly don't want to be wandering around Shanghai looking for him.'

The ship's engines suddenly thrum back into noisy, purposeful life, as though the mention of the word 'Shanghai' has reminded them of the task in hand.

'And what about you?' she asks Esther.

'Me?'

'Do you know anyone there?'

Esther shakes her head. 'No. No one.' Kitty thinks she hears a catch in her voice, but she isn't sure.

Esther gets to her feet unsteadily, appearing slightly dizzy from the heat. 'I'd better go and fetch Anni out of the sun,' she says.

ESTHER

'I wonder what they do with all the leftovers,' says Kitty, dropping her knife and fork onto the plate and dabbing the corners of her lipsticked mouth with a linen napkin.

They are sitting in the first-class dining room, which, as the majority of passengers have succumbed to seasickness, is practically empty. On a dais at the far end of the room, a forlorn string quartet plays a piece – Schubert, is it? Or Strauss? – somewhat discordantly against the swaying of the ship.

Apart from Kitty, and Anneliese of course, who sits on Esther's lap, there are only a handful of passengers scattered around the room. An older woman, who is usually in the company of her sister, is sitting alone at her table looking rather wistful. The Rosenbaum couple sits a short distance away, and Anneliese has already visited their table several times. Close to the buffet counter sits a smartly dressed couple, together with their three placid children, none of whom appear to have Anneliese's energy. They all look sluggish and horribly bored.

The gusty winds coming in from the sea make a relaxed stroll on the promenade deck impossible, and even if the weather were fine, the reek of vomit coming from the lower decks is overpowering. Unlike the first-class decks, which are mopped and cleaned several times a day, the sections of the *Conte Biancamano* to which the second- and third-class passengers are restricted are serviced infrequently.

'Perhaps they take the leftovers down to the lower decks,' Esther says, trying to feed Anni some veal casserole. 'I mean, they can hardly tip all that food overboard, can they?'

She looks at the remains on Kitty's plate, a scooped-out lobster shell the colour of coral. The choice of dishes is beyond her imaginings, but she has avoided the glazed ham and lobster thermidor, delicious though they look. She has promised her parents to observe her faith wherever possible, and she means to. She thinks of them every day, and not a night has gone by when she hasn't woken from some strange and terrible dream and the heart-stopping anxiety that she might never see them again.

Kitty, it seems, eats anything with abandon: pork, shell-fish – look at her now, tucking into the jelly trifle! She has a fiancé in Shanghai, she says, but hasn't she left anyone behind? Despite their sharing a cabin, their paths hardly cross most days. Kitty usually sleeps until midday, getting up and leaving the cabin when Esther puts Anneliese down for her nap, then returning to the cabin quietly late at night, long after Esther and Anni have gone to bed. Now, at their first lunch together, the conversation is agreeable but, Esther feels, insubstantial. They have discussed the weather, the ship's progress through the Arabian Sea, the weather again, and now, the food. Kitty is pleasant enough – and there could be far worse cabin companions, of course – but with so little in common, what is there to talk about, really?

Esther is about to take her leave to put Anni down for a nap when a man in his forties, dressed in a cream linen suit, threads his way through the dining room towards them. He has a deep tan, and his hair is parted sharply on the left of his head and greased down close to his scalp. He is really quite handsome, and it is only on second glance that Esther notices the swastika pin on his lapel. She tenses and slips her arm tighter around Anni's waist.

'Heil Hitler,' the man says, raising his right hand in a limp half-salute. He smiles and his cheek creases to reveal a razor-thin duelling scar on his left cheek.

'Heit-ler,' echoes Anneliese, and Esther is torn between shushing her and not wanting to attract his attention unnecessarily. But the man's gaze skirts over them. His eyes are fixed on Kitty.

'Fräulein Blume,' he says smoothly. 'Will you be gracing us again with your presence in the ballroom tonight?'

Kitty leans forward and props her elbows on the table, taking a long drag on her cigarette before exhaling in the direction of the ceiling.

'You'll just have to wait and see,' she replies, raising an eyebrow.

He stands there for a second longer, evidently considering his response. But then he just smiles, gives a small bow and turns to leave.

'Günter von Schönhauser,' Kitty says quietly once he is out of earshot. 'The designated cultural attaché to Shanghai.' She clicks her tongue. 'Terrible dancer.'

Esther watches him step briskly out of the dining room. She turns to Kitty. 'He doesn't know, does he?'

Kitty stubs out her cigarette. 'What?'

'That you're a Jew.'

Kitty lets out a puff of air. 'Well, no. It isn't something I go about announcing.' She shrugs and takes her handbag from the back of her chair, placing it onto her lap. 'This fell out of his pocket last night.' She reaches inside and pulls out a slim cigarette case, a twitch of a smile around her lips. 'Sterling silver. I checked the stamp.'

Esther gasps softly and looks from the cigarette case back up to Kitty. 'Did you – did you steal it?'

'My motto: if you can't beat them,' Kitty says, looking Esther straight in the eye, 'then take them for all they're worth.'

Esther blinks. Is she talking about Nazis, or men? It impossible to tell – Esther feels her own naïvety beside Kitty; she's like no woman she's ever met before.

Kitty slides the cigarette case across the table. 'Have it,' she says.

'No, I couldn't possibly –'

'Have it,' Kitty repeats. 'I don't need it, and –'

Quick as a flash, Anneliese reaches out, grabs the case and begins toying with the catch.

'No, Anni, give that to me!'

Esther wrestles it from her, and sure enough, the girl's chin begins to tremble. Out of nowhere, a waiter approaches and asks if the *bambina* wouldn't like to have some cake? With her heart beating quickly now, Esther slips the case into her jacket pocket, out of sight. She strokes Anni's cheek.

'Yes, why don't you go to the dessert table and see what you might like.'

Anneliese doesn't need to be told twice. She jumps off

Esther's lap and runs towards the long table at the far end of the dining room that heaves beneath the lavish weight of cakes and gateaux and petit fours and pastries.

Esther's attention is drawn again to the Rosenbaum couple, who appear to be exchanging cross words. Frau Rosenbaum is saying something contentious, it seems, for her husband's expression darkens and he clamps a hand around her arm. But she shrugs it off and snatches her handbag from the back of her chair. Esther looks away quickly, not wanting to be seen witnessing an awkward moment between them. But a moment later, Frau Rosenbaum approaches their table. She stands in front of them for a long minute with a hesitant smile on her face, the thrum of the engines sounding louder than ever.

Esther smiles at her encouragingly, but when the woman doesn't speak, she says, 'This is my ... my friend, Fräulein Blume.' She turns to Kitty. 'Kitty, this is Frau Rosenbaum. She and Anni have made friends.'

Frau Rosenbaum's eyes flicker towards Kitty and quickly back to Esther. 'Actually, Frau Niermann ...' she begins. She throws a brief glance over her shoulder towards her husband and when she turns back to Esther, she looks flushed. 'I don't mean to –' She pauses and begins rummaging through her handbag. 'I don't mean to bother you,' she continues, pulling something out of her bag. 'But I was wondering if you might have any use for this.' She holds out a man's watch, her hands trembling slightly. 'It's gold-plated. Very good mechanism. My husband has had it for many years. Never let him down.'

Esther frowns. 'I'm not sure I –'

'It's Swiss,' Frau Rosenbaum continues, with an urgent look at Esther. 'I thought perhaps –' She swallows and drops her gaze back to the watch. 'Ten dollars, I think. Would be a good . . . a good bargain.'

'Oh,' Esther says, beginning to understand. 'Frau Rosenbaum, I'm sorry, I –'

The woman gives her head a quick shake. 'No, forgive me. I didn't mean to intrude. Please.' She stuffs the watch back into her bag, her cheeks now as red as her nose. 'Please enjoy your lunch.'

She turns and hurries off, sweeping past her husband, who still sits on his chair with his shoulders slumped forward and his head down. After a moment, he gets to his feet heavily and follows her.

'Well, that was awkward,' Kitty says after a long silence. 'Poor woman.'

KITTY

The floor dips and heaves. The ship feels like a living thing; yes, like some sort of wild beast in whose belly she is eternally trapped. The pins on the ship's map suggest they are somewhere between Colombo and Singapore, but she feels like she is in the pit of hell. The seasickness is worse than the worst hangover she's ever experienced. Worse than the skull-scraping headaches and wrenching nausea after a night at the Nachtfalter, when the only way to get through the evening was to drink her way into oblivion.

She is too tired to sit up, so when her stomach flips again, she just turns her head and vomits into the bucket at the side of the bed. It hits the target, more or less. The sight and sound and – worst of all – the smell of it makes her retch again. Her mouth tastes fetid, like something is rotting in her throat. The sheets are damp with sweat and she shivers.

She hasn't eaten for two days, can't keep down more than a sip of water, although her body is so dehydrated she is drying up from the inside out. Her skin already feels papery, and God knows how many wrinkles she'll have by the end of it. She is exhausted. If only the vomiting would stop, give her an hour – half an hour even! – to sleep.

A hangover lasts only a couple of hours; a day if you're unlucky, and even then there are ways to ease it off gently. A shot or two of schnapps, a glass of sparkling wine. But this – *this* – is never-ending. She lies back on the bed, then curls up on her side, turns again, trying to find a position that alleviates the queasiness. It is hopeless. The relentless droning of the engines and the lurch and swell of the ship penetrate her entire body. The last time she felt this awful was twelve years ago, in November 1927, when she and her sister Elli got sick. That too had seemed to last for ever, although she recovered after six long days of fever and excruciating headaches and sore, aching joints.

They wouldn't have become ill if it hadn't been for their father. Salomon Blumenthal was Rabbi at Beth Hachneseth Temple, a petty, vicious man who hated his daughters for being born female, and his wife for failing to produce a son. It was inevitable, Kitty supposes, that he would sooner or later be confronted with his fear and disgust of her womanness. And indeed, the day came when he witnessed the prayer leader, Ari Fleischmann, fondling Kitty's backside on the way out of temple. The men did it all the time, and in truth Kitty rather liked the feeling of power the attention gave her. But her father went completely *meshugge*. Although she was only thirteen, and Fleischmann was three times her age and married with six children, in her father's eyes Kitty was a *nafka*, a dirty whore. He grabbed her, screaming, from the temple and beat her all the way home. When nine-year-old Elli came to her defence, tugging at her father's *gartel* so that it fell into the dirt, he locked them both out on the balcony, where they spent a bitter, icy night, huddled together and sobbing until they had exhausted themselves. Their mother fetched them wordlessly at dawn, when their skin had gone from red to white to ghostly blue. Shortly afterwards, the fevers began. A doctor was called, who diagnosed influenza and charged heavily for his visits. But then Elli went from bad to worse, and worse again. She never recovered, dying a week after Kitty returned to her usual plump glossiness.

The ship makes a sudden lurch up and forward, slamming down a second later and sending the bucket rolling across the cabin. Kitty watches miserably as it spills its contents on the carpet. Someone will be in to clean it up – a maid comes three times a day – but she will have to put up with the stench until then.

She twists and turns in her damp sheets, fighting against a fresh bout of heaves in her stomach. She closes her eyes. Surely this sickness is a price worth paying for a fresh start, a new life.

She doesn't hear the door open, but there Esther is, sitting on the bed beside her.

'How are you feeling?'

'Like I've been chewed up and spat out,' she replies weakly.

Anneliese stands there with a wide-eyed frown, her expression a combination of astonishment and dread.

'Oh, no, I didn't ... I didn't mean that literally. I –' Her stomach turns and she retches onto the carpet, leaving a viscous liquid hanging in a thread from her trembling lips. There is nothing of substance left in her stomach. 'God, when is this going to end?'

'The doctor said it was probably *mal di mare*,' Esther says, handing her a napkin. 'Are you sure I shouldn't fetch him?'

Kitty wipes her mouth. Her tongue is raw and swollen. 'No, I don't want anyone seeing me like this.'

'He said to rest and drink plenty of fluids. I think he said something about an injection, if it gets too bad, but' – she shrugs apologetically – 'he kept switching to Italian and I couldn't follow most of what he said. I'm sorry.'

Kitty shakes her head. 'Fluids it is, then.'

Esther gets up and unpacks a wooden puzzle she must have brought from the games room. 'To keep Anni busy,' she says.

'You don't have to stay here with me,' Kitty says, though she has enjoyed Esther's care and attention more than she'd like to admit. When was the last time someone looked after her when she wasn't feeling well, mopped her brow, brought her drinks, plumped her pillow?

Esther lays a damp towel on her forehead. 'They've been searching the lower decks,' she says quietly.

'What?' Kitty swallows and winces. Her throat is sore.

'Von Schönhauser is having the cabins on the lower decks searched. For his cigarette case.' She avoids Kitty's eye.

'Let them,' Kitty growls.

'But don't you think –?'

'They won't find it there, will they? And they're not likely to search here in first class.'

Esther looks down at her hands and begins to twist her ring around her finger. 'I know, but these people, what they've been through, I . . .'

Kitty grabs Esther's wrist and hauls herself into a

semi-upright position. 'What do you suggest then?' Her voice is an ugly croak. 'Do you want to walk up to him and hand it back? Tell him it must have fallen out of his pocket?'

Esther recoils from the smell of her breath. 'I don't know, I –'

The attempt to sit up has exhausted her. She falls back onto the pillow. 'I'm sorry. It was a stupid thing to do. And I'm sorry I involved you.' She means it. She is forever acting on impulse, taking silly risks, grabbing at snatches of life before life can grab at her and pull her down into its depths. But it was unfair to implicate Esther.

Esther gives her head a tiny shake, but before Kitty can repeat her apology and promise she would try to find a way to get the man his blasted case back unnoticed, her insides heave and she succumbs to a spasm of retching.

When the water finally becomes calmer in the Andaman Sea, Kitty is a wreck. She doesn't dare eat, although she hasn't experienced hunger like this for many years, and she is so leached of energy her legs buckle when she gets up to shower.

They have less than a week left on the ship, and aside from a short walk outside on deck to recover some of her strength, she remains in the cabin. She hopes the scandal surrounding the missing cigarette case has died down but thinks it would probably be wisest to avoid the dining room. Besides, she can order food and drink to be brought straight to the cabin, and why not make use of the first-class perks while she can?

It is a beautiful day – the sky outside the porthole is a vibrant blue and the waves caress the sides of the liner with playful slaps – and she sits in bed sipping an oxtail broth. On the bed beside her, Esther is trying to coax an unwilling Anneliese into taking her nap. From the wireless comes a soft, gentle concerto at low volume.

The knock at the cabin door startles them all.

'Signorina! Signora!'

Anneliese sits up, evidently delighted that her nap has been cancelled. Kitty and Esther exchange glances. There is another knock.

'Have you ordered something?' Kitty asks.

'No.' Esther shakes her head and gets to her feet, but at that moment, the knocking turns into banging.

'*Aufmachen! Sofort!*'

'Shit.' The word escapes Kitty's mouth. 'It's von Schönhauser.' She sits upright and the oxtail soup sloshes over the side of the bowl onto the sheets. 'What are you doing?' she adds breathlessly as Esther crosses the cabin. 'Don't let him in!'

Esther frowns and opens her mouth, but she is cut off by another shout.

'Open the door! Now!' He sounds livid. The banging makes the door tremble in the frame. 'I know you're in there, *Judenschlampe*, you filthy Jewish whore!'

There is a brief silence, followed by a mumbling of male voices from the other side of the door. Then: 'Don't tell me to calm down! She's a fucking thief!'

Kitty's heart is banging hard against her chest and she feels a vestigial flutter of nausea. 'Where is it?' she whispers to Esther. But Esther stands frozen in the middle of the cabin, white-faced and trembling.

'Where's the cigarette case?' Kitty repeats, and thankfully, Esther snaps out of her daze and rushes over to her suitcase, rummaging around for what seems like an age before retrieving the stolen item.

For a moment, she stands there, looking down at the case as though wondering how it got there. The banging and shouting resume.

'Out of the window – quick!' Kitty urges.

Esther climbs onto a chair and unscrews the porthole, while Anneliese, clearly enjoying the excitement, claps her hands in delight. Kitty watches, her heart throbbing in her mouth now, as Esther squeezes her head and one arm through the small opening and tosses the case away as far as she can. She has just managed to climb back in and slam the porthole shut when they hear a key in the lock.

'It landed in one of the lifeboats,' Esther whispers, and as the door flies open they begin to giggle helplessly like schoolgirls.

ESTHER

During their final evening on board the *Conte Biancamano*, the engines remain silent. The ship lies at anchor in the estuary of the Yangtze River, waiting for the tide to come in before it sails into port. It has taken over an hour to get Anni to sleep, and Esther is tired and nervy. She tries to push tomorrow's arrival to the back of her mind, but there is precious little to distract her. She sweeps the room one last time to make sure she has packed all their belongings.

The door opens and Kitty comes in, carrying a plate of pastries and a sweating champagne bottle.

'Here,' she says quietly. 'I thought you might be hungry. I worked my charm on the kitchen staff.'

Esther smiles a thank you. After the cabin was searched – and nothing incriminating found, much to von Schönhauser's brittle displeasure – they were told politely but firmly by the First Officer to stay away from the communal first-class areas of the ship. Esther's relief that the whole incident had not resulted in something more serious is tinged with an odd, residual sense of exhilaration.

She has never experienced anything like it – the thrill of danger, of almost being caught – and feels slightly wistful that there is no one, other than Kitty, she can share it with. From the way Kitty later brushed off the incident, she suspects she is no stranger to such excitement.

Kitty sits down and nods towards Anneliese. 'She's finally asleep, then?'

'Finally,' Esther says and looks down at Anni. Asleep, the girl looks no different than she did when she was a baby, plump arms flung up either side of her face, as though in surrender, her features melted, soft lips slightly open. Esther retrieves a spare blanket from a drawer and spreads it out on the carpet at the foot of her bed.

'What are you doing?' Kitty whispers.

Esther plumps up a pillow and places it on the blanket. 'She took so long to settle, I'd rather not risk waking her. I'll sleep down here tonight.'

Kitty puts the champagne bottle down on her bedside table. 'Don't be silly,' she says. 'You can't sleep on the floor.'

'It's fine. The carpet is very soft.'

Kitty tilts her head to one side. 'Do you really think I'm going to let you sleep on the floor?' Her cheeks are flushed, from her foraging trip to the kitchen, perhaps. 'Here, the bed's big enough for both of us.' She pulls down the blanket on her bed and steps out of her shoes. 'Come on, it'll be fun.'

Esther glances down at the makeshift bed on the floor.

'I used to slip into my sister's bed all the time,' Kitty continues, unbuttoning her dress and letting it slide to the floor. Underneath, she has on an ivory-coloured satin shift, shimmery but worse for wear with a frayed hem and several dull patches. 'Thunderstorms, monsters underneath the bed, whatever. Then we'd stay awake all night talking.'

'Well –' Esther begins.

'I insist. Otherwise I'll make you take the bed and I'll sleep on the floor. And I will have a horrible sleep and be perfectly grumpy in the morning.'

'If you're sure you don't mind.'

In response, Kitty pats the far side of the bed and smiles. Esther removes her slippers and climbs in. This close, she can smell Kitty's perfume and a starchy whiff of face powder.

'This is nice, isn't it?' Kitty says, reaching over to the bedside table for two glasses. As she does so, Esther spots two pale scars, lines no more than a hair's width, stretching across her back. 'Here, take these.' Kitty pours the champagne and they clink glasses.

Kitty shuffles into a more comfortable position, her back against the headboard and her knees up, forming a tent shape with the blanket. From elsewhere on the ship, the sounds of a big band can be heard – the farewell bash in the ballroom, Esther presumes – and smatterings of laughter and conversation. Across the cabin stands Kitty's large leather suitcase. A shaft of moonlight illuminates the gold monogram, *K. B.*, embossed on the sides.

'You have such a lovely name,' she remarks.

'Thank you,' says Kitty. Then she frowns. 'But you do realise it's a stage name?'

'Really? Are you an actress? Should I have heard of you?'

'I hardly think so. But yes, I act if they let me, but mostly I sing. And dance. Revues, cabaret, that sort of thing.'

'So what's your real name?'

Kitty pulls a face. 'Käthe Blumenthal.'

Esther laughs. 'That's not so bad!'

'But I'm hardly going to get anywhere in Hollywood with a name like that.'

'You want to go to Hollywood? But what about your fiancé?'

'Ah.' Kitty brushes some crumbs off the blanket. 'Let's say that Hollywood is my contingency plan.'

Esther's eyes widen. Hollywood! A real-life actress! This woman really is from another world entirely.

'But where's your engagement ring?' The words just rush out of her mouth and she is afraid Kitty might think her terribly nosy.

But Kitty seems unruffled by the question. 'Oh, it's waiting for me in Shanghai,' she says with a shrug. 'Vitali said it would be too risky for me to try to take valuables out of the country.' She pauses. 'That's not to say I didn't take any. My mother's pearls, a couple of gold necklaces.'

'Really?' Esther thinks back to the wretched scenes at the Brenner Pass, where people wailed in anguish and disbelief as German customs officials rifled through their suitcases, tearing up the inner lining and extracting jewellery, watches and even gold-plated menorahs. 'Did you hide them?'

Kitty gives her a sly smile. 'I sewed them into a sanitary towel. Just in case they searched me, which they didn't, as it turned out. But that was the most uncomfortable train journey I've ever taken, I can tell you.'

They both laugh. Esther sips her champagne, relishing the sensation of lightness it causes in her head. She feels drowsy now, yet quite serene, and dares to think that perhaps tonight she might have a dreamless sleep.

Kitty drains her glass and gets up to use the bathroom. When she returns, her face is free of make-up and her hair falls soft and loose onto her shoulders.

'All yours,' she says, and Esther takes her turn in the bathroom, taking the time to rub hand cream into her cuticles, pushing them back gently to reveal the pale half-moons. Then she climbs back into bed beside Kitty, the two of them laughing a little shyly as they each nestle into a comfortable sleeping position. Kitty switches off the bedside lamp. The moon over the South China Sea has swelled to its fullest, throwing a silvery light into the cabin. The small form of Anneliese lies motionless on the other bed.

'Where's your sister now?' Esther whispers.

Kitty doesn't answer straight away. When she does, her voice is thick. 'She died when I was thirteen. Pneumonia.'

Esther swallows. 'I'm sorry.' She listens to Kitty's breathing for a while. 'My husband died last year.'

They lie there without speaking for some time. Esther feels the warm softness of Kitty's body beside her. She hasn't experienced such physical closeness to someone else for the longest time – aside from Anneliese of course – and it makes something inside her ache.

'Kitty?' she says softly.

'Yes?'

'Let's stay friends, shall we?'

Kitty places her hand on top of Esther's and squeezes gently. 'Yes. Let's.'

'I'm so frightened, Kitty.'

'Me too.'

'You're not frightened. You're fearless.'

Kitty says nothing at first, but then she lifts her head from the pillow and turns towards Esther, her face hovering only inches from Esther's.

'That's the nicest thing anyone's ever said to me,' she says, her breath a minty, fruity combination of toothpaste and champagne, and a moment later she touches her lips to Esther's mouth. For some reason, Esther isn't at all surprised. She holds the kiss; it is dry and soft and – Esther feels – inviting. But before she can even consider yielding to it, Kitty pulls away. She turns away, quite suddenly, and from the ensuing silence, Esther guesses she has fallen asleep.

Much later, the dawn creeps into the cabin, turning the night shadows soft and the light grey-blue. Esther surfaces from a shallow sleep when Anneliese lets out a small murmur and turns onto her side. She gets out of Kitty's bed and slips beneath the blanket next to Anneliese.

She wakes to a pale, hazy light – and an empty cabin.
'Anni?'
She scrambles out of bed, suddenly aware of the vibration of the engines – after their silence they seem louder than ever – when the door opens.
'She's awake, finally!' It is Kitty. She is clutching Anneliese's hand, and they both have a flushed, outdoor glow in their cheeks.
'Where have you been? Is everything all right?'
Anneliese's head bobs up and down. 'Shanghai,' she says brightly.
'I taught her that,' Kitty says, adding, 'you were sleeping so peacefully, we didn't want to wake you. But we were both dying to get out and look. Come on.' She grabs Esther's dress and slip from the back of a chair and hands them to her. 'We're almost there!'
The upper decks are crammed full of passengers. Esther picks up Anneliese and follows Kitty, who pushes through

the crowds towards the railing, ignoring the protests and complaints of those lined up, equally eager to get a first glimpse of their destination.

'I should've warned you, it stinks!' Kitty says, wrinkling her nose. And indeed, seconds later Esther is assaulted by a stench that takes her breath away. Fish, gasoline, sewage, something sweet and decaying that Esther can't identify.

'And it's so bloody hot!' Kitty adds.

'I've heard it gets even hotter,' Esther says, trying to breathe through her mouth. But Kitty isn't listening. She is standing on tiptoe, craning her neck towards the crowds standing on the pier. Beyond them, a congealed mass of people swarms on the wharf among barrels and containers and trunks and huge straw-wrapped parcels. It is a moving, heaving, throbbing ants' nest – it is impossible to pick out any individual forms.

Kitty gives out a sudden shriek and points to the shore. 'There! There he is! There's Vitali!' She hops up and down, waving her scarf furiously and grinning from ear to ear.

Esther scans the crowds, but it is impossible to see exactly where Kitty is pointing to. The ship has almost come to a complete standstill and, suddenly, the people around them begin moving. First, Esther is shoved from the back, crushing Anneliese's leg against the railing, and then the crowd seems to sway as one to the right. Anneliese starts to cry, but she can hardly be heard above the shouts around them. Esther pushes backward, desperate to get out of the crush. She grasps Anneliese tighter and retreats to the back of the deck. But where is Kitty?

She tells Anneliese not to move from their spot and pushes back into the crowd, calling Kitty's name, but her voice can't be heard above the clamour. There is a sudden surge to the left as a woman, overcome by the pressing heat, collapses. Several people rush towards her, and Esther, anxious not to be swept too far from Anneliese, is struck several times on the shins and knees by the heavy suitcases people are reluctant to let go of. She finally returns to Anneliese, who sits timidly on a bench, her knees drawn up to her chest. Esther gives up her search for Kitty; surely she will be waiting on the pier, if only to say a proper goodbye.

May to September 1939

KITTY

———

From where she stands, the apartment looks... not *small* exactly, but not quite what she was expecting. She was expecting something grander. A balcony perhaps, certainly a spacious entrance hall rather than that dark poky antechamber Vitali showed her in through. She takes a step forward, assessing the thickness of the Turkish rug beneath her shoes. The rug, at least, looks expensive. And the furniture is elegant: a sleek tailored sofa in powder blue, a low walnut coffee table, a glass-and-cherry-wood sideboard, and a marble-topped bar that curves around the far corner of the room. On the wall behind the bar hangs a print, an abstract that looks vaguely familiar, but she can't quite call the artist to mind. The room speaks of style and good taste. Perhaps there is a whole other wing of the apartment she hasn't yet seen; in fact, perhaps he brought her through the servants' entrance, as a joke. A poor joke, of course, considering how exhausted she is after her travels, but she is willing to forgive him.

'What do you think, *chérie*?' Vitali says. He slides his

arm around her waist and places a warm, moist kiss on her neck.

'It's lovely,' she replies, pulling away from him slightly and lifting a gloved hand to her neck. 'That tickles.' He seems a little different than she remembers, though not in a way she can quite put her finger on. On the drive here from the port, he prattled on endlessly – nervously almost. But then again, they have been apart for over two months and perhaps it will take a few days to recover the familiarity they had in Vienna.

'Come now, *chérie*,' he says in a thick voice. 'I haven't held you for so long.'

Kitty plucks her gloves off, finger by finger. 'Don't you want to show me around first?' As she speaks, she notices that her own tone is polite, rather than affectionate.

'Oh. Well.' He straightens up and points to a door that leads off on the left. 'That's the bedroom, and that' – a nod to the right – 'is the kitchen. I'll give you the grand tour in a moment. But first' – he grabs her waist again and pulls her down onto the sofa – 'I want to make sure you've arrived in one piece.'

Kitty, too tired to resist, lets herself flop down onto his lap, although she is self-conscious of the stickiness of her skin and the dampness in her armpits. From this position, she notes gratefully, she can see a large fan hanging from the ceiling.

'Mmm, I've missed you,' Vitali says, pressing his face between her breasts. 'It's been so long.'

His chin feels harsh against her skin and scrapes the silk of her blouse, his afternoon stubble growing back thick and relentless, although she knows he shaves meticulously every morning. He smells of sweat and cigar smoke, though it is not entirely unpleasant; manly, she thinks, with a slight catch of her breath as his hand travels beneath her skirt. She feels her apprehension melt. So what if there is no other wing! The apartment is immeasurably better than her lodgings in Vienna. And the nauseating, dizzying smells and noises she endured on the drive from the port haven't managed to penetrate the thick walls of the building. Most importantly, she reminds herself with a thrill of triumph, she has made it! She has made it to the other side of the world to be with Vitali.

A sudden noise from the kitchen makes her jump. 'What was that?' she asks, pushing his hand away and sitting up hurriedly.

Vitali groans and smooths down his hair. 'Oh, I forgot. That's Wing.' He gets to his feet and calls out. 'Wing, come in here, won't you? The mistress has arrived.'

There is a scuffling noise, the sound of a cupboard door being closed, and then a Chinese boy, no more than fourteen perhaps, enters the room. He keeps his head low, peering up every couple of steps to avoid bumping into the furniture.

'This is Wing,' Vitali says.

The boy comes forward hesitantly and stops a few metres in front of Kitty. His skin is smooth, his features girlish, and he looks frightened out of his wits. He makes a small nervous bow. His timidity seems to reflect and enhance her own uncertainty: she's never had servants before, let alone foreign ones, and she isn't sure whether to speak first or offer her hand.

'Nice to meet you,' she says finally with a semi-wave in his direction.

Wing bows again, a smile fixed on his face.

'Wing is your number-one boy,' Vitali says.

'There are others?'

'What?'

'If he's number one, that suggests there are more?'

'Oh.' Vitali looks flustered. A deep crease appears on his forehead, giving him, Kitty thinks guiltily, a rather Neanderthal look. 'No. Just the one, I'm afraid. It's what they call them here. And' – his face brightens suddenly and he claps his hands – 'I've taught him how to make Manhattans.'

He ushers the boy around the bar and, in a strange choppy English that makes him sound a little lack-witted, instructs him to make two drinks. Kitty's protests that she'd rather have a glass of iced water go unheard. Finally, with a drink in hand, they make themselves comfortable on the sofa, while Wing retreats to the kitchen.

Kitty glances around the room again, trying to envisage her and Vitali sitting by the window, eating breakfast together, or perhaps playing canasta in the evenings. And entertaining friends – surely he has plenty in the city? But she is tired and hot and the images refuse to take shape. She leans back and sips her Manhattan. A little heavy on the bitters, but still good. Then she puts her glass down. Last night on the ship, she resolved to cut down when she got here – a new start. A clean start.

'Your drink isn't good?' Vitali asks.

'No, it's fine, I . . .' The heat is making her skin prickle, and she is about to ask Vitali to switch on the ceiling fan when he puts his hand on her thigh, heavy with desire.

'So, you like the apartment?' he says.

'Yes, I . . . I have to get used to it first, I suppose. Add a few touches of my own.'

Vitali sips his drink. 'Good,' he says after a moment, with a distracted smile.

'Would you mind switching on the fan?' she asks. 'I'm awfully hot.'

'Of course.' He gets up and looks around, as though not quite sure where the switch is, but then locates it on the wall behind one of the drapes. 'There,' he says with satisfaction, as the blades whir into life.

They sit in silence for a while, and she senses it again, the awkwardness between them, a vague feeling of unfamiliarity. She rather wishes he would grab her and put an end to this polite, uncomfortable silence. But with the Chinese boy just next door in the kitchen, she isn't sure she would want that, either. Does the boy live here? Will she have to become accustomed to sharing her home with a stranger?

'Kitty,' Vitali says, startling her out of her thoughts. 'There's something –'

A breeze of air from the fan passes over her. Her skin feels instantly clammy and she shivers. 'What?'

He lets his head fall between his shoulders.

'Vitali? What is it?'

But instead of answering, he springs up and crosses to the window, as if suddenly remembering there was something to see outside. Kitty perches on the edge of the sofa, knowing with a flutter of panic that whatever it is he has to tell her, it isn't good. For a terrible moment, she is torn between needing to know what he is about to say and wanting to never hear it.

He turns and looks at her, single strands of his black hair being teased this way and that by the air of the fan.

'You are a very attractive woman, Kitty,' he says.

Kitty swallows and says nothing.

'I . . . Look. Here's the thing.' He steps forward and pulls his shoulders back, reminding her of a boxer about to deliver a punch. 'This is to be your apartment. I . . . I shan't be living here with you.'

She feels her mouth dropping open. She snaps it shut.

'So . . .' he says, and then falters.

'But of course,' she says, feeling the throb of her heart in her throat. She squeezes out a smile. 'Of course. We're not married yet. We'll have to wait until after the wedding . . .' She trails off at the sight of his expression. It is quite clear this is not all he has to tell her.

'No. I mean, yes. We're not married. In fact, here's the thing, Kitty,' he says again. 'I am already married.'

The flutter of panic amplifies in an instant. 'Oh God,' is all she manages in response.

'I know. *Chérie*, I'm sorry.'

Her cheeks are burning. Vitali stands in front of her, wringing his hands. She can sense him willing her to break the silence, but she won't. She can't.

He reaches over to stroke her face. 'I didn't know how to tell you. I saw you, I fell in love with you –'

His gesture transforms her panic into rage instantaneously. She hits his hand away and he flinches. 'Don't you dare!' she shouts. 'Don't you dare tell me that you are in love with me!'

Her shout must have alerted Wing; a second later, the boy's smiling face appears at the kitchen door. 'Monsieur?'

But Vitali waves him away and the boy retreats. Vitali continues in a forced hush. 'You must understand, Kitty. When I . . . in Vienna, well, I had already parted from Anastasia. At least in my heart.' He places a closed fist on his chest.

Kitty finds herself trembling. 'Anastasia. That's your wife.'

'Anastasia, yes. But she is not a good woman, like you. She is . . . cold, and hard. But she is sick. I found out when I returned from Europe. I thought I could tell her that it is over, that I have met –' He crouches down to her eye level. 'That I have met the most beautiful woman in the world.'

She squeezes her eyes shut. 'Don't say that, Vitali, please.'

'But what would you expect me to do, hmm?' he asks, straightening up. His tone is sharper now. 'Send you a telegram and tell you not to come? I thought it would all be dealt with by the time you arrived, but –'

'You were married when you proposed to me. You led me to believe I would be coming here as your bride!'

'But at least you are safe here, no? You couldn't have stayed in Vienna – you know that. And here . . .' He gestures around the room. 'Here you are safe. And it is not too bad, is it?' He ends on a pleading note.

For a long moment, neither of them speaks. The fan continues to chop the air above their heads, its motorised purring filling the silence. Kitty is aware of Vitali staring at her and feels a strange sensation rising up inside. Usually, this would be the sort of moment in which she would feel her power – her power over men, that is – most keenly. The moment when it is up to her to decide whether to acquiesce or to challenge, under her own terms, always. The feeling catches and holds for a moment. She toys with a half-broken fingernail on her left hand. Her ring finger to be precise, the finger that should right now be decorated with an engagement ring. The nail tore earlier that day, in the commotion on the ship, where one minute she was standing next to Esther, and the next swept away in the rush and noise of hundreds disembarking. She looks down at her shoes. They are dusty and scuffed. It is all so clear now. His reluctance to give her an engagement ring in Vienna. His wanting to return to Shanghai before her to 'set everything up'.

The ebbing of her power is a physical sensation. She is such a fool! And yet, he is right. She would have had to leave Vienna along with the rest, or stay behind and face an uncertain, dangerous future. Which means that now she is no different to the other refugees. To Esther and her little girl. She has no power at all. She leans forward, weak and queasy.

Clearing her throat, she asks, 'And what happens now?'

'I will take care of you, *chérie*,' he says soothingly, and his tone carries the affirmation that he understands: the power has passed from her to him. 'Let me fix you another drink.'

'No.' She glances around the room, blinking. She isn't going to cry. Not now, in his presence. 'I need . . . I need to think. Please, just . . . just leave me alone to think.'

Vitali hesitates for a moment, but then nods firmly. 'Yes, you must think. Of course. I shall call here tomorrow.'

As he strides across towards the door, she notes his strong, straight back, the fine muscular legs beneath the fabric of his tailored trousers. Her attraction to him is undeniable and for a moment she despises herself for it. He stops just before he passes the bar and pulls some paper bills from his jacket pocket.

'Here,' he says, sliding them onto the countertop, not turning to look at her. 'For, you know, anything you might need.' And then he leaves, closing the door firmly behind him.

ESTHER

Those lucky enough to have garnered a seat on the back of the truck are merely jerked forward into their neighbour when the driver treads on the brakes, but those standing are less fortunate. Without a handhold, they are thrown forward, falling to their knees, or clinging to others' arms, shoulders, hair – anything to avoid being thrown clear of the truck altogether. The driver, a scruffy, deeply tanned young man, allocated Esther and Anneliese a seat nearest the front of the loading space, squashed up against the driver's cab. Although he took the opportunity to squeeze Esther around the waist, rather inappropriately, as he helped her and Anneliese aboard, she is thankful to be sitting down.

Some ten minutes into the drive, a young boy vomits onto the floor of the truck, narrowly missing Anneliese, who sits wide-eyed and tight-lipped on Esther's lap. They drive past a creek, and above the stench of the vomit slopping about near her feet, Esther recognises the source of the sweetish decaying odour she smelled from the ship:

faeces, human or otherwise, float atop the mud-coloured water. She presses her hand to her face, pinching her nostrils shut. The creek is crammed full of small narrow boats, 'sampans' she hears someone say, that appear to be the homes of entire families. Men stand, balancing precariously on the sides of the boats, openly urinating into the creek, while others – mostly women – use buckets to haul up the stinking water to wash their clothes in.

Just before the truck takes a sharp left turn onto the bridge that spans the creek, Esther spots a sampan containing three small Chinese children tied by a rope on their wrists to a hook on the side of the boat. There are no adults in view.

'To stop them from falling off and drowning, I presume,' the woman sitting next to Esther says, and the driver of the truck, who is visible through the partition between the driving cab and the loading space, adds, 'Animals.'

Esther clutches Anneliese more tightly to her chest. The truck drives onto a bridge – Garden Bridge, she later discovers, the connecting link between the richest and poorest parts of Shanghai, the British-run International Settlement and the Japanese-run district of Hongkew, respectively – and is stopped by two armed guards in dark green uniforms. To Esther, who has yet to learn to distinguish between the many different nationalities here, they look like slightly taller Chinese men.

'Japs,' the driver hisses over his shoulder. 'You'll want to watch out for them. Vicious bastards.'

Just as an elderly woman is telling him to mind his language in front of the young children, one of the guards steps forward and pulls a hapless Chinese man from the pavement, forcing him to his knees in the process. The man was pushing a huge cart in front of him, loaded with a dozen or so canvas bundles, and it now rolls forward, unmanned, towards the side of the bridge. He lunges forward, still on his knees, to grab hold of the cart handle, and the Japanese soldier begins shouting at him in harsh, choppy phonemes that even Esther can identify as curses. The soldier takes a step forward and slashes open one of the bundles. The Chinese man lets out a long wail as thousands of kernels of rice spill onto the street. His outcry is met with a sudden whack to the head from the soldier's rifle.

Esther gasps, and several others on the truck let out small cries.

'Shut up back there!' the driver hisses from the front. 'And keep your eyes down. No talking.'

Esther, along with everyone else, stares dutifully at the floor. She turns Anneliese's head to face in the opposite direction and holds it close to her chest, but she can't prevent her from hearing the agonised cries of the Chinese man as the guards continue to beat him. After what seems like an age, the cries die down, and the truck begins driving forward slowly. Although she means not to, Esther can't help but turn back as they get to the end of the bridge. The Chinese man has been dragged to the side of the street and lies there in the heat, bruised and bleeding. He emits a series of low groans, indicating that he is, at least, still alive.

Esther finds herself trembling. What is this hell they've landed in? Like a fool, she thought she might escape a place where helpless people are beaten on the streets by uniformed brutes. She chokes back tears.

Anneliese shifts on her lap. 'Mama. Thirsty.'

'We're all bloody thirsty,' says a man standing in front of Esther.

She ignores him and leans forward to the driver's window. 'Have we long to go?' she asks. 'My daughter is thirsty.'

'Good timing,' he replies. 'We're just about there.'

And indeed, moments later, the truck pulls up and the driver switches off the engine. When Esther finally steps off, with Anni still clinging to her, she is covered in a fine layer of dust. She can even taste it in her mouth. They have arrived at a tall building; looking up, she counts five storeys. The smell from the creek opposite is overpowering, turning the already hot air into something thick and viscous.

'Welcome to Embankment House,' the driver says, and leads the group of sweating, dusty, bewildered passengers through the front door of the building and into a large room on the ground floor. They are offered water to drink, which they all take gratefully. Esther has to help Anneliese drink hers first, lifting the beaker to her mouth with one hand while cupping the other beneath the girl's chin to catch the drips. Then she drains her own beaker in a few large gulps, noting the unusual taste and hoping it has not been extracted from a source anywhere close to the stinking creek.

For the first time since stepping off the *Conte Biancamano*, Esther's thoughts turn to Kitty, and she feels a sudden surge of resentment. She left without so much as a goodbye. Where would she be now? Probably sipping a cool cocktail somewhere in the grand apartment of her fiancé, with no thought of what has become of her and Anni.

The remainder of the afternoon passes in a blur, mostly spent standing in one queue or another. Filling in the application and registration forms of the Jewish Relief Committee; a scramble at the overcrowded telegram station, where she sends two short lines to her parents; a scratch on the skin to vaccinate them against smallpox; a bowl of watery rice pudding topped with cinnamon powder that tastes of dust, and a cup of pre-sweetened tea. By around five o'clock, Esther finds herself in yet another queue, although she has no idea for what. She is too stunned to process her surroundings any longer, and although her head is buzzing with questions, she would be hard-pressed to formulate a single one coherently. She feels hot, tired, thirsty – always thirsty – and disoriented. Her arm is tight and crampy from holding Anneliese. Finally, she can hold her no longer. She prises a very sleepy Anneliese from her, feeling an instant delicious cool on the part of her body the child was attached to, and places her on the floor. Immediately, Anneliese stretches up her arms and begins whining to be picked up again.

'I can't carry you all the time,' Esther says. 'You're getting too heavy.'

Unsurprisingly, Anneliese isn't convinced by this logic. Her whining rises in pitch, until several people in the queue ahead turn towards her.

'For heaven's sake, you're not a baby!' Esther snaps, ignoring the clicking of tongues and disapproving mutters that follow. But she immediately regrets her sharp tone and crouches down to her daughter.

'Not long now, *liebling*,' she says softly. 'Then we'll see if we can find somewhere to rest.'

Anneliese nods, placated by this. Esther kisses her on the forehead and straightens up. As she does so, the queue shuffles forward and Esther finds herself standing in front of a desk, behind which sits a tall, bulky man with round spectacles. She hands him her papers, and he starts writing down her details.

'What are your qualifications?' He doesn't look up as he speaks.

'I'm sorry?' Esther says.

'Your qualifications,' he repeats. 'We do our best to place you in employment appropriate to your qualifications, but there are no guarantees. If you wish to work, there are only so many options.'

Esther hasn't worked in almost three years, having handed in her notice when she got married. She had then just completed her clerical training at the Victoria Versicherung insurance company, learning to type and file documents, shorthand, bookkeeping, and – the most useful of all, she is to discover – basic English.

'Well?' The man rests his pen on the desk and now looks up at her. 'Any qualifications? Any skills? I'm assuming you are not illiterate.' He sighs. 'Can you cook, for example, or sew?'

Esther blushes. 'Yes,' she mumbles. 'I mean, I can read and write, of course. And I can cook, and sew a little. And I'm a trained clerical assistant.'

The man's face brightens. 'Ah,' he says, smiling, 'now don't you be telling me that you speak English.'

Esther returns his smile. 'Yes. Well – a little.'

'Wonderful. Wonderful.' He shuffles through some papers in front of him and extracts a sheet. 'Here.' He pushes the sheet towards her. 'Mr Yang's Books. They're looking for a sales assistant.'

'A Chinese bookshop?'

'Yes. The clientele is international, so they need someone

who speaks some English.' He smiles again. 'I hadn't thought we'd fill the position so quickly. To commence next Monday. It's three hundred dollars a month.' He looks up at her. 'That's Shanghai dollars, of course.'

Esther nods, although she has no idea what that amounts to in Reichsmarks, or American dollars, or any other currency she's ever heard of.

The man seems to read her thoughts. 'That's a good salary,' he says, with a little more warmth in his voice. 'It won't stretch to a suite at the Cathay Hotel, but it should more than cover the rent for a place of your own. Keep you out of the camps. Unless you already have somewhere to stay?'

Esther thinks of Aaron's address on its crumpled slip of paper in her bag. She thinks of Kitty. She shakes her head. 'No. I would like to find a place of my own.'

'Good. Well that's settled then.' The man points towards the paper in front of him. 'There are the details, if you would just complete this form and hand it in to the secretary, Fräulein Levin. She'll tell you who to report to on Monday.'

Esther takes the form. There are impatient mumblings in the queue behind her. 'But what about my daughter?' she says.

'Hmm?'

'My daughter. She's two years old. Can I take her with me? To work? I'm a widow, you see.'

The man frowns and lets out an impatient sigh. 'You'll have to find someone to look after her. A friend or neighbour, perhaps, or ...' He scratches his head, looks disappointed. 'There are some nuns, Christian nuns, at a convent in Hongkew. I've heard they take in children for safekeeping. I'll write down the address for you.'

'Safekeeping?'

He shrugs, as if to indicate it is nothing to do with him. 'That's what I've heard.'

She waits for him to elaborate, but instead he begins to write something down.

'Well, I'm not sure...' She lays a protective hand on Anneliese's head.

'Here,' the man says, a hint of finality in his voice. He thrusts another piece of paper towards her. 'The address of the convent. I'll hold the position free until Monday morning. I'll need to know by then whether you will take the job.' Then he takes a new sheet of paper from a file on his desk and looks past Esther to call up the next person waiting in line.

Later that evening, they are squeezed onto a bus to be taken to a *heim*, one of the refugee camps set up by the Shanghai Jewish community. Within minutes, Anneliese falls asleep on Esther's lap. The sun has almost set; only a few thin threads of light snake into the sky, but the heat is still oppressive. They ride along a wide street before turning into a maze of smaller roads, the bus grinding its way through traffic, past open-fronted houses, women openly nursing their babies, beggars squatting on the pavements; past Chinese coolies, calling out *'ay-ho, hah-ho'*, carrying long bamboo sticks across their shoulders with cargo so heavy it threatens to snap the sticks in two.

They drive past skeletons of houses, destroyed buildings, ruins from a war most Europeans have never heard of. And a thousand different smells mingling, some unexpectedly pleasant, and others – most others – stomach-turning. The five-week journey on the *Conte Biancamano* seems a lifetime away. Esther has already been bitten by hundreds of gnats, and so, despite the heat, she wraps her jacket around Anneliese and spends the journey swatting away mosquitoes from her face. On the seat beside her, an old man wearing a skullcap sits with his eyes closed, swaying backward and forward, reciting a prayer.

When they arrive at the *heim*, they are issued a blanket and bed sheets, a tin dish, a cup, a spoon. From the efficiency with which the new arrivals are dealt, it is obviously a practised routine. Those running the camp are calm, friendly, competent, but it is clear that they themselves have no special status: they are, all of them, refugees. The new arrivals are shown the washroom and the food hall, before being allocated to one of the dormitories – men on the first floor, women and children on the second.

Esther holds Anni's hand as they climb the stairs with a dozen or so other women, her clothes clinging to the sweat on her skin. When she was a little girl, and frightened or anxious or upset, her mother would assure her that things always looked better in the morning. She hopes so. They enter the dormitory and some women let out small moans, and one bursts into tears on the spot, but most of them trudge into the room wordlessly, either because they are too weary and dazed from their journey, or because they have simply resigned to their fate. Only some of the younger women and girls seem to have retained some energy, as they push through and begin bagging the lower bunks that are still available.

Anneliese slips her hand and scampers across the dormitory to a bunk bed close to the far wall. Some of the women who arrived before them have strung up clothes lines between the beds, hanging sheets or garments across them to afford them a little privacy. The light in the room is dim. Esther fights her way through the various pieces of cloth to find Anneliese sitting on the lap of a woman. It is Frau Rosenbaum.

'Baum,' Anneliese says and beams at Esther.

Esther and Frau Rosenbaum exchange surprised looks. Frau Rosenbaum is the first to speak. 'When I heard her voice, I thought I must be mistaken. But' – she smiles and bounces Anneliese gently on her knee – 'here you are.' She pats the bed beside her, inviting Esther to sit down.

'Thank you,' Esther says, taking a seat. She is absurdly grateful to see a familiar face and it takes some effort not to burst into tears on the spot. 'I didn't see you disembark. Or at the registration centre either.'

Frau Rosenbaum nods slowly. 'Yes, we were there, Fritz and I.' She passes a tired hand across her face. 'So many people. So many questions. We are too old for all of this.'

Esther is silent. She thinks of her parents; perhaps they really are better off with the devil they know. Anneliese yawns and snuggles into Frau Rosenbaum's arm, resting her head on the woman's large, soft breast.

'I have to apologise to you,' Frau Rosenbaum says to Esther.

'Whatever for?'

She lets out a heavy sigh. Anneliese's head rises and falls with the movement of her chest. 'For judging you on appearances.'

'I'm not sure what you mean,' Esther says.

'I thought you were one of them. You know, you and your blonde friend. You don't look very Jewish.' Unexpectedly, she tips back her head and lets out a short laugh. 'Now if that isn't just a ridiculous thing to say!' She strokes a damp curl from Anneliese's forehead. The girl has fallen fast asleep. 'So I'm sorry for all the things I might have thought about you. It's just . . . Fritz and I have been treated so . . .' She presses her lips together. 'So abominably.'

'I – I don't know what to say. You need not apologise.' Her head is throbbing and she can feel the dust clinging to her moist skin. She yearns for a cool shower.

Frau Rosenbaum shakes her head. She is trembling slightly. 'But self-pity won't do, will it?' She twists around and lets Anneliese slide onto her mattress. 'It won't do at all.' Then she gets to her feet with an air of resolution. 'The first thing you need to do is bag that bed.' She indicates the bunk opposite hers. A thin, pale-faced woman is making a beeline for the bed, but Esther is quicker. She lugs one of her cases onto the mattress just as the woman approaches.

'Sorry, this one's taken,' Esther says. The woman looks as though she is about to argue, but then just pulls the corners of her mouth down and walks off.

Esther turns back to Frau Rosenbaum. 'Thank you.'

But Frau Rosenbaum isn't finished yet. 'And we should get our hands on that cot.' She points to a small metal-framed bed on the far side of the room. 'Or you'll have to share your bed with this little one.'

Together, they cross the room and carry the cot back to their corner.

'It's every man for himself in this place,' Frau Rosenbaum says, out of breath from the effort.

'Or woman,' Esther adds, smiling. Nothing will stop this place feeling like hell, but she is glad to have found an ally in Frau Rosenbaum.

KITTY

———

Kitty can't sleep, despite the five Manhattans she ended up drinking to try to stop her whirring thoughts. Or at least slow them down long enough to fall asleep. Earlier, the young Chinese boy eagerly fixed her one drink after the next, but at one point – when the room began spinning – she shooed him away. She didn't want a child witnessing her humiliation.

She turns to her side, the sheet sticking to her damp skin. It seems even hotter now than during the day. Finally, when the silver-plated clock on the dresser strikes out three thin chimes, she gets out of bed and goes to the window. The street below is dark and quiet, just a few lone vendors sitting here and there in front of charcoal braziers, calling out to the occasional passer-by. The apartment is located in the French Concession, the section of Shanghai under French authority, Vitali explained at length on the drive from the port. Of course, he knew all along what he intended to tell her once they'd arrived and just wanted to cover his own uneasiness with a pretend air of nonchalance.

As soon as he left, Kitty began to panic. Her first thought was to get out of there, to head back to the port before the ship started out on its return journey and get as far away from Shanghai as possible. But even before she carried her suitcase to the door, she realised it was futile. Pride has so far prevented her from counting the money Vitali left behind, but she knows there is no going back. She placed all her bets on one card – Vitali, the coward – and now, it seems, she has lost.

She presses her cheek against the cool window glass. If she cranes her head, she can make out the intersection, see the red, blue, yellow glow from the electric neon signs that line the façades of the buildings, can hear the noise of cars and trams and the shouts from rickshaw runners.

She yawns, then shivers, in spite of the cloying heat.

A shriek of laughter travels up from the street, and somewhere in the distance a car backfires. Four Chinese women in skintight embroidered dresses walk, arms interlinked, along the pavement towards the intersection fifty metres away, chatting in sweet sing-song voices. Kitty can well imagine what they are talking about. For all their exoticism, the women's conversation is unlikely to be much different in content from those Kitty had with Resi, walking home along Stuwerstraße at dawn.

She and Resi parted on poor terms. Another dancer at the Nachtfalter accused Kitty of accepting tips that weren't rightly hers; there was an ugly row, allegiances were formed, and Resi ended up taking sides against Kitty. Because she'd found out she was Jewish, Kitty is sure. And then, the following evening, Vitali came to the bar – the proverbial dark handsome stranger – and all seemed suddenly well. And now . . . Her breath is crushed in her chest as she fights down another surge of panic. Eyes closed, forehead resting on the windowpane, she takes several deep breaths. She has survived before. She has endured fear and suffering and humiliation at an age at which most girls would be sitting pigtailed behind school desks. She is fearless – isn't that what Esther said?

And if Vitali really does love her, all will be good. She won't force his hand but will wait until that wife of his has recovered from (or succumbed to, she thinks spitefully) whatever illness she is suffering from, and she will be ready and waiting and irresistible. It is far from what she envisaged, but if this is her only choice, well, then she will make it her own. She wipes her tears away with her hand. There is no use in crying. Life is hard, and it is a vanity to believe any different.

Several hours later, she surrenders to the dawn and goes to the kitchen to get some water. She briefly notes the absence of a hangover before stumbling over Wing's small curled-up form in the half-light and letting out a curse so strong she surprises herself. He is lying on a rush mat on the kitchen floor.

'Sorry sorry,' he pipes, getting to his feet and rubbing his hand where she inadvertently stepped on it. He begins to roll up the mat while simultaneously bowing.

'No, *I'm* sorry,' says Kitty, leaning forward in an attempt to see if she's caused any real damage to his hand. To an observer, it would appear that they are both bowing to each other while at the same time apologising. This notion strikes Kitty as so comic she laughs out loud. Instantly, Wing straightens up, staring at her with startled eyes.

Now he thinks I'm mad, she thinks as, feeling flustered,

she crosses to the refrigerator to get some water. Sipping slowly, she watches the boy finish rolling up his mat to store it neatly beneath a counter. His movements are graceful, a precise domestic dance.

'How old are you?' she asks.

Wing frowns. 'Please?'

'How old?' she repeats. 'You. How many years?'

'Ah.' His face brightens and he begins counting off his fingers, mouthing the numbers. 'Thirteen,' he says finally.

Kitty sits at the kitchen table. 'Goodness, you're so young,' she says. Only a year younger than she was when her father disowned her.

'Please?'

'Oh, nothing.' She gives her head a quick shake. 'Your English is good.'

He smiles and lowers his eyes. His eyelashes are as long and soft as a moth's wing. 'I go one year to Catholic missionary school. Before I –' He frowns and looks up to the left, as though casting around for the words. 'Before I boy of Monsieur.'

'Do you live here? In the apartment?'

He gives her a sudden look, as though he is momentarily confused, but then nods and smiles.

'And your family? Your parents? Do they live in Shanghai?'

Wing looks down at his feet. 'No parents. My *nǎinai*, um, father's mother.'

'Your grandmother?'

'Yes-yes. And my brother, Huà. But he no good.' He shakes his head fiercely. 'He a communist.'

Kitty finishes her water. She knew several communists back in Vienna, most of them brave and defiant men – and women – even if they did appear constantly angry. But then, they had a lot to be angry about. And who knows, perhaps their anger might yet be enough to change the direction Europe seems to be headed in. Though she doubts it, somehow.

'Well, Wing,' she says, getting to her feet. 'I think I shall go back to bed for a bit. I'm not really much use at this hour.'

And, guessing that the boy has not understood most of what she just said, she heads back to the bedroom, leaving him behind to sweep or mop or wipe, or run errands, or whatever it is number-one boys do for hours each day.

ESTHER

The convent is easy to find – located on Kwenming Road, only ten minutes' walk from the *heim* – but the skies have opened and Esther and Anneliese are pelted by a torrential rain that leaves them dripping wet on their arrival. It is a small, two-storey building, squatting next to the bombed-out remains of a larger building, whose carcass juts into the dark grey skies. An iron fence with large, dagger-like spikes separates the front yard of the convent from the pavement.

At the gate, two desolate Chinese men sit on straw mats – one of them with a severe cleft lip that makes the centre of his face a single gaping hole, the other covered in angry pustular sores – who begin begging as Esther and Anneliese approach, holding out tin cups which they rattle incessantly. Esther hesitates, moved by their wretchedness, but her own pockets are empty so she sweeps past, trying to shield them from Anneliese's view, and tugs at the ring-pull on the gate. For several long minutes, nothing happens, so she pulls again, hearing the muffled sound of a bell from inside the building.

'Mama?' Anneliese says anxiously, and Esther turns to see both beggars now facing her and the child, arms outstretched, calling something that sounds like '*nu-high, nu-high*'.

Startled by the increased urgency in their calls, and the way they come shuffling forward on their mats, Esther tries the handle on the gate, which, to her surprise, gives way with a squeak. She pushes Anneliese through and closes the gate behind her. They walk down the short path to a large wooden door and take cover from the rain beneath a brick canopy. Esther looks around for a doorbell or knocker, but then the door opens a crack and a small, pink-skinned nun pokes her head through. She smiles up at Esther.

'Hello, I . . .' Esther begins, and then falters as she tries to mentally assemble a coherent sentence in English. 'I am –' She pauses again. She is – what? A refugee? German? Jewish? Looking for someone to keep her daughter safe while she is at work? Yes, all of these. 'My name is Esther Niermann,' she finally manages. 'I look for kindergarten, for my daughter.'

But the nun gives no indication that she has understood and just keeps smiling at Esther, nodding.

'This is' – Esther takes the piece of paper from her bag and looks at it – 'the convent of Our Lady of Sheshan?'

More smiling, more nodding.

Esther sighs and looks around. But apart from the two beggars still sitting and lamenting on the far side of the fence, she sees nobody who might be able to help her.

'Well . . .' she says, about to give up and leave, but then the door opens wider and another woman, at least a foot taller than the old nun, appears.

'Yes?' she asks. 'Can I help you?'

'I have your address from the Relief Committee,' Esther says, conscious of her wet hair plastered to the sides of her face. 'They tell me you look after children? I am offered a job and –' She stops, not knowing how much information she needs to give.

The taller nun nods and smiles. 'You are from Germany?' she asks. Her hair is covered entirely by her cap, and her round cheeks give her face a jolly look.

'Yes. From Berlin. My name is Esther Niermann and this is my daughter Anneliese.'

Anneliese looks up at the nun without blinking.

'Ah, a shy one,' the nun says. 'Well, never mind, I'm sure you can be chatty when you want to be.' She turns back to Esther. 'My name is Sister Ruth, and if you like, we can speak German. I am originally from Switzerland, though that is many years ago.'

Esther is so relieved she almost sighs out loud. 'Yes, that would be helpful,' she continues in German. 'My English needs a lot of work.'

'You have recently arrived?'

'Yes, two days ago. On the ship from Genoa.'

Sister Ruth shakes her head. 'So many of your people forced to flee their homes. It's terrible.'

Her benevolent tone puts Esther at ease. 'It's hard for my daughter. The place we're staying at now, the *heim*, it's – it makes me wonder whether we shouldn't have stayed in Germany.'

With a solemn nod, the nun beckons Esther inside. 'I'm glad you came to us.'

Esther takes Anneliese's hand and steps inside.

'Now, come with me,' Sister Ruth says brightly. 'I will

show you the house.' She turns and walks ahead, her rosary beads clicking as she does so. Esther gives Anni an encouraging smile and follows. The corridor grows colder and gloomier as they go further into the building.

'A little grim when the weather turns colder,' Sister Ruth says over her shoulder, reading Esther's thoughts. 'But at this time of year, we're grateful for the cool.' With her right hand, she draws a cross from forehead to stomach and shoulder to shoulder. Then she stops walking abruptly.

'And this is the children's room,' she says, opening a large wooden door to her left.

Surprised by the quiet – in fact, the complete absence of any kind of noise that might hint at children – Esther steps forward into the room. And indeed, there are no children here. The room – large and bright, although from the peeling wallpaper and scuffed floor it looks as though it hasn't been decorated in years – contains some twenty iron-framed bunk beds, each smartly made up with clean starched sheets. An enormous wooden crucifix, with the naked, suffering Jesus mounted on it, hangs on the far wall. It is a disquieting image, and for a moment, Esther longs for the comforting song and familiar sway of worship at the shul on Fasanenstraße she used to attend as a child.

She turns to Sister Ruth. 'This is where they take a nap?'

'Well, yes, the younger ones,' Sister Ruth replies, frowning ever so slightly. 'This is the bedroom. We're very strict on bedtime discipline. But most of them adjust quickly,' she adds with a reassuring smile. 'Children are so adaptable. We're currently caring for twenty-three boys and –'

Esther interrupts her. 'I don't understand. Caring for?'

'Yes. Twenty-three boys and eighteen girls live here with us.'

Esther tightens her grip on Anni's hand. 'I'm sorry. I think I have misunderstood. I don't . . . I'm not . . .'

Sister Ruth raises her eyebrows. 'You're not . . .?'

'My daughter is not here to stay. I mean, just during the day, while I'm at work.'

'But you yourself said that the *heim* is not fit for children.'

Anneliese tugs on Esther's hand. She is staring wide-eyed at the crucifix, obviously unsettled by the image.

'But we're not even Christians!' Esther says in exasperation. They may share a language, but that doesn't dispel the stark disparities between them.

The nun smiles and tilts her head, her cap now shading the left side of her face. 'The Jews will also one day stand before the Lord,' she says, reaching out to stroke Anneliese's hair. The girl, perhaps sensing her mother's bewilderment, takes a step backward and slips an arm tightly around Esther's leg.

Sister Ruth continues in a tone that might be reserved for particularly slow children. 'She will be given a uniform, but if she has a winter coat, some thick stockings and sturdy shoes perhaps, we would be grateful if you could bring those. It might not seem like it now, but it can get quite cold in winter. You may visit her, of course, but once a month at the most. We don't encourage frequent contact. It can upset them – quite unnecessarily.'

'But she has a home with me! I'm not leaving her here!' Esther says, raising her voice without meaning to. The high, cold walls echo the shrill in her voice, and Anneliese begins treading the floor as though she needs the toilet.

The nun gives a disapproving shake of her head. Her earlier jolliness has vanished. 'Think what is best for the child. Not what is best for you. We can give her everything she needs. Not least' – she straightens up and raises her chin – 'salvation.'

'No,' Esther says firmly. 'No. I was told... Never mind. I'm sorry to have bothered you.' And she picks up Anneliese and turns, hurrying back down the dark corridor, conscious of the echo of her heels on the stone floor. She squeezes past the short nun who smiles up at her and finally wrenches open the front door. She is grotesquely relieved that it opens so easily.

The two beggars are still outside; the one covered in sores appears to have fallen asleep, and the other one thrusts out his tin cup at her as she passes by, this time rather half-heartedly, as if he recognises Esther's despair.

That evening, back at the *heim*, Anneliese lets herself be put to bed without protest. It is quiet in the dormitory now, the air thick and close and smelling of sweat and camphor. Most women lie asleep on their bunks; two sit wordlessly side by side, knitting, the needles click-clicking as if in conversation, and a young woman stands at the grimy window, looking out at the dark and crying soundlessly.

Frau Rosenbaum's entrance is thus all the more noticeable. She strides through the room, her feet slapping the floor on her way to her bunk.

'I've got good news,' she says, flopping down opposite Esther with a loud *uff*, as though she has just undertaken some strenuous physical exercise.

Esther puts her finger to her lips and nods towards Anneliese.

'Sorry,' Frau Rosenbaum says more quietly. 'But I have good news.' She smiles, sticks her hand in her coat pocket and pulls something out. A key. Her eyes flash as she holds it up. 'Fritz and I are leaving this place tomorrow. We have just signed a rent contract.' She places a plump hand over her mouth and opens her eyes wide, as though she can hardly believe it.

Esther leans forward and places a hand on Frau Rosenbaum's knee. 'I'm so happy for you,' she says.

Frau Rosenbaum squeezes Esther's hand. 'Thank you, my dear. I'm not sure how long Fritz would've survived in this place.' Her eyes sweep the dormitory and she sighs. 'To be living like this. Terrible.'

Esther slips her hand out from under Frau Rosenbaum's. Terrible. That's what it is. And how much longer will she and Anneliese have to endure it? The filth; the nocturnal coughing and snoring and sobbing; the rats that scurry across the floor at night, and occasionally during the day; the hundreds of insect bites they wake to that itch like fire. This afternoon, for lack of nail scissors, she bit Anni's nails to the quick – the child squirming and fussing the whole time – to stop her from scratching her skin raw while she slept.

Already, Esther's memory of what it feels like to sleep in crisp, clean sheets has all but disappeared. She picks at the skin around her fingernails and pulls on a hangnail; it peels away painfully, leaving behind a bead of red. She quickly sucks the blood from her finger. Perhaps the nun was right – perhaps Anni would be better off with them.

Frau Rosenbaum begins to get undressed. She unclasps her skirt and lets it drop to the floor. In the heat, she isn't wearing stockings, and her legs are covered in bluish spider veins. When she gets to the buttons on her blouse, she pauses and looks at Esther. 'You should come with us,' she says.

'What?'

Frau Rosenbaum hangs her skirt on the bedframe and climbs into bed. Her voice is hushed. 'The house is on Alcock Road. Six rooms, of which we now have one. The landlord lives on the first floor with his family. I – I took the liberty of mentioning your name to him, asked him to hold one of the rooms until tomorrow. It's nothing grand, but it's a thousand times better than here. I'll take you there myself, if you like. It isn't far.'

'I won't be able to afford it,' Esther says quietly.

'But you will have a job now, won't you? The rent isn't much, and I'd be happy to loan you the key money until you get your first pay.' She blushes and adds, 'Fritz and I managed to sell some ... some things.'

Esther plucks at the fabric of her shift and tells Frau Rosenbaum about her encounter with Sister Ruth.

Frau Rosenbaum clicks her tongue. 'They wanted to keep her? Christian nuns? That doesn't seem right. Separating a child from her mother.'

Outside, the rain begins to fall again, first soundlessly, and then in a roar of heavy drops that ricochet off the windowsill. Esther yawns. She has never felt more exhausted in her life. She takes a final look at Anneliese and then climbs into her own bunk.

The beds are less than half a metre apart, and Esther can feel Frau Rosenbaum's warm breath on her face, and catches the smell of cold cream, the same brand her mother uses. Once again, she is stricken by the suffocating thought that she will never, in all honesty, be able to bring her parents here. It would kill them.

There is a loud clunking noise as the room falls into darkness. Lights out. Esther turns onto her side and tries to ignore the buzzing of mosquitoes. She is alone and frightened. In the dark, she lets her self-pity rise and swell, doesn't swallow back the lump at the base of her throat, allows her thoughts – for the first time in weeks – to turn to Aaron. He is out there somewhere, perhaps only a mile or two away, who knows? Should she seek him out? Would it –?

'Esther dear?' Frau Rosenbaum speaks quietly.

'Yes?'

She clears her throat gently. 'It is perhaps none of my business to ask, but what about your husband, Anni's father? I noticed your ring, but I've only ever seen you and Anni alone.'

Esther waits a beat before answering. 'He died.'

Frau Rosenbaum lets out a small murmuring sound and stretches out her arm, placing her hand on Esther's shoulder. The feel of her fingers is warm and moist and comforting.

'I'm so sorry, my dear. Was he ... Did they –?'

Esther shakes her head in the darkness. 'No. They didn't take him. He ... he died over a year ago. It was a road accident.'

Frau Rosenbaum gently squeezes Esther's shoulder and then removes her hand. She turns onto her back, making the bedsprings groan.

'We didn't realise he was that hurt, to begin with,' Esther continues very softly. It is the first time she has spoken of Carl's death since it happened. It feels all right to do so now, so far away, in the dark. 'He'd been hit by a tram but insisted on being brought home. I thought it was just severe bruising, perhaps a cracked rib, but once he'd gone to bed, he never got up again. For hours he lay there, slipping in and out of consciousness. He was too weak to talk, even. I couldn't get a doctor out to see him, because ... you know, there were no more house calls for people like us. A friend of my father's, a retired surgeon – he must have been over eighty – finally came. He said Carl had severe internal bleeding and should have been taken to hospital straight away. By then it was too late.'

A slow rhythmic wheeze can be heard from Frau Rosenbaum's bed. She has fallen asleep, as if Esther had been telling her a bedtime story like a child.

'And it was my fault he died,' Esther whispers into the space above her head. She can't stop now. 'The accident was all my fault.' And she knows, as she says this, that shame alone will prevent her from seeking out Aaron, however close by he might be.

KITTY

She wakes with a throbbing head and eases out of bed, cursing the fourth cocktail she drank last night. It's always one too many, especially when she has to spend the evening alone. As she pulls on her dressing gown, she suddenly remembers and her spirits lift like bubbles in a glass. Tonight, Vitali is taking her to a dance! To a proper dance at the Cathay Hotel, not a miserable evening spent propped up at a bar or squashed into a dilapidated faux-leather booth at one of the seedy nightclubs he seems so fond of, listening to him and his ugly, thick-fingered business partners discuss the communist-initiated strikes in the north and make loud, coarse jokes about the Chinese hostesses that bring drink after drink, as though she, Kitty, were invisible. But she has endured for two long months and her patience is finally going to pay off. Tonight, she will enter the Cathay Hotel, the finest building on the Bund, on Vitali's arm.

The best cure for a hangover is a hearty breakfast, so she smooths down her hair and calls out for Wing. No response. He must be out shopping or running some other errand. All the same, she calls out his name again, just to be sure. He reminds her a little of a timid house ghost, popping up when she isn't expecting him, only to disappear to God-knows-where the moment she turns her back. The kitchen and drinks cabinet are always well stocked, although she has no idea where he gets the money from. Perhaps Vitali pays him in advance, or perhaps the boy has a tab somewhere in his master's name.

Squinting against the sunlight that comes pouring in through the window, Kitty pads into the kitchen. No sign of Wing. With a vague sense of relief that she is on her own in the apartment, she opens the fridge, then the kitchen cupboards, but can find nothing appealing to eat. In fact, she feels a curl of nausea in the pit of her stomach. She will have to eat something soon to quell it, or she will feel sick for the rest of the day. And that won't do at all, because she has things to attend to before tonight. She drinks a large glass of water and heads back to the bedroom to get dressed.

Outside, the July air is thick and hazy. And, incredibly, even hotter than the day before. Kitty already feels a film of dirt forming on her skin. Surely the heat and humidity can't get much worse than this? She wouldn't be willing to bet on it, not in this place.

She hasn't taken two steps from the building when she stumbles against a metal pail. She hits it hard with the toe of her shoe, making it topple from side to side before falling over. The owner of the pail, a young Chinese man with a deep scar on the side of his face, yells at her angrily as it bumps off the kerb. Kitty's stomach turns and she almost retches as a black cloud of flies swarms off into the air, leaving behind a sheep's head, its stiff purple tongue sticking out of its mouth. Its dead eyes are dull and cloudy, and the stench is overpowering. The curl of nausea threatens to spring into foul life.

She cups her hand over her nose and then waves to a rickshaw coolie on the opposite side of the street. He immediately turns and drags his contraption across the street towards her, bashing into cars and bicycles as he sprints through gaps in the gridlocked traffic. Kitty climbs on and gives the man her directions, and he begins weaving his way down the street, the muscles on his bare back straining against the weight, sweat glistening on his skin. She doesn't plan to go far, but with any luck, the headwind will cool her down a little. Though her head is fuzzy and the sight of the sheep's head has made the sickness in her stomach blossom again, her mood is bright.

The headwind she hoped for is a feeble breeze at best, but she dabs at her forehead with a handkerchief and tries to ignore the prickling of sweat in her armpits. She plans to breakfast somewhere on Rue Lafayette, which will hopefully settle her stomach, and then go and buy the finest dress she can find. The money Vitali leaves discreetly on the sideboard at every visit is a very generous amount. Enough for her to stock up her wardrobe with clothes she has always dreamed of wearing: two-piece suits with matching hats, and tailored dresses in chiffon, crepe and silk; all purchased in the boutiques that line the busy Rue Lafayette; boutiques with perfume-scented air and banquettes upholstered in the softest calfskin – or, more daringly, in leopard skin – and discretely placed garment rails displaying the finest gowns by Balenciaga, Schiaparelli, Vionnet and Mainbocher. Boutiques, in other words, that wouldn't look out of place on Kärntner Straße in Vienna – except that there, she was never more than a window shopper.

At first, she spent the money like water, feeling slightly intoxicated by the rush of pointing to a gown or hat and confirming her purchase. When she arrived home, however, with an empty purse, she didn't dare wear any of her new outfits for fear she might have to return them. And although Vitali doesn't ask for receipts – he isn't vulgar like that – and never fails to leave her a bundle of banknotes when he visits, a part of her knows it is wise to be cautious.

It was almost on instinct that she began spending more thriftily, and then, albeit with a whisper of guilt, she began asking him for extra money.

'It's Wing's birthday next week,' she lied recently, and he pulled a hundred-dollar note from his pocket, frowning slightly.

'You shouldn't spoil him,' he said. 'Does these types no good at all.'

A week later, she claimed she'd been the target of a pickpocket – a plausible lie, for there were enough of them in the city – and he replaced the money without a murmur. She invented a tab at a nearby restaurant, claiming she had forgotten about it – she had no head for numbers, after all – and that if she didn't pay up at the end of the week, they wouldn't serve her anymore, and then where would she go for breakfast? Soon, she had saved a tidy sum, tucked away together with the pearl necklace she'd stolen from her mother's jewellery box after her father disowned her, among her sanitary napkins, one of the few places she trusts Wing won't look.

The rickshaw bumps to a halt, jerking her forward. The

man turns to her and says something she can't understand, gesturing at the traffic ahead. Assuming he is trying to tell her that he can't take her any further, that the street is just too congested, she steps off the rickshaw. But then he drops the handles and rushes towards her, addressing her in an urgent tone that sounds pleading and angry at once.

'I'm sorry, I don't understand,' Kitty says helplessly, stepping back as he puts out his arm to guide her back onto the rickshaw. She fumbles in her handbag and takes out two paper bills, far more than the ride should probably cost. 'Here,' she says, thrusting the money towards him. The man snatches it from her hand and with a short barking laugh takes up the handlebars of his rickshaw and plunges back into a gap in the traffic.

Kitty looks around. As far as she can tell, she is on Rue Corneille. She has only been here once before, but she is sure there must be a restaurant or café somewhere close by. A Chinese boy, no older than five, approaches her and tugs at her sleeve.

'No mama, no papa, no whiskey soda!' he cries, holding out his palm. Kitty shakes him off. She is jostled from behind, as two old women carrying bamboo poles nudge past her, live chickens squawking in cages on either end. She turns to her right and begins to walk. Shanghai pavements do not lend themselves to idling about. After several minutes' walk her mouth is dry and she is beginning to feel faint from the exhaust fumes. At the next junction, she turns off the main road to get away from the noise and smells. The side road is quiet and unexpectedly leafy; a line of sycamore trees stretches out along the pavement. For an instant, she is afraid she might be lost in a completely unfamiliar part of the city. But then she spots something

– a painted sign hanging over a door: *Wiener Kaffeehaus*.

She pushes the door open, hearing the chime of a bell hanging over the door, which seems to echo her sense of childish delight at what she has discovered: an Austrian café, here in China of all places! It is no cooler inside than out, but the smell of roasted coffee beans and dark chocolate makes it cosy – pleasant, almost. The café is small, eight tables perhaps, of which most are occupied. They are covered with starched linen tablecloths; only the chairs, made from bamboo and appearing a little wobbly, look out of place. In a corner sit three Japanese officers in stiff uniforms devouring enormous portions of *apfelstrudel*. The other customers are all European.

Almost immediately, a short moustached waiter approaches Kitty and guides her to one of the empty tables. Delighted with the waiter's broad, familiar dialect, she orders coffee and a slice of cake and then sits, giddy with pleasure that fate has led her to this place. She must tell Vitali about it – in fact, she will bring him here to eat proper cake and drink proper coffee. It won't be long now, she is sure of it: visits to the racecourse on his arm, dining in exquisite restaurants, living in a beautiful grand house with gardens and servants. She will take Wing as her number-one boy, of course, but he will only be the first in a whole number of boys. And one day, in a year or two perhaps, she will need an amah, one of those Chinese nannies who take the children of their white employers for walks in Jessfield Park. Tonight is where it all begins, she feels sure of it!

A rich, dark slice of Sachertorte, barely managing to retain its shape in the humidity, is placed in front of her. In Vienna, she never ate Sachertorte, conscious of her figure's tendency to plumpness, but the sheer comfort of having something here, in this exotic place, that is so intrinsically familiar, is overwhelming. She knows that she has already put on weight since arriving, but 'all in the right places', Vitali assured her, as he cupped her breasts in his large hands. She takes a small bite, instructing herself to savour it properly, but before she knows it, the plate is empty. She moistens a fingertip and scoops up the last of the chocolate crumbs into her mouth. Still deliberating whether to order another piece, she becomes aware of three women talking at the table behind her. In German. Again, it strikes her as immensely comforting, hearing her native language so far from home. But then, as she listens, she realises what they are talking about.

'They made us get down on our knees and scrub at the pavement with a toothbrush. People just stood by and gawped; some of them spat at us.'

'My niece was dragged from the restaurant she worked at and they shaved her head, right down to the scalp.'

'He weighed one hundred and eighty pounds when they came for him. When they released him from the camp, he weighed only half that. And he still screams at night in his sleep, though it's been six months since we left that hell.'

It isn't a conversation. They are talking alongside one another, urgently, almost breathlessly. The café is suddenly airless. Kitty feels a stab of irritation. She isn't unsympathetic to these dreadful stories, of course not. But there is something distasteful about the way in which they are told, almost as if the women are trying to outdo one another in terms of dreadfulness. It is so ... *Jewish*, she thinks bitterly, these people so ostentatious about their suffering, competitive in their misery. Like at her sister Elli's funeral, for example. Her father, who never betrayed any emotion other than anger, wailing and blubbing throughout the entire Kaddish, as though this lost daughter actually meant anything to him; her mother, who rarely spoke a warm word to either of her girls, gushing forth to those assembled about her wretchedness at suffering the death of her own child. And Kitty – or Käthe as she was back then – rubbing a smarting cheek where her father had struck her hard across the face for lifting back the mourning sheet that covered the living-room mirror to check her reflection.

She lights a cigarette, inhales and blows out a cloud of smoke. The chocolate cake feels heavy in her stomach now. She finishes her coffee and signs to the waiter to bring her the bill. Although she means not to, she turns to look at the women. Two of them are aged upwards of sixty, the other woman a little younger. Their clothes are shabby; the younger one wears a thin print dress, its colours bleached out almost completely. Large semicircles of sweat spread out from beneath her armpits. The other two have on darker clothes, dusty and scuffed at the collar, and entirely unsuited to the hot weather. The women sit silently now, exhausted perhaps by their tales of woe, each apparently immersed in some private reminiscence.

For the first time in months, Kitty thinks of Esther and is instantly ashamed. She is somewhere in this city, in one of those dreadful refugee camps perhaps, with her own story to tell, and this is the first time Kitty has had cause to think of her since she arrived. And what of that adorable little girl, Anni? Only a moment earlier she was thinking of what it would be like to be a mother herself.

She stubs out her half-smoked cigarette and then she

realises the women are looking at her, have caught her staring. She turns away, a hot flush rising from her chest up to her face.

She gets to her feet to head off the approaching waiter. Catching him between the service counter and the table with the Japanese officers, she says quietly, 'I'd like to pay their bill, too.' She inclines her head to the table where the three women sit.

The waiter raises his eyebrows and looks over Kitty's shoulder at the women. He smiles. 'That is very generous of you.'

Kitty dismisses his words with a small shake of her head. *It's not my money and there's plenty more where that came from*, she wants to say, but doesn't. Instead, she waits for him to calculate the total and then hands him some banknotes. She includes a generous tip.

'And please,' she says. 'Don't say anything until I've left.'

She crosses the café and pushes open the door. The bell tinkles a goodbye as she steps outside.

The bustle of the main street soon removes any space for thought. Kitty has to pay attention not to step on vendors crouching on the kerb, or trip over calligraphers sitting at low tables with their inkwells and quills, as she squeezes past groups of perfumed girls wearing impossibly tight dresses with slits up to the thigh, and generally tries to avoid being knocked over by the many vehicles – cars, buses, rickshaws, bicycles – that swerve dangerously close to the kerb. Across the street, she spots an elderly man in a large black hat stepping off a rickshaw, four tassels dangling from beneath his jacket. She stops, startled by a brief, unwelcome memory of her father. The man must have felt her stare, because he raises his head to look straight at her. She blinks and looks away quickly. With some effort, she reminds herself of the task in hand, and sets off purposefully, her mental map of the shops, boutiques and dressmakers firmly back in place.

When she arrives home it is just after four in the afternoon. Vitali is picking her up at eight, so she only has a few hours to get ready. Her stomach flutters. She feels like a schoolgirl before an examination – although she left school long before taking any exams, so what does she know, really? Her spirits are high; her shopping expedition was an unequivocal success. In only the third boutique she visited, she struck lucky and found the perfect dress for her night out. It is a high-necked, backless gown in blood-red chiffon and gold lamé stripes. The dress of a film star. Vitali will love it, she is sure! She could hardly wait to get it home but had to endure almost an hour of fitting as the dressmaker pinched in the waist and adjusted the hem. It is by far the most expensive dress she's ever owned; the mere feel of the fabric between her fingers gives her a childish thrill of excitement.

Back at the apartment, she comes across Wing dusting the blinds and tells him he can go, for she won't be needing him that evening. As soon as he has left, she opens the box – embossed with a golden rose – and unfolds the tissue paper with care, before sliding the dress out and holding it up, marvelling at it. Then she drapes it over the back of the sofa, changes her mind and quickly undresses, slipping it over her head. She assesses her reflection in the full-length mirror standing in the bedroom. It is beautiful, just beautiful. But she will have to wave her hair and paint her nails to match the blood red of the fabric. And shave her legs. And pluck her eyebrows. So much to do! She slips out of the dress and hangs it on the back of the door. This way, she can look at it for inspiration while she makes herself beautiful.

In fact, time passes in an oddly distorted way, stopping and starting, gathering speed and then dropping to a sluggish crawl. One moment it is half past five, then quarter past six, and when she next checks the time, after she has set her hair in neat, obedient waves and her legs are as smooth as silk, and her nail polish dry, it is only twenty to seven. She picks up a magazine and flicks through it, scans a couple of articles and then checks the time again. Only five minutes have passed. She crosses to the bar and pours herself a finger of whisky, knocks it back and pours another. Should she put on the dress now? She doesn't want to risk creasing it, and although the ceiling fan has been on since she arrived home, her skin is damp with perspiration. But then again ... Finally, she gives up the deliberation and gets dressed. It is only another hour until Vitali will call for her. She saunters across the room to the gramophone. A little music, that will help pass the time nicely. And she can practise her foxtrot! She is surely getting a little rusty.

Just as she lowers the needle to the record, anticipating the thunk and scratch that precede the music, the doorbell rings.

He's early! She rushes to the door, thinking of how she might playfully scold him for arriving before the agreed time – a woman cannot be rushed! – and preparing to delight in his reaction to her outfit. She pulls the door open, almost snagging the hem of her dress in the process, to come face to face with the Chinese concierge.

'A message from Monsieur Petrov,' he says, bowing in his oversized uniform and handing her a small cream-coloured envelope. 'He say he indisposed this evening.'

Kitty takes the envelope from him. 'But –' Her voice fails her.

The concierge opens his mouth, but Kitty very softly closes the door before he can say any more.

ESTHER

The days congeal into a sticky mass, the time of day meaningless and marked only by the gong that rings out mealtimes. At times, it seems the only way to tell the days apart is when the storms come and wash the humidity out of the sky. Then, the relief is exquisite, but painfully short. Esther spends her days trying to pass the time, and will do anything asked of her in exchange for a small allowance: scrubbing mattresses soaked in Lysol to remove the lice until the skin on her hands chaps and reddens and bleeds; wiping the small bloodstains and crushed insects off chalky walls; sweeping thick yellow dust from the floors.

It is mind-numbing, exhausting work. But the monotony, the lack of privacy in the dormitory, her ruined hands, the stifling heat – none of these cause her as much concern as Anneliese. The girl has become tearful and anxious, quick to cry when she runs in to one of the smelly, unshaven old men in dishevelled clothing who roam the building as if they aren't quite sure where they are, refusing to join in with the other children who run up and down the hallways in a game of tag. Instead she sits for hours on the dusty ground, scraping a chipped, wheel-less toy truck across the floor.

Nothing Esther does can encourage her to break out of her stupor – not an extra hard-boiled egg at dinnertime, nor the promise of sweets from a vendor on the corner, nor a tickle, nor a cuddle. Last Friday, at Shabbat service at Ohel Moshe Synagogue, Esther overheard two women behind her whispering about 'that poor little retarded girl'. Esther turned to Anneliese, who was sitting slumped and dribbling in the gloom amid the heat and the monotonous chanting of the *shaliach tzibbur*. Mortified, she snatched her up and rushed her back to the *heim*. She had to restrain herself from slapping her daughter back into life.

Then, in early September, the monotony is ruptured. On a grey, airless morning, Esther takes Anneliese to fetch some boiled water from a water store on the corner of Seward and Kungpin Roads. The water from the tap is undrinkable, and although clean drinking water is available at mealtimes in the *heim*, Esther is constantly worried that she or Anneliese might get sick if they use the tap water to brush their teeth. And boiled water is relatively cheap. She reaches into her pillowslip to retrieve a bundle of bamboo tokens – there is no currency small enough to pay for a canister of water, and so local vendors sell short bamboo sticks with the initials of the water store to ensure repeat custom.

On the way to the water store, they pass by a small square where refugees have set up a street market: dozens of people who have something to sell or barter stand behind makeshift stalls, some of them raucously tout their wares and others, out of shyness or embarrassment, stand silently behind their tables, looking on in dismay as strangers pick their way through their personal belongings.

The quality items on sale include embroidered table-cloths, silver cutlery, Meissen porcelain, Hummel figurines, candles and razor blades. Those refugees who haven't anything better, or who have already sold most things of value, offer out-of-date medication, books with pages missing, blunt knives. Who on earth would buy such things – let alone imagine that you could sell them? The depth of desperation frightens Esther. Most pitiable of all is a man who sits on the ground with a blanket spread in front of him, displaying items of use only to those with unlimited imagination: old spark plugs, a pair of broken spectacles, a set of false teeth, rusty keys, and even a long braid of reddish hair tied with velvet that perhaps once belonged to the man's wife or daughter.

Anneliese leans over to stroke the braid of hair, but Esther pulls her back. Her fear of infectious disease is becoming a compulsion. Just as Anneliese draws down the corners of her mouth to cry, a woman pushes through the crowd and presents the girl with a lollipop shiny with sugar. Frau Rosenbaum.

'This is only for girls who aren't crying, mind,' she says, placing the lollipop in Anneliese's hand.

'Baum!' Anneliese chirps. '*Danke!*' It is the most animated Esther has seen her in weeks.

Frau Rosenbaum strokes the girl's cheek and turns to Esther. 'How are you?'

Esther pats down her hair, which is unmanageable in the humidity. 'I'm ... We're managing,' she says. 'How are you?'

'I can't complain.' Her eyes dull for a moment.

Esther holds up the canister. 'We're just out for some water.' When Frau Rosenbaum doesn't respond, she adds, 'Would you like to accompany us? If you aren't busy, that is.'

'I would be happy to,' Frau Rosenbaum says. 'I haven't much else to do. And it would be nice to have someone to talk to.'

There is already a queue outside the water store when they arrive. Queues used to represent a nightmare; Anneliese couldn't stand still for two minutes without feeling the need to hop, skip or jump about. Today however, she holds on to her mother's hand as docile as a lamb, clutching her Kitty-doll in the other hand, and Esther is grateful for this. The queue moves forward a little. Anni tags along like a sleepwalker. Esther can't stop thinking she might be sick – what else could explain this change in temperament? There was an outbreak of scarlet fever two weeks ago in one of the dormitories, and the younger children were all examined for symptoms. Anneliese was fine, the doctor told her: a healthy, robust child. She should be pleased to have such a quiet, obedient daughter, he added impatiently, when Esther insisted Anneliese was not herself.

Frau Rosenbaum gives her arm a gentle nudge. It's her turn. She snaps open her bag and hands over two bamboo tokens to the vendor. He lifts the lid of the cauldron a fraction and scoops out some water with a large dipper. But before Esther can hand over her canister, Frau Rosenbaum takes it from her.

'Has the water been boiled properly?' she asks the vendor.

'Yes yes.'

'There isn't enough steam. Please, lift the lid. Show me that it's boiling.'

He pretends not to understand and goes to take her canister from her hands.

'No! I want look-see!' Frau Rosenbaum says, raising her voice and holding the canister out of his reach.

The man spits out a curse and reluctantly lifts the lid from the cauldron. Frau Rosenbaum guessed correctly: the water is hot, but not boiling. So they wait another few minutes until it has come to a vigorous boil and then Esther lets the man fill her canister.

'Thank you,' she says to Frau Rosenbaum as they push through the crowds onto the pavement.

'One can't be too careful. Oh goodness, you've got a tired little one there!' She nods at Anneliese, whose mouth is stretched in a huge yawn.

Esther nods. 'It's time for her nap.'

They walk back to Seward Road in silence. At the entrance to the *heim*, Esther thanks Frau Rosenbaum for her company and wishes her all the best. But Frau Rosenbaum remains standing there, looking up at the shabby red-brick building.

'Come,' she says, taking Esther's elbow. 'I'll just see you inside.'

Esther picks up Anneliese, who is unwilling to walk up the stairs, and carries her to the dormitory. They pass the recreation room on the way, full of residents playing cards, or noisily discussing the latest gossip. By contrast, the women's dormitory is beautifully quiet, apart from the ever-present scratching and scuttling of insects across the floor. Frau Rosenbaum takes a seat on the bunk opposite Esther's – the one she slept in all those months ago – and

Esther lifts Anneliese into her cot. She falls asleep almost immediately. Esther leans over the cot and listens out for signs of wheezing, but her breathing is regular and silent. Then she tucks the mosquito netting tightly down the sides of the mattress and goes to sit on her bunk. 'She's been sleeping a lot lately,' she says quietly.

'She's growing.'

'Yes. Yes, I hope that's it.' She turns to Frau Rosenbaum. 'I forgot to ask. How is your husband?'

'Oh, he's . . . surviving.' Frau Rosenbaum sighs. 'It isn't easy for people our age to adjust. We're like two old oak trees, you know? You can't just uproot us and expect us to flourish in such . . . different soil. Sometimes I think I shall go mad, with nothing to do all day except sit around and mourn my lovely apartment and all the wonderful things I had to leave behind. I had the most beautiful tableware from the Königliche Porzellan-Manufaktur, did I tell you? And Fritz's pipe collection. And all our leather-bound books!' She blinks back a bead of sweat that has dripped into the corner of her eye. 'But what else could we do? And there are those far worse off than we are, I suppose.' She takes out a handkerchief and wipes her forehead.

Esther glances across at Anneliese, who has stuck her thumb in her mouth – a habit Esther has tried to break, so far without success.

Then, from downstairs, there is the sound of a gong.

'Lunchtime,' Esther says, getting to her feet. 'It always coincides with Anni's nap, unfortunately. I hate to wake her, but otherwise we'll be last in the queue.'

'Well, it was good to see you again,' Frau Rosenbaum says.

'It was.' Esther casts a dispirited look around the

dormitory and a thought forms in her mind. 'Anni took an awful shine to you on the boat.'

'She did. And Fritz and I to her.' Frau Rosenbaum stands up, leaving a hollow behind on the lumpy mattress.

Esther reaches through the netting and gently eases Anni's thumb from between her lips. The child stirs and, for a few moments, continues to make small sucking movements with her tongue, but soon lapses back into sleep.

Esther continues, 'It's just a thought, and I wouldn't want to impose, but –'

'Yes?'

'Perhaps, I mean, if it isn't a bother... Perhaps you might like to look after Anni. So that I can find work. I'd be happy to pay you. It's just – I can't possibly leave her with the convent, and I don't see any other way out of here.' Her voice catches. 'And I really don't know what else to do.'

Frau Rosenbaum looks down at her hands.

'I'm sorry,' Esther says quietly. 'I've embarrassed you.'

But when Frau Rosenbaum looks up, she is smiling. 'Nonsense! I would be delighted. I thought you'd never ask! You know, Fritz and I were never blessed with children. And I always thought I would be such a nice grandmother. Just the right combination of indulgence and firmness. It would be –'

She is interrupted by a small voice. 'Mama?'

They turn to see Anneliese sitting up in her cot. Her hair is ruffled, her face pink and hot with sleep.

'Mama, I'm awake,' she announces. 'I'm thirsty.'

Esther sweeps back the mosquito netting and picks her up. 'Anni?' she says. 'Frau Rosenbaum and I have been talking, and we think it would be nice for the two of you to spend some time together. Do you think you might like that?'

Anneliese gazes at her, open-eyed, and for a moment, Esther thinks she might burst into tears. But instead, she turns to Frau Rosenbaum and grins. 'Baum,' she says.

There is the sound of heavy footsteps ascending the stairs to the dormitory, and a young man bursts through the door. He looks darkly excited.

'It's just been broadcast,' he says, hands on his thighs to catch his breath. 'Just now, on the radio.'

'What?' Esther and Frau Rosenbaum speak at the same time.

'They've declared war. The British and French. They've declared war on Hitler.'

October 1939 to
February 1940

周翼

———

Wing's real name isn't Wing. It is Yì. Zhōu Yì. But when he hired him, Monsieur Petrov said that Yì was a ridiculous name; that it made him, Monsieur Petrov, sound like a demented donkey having to call out 'Yì, Yì!' all the time when he needed the boy to run some errand, or bring him a drink or a snack, or massage his sweaty temples or feet when he was tired. So his employer chose another name – Wing – one he prefers the sound of. And it could be worse. There are many Chinese servants who have been given names whose meanings are bound to bring bad luck, or invoke demons. So Wing doesn't mind, not really.

At night, when he isn't sleeping under the kitchen counter at Mamselle Kitty's, he sleeps on a rush mat beside his *nǎinai*, his father's mother. She lives in a north-facing room in a narrow, smelly lane off Whashang Road, close to the river. It wouldn't matter if the room were south-, east- or west-facing: it is windowless and perpetually dim. The front door opens onto the lane. It doesn't close properly; the hinges are corroded and the frame warped. The building was lucky to escape a direct strike by a Japanese bomb three years ago but has since developed worrying cracks. It is Yì's dream to save enough money to rent a room for himself and his *nǎinai* not so close to the river. Here, the slightest breeze sweeps in smells that are terrible in winter, and unbearable in summer. The river is a cesspool. The city's rubbish tip: bottles, jute sacks, paper flowers in vivid reds and purples, and occasionally – though disturbingly more often than one might think – a bloated corpse. The only thing keeping the noxious smells at bay is the bunch of continuously burning incense sticks placed on the spirit tablet, purchased for a couple of jiǎo from the nearby Xiàhǎi Temple.

Yì tries to come home at least once every week, for his *nǎinai* is almost blind and can no longer provide for herself. Yì isn't exactly sure of her age, but she seems ancient to him, her skin the colour and texture of bark, her feet so impossibly tiny she can only manage an arduous hobble across the floor of the dim, cluttered room that is their home. Nǎinai has been with him for as long as he can remember, making sure he knows where he's from and that he must never go back. He wasn't born in Shanghai; according to Nǎinai he was born on a dirt road somewhere between Xuzhou and Huai'in, to peasant parents fleeing poverty and famine in general, and the brutalities of northern warlords and the Kuomintang in particular. His mother died when he was three years old, and two years after that his father disappeared – abducted by Chiang Kai-shek's hoodlums for taking part in a railway workers' strike, according to Yì's older brother Huà; or – more plausibly, says Nǎinai – disappeared one night to escape his gambling debts.

When Huà comes to visit, when he has run out of food or money, or needs a place to hide (*Why come here?* Yì thinks. *It is the first place they will think to look, and it puts Nǎinai in danger every time*), he scoffs at the buildings opposite, where the Europeans are constantly building, renovating and patching up ruinous buildings, perched uncertainly on bamboo scaffolding, with a tenacity that seems to feed itself. Tap tap, hammer hammer, saw saw. Until the buildings that were not so long ago ruins are once more solid structures that can provide a home. They have been arriving in a steady stream for many months; these tall, hook-nosed, strange-smelling, round-eyed foreigners – these *lǎowài* – arriving here, in the poorest part of the city, in an unspoken battle for resources, housing, food, employment against the filth that threatens to engulf them all.

'Why do they come here?' Huà complains, spitting out a piece of chicken gristle onto the floor. (On rare occasions, Huà doesn't come back home for food – on the contrary, he brings food with him: parcels of rice, small pink pork feet, or even live, squawking chickens. Yì and Nǎinai know better than to ask him where he gets it.) 'We cannot be expected to share the little we have. Let them go across there' – he gestures with an outstretched arm in the direction of the river – 'to their rich friends.'

'They have no friends there, Huà,' says Nǎinai, fanning the small stove and sending a cloud of thick smoke spiralling upwards. 'They are like us, the lowest of the low.'

Yì's eyes flick towards his brother, at once afraid and eager to see his response. Huà's temperament is unpredictable. Yì often feels trapped in his feelings towards Huà. He admires his brother's passion, his devotion to what he believes in, his unwavering dedication to creating a more just world; but at the same time he is angry at his disrespect for their father's mother, and that he is prepared to risk not only his own torture or death, but also that of his family. Whenever Yì catches sight of the severed heads of captured communists placed on spikes around the city, he gets a dark, twisted feeling in his gut and must force himself to look up at those bloodless empty-eyed heads, terrified that he might recognise the face of his brother. And his relief that Huà is not among them is quickly replaced by rage. Rage at his brother's pride and arrogance and unwillingness to accept his fate: that he is, as Nǎinai says, one of the lowest of the low.

Huà hawks noisily and spits onto the ground, and then holds out his bowl for another serving of the chicken soup Nǎinai has cooked. 'The chicken is tasty, Nǎinai,' he says and gives the old woman a lopsided smile, indicating that he is not in a fighting mood.

Nǎinai clucks her tongue. 'It would be tastier if you'd worked for it.'

Huà shifts on his haunches. But before he can flare up, or knock the bowl from the stove in anger, or just walk out and disappear for months without a word, Yì jumps up and rushes to the corner of the room to where he keeps a sack with his belongings.

'I have something for you, Nǎinai,' he says brightly. He opens the sack and carefully removes a small parcel wrapped in paper. He blinks as he hands it to her. His eyes are watering from the black smoke. The stove is useful for cooking, but it provides very little warmth and makes the air almost unbreathable. 'It is a gift from Mamselle Kitty.'

The old woman brings the parcel to within an inch of

her face. She peers at it, sniffs at it, then begins to peel back the paper.

'It's cake,' Yì says and notices the saliva gathering in his own mouth. 'Mamselle Kitty gave it to me as a treat.'

'Did she bake it herself?' Năinai asks.

'No. She gets it from a special shop. She likes it very much. Go on' – he gestures with his hand – 'taste it. It is very sweet. Very good.'

Năinai breaks off a corner and puts it in her mouth, working her tongue around her toothless gums. Then she smiles. '*Hăo*. Very good, very good.' She takes another bite. 'Give my thanks to Mamselle Kitty. This was very kind of her.' Yì knows she is proud that he is employed as a taipan's number-one boy.

Huà has lit a matchstick-thin cigarette. 'So she keeps you as a slave and you should thank her for a small morsel of food.' He draws heavily on his cigarette and exhales, adding to the smoke from the stove and the incense sticks. Then he spits again and releases a string of filthy curses.

'Enough!' croaks the old woman. Her voice is surprisingly loud.

Huà falls silent. Yì knows his brother regards Mamselle Kitty as a rich, spoilt, good-for-nothing *jì nŭ* – a kept woman living in decadence while others work all the hours life gives them to scrape a survival; others, like their neighbours the Wangs, who have sold three of their five children in order to feed the remaining two. But Huà has never met Mamselle Kitty, hasn't encountered her beauty and kindness.

Yì likes to imagine – for of course he cannot remember – his own mother as having Mamselle Kitty's generosity and kind-heartedness. In fact, when he plucks Mamselle

Kitty's clothing from the wicker basket in the bathroom, to be bagged and taken to Chong's Premium Laundry Service on Rue Corneille, he sometimes lifts the garments to his face and inhales the warm fragrance of her perfume and body odour – honeyed and spicy, with traces of cigarette smoke and occasionally a slight, pungent muskiness – and imagines that this is his mother's smell. Lately, though, he has woken several times in the early morning with this scent in his nose and a warm stickiness on his blanket, causing him to feel a shame and confusion that linger throughout the day.

'Here, eat some too.' Nǎinai holds the remaining cake out to him.

Yì shakes his head. 'Give it to Huà.'

Huà eyes his younger brother, tilts his head back and exhales a thin stream of smoke. Then he laughs, a soft low laugh that holds no residue of his earlier contempt.

'When we take over,' he says, reaching for the cake, 'we will ensure that everyone has as much as he needs, including cake.' He stuffs the last piece of sweet luxury into his mouth, still laughing.

In the early hours of the following morning, Yì is woken by the cold that creeps through the cracks in the door frame. It is only October, but the dawn air already has a bite to it. He rises quietly, so as not to wake Nǎinai, who is sleeping beside him on her back, emitting soft rattling breaths from her open mouth. He shakes the damp chill from his limbs, urinates in the bucket that stands in the corner of the room and then slides his feet into his shoes. There is still some chicken and sweet potato left in the cooking pot, so he scrapes them out with his chopsticks, the final scraps with his hand, and stuffs them into his mouth. He checks the shelf – mounted high on the wall to prevent the mice from getting to it – to make sure there is a bag of rice for Năinai. It might be several days, a week even, before he can come home again. He makes a small bow in the direction of his sleeping *năinai* and then takes the bucket out to empty it. It is dark outside, and he shivers at the sound of the rats scuttling alongside the building.

'Tsss tsss,' he hisses to frighten them off as he pours the contents of the bucket into the gutter, although he knows his fear of them is greater. He doesn't like the darkness and carries a talisman around his neck – a *hù shēn fú* amulet in the shape of a tiger's claw given to him by Huà on Lunar New Year – to ward off sudden fright and give him the courage of the tiger. To be on the safe side, he also carries a bamboo rod when he is out at night. He uses it to dispel evil spirits by whacking it noisily against walls or off the ground. It could also serve as a makeshift weapon, he thinks, should he encounter any thieves or kidnappers.

As he sets off towards the bridge, a narrow flat light appears on the eastern horizon. He takes the shortest route, along the waterfront. On the river, the water makes a soft slapping noise against the sides of the sampans. Dozens of wharf coolies lie huddled beneath burlap sacks, waiting for ships to dock and their workday to begin. A few bars along the waterside are still open, music and electric light spilling out into the street. Yì hurries past, trying to walk the cold stiffness out of his legs. In these bars, he knows from Huà, women sell their bodies for money, or even just for a few glasses of whisky. The act of 'selling their bodies' is still part mystery to him, but the thought of them, in tight satin dresses that show an immodest amount of thigh, creates anxiety and thrill in equal measure.

A man calls out, 'Hey, you, pretty boy!'

Yì throws a glance to where the call has come from but doesn't slow down.

'Hey, pretty boy!' the voice calls again. It is a pimp from one of the bars. 'Want to earn some money? Good money! For a pretty boy like you. Five yuan – only ten minutes' work!' He barks a laugh.

Yì keeps his head down and breaks into a slow run until the pimp's laughter has faded and he finally glimpses Garden Bridge. He slows his pace to catch his breath. The Japanese guard at the near end of the bridge gives Yì no more than a cursory glance as he passes with a low grovelling bow from the waist. Crossing the bridge isn't always this uneventful, he knows from experience, having once ended up with a bloodied lip and a chipped tooth.

For the final part of his journey he hops on to the third-class car of the tram that travels up Amherst Avenue and Szechuan Road, and from there it is only a few minutes' walk to Mamselle Kitty's apartment.

He stops off on the corner of Rue Voyron to buy some sweet sesame crust buns for Mamselle Kitty's breakfast. Food and drink are usually delivered directly to the apartment from one of the fancy French food shops on Avenue Joffre, but Mamselle has developed a taste for these steamed, fragrant buns, and so Monsieur Petrov told Yì he'd set up an account at the bakery so Mamselle could have her pastries whenever she pleased. The account has been set up on trust ('If I ever discover you've cheated me, I'll hang you by your ears,' Monsieur warned Yì while bending the boy's wrist back so far he was afraid it might snap), and Yì always makes sure to select the buns with the heaviest sprinkling of sugar. He loves to watch Mamselle bite into the pastry, see the crinkle appear on the bridge of her nose as she chews and smiles at the same time, hear her laugh as she licks the powdered sugar from the corners of her mouth. Sometimes, but not always, she leaves a bun or two for Yì to eat.

The sun has risen fully by the time he arrives at the apartment building, providing a flat unchangeable light, but little warmth. The concierge, a round-cheeked Shanghainese with black wiry whiskers and a too-large uniform, lets him into the apartment, cuffing Yì around the back of the head as he always does to show him his place.

Yì tiptoes through the apartment into the kitchen, although he knows that Mamselle Kitty will not be awake for many hours, and changes into his uniform, a long-sleeved blue gown and a black cap. His next few hours are taken up with general chores: cleaning out the grate and lighting the fire, washing dishes, boiling water to put in the refrigerator to drink and prepare food with, sweeping and mopping floors, beating out rugs in the courtyard below (he props the apartment door open so as not to bother the concierge on his way back inside – and to avoid another smack to the head) and bagging up Mamselle Kitty's laundry. The work keeps him busy, but it is light in comparison to his previous position at Monsieur and Madame Petrov's residence. There, he reported for duty at five in the morning, was treated like vermin by the other staff, was often subjected to beatings and insults, and was put to work until everyone – Monsieur, Madame, all the members of the household staff – was tucked into bed.

He shudders to remember Madame Anastasia – a skinny, soulless woman, so unlike her coarse, boisterous husband – who either pretended that Yì was invisible (stepping on his hand when he was scrubbing the tiled floor), or treated him as an uninvited nuisance (shooing him out of a room when he was in the middle of some task, so that he would receive a beating from Lăo, the butler, for neglecting his duties). When Monsieur Petrov approached him one day to ask if he'd like to take up a position as number-one boy at a lady's apartment on Avenue Dubail, Yì's head bobbed up and down on his neck in affirmation so many times he thought it might fall off. And so here he is, number-one boy in a lady's small, elegant apartment, with enough duties to keep his mind from worries over his *năinai's* failing health or his brother's misadventures, but not so many that he cannot hum a tune as he works.

In the early evening, he returns from the cleaning service with a box of freshly laundered clothes for Mamselle Kitty and steels himself for another run-in with the concierge. He manages to avoid the man's hand as he opens the apartment door, however, and slips inside laughing, knowing the concierge would never dare to enter without instruction or invitation. The yeasty fragrance of the dough he prepared earlier – Mamselle Kitty requested *xiăolóngbāo* for dinner, succulent dumplings whose recipe he has from his *năinai* – drifts from the kitchen into the hallway.

'Wing, is that you?' Her voice rings out from the living room.

Yì enters, the box of laundry still in his arms, and makes a small bow. Mamselle Kitty is sitting on the sofa, legs tucked beneath her, with a magazine on her lap.

'You've brought my clothes,' she says. 'Good. Just pop

them in the bedroom please. I'll need to get changed before dinner. Monsieur Petrov will be dining with us tonight.' For a second, she seems pensive, chewing on her bottom lip. Then her expression brightens. 'What's for dinner?'

'Dumpling, Mamselle,' Yì answers, suppressing a gentle surge of disappointment at her news. He enjoys his evenings alone with Mamselle Kitty. Usually, she will call him into the living room after her dinner to make a drink, and tell him about what she's seen or done that day. She has taught him to use the gramophone, and tried once to teach him a card game. but the rules refused to stick in his mind. To Yì, it seems she dislikes solitude as much as he does. But tonight, Monsieur will be there, which means he will be banished to the kitchen.

'Dumplings? Lovely.' Mamselle gets to her feet and reaches for the silver cigarette box. 'How do you say "delicious"? *How che?*' She smiles.

'Yes. *Hǎo chī,*' Yì replies, feeling a little shameful at correcting her pronunciation but delighted she has remembered the word.

Mamselle Kitty lights a cigarette. 'Well then, I'd better go and get ready,' she says and disappears into the bedroom.

In the kitchen, Yì sets about thumping the air out of the dough and rolling out small circles, topping each with a filling of vegetables and shredded pork. It is a pleasant and rewarding task; Yì enjoys the feeling of the smooth, springy dough between his fingers. He prepares three large batches in the hope that there will be some left over for him when Mamselle Kitty and Monsieur have eaten. He rarely experiences the joy of a full belly.

He is just twisting the top of one of the dumplings to form a neat parcel for steaming when he hears the apartment door open and close. He wipes his floury hands on a cloth and goes into the hall, already in a half-bow, but Mamselle Kitty has opened the door and is relieving Monsieur Petrov of his bulky fur coat. They embrace; Yì lowers his head even further but through his long eyelashes he can see Monsieur's hand cupping Mamselle Kitty's behind and giving it a squeeze. Mamselle makes a silly squealing sound and slaps the indelicate hand away. They fumble about with each other for a few moments, until Monsieur turns to look straight at Yì. Yì cannot lower his eyes fast enough.

'What are you gawking at?' Monsieur says, then adds, 'Wanchee eat chop-chop. Can do?' He uses his fingers to gesture placing something in his mouth. Yì nods, blushing, and heads back towards the kitchen. He over-hears Mamselle Kitty saying, 'He does speak quite good English, you know,' but Monsieur's response is lost to him.

When he comes in later to clear the table, Yì is disappointed to see only three dumplings remaining. But better than nothing. He retreats to the kitchen to eat and clean up, and then waits for Monsieur to leave. They will go into the bedroom for a while, this is their usual routine, but eventually – it might be an hour, it might be four – Monsieur will call for his coat and leave. He never stays the whole night – Yì is sure that Madame Anastasia would never allow it. He has often observed Mamselle Kitty sitting at the window, staring out longingly as though she is waiting for a dear friend to arrive. When she catches him watching her, though, her face softens and she smiles, making her as beautiful as a peach blossom. It triggers in Yì a profound feeling of gratification that he can make her smile when anyone can see that she carries in her a dark, hollow sadness.

He rolls out his mat but has to wait until Monsieur has left before he can lie down. Sitting at the kitchen table, he lowers his head onto his arms and closes his eyes. He dreams. He dreams that one day, Monsieur will take Mamselle Kitty as his second wife – she will move into the big beautiful house and take Yì along as her personal number-one boy (he will be given his own room, like the butler). He will bring Năinai to live with him where they cannot be found by Huà, or the police, or the nationalists.

A loud noise from the other room stirs him from his dozing. A bang, then harsh yelling. Yì sits up, startled. The kitchen is now almost entirely in darkness, just the yellowish glow from the street lamp outside providing some dim light. They are arguing, their voices hard and angry. Monsieur's coarse voice surges, drowning out hers, then there is a ripping sound, Mamselle's voice again, thick with tears, and a series of smashes and bangs, and finally the thunderous slamming of a door.

Yì waits several minutes before he dares to leave the kitchen. When he opens the door, he gasps. The living room is a mess. Several records lie broken on the carpet; one of the curtains has been half-pulled from the rod; a pool of amber liquid is soaking into the rug; and the silver-framed photograph of Mamselle Kitty lies in the corner of the room, the glass fractured into a perfect spiderweb. Yì stands in the doorway, half-hiding behind the door frame. Has Monsieur Petrov left? Yì holds his breath and squeezes his eyes shut to enhance his hearing, and after a moment pads into the hallway. Monsieur's coat is gone. From the bedroom, he hears a noise: a strangled, wretched sob, then murmuring – a string of words he cannot understand – spoken first quietly distressed and then rebuking. He creeps towards the door.

'Mamselle?' he says quietly. There is no response. The door isn't fully closed and he peers in through the gap. She is sitting on the edge of her bed, playing with her hands, interlacing her fingers and pulling them apart, clenching her hands into fists and rubbing them hard against her thighs.

'Mamselle Kitty?' Yì says and pushes the door open a little.

She looks up. Her pale wide face is blotchy, her eyes swollen. Thick black streaks run down her cheeks. For a moment, she looks startled, but then her expression hardens.

'Get out!' she shouts. Her voice cracks. She leaps up and waves her arms about wildly. 'Get out! Get out!'

Yì is suddenly frightened she might strike him. 'Sorry sorry,' he says, backing towards the door. 'Sorry, Mamselle.'

Mamselle Kitty flops down onto the bed and Yì runs back into the kitchen. He throws himself down onto his mat and slaps his face several times to stop himself from crying. His heart is beating painfully in his chest, so he inhales and exhales deeply. Four times, five times. His pulse slows. Then he closes his eyes and, thankfully, sleep finds him.

ESTHER

'It's a bit shabby,' says Frau Rosenbaum as she greets Esther at the door to the building. 'But I'm sure you'll spruce it up in no time.'

She wheezes as they climb a steep narrow staircase. Esther and Anneliese follow, their steps oddly cushioned, as though the wood is rotting beneath their feet.

'Just a bit shabby,' Frau Rosenbaum repeats, though less confidently this time. When they reach the second floor, she pulls out a handkerchief and wipes her face. 'You're just up there,' she says, nodding up the staircase. She tucks the handkerchief into her sleeve and adds, 'Do you want to leave Anni with me while you sort yourself out? Give the two of us a chance to become properly acquainted.' She strokes Anneliese's hair. 'I'm sure I've got a sweet or two hidden somewhere.'

Anneliese's eyes widen and she nods eagerly.

'All right,' Esther says. The suitcases are straining at her arms. 'I'll be back down shortly.' She turns to climb the final set of stairs.

The room, when she gets there, is beyond disappointing. Although alone, she lets out a gasp of dismay. The room is tiny, ten square metres perhaps, with black wooden floorboards, a bedframe without a mattress, a worn chest of drawers, and three shelves attached haphazardly to the far wall. A dirty paper screen with a bamboo frame hides a stained tin bucket in a corner near the window. The walls are unpapered; their scuffed chalky surface gives off an odour that is sharp and musty at the same time.

Although the room is on the top floor, the street noise travels up from below: the shouts of peddlers pushing wheelbarrows with squeaky ungreased axles; the wails and groans of beggars; conversations being held between neighbours in German, Russian, Polish, Chinese; and from somewhere distant, the strains of a gramophone record. Esther places the suitcases on the floor. Her legs are heavy, but there is nowhere to sit. The room's only redeeming feature is that, being just beneath the roof on the top floor, it is not quite as dark as the rest of the house. But even as she thinks this, she looks up and sees that some of the light is coming through a gap in the roof – a small hole that has been patched up inexpertly.

'No worry, will fix better.'

Startled, Esther turns to find her landlady standing behind her. Mrs Kavalchuk is an elderly Belarusian woman, with a pink scalp that shows through her scraped-back white hair. 'Will fix, later,' she says, waving at the hole. 'Japanese bombs.' She lets out a series of tuts.

'Yes,' Esther says, already disliking the woman for charging twenty-five dollars' rent for a room that is barely habitable. 'It'll need to be fixed before it rains again. And —' She glances around the room, beset by a sudden surge of exhaustion. 'Where can I get a mattress from? My daughter and I can't sleep on the floor.'

'Mattress in yard. My husband bring it up later.'

'Thank you.'

'And the honey pot must be downstairs in the morning, or not be emptied.'

'I beg your pardon?'

The woman crosses the room towards the bamboo screen and gives the tin bucket a sharp kick. 'Honey pot,' she says tersely.

'Oh,' Esther says, blushing.

Mrs Kavalchuk tilts her head slightly and narrows her eyes. 'Rent pay every Monday. No be late.' Then she turns and clomps back down the stairs.

But it is still preferable to the *heim*, Esther thinks, and smooths down the front of her dress with clammy hands.

'They've sent a girl!'

The man leads Esther into an office so full of cigarette smoke she can barely see beyond the four desks to the far wall. The place is in chaos; cardboard boxes piled all over the place, pictures in their frames propped up against the wall, ashtrays overflowing with ash and butts, and everywhere paper, paper, paper. The clatter of typewriters is so loud, Esther can hardly hear herself think. Three scruffy-looking men turn towards her briefly as Joseph Grünblatt, the man who introduced himself to her as the editor of the *Shanghai Jewish Post*, shows her inside.

'This is Esther Niermann,' he says, addressing the men. 'From Berlin. Stepped off the boat' – he turns back to Esther – 'a couple of months ago?'

Esther nods. The smoke is making her eyes water. She

takes out the slip of paper Fräulein Levin gave her, still a little dazed that she is here at all. The Committee, whom she turned to first, confident they would place her immediately, couldn't – or wouldn't – help.

'There are hundreds of refugees arriving every week,' she was told by the same man she'd spoken to when she first arrived. 'And unfortunately for you, many of them are skilled.'

'But I am trained. I have qualifications!'

'They are more . . . experienced,' the man told her. 'They are men who have families to feed.'

'I have a daughter to feed,' Esther insisted, exasperated by this logic.

The man shook his head. 'That's not quite the same thing. Look, I'm very sorry, but perhaps you'd like to try again in a month or two?'

On her way out, trembling with frustration and humiliation, she was approached by a red-faced Fräulein Levin, who slipped her a sheet of paper. 'You'd better get round there within the week,' she said quietly, 'before they give the job to someone else.' She smiled, blushing hard. 'We have to stick together, don't we?'

Esther looked down and saw the advertisement for a position as a typist, signed illegibly, and stamped: 'Position Filled'.

Her hand shakes now as she hands it to Joseph. But he scans the paper and then shakes his head.

'Oh dear. There's been a mistake.' He looks at Esther and rubs the side of his face. 'I'm sorry, but we won't be needing a typist.' He waves his hand around the room. 'These are our reporters, and they can all type.'

Esther tries to swallow, but her mouth is so dry she can

hardly move her tongue. She wants to cry. Of course they don't need a typist; what they probably need is a cleaner. And she would take that job – *any* job – if she were offered it. She has little choice. She has signed the rent contract, and borrowed one hundred dollars from Frau Rosenbaum for the key money.

Beside her, Joseph is overcome by a sudden coughing fit. It is a harsh, wretched cough that lasts for a minute or two. When it is over, he spits into an oversized grubby handkerchief he pulls from his pocket. 'I'm sorry,' he says finally. 'The Committee, well ... I know they're a bit overwhelmed right now, so ... there's been some sort of mix-up. We need a bookkeeper, not a typist.'

'I can do that,' Esther blurts out, louder than she intended.

Joseph frowns. 'Well, I'm not sure –'

He is interrupted by a dark-haired man who hurries into the room, a sheet of paper in his hand. 'We discussed this, Eli,' he snaps, addressing one of the reporters and slamming the paper down on the desk. 'We do not publish personal advertisements alongside news of British losses on the Western Front.' He snorts. 'It's distasteful. And before you start –'

He stops abruptly when he notices Esther. 'Who's this?' he asks, staring at her through sharp dark eyes.

'This is –' Grünblatt looks down again at the piece of paper Esther gave him. 'Esther Niermann. Frau Niermann, this is Franz Hohlbein, our deputy editor.'

Hohlbein's lips twitch impatiently. They are very red and wet, almost as though he is wearing lipstick.

'She's here for the job,' Grünblatt continues. 'The Committee sent her.'

Hohlbein's eyes dart from Esther back to Grünblatt. 'But she's a – a woman.' He says it as though her sex is a personal insult to him. 'They can't possibly be serious.'

Esther throws a glance at Grünblatt.

'I trained as a clerical assistant at an insurance company,' she says quickly, before Hohlbein's objections have time to settle. 'It's a few years ago now, but I'm fully qualified. And I'm a quick learner.' She looks around the room to avoid Hohlbein's stare and takes in the mess again. She hopes she isn't overestimating her capabilities, but she has always been good with numbers – and besides, what choice does she have?

'Don't listen to him, Joe,' the man called Eli says suddenly. 'Give her a chance, I'd say. It's not as though she can do any worse than the last chap.' He smiles at Esther and then nods towards a pile of papers perched precariously on the corner of one of the desks. 'Those are the invoices for our advertisers. Here' – he points at a couple of folders lying on a corner of the floor – 'expense accounts, payroll accounting – not that we get paid much' – he winks at her – 'but we definitely need someone to do the sums.'

Esther looks back to Grünblatt and realises she is holding her breath.

'All right, all right,' Joseph says. His voice is cracked, the cough still lingering in his breath. 'Very well. You can have a go, by all means. Can we agree on a trial period, say ... two weeks?'

Esther suppresses a nervous laugh of relief. She doesn't want to appear unprofessional, or give him any reason to change his mind. 'Yes, thank you, two weeks sounds perfect.'

'Well then,' says Joseph, 'let's get you to work.'

★

The trial period passes unmentioned, and for the first time since Esther arrived in Shanghai, life seems to be taking on some tangible, malleable shape. Her wages cover her rent, and she is able to repay her debt to Frau Rosenbaum. She feels bad about not paying for childcare, but Frau Rosenbaum won't hear of accepting payment.

'She's all I have from wasting away with homesickness,' she says. 'If anything, I am in *your* debt. No, you keep your money. Anni is good for us. I can think of no other reason for getting up every morning.'

Esther leaves it at that, knowing that if it hadn't been for Anneliese, she too would have struggled to find a reason for getting out of bed when they were living in the *heim*. Now, each morning starts with the promise of a new day of doing something meaningful, and she is surprised by how quickly her training comes back to her after all these years. Never once had she imagined going back to work after she married Carl, certainly not after Anneliese was born, and yet it is as though the keenness in her brain has been lying dormant, waiting patiently for the moment when it can get back to the methodical task of adding and subtracting, lining up numbers on either side of a straight line, entering accounts received and accounts payable.

Esther's quick progress is greeted with warm words of praise by Grünblatt, and the occasional nod by his deputy, Franz Hohlbein. The coarse language and bluster of the reporters takes some getting used to, but Esther soon learns that, although loud, their bark is worse than their bite. Hohlbein, by contrast, rarely speaks. Does his absence of a bark mean his bite is something to be wary of? Esther isn't sure. But this is a trivial concern compared to the grim realities faced by many of the other refugees, and Esther returns to Alcock Road tired but content most evenings, and grateful at how Anni and the Rosenbaums bookend her days.

Four months after starting work at the *Post*, in February 1940, Esther returns home one evening to find two boys sitting on the front step playing marbles. They are the sons of the Brauners, who live on the first floor. They get up to let her pass.

'Isn't it a bit cold to be playing outside?' she asks.

The older one, nine-year-old Manfred, is wearing trousers that stop a good few inches above his ankles. He looks up at her and blinks. 'We're just playing marbles,' he says dully.

'Perhaps you should go inside now,' Esther says gently, thinking she will buy the boys some new trousers when she is next at the market. 'You don't want to catch a chill.'

Manfred blinks again. His brother Isaac stares down at his shoes, wiping a thick glob of snot from his nose with his sleeve. Neither of them makes a move. Esther can guess why they are sitting outside, and indeed, as she enters the house, she hears ugly, bitter snatches of an argument coming from the Brauners' room. As she steps quickly and quietly past, the door opens and Frau Brauner pokes her head out. She is a slight woman, a few years older than Esther, with nut-brown hair and delicate features. But now her face is pale and puffy, and Esther can smell alcohol on her breath. She smiles at Esther. It is a pinched smile and costs her some effort.

'Could you –' Her voice cracks. She clears her throat and tries again. 'Could you please tell the boys to come in? Their supper is on the table.'

Though Esther is tired, she nods and heads downstairs again. The boys' cheeks and noses are bright red, and Manfred is using a stick to poke at a small bundle lying beside a concrete bin overflowing with refuse.

'Boys, your mother says it's time for supper,' she says as warmly as she can, and glances down the short lane to the street, to where a scuffle has broken out between three or four Chinese men. A wheelbarrow lies upturned beside them, spilling its contents, a pile of rotting sweet potatoes, onto the pavement. From further down the street come the familiar sounds of whooping and yelling from one of the bars, squeaking rickshaw axles, and from behind the nearby bins, the scuttling of rats. It doesn't matter whether it is day or night, winter or summer, the street never seems to come to rest.

Manfred continues to poke at the bundle, something wrapped in a straw mat.

'Manfred,' Esther says, adding a sharper edge to her voice. Unlike Anni, these boys seem more responsive to commands than requests. As she steps forward, she catches sight of what Manfred is poking at. She lets out an involuntary cry and her stomach heaves. Shivering with cold, or disgust, she leans over to peer more closely at the bundle, hoping she is mistaken. But there it is – a tiny baby, its skin tinged blue, a shock of black hair, its face wrinkled. Esther doesn't have to touch it to see that it is dead, lying next to the waste that is due to be collected the following morning.

Sick to her stomach, she orders the children upstairs and climbs the stairs to the Rosenbaums' room. Anneliese jumps up to greet her.

'Rosie made me soup, Mama!' she says, waving a spoon

in the air. She has been in Frau Rosenbaum's care for only a few months, and she has been transformed from the dull and fearful child Esther knew in the *heim* into a sparkling, animated three-year-old. Esther has long since repaid the one-hundred-dollar loan, but she will always be in Frau Rosenbaum's debt for what magic she has done for Anni.

'Yes, I can see that, *liebling*,' Esther says, stepping forward to wipe Anneliese's chin with a cloth before gathering her up in her arms and giving her a kiss. She holds her for a while and then smiles at Frau Rosenbaum, who sits on a wooden stool at a tiny scuffed table next to the window. A narrow brass bed stands pushed up against the far wall beside a washbasin. Despite Frau Rosenbaum's attempts to make it homely – a patchwork blanket thrown across the bed, framed photographs of her and her husband nailed to the chalky walls, even a square of lace tablecloth on the deeply scarred table – the room has never lost its wretched shabbiness.

There is an angry yell from downstairs, followed by a child's wail of despair. Anneliese looks up sharply at her mother, but Esther just shakes her head a fraction and kisses her on the forehead.

'Have you been a good girl today?' she asks.

'Oh, she's a very good girl,' Frau Rosenbaum replies, rising from the stool and wiping her hands on the front of her apron. Her dress, a brown woollen garment that has seen better days, hangs loosely from her body. She is no longer the stout, well-upholstered woman Esther met on the boat.

Esther lets Anneliese slide out of her arms. 'Go and finish your soup, Anni.'

Anneliese goes to sit back at the table. 'Goulash,' she says. 'I like goulash – it's yummy.'

Frau Rosenbaum lets out a small puff of air. 'Goulash without the meat. Just potatoes, onion and tomato. But it's good that she eats,' she adds, reaching over to ruffle Anneliese's hair. 'Please, sit down,' she says to Esther. 'And at least we don't have to worry about it not being kosher. There's enough for you, if you'd like.' She goes to the stove, a contraption shaped like an upside-down flowerpot with small briquettes used to produce a feeble heat, and spoons a ladle of watery goulash into a bowl.

'Any news?' she asks, setting the bowl down in front of Esther. She does, of course, read the newspaper herself, but never fails to question Esther about what she might have learned at the office – a nugget of information from Europe, perhaps, that didn't make it into the paper.

Like all the other newspapers, the *Jewish Post* is under pressure from the Japanese to report only German victories. And, as things currently stand, there wouldn't be anything more hopeful to report anyway: the Wehrmacht continues to spread eastwards like a cancer, and recent reports suggest they will soon advance to the north. Almost every day brings the same sobering truth – that the Germans are outclassing their opponents not just in military dominance and strategy, but also in fanaticism. Esther blows on her food and shakes her head.

'Well, it can't go on for ever,' Frau Rosenbaum says with a sigh, leaving the most important thing unspoken: what will happen when 'it' is over.

Esther doesn't respond. This is not the first time Frau Rosenbaum has reminded her of her own mother. She concentrates on eating her goulash, trying to ignore the draught that plays at her ankles and the horror of the bundle outside.

A loud grating noise can be heard from downstairs, then a door slamming. The shouting has stopped. Frau Rosenbaum sighs heavily. 'Let's hope they give us a rest for a while,' she says, 'and those poor boys, too.'

'They were playing outside when I arrived.'

Frau Rosenbaum shakes her head and frowns. 'It's hard for them, of course it is, but it's hard for all of us. Fritz and I have never argued like that. Never.' She strokes her wedding ring, as if for good luck. 'We –'

She is interrupted by the sound of the door scraping open. Herr Rosenbaum steps in without a word and turns to close the door behind him, using his shoulder to press it shut into the warped frame. Frau Rosenbaum lets out a groan – barely audible, but it is there – before saying, 'How was your day, dear?'

Without answering, he shuffles to the bed and sits down with a thump, making the springs squeak. Anneliese goes and sits on his lap. He manages a tired smile.

'Your Uncle Fritz used to have a very important job,' he says to Anneliese. He has told her this story numerous times, but she never tires of hearing it. 'I was a pharmacist. Do you know what that is? Hmm? A very important job, very important. Part healer, part magician.' At this, he lifts his hands to mime a magician's trick, letting his fingers flutter around Anneliese's face. 'And everybody knew me, and . . . oh, never mind, that's not what was important. What's important is that I was happy. Oh' – he tips his head back, causing the loose skin beneath his chin to tauten – 'oh, I was happy to be helping people.' He lets his head fall forward again.

Esther is horrified and embarrassed to see tears running down his face. Anneliese reaches out to stroke his cheek. 'Why are you crying, Uncle Fritz?'

He doesn't answer her question. Instead, he says, 'And do you know what I did today?'

'No,' Anneliese whispers. Her eyes are wide. This part of the story is new.

'I swept out a warehouse. An enormous building with the dirtiest floor you can imagine. Swept it out. All day. Sweep, sweep, sweep, with a besom made from bamboo, until my back was so sore I couldn't stand up straight.'

'Oh, Fritz, my love.' Frau Rosenbaum gets to her feet. 'Leave the little one,' she says softly. 'She doesn't understand.'

'I'm not little, I'm three,' Anneliese complains, holding up three fingers to prove her point.

Esther stands, scraping the floor with her chair. 'Anni, *liebling*, it's time to get cleaned up for bed.' She suddenly can't bear the scene in front of her, can't bear the wretched intimacy of it all. 'Come on, time to go.' She has to pull hard on the handle before the door yields.

'Nightie-night,' Anneliese says cheerfully and dashes out into the hallway.

Before closing the door, Esther turns to see Frau Rosenbaum standing in front of her husband, his arms clinging wearily around her waist and his head resting on her stomach.

*May 1940 to
December 1941*

KITTY

When the bruising has faded sufficiently to be concealed with make-up, Kitty's roots have grown out by half an inch. Her ribcage still aches when she breathes in too deeply, but after almost two weeks indoors, she has become desperate for some fresh air. She finishes touching up her face with powder and pins on a tilted hat, grateful that this fashion lets her hide the left side of her face.

The air outside is not as fresh as she hoped, perpetually filled, it seems, with a sour-smoky odour. But it is May, and one of those few days of the year when the weather isn't either oppressively hot or miserably cold, and so she decides to walk the fifteen minutes or so to the salon, rather than take a rickshaw. She fastens her coat and walks briskly down Avenue Joffre, ignoring the crush and noise around her. She clutches her handbag tightly to her chest. It holds her passport, and a scribbled note with the address of the US consulate. She steps past a beggar, almost tripping over the man's rag-wrapped feet, and picks up her pace. Her legs are getting tired and she is a little out of breath, but no matter – soon she will sit and enjoy a few hours of pampering.

It is a popular salon among the Europeans living in the French Concession, but Kitty is a regular enough customer not to need an appointment. The owner and stylist, Marcel Chang, greets her with a kiss on either cheek and shows her to a chair in front of a large mirror. Standing behind her, he fiddles with her hair for a moment or two, and then clicks his tongue, clearly unimpressed. 'Hmm, these roots.'

'I haven't had a chance to –'

'Yes, definitely some colour. And a wave. A cold wave, I think, just the thing.'

Kitty nods. 'Yes, of course.'

She settles back in her chair, picking up a copy of *Lin Loon Lady's Magazine* to flick through while Marcel mixes the colour. Then he brushes on the dye, clucking and tutting occasionally at how long she has allowed her dark roots to grow. Kitty knows he enjoys scolding her as much as he will enjoy praising his own handiwork when it's done.

Marcel gives the colour half an hour to take, during which Kitty smokes a couple of cigarettes and sips at a cup of very bitter green tea. Marcel returns to wash out the colour and then trims the split ends, humming along to a *shídàiqǔ* tune that is playing on a wireless in the corner. A Chinese girl with an impressively long braid that reaches almost to her knees comes to sweep up the cut-offs with a bamboo broom. Kitty doesn't know her name, and the few times she has addressed her, the girl responded with a tight-lipped smile and a shake of her head, indicating that the two of them don't share a language.

Marcel begins to twist Kitty's hair firmly onto the rollers, grinning at her reflection whenever she winces at the tightness of his actions. 'I make you beautiful, Mademoiselle Kitty,' he says.

'I hope so, Marcel,' she replies with a practised grimace.

'Ah, but *il faut souffrir pour être belle, n'est pas?*' He grins again, and Kitty can't help but think he might be enjoying himself. But he doesn't try to hide it; not like her father when he would chastise her – for her own good – beating and punching and kicking until she learned that the more she resisted, the harder the blows would fall.

Looking in the mirror, she catches the shadow of a bruise on her left cheekbone. Instinctively, she raises a hand to it but drops it again quickly. She doesn't want to draw Marcel's attention to the bruising, and feels suddenly foolish for not having prepared a plausible excuse in case he notices anything. Bruises or marks on the face – that could have cost a girl her job at the Nachtfalter, back in Vienna. They all knew this; all of them knew to anticipate the violence of an angry, drunk or plain sadistic customer, learning fast to raise their arms and take the blows on their ribs, back, legs. But of course, Vitali isn't a one-night-only customer, and so Kitty had trusted him too far; she hadn't been prepared.

It came out of nowhere – she can't even remember when things got quite so heated. All she knows was that when the punch fell, she felt immense surprise before the pain seared through her head. And before she could open her mouth to ask him why, or to tell him to stop, or to scream and curse him to hell, the next punch came, delivered precisely to her nose, snatching her breath away and setting off an explosion of bright dots in front of her eyes. She fell back onto the bed, where a mere half an hour earlier he had pinched her earlobe between his teeth and run his hand up her thigh, and she had felt his stiffness against her belly, his hot scruffy breath in her ear as he lifted her on top of him, and the poison of her anxieties and jealousies melted into nothingness. And afterwards, in the comforting warmth of his arms, she asked him to stay for a whole night – a single night after almost a year! – and the familiar row started, and then she felt blood running from her nose, dripping onto the white bed sheets, making patterns as pretty as any calligrapher's quill, then more punches, though now she thought to raise her arms in protection, taking the blows to her ribs as she had learned, until he was out of breath and sweating, and spitting words at her, 'Who the hell do you think you are? A fat dirty Jew whore, that's what you are! You are nothing. Nothing!' before shaking out his fists and fumbling into his clothes, and throwing the money into her face, not leaving it discreetly on the counter as always.

Three days later, he appeared at the apartment door, sheepish behind a bouquet of lilies. Kitty let him in, listened patiently to his abject and lengthy apology, let him take her into his arms, into the bedroom – and as his large sweaty hands roamed her body, stroking, teasing, pinching, she contemplated the practicalities of implementing her contingency plan.

The bell above the salon door tinkles, and the buzz and roar of the outside traffic sweeps in and fades again as the door opens and then closes. Kitty turns her head a fraction. Two women, one middle-aged, the other somewhat younger, stand at the door waiting to be attended to.

'*Vite, vite!*' Marcel hisses at the young Chinese girl, who immediately lays her broom aside to take the women's hats and gloves. They are seated beside one another in front of large mirrors. Marcel leaves Kitty's hair and slides over to greet them effusively. The women give their instructions, and Marcel promises to attend to them as soon as he has finished setting his other customer's hair. The older woman glances over to Kitty with a prim smile and looks back at her reflection in the mirror.

'Not really a surprise,' she says to her friend, clearly picking up the thread of a conversation they started earlier. 'But shocking, all the same.'

The other woman mews her agreement as the young assistant drapes covers over their shoulders. 'One does feel very grateful to be so far from it all,' she says. 'It seems like only yesterday that we came through the last one. Hugh, you know, lost his brother at Ypres. His poor, poor mother.' She shakes her head.

'Well, we can only hope that the new prime minister shows this Herr Hitler what's what pretty quickly now. The war's been dragging on for what, eight months now? And it's all very well being over here, but we are already seeing the effects.'

The younger woman raises her eyebrows. 'On Henry's business, you mean?'

Her friend snorts. 'Oh no, far from it. But all these Jews spilling into the place. A few hundred of them are landing every week, I've heard. I wonder why the shipping companies take them on board at all.'

'But one hears of the most awful things going on in Germany. About what's being done to them.'

'I know, I know. It is all rather frightful. But that doesn't make these people our responsibility. All the civilised countries have quotas. Even the Yanks. And they're full, from what I hear.'

Kitty swallows. A wave of heat rises up and over her, only to turn to ice as Marcel squirts the permanent wave solution onto her curled-up hair.

'Head to the front,' he orders. 'You don't want this in your eyes, no no no.'

Kitty straightens her head and has no choice but to sit face-to-face with her own reflection. The women continue their conversation, not bothering to lower their voices. But why should they?

The older one speaks again, and Kitty can just about see her at the corner of her vision. 'Without a doubt, Felicity, without a doubt. But . . .' Here, she raises an eyebrow and gives her friend a strained, conspiratorial look. 'The truth of it is – however awfully they're being treated in Germany – they might perhaps want to ask why it's always the Jews who are the target of such measures, pogroms and such.' She waves her hand dismissively. 'I mean, they might want to take a good, hard look at themselves, you know.'

'We-ll, perhaps,' her friend replies, her tone indicating she does not quite agree.

The sharp smell of the wave solution makes Kitty's eyes water. Her scalp is on fire and she feels like she could tear her own skin off in hot chunks.

The younger woman continues. 'They're not *all* bad though, are they? There are the Sassoons, for example.'

Kitty recognises the name. Sir Victor Sassoon is one of the wealthiest men in Shanghai, a taipan, owner of numerous properties and a man with whom Vitali is desperate to do business. But he is a Jew, nonetheless.

The older woman lets out a little sniff. 'Sir Victor has

breeding, I grant you. But you know –' Here she turns in her chair to face her friend. 'There's been talk of letting them into the Club. Of course, Henry – he's on the board now, did I tell you? – put a stop to that right away.' She sits back and inspects herself in the mirror, tracing a lofty eyebrow with her finger. 'We had enough of that nonsense in India. But one does wonder, what with France on its knees and that dreadful little Vichy man on the Municipal Council now – did you hear about that?' She sighs. 'One does wonder if one might not be better off somewhere else.'

'Are you and Henry thinking of going back to England?'

'Oh goodness no! But we are considering Hong Kong. Now' – she says with another sniff, looking around the salon – 'where has that peculiar little man got to? We haven't all day. And do switch that awful racket off!' she adds to the assistant with a dismissive gesture towards the wireless.

ESTHER

Esther wakes to calls and whoops from outside. She stirs from sleep and a queer dream that surfaces briefly but slips away before she can grasp it. She shivers and slides out of bed, wrapping her blanket around her. Her throat is dry and raspy and she feels the beginnings of a dull headache. She walks to the window and rubs on the glass with her hand to remove the condensation. She lets out a surprised 'Oh!'

The New Year has begun with snow. The shouts and whoops are coming from a group of children playing on the street; the Brauner boys, the Goldstein twins from next door, several Chinese children Esther recognises from the building opposite, and in their midst, the small blonde head of Anneliese. The children run about, their breath coming in short bursts of cloud, shouting to each other in a strange mix of German, Yiddish and Chinese that has emerged as the children's common language.

Esther raps on the glass, but Anneliese doesn't look up. She opens the window, wincing as the cold sulphurous air squeezes her lungs, and then calls out, 'Anni! Anni!'

Anneliese looks around and then up. She beams at Esther. 'Snow, Mama! It's snow!'

'Happy New Year, *liebling*!'

Close by, someone sets off firecrackers. The children greet this with more whoops of joy, and then Manfred and Isaac lie down in the scrawny snow and begin flinging their arms and legs from side to side. Immediately, Anneliese lets herself fall to the ground and does the same.

'It's freezing, Anni!' Esther calls. 'It's too –' She stops herself. Who knows when Anneliese will next have the opportunity to make a snow angel? Her chest tightens. Angel – *malekh*. That was her mother's pet name for Anni. She locks away the thought and starts getting dressed, rubbing her arms and legs vigorously to warm them. The children's excited shouting continues. More firecrackers go off. What a racket! Esther smiles as she pulls on a second pair of socks. A new year. Perhaps the snow is a good omen; perhaps this will be the year that everything changes for the better. Hope dies last, isn't that what they say? She begins to draft a mental letter to her parents: *New Year is celebrated three times here, can you imagine? Rosh Hashanah, 1 January and Lunar New Year, which is spectacular beyond imagination. The costumes, lanterns, fireworks, pageants – Anni loves it!*

It will be one of countless letters she has written, each of them injected with as much cheerfulness as she can muster. She has not yet received a single reply. With the war in Europe raging, her hopes of her parents receiving her letters have dwindled – either because they get lost on the way in all the chaos, or because ... No, she refuses to take that thought to its dreadful conclusion.

She rubs her toes, cold despite the two pairs of socks,

143

and gets to her feet. Then, through the children's yells and the crackle of fireworks, she becomes aware of another sound, very different in quality, vague at first and then growing louder and more insistent. A howling noise, deep and urgent. With a painful start, as though her heart has been snagged by a wire, she realises it is Frau Rosenbaum.

She rushes down the stairs in stockinged feet and bursts into the Rosenbaums' room without knocking. She goes blank with shock. Frau Rosenbaum is kneeling on the floor next to the bed; her head is thrown back and her shoulders heave uncontrollably as she lets out a distressing wail that fills the room, the house, the whole city of Shanghai. On the bed lies Herr Rosenbaum. He is on his side, his face a yellowish-grey, contorted into an expression of pain. His lips are dark purple, almost black, and his chin is caked in a white, chalky substance. It appears regurgitated. His left arm hangs at an odd angle over the side of the bed, but it has already begun to stiffen.

The funeral takes place two days later. Esther takes a half-day off work – unpaid – to attend. At the *Post*, Franz Hohlbein is standing in as editor-in-chief for Joseph, who has been laid up with bronchitis for the past week. Esther is certain Joseph would have granted her a day off, no questions asked, but Hohlbein runs a tighter, more stringent ship. She leaves Anneliese in the care of Frau Brauner; reluctantly, but a funeral is no place for a child.

The cemetery is on a low hill at the outskirts of the city. Frau Rosenbaum walks behind the coffin, leaning heavily on Esther's arm. The pallbearers are all refugees like themselves, haggard young men in kippot who carry the coffin awkwardly, stumbling occasionally on the snow-covered ground. A sharp wind carries in the thick, acrid smoke of a nearby cotton factory.

When the procession reaches the grave, the Chinese gravediggers, whose services are paid for by the Jewish Relief Committee, are still battling against the frozen soil. The threadbare congregation – neighbours, acquaintances, the young rabbi from Ohel Moshe Synagogue and a tired-looking representative from the Committee – is forced to wait for twenty freezing minutes until the hole is deep enough. Then the coffin, with the Star of David painted neatly on its side, is lowered, weighted with rocks to prevent it from rising with the groundwater when the rainy season comes, and covered.

The rabbi recites psalms and speaks some words about 'the infinite suffering of our people', omitting any mention of the cause of Herr Rosenbaum's death. But Esther had guessed it immediately: he poisoned himself, a skilled pharmacist; of course he knew just how to take his own life with a minimum of fuss.

The biting cold makes the congregation impatient. They fidget, stamp their feet as inconspicuously as they can, check their watches – as tragic as the occasion is, it is nothing special. Death has become their constant companion.

Frau Rosenbaum stares vacantly into the distance. 'I don't exist without him,' she says, to no one in particular. 'Just as he wouldn't exist without me.'

Esther uses her lunch break to go to the post office. She shivers at the chilly air inside. The grandiose marble panelling radiates a coolness that is pleasant in the summer, but now, in February, makes the place resemble a meat locker.

A huge electrified chandelier hangs from the ceiling of the large main hall, beneath which queues have formed at the open counters. Esther reaches into her pocket for the letter and joins the shortest queue. She smiles a greeting at one of the customers up ahead, a man from her neighbourhood who recently tried to sell her his wife's rather ragged fox wrap and is nudged rudely in the back. She turns; the customer behind her nods with a scowl. 'Your turn,' he says in German. 'I haven't got all day.'

Esther steps forward and places her letter on the counter. 'A letter to Germany,' she says to the clerk, pushing the envelope through the slit at the bottom of the glass. 'And would you please check to see if I have any mail? For Esther Niermann.'

The clerk, a tall Chinese man of indeterminate age with large black-framed glasses, nods and turns around to face a huge mahogany shelf that reaches from floor to ceiling. The shelf contains hundreds of small boxes, some stuffed full of letters and papers, some gapingly empty. The man reaches up purposefully to a box – obviously expertly acquainted with whatever sorting system they have – and pulls down an envelope.

'Yes,' he says, turning to Esther and smiling. Her heart gives a jolt. Finally! After all this time, a sign of life! But then the clerk adjusts his glasses on his nose and peers more closely at the envelope in his hand. 'What your name again?'

'Niermann.' Her voice comes out as a squeak. She clears her throat. 'Esther Niermann.'

'Ah.' The man squints down at the envelope for what seems like an age, and then slowly shakes his head. 'Ah, no. This addressed to Niemann. Eva Niemann.' He speaks very precisely, emphasising the *Nie*. He pushes his glasses back up. 'Sound the same, but not the same.'

'Oh.' Her heartbeat seems to slow down so much she thinks it might stop altogether. She feels the clerk's stare on her, but for a moment she can't move. Behind her, the next customer taps his nails impatiently on the counter.

'Then it's just the letter,' she says finally. 'To Germany.' She counts out the coins for the stamp and slides them across the counter.

The clerk shrugs, though not unsympathetically, and then sweeps up the coins. 'Next time,' he says with a firm nod. 'You come and get letter next time.'

'Yes,' she says, and tries to stop her voice trembling. 'Next time.'

She has overrun her lunch break by ten minutes by the time she arrives back at work and hurries into her tiny office, quickly removing her hat and coat.

A moment later, Franz Hohlbein taps on the door frame. 'Fräulein Niermann? Would you step into my office please?'

'Of course.' She follows him through the press room – the men smoking and typing and speaking on the telephone – and into his office, where he takes a seat behind the desk.

'I'm sorry I was late,' she says, a little breathlessly. 'I had to wait in line at the post office. I'll make up for it this afternoon.' She says this with a tinge of guilt. Frau Rosenbaum has recently been complaining of headaches and general fatigue – she has lost her husband, after all – and Anneliese is a handful at the best of times.

But Hohlbein doesn't respond to this. He indicates the

chair opposite. 'Please, Fräulein Niermann, take a seat.'

'Frau,' she says, smoothing down the back of her skirt and sitting down. The sharp smell of Hohlbein's aftershave is making her eyes water. 'It's Frau Niermann.'

'Oh.' He frowns. 'I didn't realise you were married.'

She gives her head a small shake. 'I'm widowed, actually.'

'Ah.' Hohlbein smiles at her. It is not so much a smile as an expanded twitch, a brief pulling back of his wet lips over his teeth. As though he is not used to smiling, she thinks.

For the next few minutes, he asks her about her book-keeping. He has an odd manner about him; she isn't sure if he has some complaint about her work, or whether he is genuinely interested in the intricacies of her accounting system. But after a while, when he seems to run out of questions, he says, 'Good, good.' He places his hands, palms down, on the desk between them. 'You are an asset to the newspaper.' He says it as though it was his idea to hire her in the first place.

'Thank you.' She waits for him to tell her she can get back to work.

Instead, he offers her a cigarette, which she refuses, then takes one himself. He fumbles with the lighter. 'Frau Niermann.' He smiles – or twitches – at her again. His eyes are sharp and dark and round. 'I have it on good authority that Café Atlantic serves the best *apfelstrudel* in the city. And I thought, perhaps, you and I could go and partake of a slice. And perhaps a glass of beer or two.'

The heat rushes to her face. 'Herr Hohlbein, I'm ... well, I have a daughter.'

'You could bring her along.'

Esther shifts in her seat. The metal legs of the chair

make a scraping noise against the floor. 'I ... I don't think, I mean, thank you for the offer, but ...' All she wants now is to get away from his small dark eyes and moist lips. She gets to her feet, not looking at him. 'I think I'll ... I should really get back to work.'

On her way out, she is unsure whether to close his office door or leave it open. Finally, she decides to close it with a soft click.

That afternoon, she gets home to find Anneliese at the front door, bunching the apron of her dress with both hands.

'Look-see, Mama,' she says proudly and carefully opens the apron a little. She is holding dozens of red paper flowers that decorated the streets at the recent Lunar New Year celebrations. 'I collected them myself. For Rosie.'

'That's very nice of you, *liebling*,' Esther says, trying to ignore the thought of the thousands of germs the flowers might be covered in. 'Where is Rosie?'

Anneliese shakes her head. 'She's poorly, Mama. We were playing marbles but then she said she has to lie down. I said can we play hospitals and I would be the nurse and she would be the patient.' She frowns. 'But she didn't play very well. She kept falling asleep. So I gathered these for her' – she nods towards the flowers – 'to make her feel better.'

Esther hurries upstairs, takes one look at Frau Rosenbaum and runs out to call a doctor. He arrives half an hour later and diagnoses malaria.

'Malaria?' says Esther. 'In February?'

But the doctor just gives her an impatient look. 'Why wasn't I called earlier?' he asks crossly. 'She's barely conscious and deteriorating rapidly. When did the symptoms start?'

'I ... I don't know. She's ...' Esther trails off. 'Her husband died recently. She hasn't been herself since.' It sounds feeble, neglectful, even to her.

'Well,' the doctor says, shaking his head as he packs away his stethoscope, 'sit with her, keep her comfortable. I'm afraid there isn't much I can do for her.'

'But you must have some medicine! Quinine or something.'

He sighs and puts on his coat. 'I'm very sorry. If I had the choice, please believe me, I would administer something. But I have to be very careful with the little I have, and this patient ...' He pauses and looks down at Frau Rosenbaum. His face is gaunt and pale. 'She won't recover. I'm sorry,' he repeats, and leaves.

Esther sits with Frau Rosenbaum in the near darkness, with only a thick candle to provide some light. She cools Frau Rosenbaum's forehead with a wet rag and drips clean water into her mouth with her fingertips. Esther can feel the heat of her body from where she sits, but when she folds down the blanket, Frau Rosenbaum moans and starts shaking violently, so she tucks it back up under her chin. This close, Esther sees the appalling state of the woman's teeth. Apart from three gold molars, most of her other back teeth are brown and carious. They've all suffered with toothache at one time or another, ensuring a roaring trade for dentists specialised in the pulling of teeth, but Frau Rosenbaum's must have been giving her real pain. She stirs and Esther takes her hand. Her face has a ghastly doughy pallor, with two bright red blotches on her cheeks, as though she's been clumsily made up to look like a doll.

At around midnight, Frau Brauner brings Esther a cup

of broth and offers to sit with Frau Rosenbaum for a while, but Esther declines.

'I don't mind sitting with her. I want to be here if she wakes up.'

Frau Brauner nods. 'Anni is sleeping with the boys,' she says. 'I didn't think she would want to sleep all on her own.'

'Thank you,' Esther says softly and gives Frau Brauner a tired smile. The woman looks terrible. Her eyes are sunk in dark purple sockets and the flesh at her jawline is as slack as that of a woman twenty years older. She has taken to wearing a headscarf to cover missing clumps of hair, and her skin is covered in red patches of scaly skin. All of her abject misery turned outward. Last month, her husband was arrested for drunk and disorderly behaviour; the Chinese judge sentenced him to two days in Ward Road Gaol. He was taken into custody kicking and screaming, knowing it was in fact a death sentence. He was right: bitten by typhoid-carrying lice that inhabit the cells, he died two weeks later. Now Frau Brauner spends most of the day in an alcoholic daze, while her sons spend hours wandering the streets. The sickening thought of the dead baby Esther found last winter crosses her mind. What other horrors might the boys stumble over on the streets now?

When Frau Brauner has left, Esther takes the cloth from Frau Rosenbaum's forehead and rinses it in a bowl of cold water. *A house of widows*, she thinks bitterly. She gently places the cloth on Frau Rosenbaum's head and then gets to her feet to alleviate the cramp in her legs. Frau Rosenbaum stirs and coughs. It is a dark rattling sound.

'Shhh, I'm here,' Esther says gently and takes her hand.

Frau Rosenbaum's eyelids flutter for a moment and she opens her mouth to speak, but the effort is too great and her face slackens again. Esther watches her closely for a moment and then leans back in her chair and shuts her eyes. She remembers the dimly lit room in Berlin, a slice of black night visible at the edge of the curtains, the smell of stale sweat and sour breath, the sound of baby Anneliese crying in the next room. And Carl, hot and feverish, lying in his bed, his eyes cloudy but resting heavily on her face, *Aaron*, he whispered, *Aaron*, as he struggled to take a rasping breath with his squashed and bleeding lungs.

She must have dozed off, because she blinks to find a grey dawn light creeping into the room. The air is freezing and there is a tart odour of sweat and urine in the room. From outside, she hears the sound of the night soil collectors come to do their early dawn business. She shivers and sits up straight, noting a painful ache in her neck, and looks at Frau Rosenbaum. Her complexion is still pale but clear, the dark red blotches have disappeared from her cheeks and for one absurd moment, Esther thinks she must have miraculously recovered during the night. She leans forward to remove the rag that still lies across Frau Rosenbaum's forehead, and her hand brushes the waxen skin of the woman's cold cheek.

周翼

July, and Shanghai is a thirsty, heaving, languid beast. The
entire city is gasping for air. Yì stands at the intersection
of Chengdu Road and Avenue Foch, where the French
Concession borders on the International Settlement,
waiting for a break in traffic so that he can cross. Like
everyone around him, he is dripping with sweat, but it is
a vain effort to wipe his damp forehead with moist hands,
so he just blinks back the drips that fall into his eyes. In
a pocket sewn into the inside of his shirt he carries five
dollars given to him by Mamselle Kitty to buy 'as many
watermelons as you can carry, Wing'. Food deliveries to the
apartment have been irregular lately – supply problems in
the north, Monsieur Petrov claims, though Yì has noticed
nothing of this on the markets – and Mamselle says she
cannot keep drinking water, water, water to quench her
thirst. She needs watermelons.

A man Yì recognises as a pickpocket shuffles past. Even
the criminals are listless in this heat. Yì's hand travels to
his chest where the money is hidden. He is humbled by

Mamselle's trust – five dollars is more than half a year's wages – and intends to show his respect by bringing back not only the sweetest, ripest, juiciest melons she has ever eaten but also a talisman. Not a tiger's claw like he has, for this is far too masculine, but perhaps a White Tara to ensure a long life and serenity, and to protect her from dangers and problems of the heart.

Mamselle Kitty has not, of course, given him permission to spend the money in this way, but for this he has a plan: here, in this part of the city, watermelons can cost up to two jiǎo apiece – a ridiculous price aimed at those who have more money than they can count – but Yì knows to go to one of the markets in the Old City, where he can buy four melons for the same price. With the change, he can haggle for a talisman and still have several dollars to give back to Mamselle. How he longs to make her smile! He can't help but feel smug with pride at his plan.

He paces up and down on the pavement as he waits to cross, even though there is no escape from the white heat of the sun. But then he is lucky: a rickshaw coolie cuts off a tram, forcing it to screech to a halt. The passengers, jerked out of their humid stupor, begin shouting and cursing complaints from the windows. Yì watches as a Sikh policeman – a red-turbaned giant with a jet-black beard – marches across the street and drags the coolie from his rickshaw. He is out of his jurisdiction, strictly speaking, but this doesn't stop him hauling the man, who is half his size and weight, to the Settlement side of the road and begin beating him with his club. The man's cries can hardly be heard above the whoops and cheers from the tram's occupants. Yì uses the ensuing traffic chaos to sprint across the street.

It takes him half an hour to get to the Old City, and the soles of his feet are burning from walking so far on baking pavements. He stops outside City God Temple to splash his face with water from the small fountain there. The water is lukewarm and leaves a strange, unpleasant smell behind on his skin, which is just as well, because it stops him drinking any in spite of his thirst. Perhaps, when he has bought the watermelons, he might use a few fēn to buy some tea. Surely Mamselle wouldn't mind, would she?

The Old City is a maze of alleyways, not much wider than an arm span. And yet, the residents use these tiniest of spaces to sit, eat, play cards and mah-jong, argue, barter and gamble. Yì hurries down a dim alley; it is as though the relative luxury he now enjoys at Mamselle Kitty's apartment has given him fresh eyes for the squalor. Strung between the ramshackle, blackened buildings are washing lines hung with a canopy of clothes in all shapes and sizes and colours. The alleys open up into small squares that serve as meeting and market places, and, occasionally, as stages for public executions. Yì shudders as he recalls how his brother Huà once described to him a public strangling, taking obvious pleasure in his younger brother's dread as he depicted the spectacle in detail: the bloodthirsty onlookers, the solemnity of the executioner, the instant hush in the crowd as the executioner raised the garrotte, the wide-eyed terror on the face of the condemned man, the darkening of his crotch as he pissed himself, and then the crunch of his windpipe as the garrotte tightened around his neck, causing his face to swell and his eyes to bulge – and the frenzied cheers of the crowd as the body fell forward onto the dust. For weeks afterwards, Yì found it difficult to fall asleep without the sequence of images crawling into his brain.

He slips his hand inside his shirt and strokes his amulet, then walks quickly in the direction of the fruit market, feeling a faint shiver of horror in spite of the crushing heat as he passes the site of a recent execution – a beheading this time, not a strangling, as evident by the bloodstain caked onto the dusty ground.

Even the concierge takes pity on Yì and spares him a box around the ears when at last he arrives back at the apartment. The weight of the melons he carries in a sack on his back seems to have increased threefold during the long walk back, and he is red-faced and soaked in sweat on his return. His tongue is swollen and he can barely swallow; his mouth is as dry as rice paper. He is sure there isn't a drop of moisture left in his body.

The apartment is gloriously cool as he steps inside, and his step is light as he goes into the kitchen to put the melons in the refrigerator. He knows Mamselle Kitty will prefer them cold. The talisman, a small porcelain pendant with an image of a White Tara, which he haggled hard for, but which in the end cost him a whole dollar, he places inside his rolled-up sleeping mat. He will wait for the right moment to present it to her.

Just then, she calls from the living room. 'Wing, is that you?'

He hurries in, bowing. 'Yes-yes, Mamselle.'

She is lying on the sofa, a cigarette in one hand and a cocktail glass in the other. Above her, the ceiling fan whirs, stirring the thick smoke-filled air above her head but creating a pleasant breeze below.

'What took you so long? I feel like I'm melting. Did you get the watermelon?'

Yì feels a swell of irritation. This is her gratitude for his efforts?

'Yes, Mamselle. Watermelon in . . .' He has tried many times but still cannot pronounce the word of the cupboard that keeps food cold and fresh. 'In kitchen.'

'Oh good.' She flicks the ash from her cigarette and then looks at him with raised eyebrows. 'Well? What are you standing there for? Go and get some.'

Yì holds his smile but bites down on his lip and goes back into the kitchen, where his smile drops from his face. He takes a large cleaver and begins chopping up one of the melons, not caring that chunks and seeds go flying through the room. It's him who has to clean the floor anyway. He stacks them carelessly onto a plate to take in to Mamselle.

'Mamselle,' he says with a stiff bow, holding the plate out to her.

She takes the plate. 'A fork . . .?' she begins, but then adds, 'Oh, what the hell!' and picks up a dark red chunk of melon between her fingers, stuffing it in her mouth. The juice runs down her chin as she eats. '*Hǎo chī*,' she says, grinning. 'Velly velly *hǎo chī*. Thank you, Wing, this is just what I needed. Here, you must try it. It's delicious!'

Between them, they devour the entire watermelon, gorging as though they haven't eaten in weeks. And at that moment, licking sticky red juice from his fingers, her smiling eyes upon him, Yì knows he will never meet a sweeter woman than Mamselle Kitty.

Monsieur Petrov arrives shortly after six to take Mamselle Kitty out to dinner. Yì wasn't told he was coming this evening and hopes Mamselle will let him go home tonight. He hasn't visited his *năinai* for over a week now and knows she suffers terribly in the heat. But Mamselle pays him no attention as he sees her and Monsieur out of the front door, and it is not his position to ask if he may leave. He closes the door and inhales the cloud of perfume she has left behind.

As always, there is a large number of small tasks to attend to: tidying magazines from the floor; placing the gramophone records back in the shelf; boiling water; sweeping dead spiders out of the cracks in the walls and floors. He gets through his tasks briskly, stopping only to nibble at some spicy chicken wings left over from Mamselle's lunch. He is standing on a bamboo chair in the living room, wiping the dust from the arms of the ceiling fan, when he hears the front door opening. They are back earlier than expected. He clambers down quietly and places the chair back at the table. He takes his place behind the bar, thinking they will want him to mix them a drink. But when they come in, they are arguing and don't notice him. He makes himself a little smaller and stands there, motionless.

'It was humiliating,' Mamselle Kitty says. Her face is red and shiny. 'Did you see how he was looking at me? Hmm? Did you?'

Monsieur takes a cigarette from a small silver case. 'What do you want, Kitty? The man was paying you a compliment. What, do you think you're royalty?' His words are a little slurred.

'No.' She shakes her head vigorously. 'No. I don't think I'm royalty. But I'm not a *whore*, either!'

Yì ducks a little lower and steals towards the door as quietly as he can.

Monsieur pulls his face into a sneer. 'Lobster, champagne, American cigarettes, these ... these dresses!' He steps forward and grabs the front of Mamselle's dress. 'Are these the clothes of a whore?'

She pushes his hand away. Her voice is trembling. 'You tell me, Vitali. Or, if you'd prefer, why don't we ask your wife?'

A bluish vein on Monsieur's temple begins to throb and he clenches his fists. Yì stands in the shadow of the doorway, ready to leap out. He isn't sure how much help he would be – in fact, he is sure he would have to take a beating – but he is prepared. A cockroach scuttles across the tiled floor and Monsieur crushes it with his shoe. At that moment, he spots Yì. A fleeting look of astonishment is quickly replaced by a flash of anger.

'What are you doing there?' he snaps. 'Come here, now!'

Yì steps forward, smiling politely, and Monsieur clamps a hand on his shoulder, hard. 'Look, Kitty, your number-one boy has decided that we are his evening's entertainment.'

Mamselle Kitty looks away. 'Leave him alone, Vitali.'

'But, *chérie*! The servant wants entertainment! Let's give him some.' He takes Yì in an awkward but firm embrace and begins to dance him across the floor. Yì tries to release himself, but cannot. 'A waltz, how about it, boy? Kitty, put on a record!'

'You're drunk,' she hisses. 'You're embarrassing yourself.'

Yì is frightened. His smile keeps slipping off his face. Monsieur's movements are clumsy and heavy, and suddenly, he twirls Yì out to the side and lets go. Yì stumbles across the room, only just managing to retain his balance. He can feel tears on his face.

'Snivelling little bastard,' Monsieur says, and curses him with some choppy, throaty words Yì can't understand.

'Leave him alone,' Mamselle Kitty says again, coming over to where Yì is crouching. 'It's not –'

But Monsieur hasn't finished with him. 'You know what I think? I think he's a dirty little spy. I think he spies on everything we do. You stand outside the bedroom and listen to everything we do in there, don't you? Is that entertaining for you, you little yellow pervert? Do you enjoy listening to me and Mamselle, hmm?'

Yì shakes his head, desperate to be away from this.

'He's probably been stealing, too. They all do. Can't trust them any further than you can throw them.' He marches into the kitchen and begins yanking open drawers and cupboards, ignoring Mamselle Kitty's protests. Yì stands silently in the doorway, his heart beating so fast he fears it will explode.

'What's this?' Monsieur says, stooping awkwardly to look beneath the counter. He uses the tip of his shoe to nudge out Yì's sleeping mat. Yì's breath catches in his throat.

'That's his mat,' Kitty says in a low angry voice. 'That's what he sleeps on. Not on a nice soft mattress like you or me. The boy sleeps on a rush mat on the floor.' She folds her arms across her chest. 'Now. If you've finished wreaking havoc in the kitchen, I think it's best if you leave.'

Monsieur lets out a noisy snort but doesn't say anything. Then, as he steps across the mat towards the door, his shoe catches, and Yì can only stand and watch in horror as the mat slowly unfurls to reveal a small paper parcel containing the amulet he bought for Mamselle Kitty.

An ugly smile forms on Monsieur's face as he – slowly, very slowly – bends to retrieve the parcel. With similar, horrible patience, he unwraps it. Mamselle throws Yì a questioning look.

'Lookee see,' Monsieur says. 'What have we here?'

Mamselle Kitty lets out a soft moan. 'Oh, Wing.'

Monsieur holds up the pendant and shoots Yì a fierce glance. 'You thieving little bastard, I should –'

Mamselle Kitty interrupts him. 'But that isn't mine.'

'If he didn't steal it from you, he stole it from someone else. Where would he get his hands on money to buy something like this? Why would he bother hiding it, if it weren't stolen?' He takes a sudden step towards Yì and, without warning, strikes him hard across the face. Yì yelps and stumbles backward to the floor. But before Monsieur can hit him again, Mamselle grabs his arm.

'Leave him, Vitali. Please. He's only a boy.'

'A thief is a thief. I don't care how old he is!' He flings the amulet in Yì's direction but misses.

'Please, Vitali.' Mamselle steps in front of him, shielding Yì. Her tone is soft and appeasing. '*Chérie*. He is worth nothing. Not the bruise on your knuckles. The red on your palm. The scuff on your shoe.' She raises her hand to stroke his cheek. 'He is nothing,' she whispers.

Monsieur takes her hand and kisses the inside of her palm. He takes a deep breath. 'You are right, *chérie*, of course. A worthless piece of yellow dirt.' He turns his head and spits on Yì.

Yì doesn't dare wipe it off. He remains motionless, crouched on the floor.

'Go to the bedroom and wait for me,' Mamselle tells him. 'I wish to give the boy a piece of my mind before I throw him out. Shoo, go on,' she adds with a teasing smile. 'I will join you in a minute.'

As soon as the door to the bedroom falls shut, Mamselle Kitty tugs Yì to his feet.

'You will have to leave,' she says softly. 'I'm sorry, but I don't think he will change his mind. You have to go.'

'I no steal,' Yì says desperately. He hides his face in his hands. He doesn't want to show her his tears.

Mamselle bends down to roll up his rush mat. 'I'm sorry,' she says as she hands it to him.

Yì shakes his head but cannot find the right words.

'Wait here a minute,' she whispers, and then crosses the kitchen silently into the hallway. A moment later, she returns, holding something in her hand. 'Take this.'

She presses a wad of banknotes into his hand. A bleat of surprise escapes his mouth.

'I can't give you any more,' she says. 'I . . . I need the rest. Now go. I'm sorry. Be safe and go. Go!'

ESTHER

———

'No. Absolutely not.' Franz Hohlbein stands at the doorway to the press room. His face is sweaty, his eyes as sharp as ever. The room is filled with the sound of the tapping of typewriters and an occasional scratching of pen on paper. Anneliese stands behind her mother's legs, quietly, as Esther begged her to.

Esther tries again. 'But I can't leave her at home on her own. The woman who was looking after her ... she had an accident.'

Frau Brauner, who has been looking after Anneliese for several months now since Frau Rosenbaum died, is lying in bed with concussion and three broken ribs. It's remarkable she isn't dead.

Hohlbein's mouth twitches. 'This is a place of business, not a kindergarten,' he says moistly.

'Oh go on, Franz,' Eli says without taking his eyes off his typing. 'She's no trouble. I think she'll cheer the whole place up.'

'Yes. That's exactly what I'm afraid of,' says Hohlbein,

with a swift look towards Eli. 'And it's Herr Hohlbein to you.' He turns back to Esther. 'Shouldn't she be in school? How old is she, anyway?'

'I'm nearly five,' Anneliese announces proudly, stepping forward. 'Mama says I can go to school next year, but I can already write my name. Shall I show you?'

'No, that won't be necessary,' Hohlbein snaps.

'But I can write it all on my own,' Anneliese insists. 'And it's a long name. It's got nine letters.'

Esther gives her shoulder a gentle squeeze. 'Not now, *liebling*,' she says. This is going far worse than she expected. She was hoping for at least a week, until she can make other arrangements. Turning back to Hohlbein, she says, 'I'm sure I can find Anni something useful to do.' Her glance falls on some piled-up boxes near the back door. 'Unpacking the typewriter ribbon, perhaps.'

'And next you'll be accusing me of employing child labour. No, I'm sorry. You'll have to find other arrangements. This isn't a kindergarten,' he repeats and leaves the room.

Yesterday afternoon, Esther returned home from work to find a small crowd of people gathered outside the house. With a stab of panic, she ran inside to find Mrs Kavalchuk standing at the bottom of the stairs with a sneer on her face.

'She have Japanese man there. I tell her they sadists,' she spat out. 'I no pay the doctor's bill, you tell her. I call doctor, but I no pay the bill.'

Esther brushed past her and ran up the stairs. There had been rumours that Frau Brauner had turned to 'entertaining' Japanese soldiers in her room to make ends meet, but Esther hadn't wanted to believe them, for Frau

Brauner's sake as well as her own – who else would look after her daughter while she worked?

'Where's Anni?' she demanded, bursting into the room, and only then took in the scene in front of her: the room was in complete disarray; a table lay overturned in the corner; one of the window blinds hung lopsided on its frame; and on the bed lay Frau Brauner, her face already beginning to swell up in an angry reddish-purple colour. She was being examined by the doctor – the same doctor who had treated Frau Rosenbaum – letting out dark groans as he pushed and prodded her chest. A fug of blood and sweat and sex hung in the air. The doctor turned and nodded a greeting.

'I've sent the children to play downstairs,' he said and turned back to wipe some blood off Frau Brauner's eyebrow with a wet cloth.

Esther was still clutching the doorknob, so hard her knuckles had turned white. She was trembling. Any sympathy she might have felt for this battered, broken figure on the bed – Frau Brauner opened her mouth to lick her bloody lips, and Esther could see bright red gaps where teeth had been knocked out – was overridden by a ferocious anger that Anneliese had witnessed this.

'How long has this been going on?' she hissed at Frau Brauner.

'It was the first time, I swear, I needed a little money, that's all.' Her voice was a low rasp. 'And Anni wasn't in here ... with us, she was with Manfred, downstairs. That's what I thought, but then, I looked up and there she was, at the door, and he ... he went berserk.' She closed her eyes and swallowed, wincing in pain.

'I felt three cracked ribs,' the doctor said to Esther,

straightening up. 'She might be a little concussed, but the bruising to her face should heal without scarring. Replacing the missing teeth' – he shrugged – 'that would be quite expensive.'

Esther hasn't spoken to Anneliese about what she might have seen, knowing she would be at a loss for words to describe it. But Anneliese slept soundly last night, and is now her chirpy, cheerful self.

'They just opened a kindergarten,' Eli says, when Hohlbein is out of earshot. 'You know, on Tongshan Road. Samuel wrote up a piece on it, right, Sam?'

Samuel nods, a pencil clamped between his teeth.

'The IC Nursery. I was there this morning,' Esther says. 'They're completely full. Anni's been put on a waiting list, but they said there was very little chance of a place before the older children start school in September.' She throws a glance towards Hohlbein's office. He's on the telephone. 'I'll have to hide her in here today,' she says, 'in the back.' She turns to the men. 'You won't say anything, will you?'

They shake their heads, and Eli gives her an encouraging smile. It seems a tenuous plan at best, but there is nothing for it. Esther clears a space behind the desk in her tiny office and gives Anneliese a pencil and some paper to keep her busy, warning her to be on her best behaviour.

It is a long, hot day. Esther's skin is clammy from the heat but also from nerves. Anneliese has risen to the challenge of the hiding game, keeping as quiet as she can, but Esther knows she will need to spend her accumulated energy later before there is any chance of her sleeping tonight.

Finally, a strangled series of chimes from the wall clock rings out five o'clock. The men throw covers over their typewriters and begin to gather their things; one of the reporters, Samuel, says he will stay on in case any news comes in on the charter expected to be signed by the British and Americans.

'The Americans have to get involved soon, Sam. They can't just sit by and watch,' Eli says. 'Not if they have any decency.'

'They're biding their time,' Samuel says. 'They're not stupid – they'll strike when the time's right.' He won't hear anything bad said about the Americans; but then, he's on the visa waiting list.

Esther gathers up some pencils and tidies them away. 'Well if they don't, we'll be stuck here for ever.'

Just then, Anneliese runs in from the back with her hands cupped. 'Look, Mama, look what I found.' She lifts her right hand to reveal a butterfly, a beautiful creature with black-and-gold-striped wings, which must have flown in through the window. Sensing an opportunity for escape, the butterfly twitches its wings once, twice, and then takes flight. Anneliese watches in wide-eyed dismay as it flies off into the corridor.

'Come back!' she cries, and before Esther can stop her, she sprints after it.

Esther throws down her bag and rushes towards the door, stopping short when she comes face to face with Hohlbein. He is holding Anneliese by the wrist.

'Anni, come here,' Esther says, trying to control the tremble in her voice. 'Anni. I told you not to –'

Anneliese shakes herself free. She gives her mother a guilty look. 'My butterfly,' she mutters.

Esther takes her hand and turns back to Hohlbein. With the typewriters now silent, the whirring of the ceiling fan is louder than ever.

'Herr Hohlbein,' she begins, feeling the sweat prickling on her upper lip.

'I told you this is no place for a child. And here she is, running about the place.'

'I know. I'm sorry. But she's been here all day and she's been as good as gold. She just draws and plays quietly. Just now – well, I think her energy got the better of her. But if you'd –'

'Do you take me for a fool?' His voice is dangerously low.

Esther tightens her grip on Anneliese's hand. 'No, it's –'

'You think you can just go behind my back, when I *specifically* said this was no place for a child . . .' He presses his lips together hard. His left cheek twitches. 'Consider your contract terminated without notice.'

'But I need this job!' Esther cries. 'I've always worked hard, I've never been late, I –'

Eli interjects. 'Come on, Franz. Have a heart. Or at least, think of the paper. She's better at her job than any man.'

Hohlbein gives a tight shake of the head. 'That's all I have to say on the matter,' he says, and turns to leave.

'Herr Hohlbein, please!' Esther has to fight back tears. 'Are you punishing me because I wouldn't eat *apfelstrudel* with you? Really, Herr Hohlbein?'

He has crossed to the door. He opens it wide and steps aside. 'Out, now.'

Esther knows she only has one last card to play, but *I won't beg*, she thinks, *not in front of my daughter*. She pulls Anneliese close. 'Come on, Anni. We're leaving.'

They step outside. Behind them, the door bangs shut. On the street, Esther barely notices the crush, the shouts and yells of the hawkers and beggars, the incessant honk of the car horns as they try to edge forward through the usual assemblage of rickshaws, cars, cyclists and handcarts that clog the road.

Anneliese tugs at her hand. 'Mama, please don't cry. Please don't be sad. I'm sorry if I was naughty. I didn't mean to be.'

Esther puts a hand to her face. It is wet. She crouches down in front of Anneliese and holds her tight.

'Oh, *liebling*, you weren't naughty at all. You are the best little girl in the whole world.' She swallows, although her throat is tight, and all at once, her mind is made up. She takes Anni's hand. 'Come on.'

'Where are we going?'

Esther tries to smile. 'It's a surprise.'

They begin to walk down Broadway, in the opposite direction of home. Esther doesn't have the money for a rickshaw, and the tram is so full she is likely to have her pockets emptied before they'd even left the stop.

On the corner ahead of them, a scuffle has broken out between a group of European Jews and some black-clothed yeshiva students. Esther crosses the street to avoid them. The recent arrival of a large group of orthodox Jews from Belarus, devout and observant Mir Yeshiva students, has created further tension and conflict in the district. The scuffle fizzles out, however, with no punches thrown.

They continue down Broadway, past Abraham's Dry Goods Store, Feiner & Reich's Broadway Pharmacy, Silbermann's stationery shop. Beggars everywhere. All the way, Anneliese drags her feet, slowing in front of every food stall. 'But, Mama, I'm hungry. I'm thirsty. Where are we going? Are we there yet?'

Esther yanks her arm, a little harder than necessary perhaps, but knows that if she stops now, she might not continue at all. From a nearby courtyard, the crack of gunfire – *bang bang bang* – and suddenly Anneliese is at her side and silent, clutching her Kitty-doll to her chest.

They walk as quickly as the crush of people on the pavement will allow, Anneliese's hand tightly in her own. And with every step comes a sharp longing to turn back. But she has no choice but to continue. She concentrates on placing one foot in front of the other, focuses on her scuffed shoes – left, right, left, right – coming into her line of vision and then disappearing again, until she feels dizzy and has to look up.

They stop in front of an iron gate, the entrance to a compound of houses. The gate opens onto a main alley running down the middle, with the entrances to the two-storey houses in smaller alleys that lead off the main path. Esther has long since committed the address to memory: 219 Lane on Broadway, house no. 37. At one side of the alley, a Chinese cobbler sits on a chair with his tools in a box in front of him. Esther recognises him from his call, '*Kaputie – ganz machen!*', a nugget of German he has picked up from the refugees. He looks up at Esther and Anneliese as they pass, then down at Esther's shoes and begins speaking eagerly, but she just shakes her head and continues on.

They turn into a dark narrow lane marked with the sign: 35–37. Two women are bent over a makeshift stove, stirring large metal pots. Esther greets them, '*Guten Tag*,' and they mumble a greeting in reply. Four children sit in a huddle near the wall playing marbles. As in every single lane in Hongkew, there is a rising odour of faeces coming from the foul brown trail the collectors of the 'honey pots' leave behind every morning, to take and sell to farmers on the outskirts of Shanghai. Esther breathes through her mouth and tries to ignore the stench. She hurries Anneliese along. The blackish-red bricks of the buildings on either side of the lane seem to suck up the little light that seeps in from above.

'Mama, where are we going?' Anneliese whispers. 'I don't like it here.'

Esther squeezes her hand gently. 'We're nearly there, I think.'

Further down, the lane opens up into a small courtyard, though the light remains dim: dozens of garments are strung up on washing lines that cross from one house to the next. Some are freshly washed and still dripping clear pearls of water onto the ground.

As they get to the end of the lane, Esther spots a bicycle in a corner of the courtyard, half-hidden by a bamboo screen, turned upside down to rest on its saddle and handlebars. The clatter of something metallic falls to the ground. The form of a man appears from beyond the screen, crouching beside the bicycle, his shirtsleeves rolled up to reveal oil-smeared forearms. His dark hair is slicked back, and his shirt is soaked with sweat, even though the sun is now low in the sky. As they approach, the man reaches out to retrieve the spanner he has dropped. Esther feels her blood quickening. She stands very still for several long moments, half-hoping he will look up and see her, and at the same time tempted to leave again unseen.

'Aaron?' she says. It is almost a whisper.

He looks up, confused at first. Then he blinks, startled, or perhaps it is the sweat dripping into his eyes. He lifts his hand to wipe his forehead.

'Esther? Is that you?' He rises from his crouching position and takes two steps towards her. 'It is, isn't it?'

He is tall, a good twenty centimetres taller than her, and all at once the small dingy space seems even more confined. He blinks again. 'I knew . . . my aunt Sara wrote that you were in Shanghai, but I didn't –'

'Aaron,' she begins, but at the same time, he says, 'You're so thin.'

The clash of words strikes them both mute for a moment.

Esther feels the flutter of Anneliese's fingers in the palm of her hand. 'This is Anni,' she says. 'My daughter.'

Aaron stares at her face for a second longer, his expression holding something she cannot read, before looking down at Anneliese.

'Hello, Anni,' he says and smiles.

Anneliese slips her hand from Esther's and wraps one arm around her mother's leg. 'Hello,' she says cautiously.

Behind them, some children have come into the courtyard. A girl, a year or two older than Anneliese, draws a circle in the dirt with her foot and their game of marbles commences.

'Can I play, Mama?' Anneliese asks.

Esther nods. 'Don't be running off though,' she says, and Anneliese skips over to the children, not minding at all that they are strangers.

Esther turns back to Aaron. 'You're repairing a bike,' she says. Her tongue is numb, dense in her mouth.

Aaron takes a cloth from his back pocket and rubs his hands, paying special attention to the spaces between his fingers. 'It's my business. I've become quite the expert.'

'But you're an architect!'

'Not here.' He shrugs. 'But it's a living. I recently had my hat mended by a professor of archaeology.' He stops rubbing his hands and looks at her. She manages to hold his gaze for a minute. She knows she has to come quickly to the point.

'Anni and I . . . I lost my job because I took her to work with me. I don't know what to do. She can't start kindergarten until September, and there is no one to look after her, so I can't work. I have no money, and my landlord will evict us if I can't pay the rent. And I haven't had news from my parents since I arrived. I've heard they're closing the port to refugees, so I'd have to let them know to come, but . . . but I just don't know what to do.'

Aaron takes a step forward. A long spill of light penetrates the drying laundry above him, illuminating his face.

'Esther.' He stretches out his arm. This movement unsettles her, and she steps back out of his reach. He rubs the side of his face, leaving behind a faint smear of oil on his cheek. He looks down at his feet.

'They're gone,' he says. 'Sara wrote to me. She's in London now. Your parents were taken about six months ago.'

'Taken? Where?'

His head snaps up. 'Where do you think?' he says, suddenly loud. 'Somewhere out east, I'd guess. Poland, or Czechoslovakia. To one of the labour camps.'

Esther flinches. She tries to take a breath but there is no oxygen in the air. She gasps. Aaron moves towards her and puts his hands on her shoulders.

He says, 'Oh God, Esther, I'm sorry. I'm so sorry.'

He draws her towards his chest and holds her there.

His smell is guiltily familiar, and instantly she can breathe again. She inhales his smell of sweat, nutty and leathery. He holds her close, murmurs some words she can't hear, can only feel the breath of his words on her neck.

'Oh, Esther,' he says, 'why did you take so long to find me?'

周翼

——

Yì walks along the waterfront in a daze, half-blind with exhaustion and hunger. It is the coldest hour, just before dawn, and although he has wrapped his sandaled feet in cloth, his toes are blue with cold. He is heading for one of the squares in the Old City, where men and women of all ages gather in the hope of garnering a few cents' worth of work as day labourers in mills, factories or – most coveted of all – private homes. At sunrise, prospective employers come here to select workers from among the motley assembly, picking out the most suitable for the variety of jobs they offer – strong men for the physical work, women for sewing, children for climbing up and into tight and narrow spaces, pretty girls for ... Yì can imagine what kind of work they are destined for, even the ones no older than eight or nine. Those left behind are forced to spend the day seeking out scraps of food or begging.

The place is a long walk from home, and Yì tries to smother the thought that as tired as he will be when he gets there, he will still have a full day's work ahead of him.

If he's lucky. Although he is fifteen now – a man – he has hardly grown over the past year. Lack of food, lack of sleep, and the weight of responsibility for his *nǎinai* have kept his body small and slight. The only work he is able to secure is children's work, and that is the most pitifully paid of all.

On the quayside, he passes a food vendor frying chunks of eel in ginger and peanut oil, and feels a painful twinge as his salivary glands stir into action. Last night, he shared the last of the rice and salted pork with Nǎinai, and he knows they won't eat again until he finds work. The money Mamselle Kitty gave him has long since been spent: shortly after his shameful dismissal, Nǎinai fell ill, and the tinctures and needles and herbs and medicines needed to keep her alive cost him every cent. They are now once again perched on the very edge of starvation.

He finds himself on the cobbled waterfront. There in front of him flows the black, stinking, oozing Whangpoo – and on the quayside, dozens of men lying on mats or squatting next to charcoal braziers, frying food. Wharf coolies waiting for the workday to begin. It is back-breaking, and pays only a few cents a day, but that is better than nothing. He slows. For a few fēn, he could buy just enough rice to stop him and his *nǎinai* from starving. Feeling nervous, but steeled by the thought of Nǎinai, Yì approaches a group of scrawny, sinewy men whose skin is so dirty it looks as though they haven't washed in months. They all wear ragged blue trousers, some of them tied at the waist by pieces of string. One of the men looks up at Yì and grins, displaying a gappy row of blackened teeth.

'I'm looking for work,' Yì says. It comes out as a squeak. He clears his throat and pulls his shoulders back, trying to appear taller than he is. The man with the black teeth shifts on his haunches and spits on the ground beside him.

'Eh? What did he say?' another man asks.

'Wants a job,' Black-teeth says.

Almost as one, the men begin to laugh. It isn't a kind laughter; it is a snarling, barking laughter that plants a tight seed of fear in Yì's stomach. He glances over his shoulder to make sure he has a clear passage, should the need of a quick escape arise. Black-teeth's laugh transforms into a hacking cough. Spitting another gob of shiny mucus onto the ground, he gets to his feet.

'See that barrel?' He points. 'Over there?'

Yì nods.

'Go and stack it on top of the others.' He nods to the left where some other wooden barrels stand, neatly stacked atop each other, three-high.

Yì doesn't hesitate to consider the impossibility of the task. He strides over to the single barrel and with a groaning effort manages to tip it onto its side. He gives the barrel a push and it begins to roll. It rolls faster than anticipated and he has to run to catch up, scooting in front and bringing it to a stop with both hands. When he has manoeuvred it into place beside the other barrels, he crouches down and tries to slide his fingers underneath it. It is too heavy. He straightens up and tries rocking the barrel back and forth, thinking he might slip his foot beneath it to then get a grip with his fingers. He rocks the barrel, places the tip of his sandaled foot underneath and yelps in pain as the weight crushes down onto his toes. Sweat is pouring down his face, despite the cold. He retracts his foot, rubs his toes and sees the faint dawn light creeping into the eastern sky. He feels a sudden clap on his shoulder and turns to find Black-teeth standing there, grinning.

'Come back in five years,' he says and laughs.

Then there is a sudden burst of noise to his left; explosions, too loud to be firecrackers. In an instant, the quayside comes to life, men scurrying and shouting all around him, ships' horns blaring across the water, freight being carried, shunted, pushed and pulled by coolies with the strength of demons. Yì ducks instinctively; he still remembers when the Japanese bombs fell from the sky four years ago, blasting houses and shops, obliterating the rickety mud-and-bamboo huts that lined the banks of Suzhou Creek and the Whangpoo, and killing thousands. But he also remembers that the bombing was always accompanied by the menacing drone of aeroplanes, and there is nothing like that to be heard now. So he crouches down behind the oil barrels and looks out towards the river. His first thought is that Huà's prediction has come to pass, that this is the beginning of the Communist uprising, the bloody battle against Chiang Kai-shek's nationalists, and against the evil Japanese oppressors.

He raises his head to peer over the barrels. Amid the hundreds of junks and sampans moored along the waterfront is the imposing structure of a huge gunship. Black smoke curls out of its gun barrels, which are pointed at a smaller gunboat upriver. Yì recognises the large gunship – it is British, and has sat in the estuary for as long as he can remember – and is momentarily confused. Why is Huà's bloody battle playing out on the water? And who are the British firing at? Then there is a blinding flash and another deafening bang, and the British ship begins to heave, creating waves large enough to upset several of the sampans. More guns flashing, more explosions, the skies ablaze as though lit by fireworks, and suddenly there it is: the drone of aeroplanes. Yì gets to his feet and runs in the opposite direction, squirreling his way through crowds of people sheltering in the entrances of the larger buildings, past frantic rickshaw runners dragging their empty contraptions at a speed their emaciated bodies hardly seem capable of.

He takes a route home as far from the waterfront as possible, feeling too troubled by these unexpected events to make his way to the Old City. Indeed, the city around him is in turmoil. Bustling at the best of times, it is now as though someone has poked a stick into an ants' nest. Several times he considers moving off the main thoroughfares and into the quieter back alleys to escape the throng. But although the dawn has dragged a little of its grey light onto the streets, the alleys are still dark and threatening, full of distorted shadows and unidentifiable noises, and he hasn't his bamboo rod with which to drive away any demons or evil spirits. And he knows there are plenty of people in Shanghai desperate enough to slit his throat for his ragged clothes alone.

He tries to reassemble the images he witnessed out on the river into something meaningful. And though he fails to make sense of it, he knows intuitively that it is the beginning of something bad. He stumbles along, pausing only when he hears the scurry of rats and the clatter of metal bins in an alleyway to his left. Without stopping to register his fear and disgust, he quickly ducks into the alley and with loud whoops and a frantic wave of his arms shoos the rats away. His instincts were right: on the ground beside the rubbish bins is a handful of sweet potato peelings and – incredibly – a few pork-belly rinds. He scoops up as much as he can, although the scraps are filthy, and stuffs them into his pockets. Rinsed and boiled, they will be edible.

He gets to Garden Bridge just as several Japanese tanks are trundling noisily across, followed by trucks and cars all flying the same flag. The Rising Sun glows on its white background like a drop of blood. At the near side of the bridge, groups of people stand queuing, waiting to cross. They must each bow to the Japanese sentries as they pass – usually a common-enough sight. But among those forced to bow are white foreigners, and this is not a common sight at all. In fact, several of them – three men and a woman – are pulled out of the queue by the Japanese soldiers and made to kneel. Then, without warning, one of the soldiers begins to beat them with a stick. Some of the others in the crowd let out shouts but are held back by soldiers. The woman on her knees receives a blow to the head and keels over like a toy on a spring.

And this sight makes Yì's uneasiness blossom into real dread – the white foreigners are now also at the mercy of the Japanese. This is the beginning of something truly bad.

At night, he dreams of Mamselle Kitty. In these dreams – no, not dreams, but fierce night terrors that leave him with a racing heart on waking – she is falling, falling, her red-painted lips luminous against the white of her skin, her mouth open in a silent scream.

He wakes one morning from such a dream to find Năinai sitting beside him, gripping his arm.

'Yì,' she says, staring sightlessly into a dark corner of the room. 'What is it?'

'Nothing,' Yì responds, rubbing his eyes. He doesn't want to worry her with stories of his dreams.

'You were calling out.' She leans towards him and he

recoils at the foul odour of her breath. Even in the gloom, he can see the skin stretched tight across her face, the gauntness making her ears appear oversized. Năinai is now completely blind and spends most of the day lying on her mat in a shallow, pained sleep.

'It is nothing, Năinai,' he says, stroking her arm. 'Lie down and sleep. I will bring some food back today.'

The old woman lies back with a whispered groan and closes her eyes.

'Where is Huà?' she asks, so quietly he is forced to lean in closely. 'Is he safe? When is he coming home?'

Yì places his palm on her cheek. Her skin is cool and dry. 'He will come home soon, Năinai,' he says, although he has long since given up hope that his brother might share his burden of caring for her. Huà does appear occasionally, usually staying only for a night, or a few twitchy, restless hours, which he spends cowering in a corner, jumping whenever he hears sounds in the alleyway. On his last visit a month earlier, he brought two young men with him, and they sat in a huddle all night, debating something in urgent, hissed whispers. Yì tried to listen in, but Huà shoved him away, telling him these were matters for men, not boys. When they left the following dawn, one of them gave Yì a small sack of rice, which sustained him and Năinai for several days.

The next morning, he leaves Năinai asleep on her mat and sets out for Frenchtown. If he finds Mamselle Kitty, it might put his nightmares to rest. And a secret, shameful part of him hopes he might be able to beg some food from her. Năinai must eat, and so must he, but he has become too weak for physical labour. Without money for the tram, it is a long walk, and by the time he arrives, the muscles in his legs are liquid.

When he reaches the building, he spots the concierge, and for a moment he feels a weird relief that it is the same man, although he appears bigger, bulkier than in Yì's recollection. Perhaps he is one of those who have prospered since the Japanese takeover of Shanghai, growing coin-heavy pockets and fat bellies. Yì edges towards him, unsure of how to pose his question, when the man notices him.

'Get away from here! Go on, off with you!' He makes a shooing motion with his hands.

But Yì doesn't move. The concierge pulls back an arm to strike him, and the action must have triggered some recollection, because he drops his arm and grins.

'What do you want, then, you little runt? Come for a box around the ears? I can give you that.' He raises his arm again but Yì ducks.

'The lady,' Yì says hastily. 'The Mamselle. Is she ... is she well?'

The concierge opens his fleshy mouth and begins to laugh, but his expression becomes serious as he looks past Yì towards an approaching Japanese officer. He shoves Yì to the side and opens the door for the officer, bowing very low from the waist and mumbling, 'Your worthless servant, *masuta.*'

The officer lets out a grunt, drops a coin onto the ground and disappears into the building. The concierge scuttles to retrieve the coin and then turns to Yì. 'Your *Mamselle*,' he utters with a sneer, 'is long gone.'

'Gone? Gone where?'

'Ksss!' The concierge manages to land a light blow on the side of Yì's head. 'Her rent not paid. She gone.'

December 1941 to
June 1942

ESTHER

A winter rain falls softly outside and the buttery smell of scrambled eggs lingers in the small room.

'What are you thinking?' Aaron asks and raises himself onto his elbow. With his other hand, he brushes his fingers up and down the curve of her neck.

'I was wondering where you managed to get fresh eggs.'

'That's for me to know,' he says, smiling, and taps the side of his nose. 'But I don't believe for a moment that was what you were really thinking.'

Esther smiles and lets him kiss her. She can't tell him what she's thinking because she can't put it into words herself. She runs her fingers through his hair. Thick, black hair. Was it the distressing news of her parents, or was it seeing Aaron again? She doesn't know, but suddenly everything has changed. *She* has changed. Not a butterfly emerging from its cocoon; no, more like a snake shedding its old, useless skin. There is no longer the fragile prospect of returning home, the naïve belief that she might wake up from a terrible dream and continue as normal with nothing more than a few bruised memories.

That belief has vanished, but it has been replaced with something else: a new, sharper kind of hope that it is not only possible to put the past behind you, but also to overcome it. Perhaps this is why it took her so long to find him.

Aaron catches her hand and presses it to his mouth, then interlaces his fingers with hers. Once upon a time, before everything, he would tell her she had the hands of an angel – pale, soft, slender. That was before Carl slipped the wedding ring on her finger. She pulls her hand away.

Aaron misreads her. 'You're right,' he says. 'Duty calls.' He climbs out of bed and gets dressed. 'You can stay in bed and watch me work if you like.'

He rolls up his sleeves and sits down at the table. In front of him lies a radio, its casing open, with protruding wires in different colours and dozens of tiny screws beside it. He repairs everything: bicycles, lamps, typewriters, ventilators. From architect to repairman, and a successful one at that.

She has known him for as long as she can remember, when he came to live with his aunt Sara after his parents died. Sara was the best friend of Esther's mother, and she recalls how they used to sit and watch her and Aaron playing, embarrassing them with their jovial talk of matchmaking. And she can pinpoint the moment – at Aaron's bar mitzvah, him the most beautiful boy in the room, with glossy dark hair and a perfectly symmetrical face – when it hit her with a physical force that this was, indeed, the boy she would grow up to marry. It took another two years for his feelings to catch up with hers, but after that they were inseparable.

She gets out of bed and pulls on her housecoat. Aaron's ground-floor flat is small but tidy, with enough room for her and Anni and their few belongings. The rent isn't much, though she still hasn't managed to find a job and money is tight.

'Where did you learn to do that?' she asks, watching Aaron tease a wire out of the radio casing and clamp it into place.

'Here and there,' he says. He lights a cigarette. 'Lots of practice.'

'Would you like some tea?' She fills the kettle from a large jug and places it on the stove. It will take ages to boil; the charcoal briquettes they've been using since the rationing began, a mix of coal dust and water pressed into egg-like shapes, produce little heat.

'There.' Aaron snaps the casing shut and begins to insert the tiny screws. His cigarette is clamped between his lips.

'Whose is it?' Esther asks, nodding towards the radio. It is illegal to own a shortwave radio, and the presence of this one makes her nervous. There is little in the way of good news, anyway. If rumours are to be believed, the Japanese are not just in control of Shanghai but have launched successful attacks on Burma, the Philippines and Hong Kong. But these are only rumours, and there is always the hope they are wrong.

Aaron shrugs. 'It belongs to some fellow,' he says, squinting against the smoke that curls up from his cigarette. When he looks up at her, he has a rakish smile on his face.

'What?' she asks.

'I was in Frenchtown a few weeks ago. You remember, to fix a generator.'

Esther nods.

'Well, the owner of the house is a senior executive at a French insurance company. We got talking, and he told me the company wants to build offices on Rue du Consulat. A huge project. Anyway' – he raises his eyebrows – 'it turns out the assistant to the principal architect jumped off the bell tower at Customs House. Girl trouble.'

Esther looks at him, aghast.

Aaron's expression drops momentarily. 'Yes, a terrible matter. But listen: I went and spoke with the man in charge, showed him some drawings, and –' He gets to his feet. 'You know what this means, don't you? I'd be working as an architect again!'

She almost claps her hands in delight. 'Why didn't you tell me?'

'I haven't anything in writing yet, but Deschamps – that's the principal architect – seemed very impressed. The job wouldn't start for a while, but . . . sweetheart!' He places his workman's hands around her waist. 'This would change everything!'

He puts his mouth on hers and a quiver of excitement builds inside her. Behind her, the kettle whistles.

'I have to pick up Anni soon,' she says. 'Let's celebrate properly tonight.'

He lets out a scruffy breath and nods. 'We'll celebrate in style.'

He begins to tidy away his tools. Esther pours the tea and gets dressed while it brews. She smiles as she pulls a stocking up her leg. The heel is darned to hell, but who cares? If Aaron gets this job, she'll be able to buy as many new stockings as she likes! And no more patched-up dresses for Anni, who has been outgrowing her clothes at a frustratingly quick rate. She attaches the stocking to the garter and remembers something.

'Oh, have you seen Kitty?' she asks Aaron, who is trying to remove some dirt from under his fingernails with a toothpick.

He looks up and frowns.

'Anni's doll,' she explains, taking the other stocking from the drawer. 'We couldn't find it this morning and I promised I'd look for it while she was at kindergarten.'

Aaron stops picking and gives her a sheepish look. 'That thing made of rags, with the floppy arms and legs?'

She nods.

He hesitates. Then: 'I cleared it out this morning, when you were out with Anni.'

'You threw it away? But Kitty's her favourite!' Her tone is sharp – too sharp.

He dismisses her words with a shrug. 'It was filthy. And besides, isn't she getting a little old for a doll?'

Esther's breath catches in her throat. She feels a spasm of anger at his utter thoughtlessness. 'How could you? It was a gift from my mother!' She tosses the second stocking onto the bed and sits there, a fistful of blanket in either hand. The speed at which her mood has shifted stuns her. When did she become so prickly, so quick to anger? She must have forgotten how to do this, how to read the rhythm and flow of a conversation. Living on her own with Anni for so long – she is out of practice. She gropes for something to say. 'It was all Anni had left of the past. What will I tell her? She'll be heartbroken!'

'I'm sorry, sweetheart, I didn't know that.' He crosses the room towards her. 'Tell her ... tell her Kitty's gone travelling around the world. To meet some other dolls.

Anni loves adventures – she'll understand.' He crouches down in front of her. 'I'm sorry. I can be such a klutz. I'll make it up to her, I promise.'

He takes the stocking, and very gently begins to roll it up her leg. He fumbles with the clasp of the suspender belt and she can see his hands trembling. She swallows. He was thoughtless, that's all. There was no cruel intent.

He looks up and she sees the Adam's apple jerking in his throat. 'I'll make it up to her,' he repeats quietly, and adds: 'Perhaps it's not such a bad thing to leave the past behind. We can build a future together, can't we?' He lays his head on her lap.

Hearing him speak her own thoughts aloud unsettles her. Oh, she would gladly forget the past if she could! She goes to stroke his hair but can't quite bring herself to touch him. This is the man she betrayed her husband for. The weight and warmth of his head are suddenly unbearable. She shifts position.

'I really have to be going,' she says. 'Anni will be waiting.'

KITTY

The music lilts, then slows almost imperceptibly, although the band is playing an upbeat tune – 'Eeny Meeny Miny Mo'. The percussionist yawns and misses several beats, causing the music to waver even further. Kitty is tired too. Her dancing partner is one of the energetic ones, swinging her back and forth across the dance floor. But she supposes she should be grateful that he just wants to dance. Not rub himself against her hips, or let his rancid breath wash over her, or slide his fingers between her legs, so that she has to raise her arm to draw the bodyguard's attention. She's lost count of this evening's number. But there have been many; the dance tickets are safely tucked away in a small satin bag that hangs from her wrist, waiting to be counted and handed in to Pavel, the taxi girls' manager, when the club closes.

She wears her walnut-brown hair in a shoulder-length wave. She has let the colour grow out and knows it makes her look older, but it's less fuss this way; she can crimp it herself, saving expensive trips to the salon. Besides, her age – twenty-six – doesn't matter to the men who come here. The customers who want the really young girls know to go to a neon-lit strip on the other side of Nanking Road, where they are supplied with five- or six-year-old girls, kidnapped, sold or rented, whose feet have more often than not been broken – arches snapped, toes bent inwards – and then bound tightly to conform to some twisted notion of beauty. Kitty thinks of these young girls most nights, when she returns to her room and relieves her own bruised and swollen feet from her court shoes.

But for all he only wants to dance, he is a poor dancer. He steps on her toes, misses the beat when he stretches his arm out to turn her. She is glad when the song is over and he gives her the ticket. She slips from the dance floor quickly before Pavel can bring her another customer and heads to the dressing room. Two other taxi dancers, White Russian girls who claim – as they all do – to be distant relatives of the Czar, are in here kneeling over a small table sniffing choppy lines of white powder. The room is poorly ventilated and smells of sweat and greasepaint. The women look up briefly as Kitty enters, eyes alert beneath inflamed eyelids, and then turn their attention back to the table. Kitty sits down and removes her shoes. She rubs her feet, gently coaxing the blood to circulate around her pinched toes and numbed heels. The two other girls get up and leave the dressing room, one of them bumping Kitty rudely in the back as she passes. Her friend says something in Russian and the other responds with a deliberate giggle.

Kitty doesn't catch what was said. She knows five, maybe six Russian words and most of them are curses, taught to her by Vitali as his idea of a joke. In the dance hall, another song starts up, but it is a slow melody, one

192

that implicates roving hands and tightly pressed bodies. She remains sitting and picks up a powder brush from the dressing table. If Pavel or one of his goons come looking for her, she'll say she needed to reapply her make-up. It is almost six months now since she last spoke to Vitali. In the end, he was too much of a coward even to tell her face-to-face – just a note from the agency to tell her that the rent had been paid until the end of the month and an instruction to hand over the keys to the concierge when she vacated the apartment.

Getting a job here was easy: Shanghai has an insatiable market for young women willing to dance – and more – for money. Kitty picks up a facial tissue and wipes a grain of dried mascara from the inside corner of her eye. From the hall, she hears the final strains of the slow song, to be followed by a livelier foxtrot. She slides her shoes back on, stuffing a small wad of cotton wool between heel and shoe to ease the pain of a blister, and heads back out to dance.

At just after four in the morning, she steps out of the Del Monte and sets off on the fifteen-minute walk home, to a single furnished room above Madame Ling's department store on Szechuen Road. It is the height of Lunar New Year celebrations and Avenue Haig is still buzzing. Nobody seems bothered by the punishing chill, but it is dark once she turns onto a narrow side street; only a few humped shapes lie scattered on the pavement here and there. The wind is knife-sharp and she shivers. She has had too much to drink and curses her shoes as she stumbles along the uneven slabs, keeping her coat tightly fastened with her hand. Some of the other dancers were heading on to a bar on Rue Maresca and invited her to join them, but she declined. She is headachy and tired and longs just to drop into bed.

There is a commotion ahead of her, and she stops to see a line of small children, tied by their necks to a heavy, abrading rope, being led by two men with sticks through a blue-painted godown doorway. The children look stiff with fatigue. Kitty dreads to think where they might be heading – to a factory and not a brothel, she hopes. She clenches her handbag tightly to her body. She made two-hundred and fifty dollars last month, a mere fraction of the cost of one of those beautiful gowns, gowns she had to sell off one by one until she managed to secure a fixed contract at the Del Monte. She has kept just one – the chiffon dress in red and gold. She has saved it for months now, forgoing a hot meal rather than face the thought of parting with it. It is superstitious nonsense of course, but as long as she is in possession of this one beautiful dress, there is the hope that things might improve. She can't bear to read the newspapers. All she knows is that since the Japanese joined the war and took over the entire city, her chances of escaping have become smaller than ever.

Drunken voices on the opposite side of the street. She picks up her pace, but her heel catches between two stone slabs and she almost falls. Resting her arm against the side of a building to steady herself, she slides off her shoe and examines the heel. It isn't broken. One detail to be grateful for, she thinks, before she is grabbed from behind, two strong hands pinning down her arms so she almost loses her balance again. She is pulled into a dark, foul-smelling back alley before the hands holding her release a little pressure and she spins around, kicking and clawing and screaming. She has heard about the kidnappings, understands how hunger and desperation can mutate into ruthlessness, that in this place a human life can be worth everything or nothing at all. Terror washes through her. She drops her handbag and lands a blow across her assailant's face, grabs a fistful of his jacket – he is alone, so perhaps she has a chance – and feels her fingernail bending back and snapping off. Pain rears up. The man grabs her hair and pulls her head back, making her catch her breath.

'*Schlampe*,' he says in German, bringing his face close to hers so she can smell his tangy, malodorous breath. '*Du Schlampe*,' he repeats. You slut. She vaguely recognises the face. A customer barred from the Del Monte the previous month after she'd made a complaint. He lets go of her hair and clasps his hand around her throat, then smacks the back of her head against the wall. It is the sound – a sickening thud – rather than the ensuing pain that makes her lose control of her bladder. For a moment, she can't move, feels the hot liquid running down the inside of her legs. But either he doesn't notice or it doesn't bother him. He fumbles with the belt of his trousers with one hand, tightening the pressure of his other hand around her throat. She tries to swallow, can't, panics, wants to scream out, but her throat is shut. The blackness around her turns crimson. His breath comes in ragged, excited bursts. Then his belt buckle snags and he removes his hand from her throat. She will never quite know how she managed to summon the strength, but she does – she throws herself against him and he stumbles backward, and she dives towards the opening of the backstreet, tripping, falling and finally crawling towards the road. A moment later, he is on top of her. She crumples beneath his weight. The air is knocked out of her lungs.

'Hey!'

A shout. A man's voice. She opens her mouth to call out but releases only a whimper.

'Hey there!' Louder, closer now. Footsteps approaching.

She can't look up; her left cheek is pressed to the freezing ground. She smells mud and oil and shit. And then abruptly, the weight lifts and she can breathe. She sees his shoes, sees him pull back a foot to kick her, but he is off balance and only lands a soft tap to her thigh before hurtling off.

'Is everything all right?' The other man, the man who shouted, helps her to her feet. 'I saw him attacking you, and I . . . here, take this.' He hands her an impossibly soft, clean handkerchief. She takes it with trembling hands.

'Thank you,' she says and wipes the left side of her face. It hurts to swallow.

'Are you sure you're all right?' he asks, reaching out an arm to touch her shoulder but then pulling back.

Kitty is shaking. 'I . . . I'm not quite sure.' Then: 'My bag. Is my bag there somewhere?'

The man steps around her and looks about in the dark. 'Yes, I've got it,' he says, bending over and retrieving the handbag from the ground. 'I should get you a taxi. Do you need a hospital?'

She shakes her head rapidly. 'No. No. I just want to . . .' She feels suddenly sick. Where a few seconds earlier she was completely sober, her drunkenness now overcomes her. Her head is pounding; the world around her starts to spin.

'Here, take my arm. Please.' He holds out his elbow and guides her to the main road. He stops, looks from left to right. Several cars drive past; a little further off, a group of young men are belting out songs.

The man seems at a loss; the authority with which he saved her has suddenly vanished. He turns to Kitty. 'Would you like me to accompany you to a police station?' he asks. His breath forms a white cloud in the air.

She shakes her head. Her whole body feels drained; she doesn't know how much longer she can stay on her feet. 'No use. He's long gone. And' – she pats her bag with a trembling hand – 'he didn't manage to steal anything.'

'You're shaking,' he says. 'We'd better find a taxicab to take you home.'

He sticks out his arm and, miraculously, a taxi pulls up beside them. The last thing Kitty remembers is climbing in, dizzy and conscious of her moist and sticky thighs, the freezing wetness on the back of her dress, and the man beside her saying, 'I'm Timothy Hamilton. Now, what's your address?'

She wakes to a swishing sound and opens her eyes to a hazy midday light. Her head throbs and her throat is raw. She is lying on a queen-sized bed, the sheets and pillow white and fragrant, in a large room. Watercolours hang on the walls, pale Chinese landscapes in greens and blues and pinks. A bulky, reddish-brown chest of drawers stands against the far wall, polished to a high sheen, atop it a collection of jade figurines that seem to glow from the inside. Kitty raises her head and catches sight of a black braid as a woman or girl scampers out of the door. From where she lies, she hears excited chatter, followed by the voice of a man. The same voice as last night (what was his name? She vaguely recalls him introducing himself), but in a cadence that confuses her until she realises he is speaking Chinese. There is a gentle knock on the door.

'Yes?' Kitty calls. It hurts to speak. The door opens again, slowly.

'Huìqín says you're awake.' The man takes a step inside. 'How are you feeling?'

Kitty sits up, making sure the blanket is covering her. 'Where am I?'

'Last night, you passed out in the taxi. I wasn't sure . . .' He comes closer and wraps his hands around the bedrail. He has short sandy hair and a fine-boned face, though his nose is perhaps a little thin. She can see hundreds of pale freckles on his skin, a complexion spectacularly unsuited to Shanghai summers. 'I asked if I should take you to hospital, but you insisted you were fine. Then you passed out, and I wasn't sure quite what to do. Chinese New Year, the hospitals were bound to be busy . . .' He clears his throat and shoves his hands into his pockets. 'I can call a doctor now, if you like.'

'No, I . . . I think I'm fine.' She scans her body, twists her head from side to side and raises and drops her knees. A slight queasiness in the pit of her stomach, that's all. 'Nothing broken.'

'Your face?'

'Oh,' she says and lays a hand on her cheek. She can feel an abrasion, sore to the touch. 'Just a graze. It's nothing.'

He takes a step back. 'Would you like coffee? Or tea? Are you hungry? I can get the cook to rustle up some breakfast.'

His English is crisp and enunciated. He is well dressed, she notes, expensively dressed, in a blue V-necked cardigan with a mustard and blue cravat around his neck. It only now occurs to her that she has been undressed and put in a white nightgown belonging to somebody else.

He seems to read her thoughts. 'Oh, no,' he says quickly. 'Huìqín, the maid, she helped you out of your clothes. I didn't . . .' He trails off and ducks his head slightly to run his hand through his hair. He is blushing.

She feels an odd urge to put him at ease. 'I'd love some coffee,' she says.

'Good.' He nods rapidly. 'Well, I'll send in Huìqín with your clothes. They've been laundered.'

Now Kitty blushes. She mumbles, 'Thank you.'

He turns to leave, and then: 'I'm Timothy, by the way. Timothy Hamilton. I'm not sure I introduced myself.'

'I'm Kitty Blume,' Kitty says. 'A pleasure to meet you.'

They sit across from one another at a neat, round table set in a bay window. From here, Kitty can see outside onto a courtyard, and beyond that, to a lane leading up to a main road. Everything is shrouded in a fine veil of mist: the ground, the stunted shrubs that line the courtyard, two bicycles leaning against the side of the building opposite. 'It snowed last winter,' Timothy says. 'The first snow I'd ever seen here.'

Kitty puts down her coffee cup but keeps her hands wrapped around it for warmth. She remembers last year's snow: it was a scrawny kind – it had no depth. Like everything here, she feels in a surge of homesickness, a poor, shallow imitation of the real thing. She feels a chill from the inside out, although the room is nicely heated by an electric fire.

A Chinese maid enters. She is young, and very pretty, her long braid reminding Kitty of the girl who works at Marcel Chang's.

'You will stay for breakfast?' Timothy asks Kitty.

She nods; if she drinks only coffee, she'll feel sick for hours.

'Good,' Timothy says with a smile. 'I can't start the day on an empty stomach, either.'

He turns to the maid and says something in Chinese, and she disappears again through a door.

'Where I come from,' Kitty says, 'the snow comes up to here in winter.' She holds her hand about a metre off the ground. 'It's beautiful.'

'Where is that?'

'Vienna,' she says, and then points at an ivory-lidded cigarette case lying between them on the table. 'May I?'

Timothy offers her a cigarette and leans forward to light it.

'You still haven't told me where I am,' she says, blowing out a fragrant stream of smoke.

'Of course. Yes. We're in my apartment, on Bubbling Well Road. I'm sorry. I hope you haven't been worried that I'm some sort of . . . some sort of . . .' He appears to run out of words.

'No.' She smiles at him. 'Thank you. For helping me last night.'

He looks bewildered for a moment. 'But of course! No need to thank me. Truly. I'm only sorry I didn't get a better look at the man who attacked you.'

Kitty lets her glance slide across the table.

'But if you don't mind me saying,' he continues, 'it's not really advisable for, well, for a young woman like yourself to be out at night on your own.'

'I was out dancing,' she says with a strained smile. It's truthful enough. For some reason – perhaps it is his slightly gauche manner, an old-fashioned bashfulness – it doesn't seem right to lie to him. She turns to look out of the window again.

Her thoughts are interrupted by the maid placing two plates on the table. Kitty stubs out her half-smoked cigarette and looks down at her plate: two fried eggs, bacon, sausages, beans in a reddish sauce and a slice of toasted bread. She sniffs cautiously. Is this what the English have for breakfast? She picks up her knife and fork. She is ravenous, and although it seems like a queer collection of food to eat first thing in the morning, she tucks in and has cleared her plate a few minutes later.

'You were hungry!' Timothy says. He still has half of his on the plate in front of him.

She smiles her response and wipes the corners of her mouth. Any queasiness she might have felt on waking has disappeared. Perhaps she should eat this kind of hot, meaty breakfast more often. If she could afford to.

'Have you been in Shanghai long?' Timothy asks, buttering a second piece of toast.

A lifetime, she wants to say, but instead replies, 'About two and a half years. I came to join my fiancé. But I don't think I'll be staying much longer.'

'That's what I said when I first arrived.' He gives her a bright smile, making him look unexpectedly boyish. 'That was five years ago.' He bites into his toast.

'Did I hear you speaking Chinese?'

He nods and swallows. 'Shanghainese, actually. I thought I should make the effort. The grammar isn't that tricky, really. It's the pitches you have to watch out for. But I find the language quite beautiful.'

He wipes some crumbs from the corner of his mouth and looks out of the window. 'I do hope the weather cheers up soon. My fiancée, Madeleine, is due to arrive next month. I don't think she'll be expecting the cold. In fact, I think she has a rather different idea of the place – warm and exotic, you know?'

'I'm sure she'll love it.'

Timothy frowns. 'I hope so.'

Kitty finishes her coffee. 'I'd better be going,' she says, getting to her feet.

Timothy rises with her. 'Can I offer to drive you somewhere?'

'Thank you, but no. I think some fresh air would do me good.'

'Of course.' Timothy comes around the table and pulls her chair out.

Kitty looks around. 'Oh. I think I left my handbag in the bedroom.'

'Hang on, I'll tell Huìqín to fetch it.'

Kitty takes a step forward. 'No, please don't trouble her. I know where it is.'

In the bedroom, the bed has been made and the curtains drawn back. Kitty's bag is hanging from the back of a chair. She pulls out her compact and checks her hair. It'll do, she decides. On her way out, she passes by the chest of drawers displaying the jade figurines on top. She reaches out to touch one, imagining it to be as warm as its glow, but it is cold and hard. Quickly, almost as an afterthought, she removes one – a small dragon statue – and slides it into her handbag. Then she hurries out of the room to say her goodbyes.

ESTHER

One afternoon in early March, as the skies have opened yet again to release a grey, ceaseless rain shower, Esther waits impatiently for Aaron to return from a salvaging trip to a scrap yard in Yangtszepoo in search of cheap spare parts. His repair business has felt the pinch of the refugees' dwindling funds and they just about manage to scrape together the rent. The cold winter has eased seamlessly into a wet spring, and the coal rationing coupled with the lack of food make the days drag on endlessly. But today, Esther finally has some good news of her own.

When Aaron arrives home, he is smiling. His trip was evidently successful. He shakes off the rain and changes into dry clothes, telling her all about the bits and pieces he found, how he haggled the scrap dealer down to three dollars for some copper cables and aluminium sheeting.

Esther makes a pot of tea and waits for him to finish. 'That's wonderful,' she says, when he has washed his hands and sat down.

He looks around. 'Where's Anni?'

'With Lí Mà, next door.' Lí Mà is the Chinese neighbour's daughter and Anni's new best friend. Despite the absence of a common language, the two girls are inseparable, and they spend most afternoons playing games Esther can make neither head nor tail of, but which cause plenty of laughing and squealing. She smiles absently.

Aaron gives her a quizzical look. 'What's going on? You look like the cat that got the cream.'

She smiles and pours the tea. 'I had a job interview last week,' she says. 'At the Sterns', you know, where I took Anni for her vaccinations. They're looking for a receptionist. They're both doctors, and they said they had one other candidate, but as I'm trained in bookkeeping, they thought I'd be perfect. They offered me the job this morning. They can't afford to pay much, but it all helps, doesn't it? And I've nothing much else to do all day.' It comes out in a garbled rush. For some reason, she feels self-conscious.

Aaron doesn't respond immediately. When he speaks, his voice is non-committal. 'So you're keeping secrets from me.'

She frowns. Why isn't he pleased? 'I didn't want to jinx it, I suppose.' She attempts a smile, but his expression is serious. 'I've been a kept woman long enough,' she adds lightly.

Again, Aaron doesn't speak. He stares down at the steaming tea in front of him, letting the silence drag.

'We should get married,' he says finally. 'Then you wouldn't be a kept woman. You'd be *my* woman.' He gets to his feet, his mood lifting again. 'I mean it, sweetheart. I'm still hopeful about the job in Frenchtown, and if that works out we could get married, move out of here ...' He glances around the small room. 'You wouldn't have to work, I could adopt Anni –'

'Aaron,' she says quietly. She places the teapot down. 'Aaron, I –'

'What?'

She takes a deep breath and thinks of what to say next. She's gone about it all wrong. Perhaps if she'd waited until he'd eaten to tell him about the job . . . but he was in such a buoyant mood when he came in, it seemed like the perfect moment. And now – this. She reaches out and touches his sleeve.

He pulls his arm away. 'You never responded to my letters,' he says.

So this is what's troubling him! The blood rushes to her face. All this time, they have avoided talking about it. About Carl's death, about the letters Aaron wrote and which she ignored because there was nothing she could possibly say. The guilt over Carl's death was the punishment for her betrayal. That guilt was strong enough to keep her from seeing Aaron for so long.

The rain comes down ever harder outside, making crackling noises as it hits the gravel. Aaron breathes out.

'That night . . . you told me you loved me.'

She turns away. She doesn't want to talk about this. Wasn't he the one who said the past should stay in the past?

'You said you loved me,' he repeats. 'Was that a lie?'

Her hands are shaking. She interlaces her fingers to calm them. 'Carl found out,' she says. 'He knew I'd gone to see you that night. I don't know how he found out, but he should never have been there. He –'

'But accidents happen. His death wasn't your fault.'

'Of course it was! If I hadn't . . . if we hadn't . . .' She takes a deep shaky breath. 'He should never have been there.' Her throat is tight, the guilt pressing its fingers around her neck all over again. 'He was dying when they brought him home. Nobody knew. We thought he'd recover after a few days in bed. He didn't survive the night.'

Aaron puts a hand on her shoulder. She shrugs him off.

'That's why I didn't write back to you. I couldn't face you, not after what had happened. Not after what I'd done. I made a mistake.'

'*I* was a mistake?'

'You know what I mean.'

They are both silent for a while. Then Aaron says, 'Why did you marry him, Esther?'

She feels, from nowhere, a flash of old anger. 'You left me, waltzed off to Paris without me!'

'Six months! The scholarship was a once-in-a-lifetime opportunity, you know that. And it didn't take you long to replace me, did it?'

'I was angry, and hurt. And Carl . . .'

'Carl – what?'

'Carl was there. You weren't.' She hears how petulant she sounds, but it's true. It was true.

Aaron runs a hand through his hair. 'Did you love him?'

'Yes. No. I mean . . .' She can't help it. She begins to cry. 'He didn't understand how low I was after Anni's birth. He thought I was being selfish, when I didn't cook his dinner, or mend his socks. I could hardly get out of bed to feed Anni. Do you know what he said? He said we should have another baby!' She sniffs and lets out an angry laugh. 'He said that would get me going. And I ended up hating him for it. But . . . but I didn't mean for him to die!'

'Of course not. I know that. It was an accident, Esther.'

There is a low growl in the sky, then a burst of thunder. It drowns out all other sounds. Aaron moves close and puts his arms around her.

She whispers into his shoulder. 'Sometimes I don't think I can bear the shame.' She wishes he could take her words and fling them away.

On a pleasantly warm May evening, Victor Stern greets Esther, Aaron and Anneliese at the door of his home with his arms open.

'Welcome,' he says. 'We're so glad you could come.'

The invitation to dinner was a pleasant surprise, as the Sterns guard their private life carefully, choosing not to mix with patients after hours for *Kaffee und Kuchen*, and declining their occasional offers of gifts. Victor and Helene Stern are both dermatologists by training – they once ran a thriving practice in Germany – but now specialise in just about everything, from colds, infected mosquito bites, diabetes and diarrhoea, to setting minor fractures and pulling teeth. Even several months into her job as a receptionist, Esther is still squeamish about what goes on in the examination rooms.

'Thank you for the invitation,' she says, as Helene ushers them in through the door. Anneliese dashes ahead.

'Anni!' Esther calls, but Helene shakes her head.

'It's fine,' she says. 'We were all that age once.' Like Esther, Helene has made an effort to dress up. She wears her hair, which is completely silver, in a neat chignon, and her green cotton-voile dress has been pressed. Esther casts a slightly dispirited look towards Aaron, in his not-quite-white shirt and loose trousers. And he wears his scuffed leather bag strung around his shoulder. But at least, she notes, Victor Stern isn't wearing a tie, either.

'I'm glad you could arrange to come at such short notice,' Helene says, taking her coat.

Esther turns to Aaron. 'This is Aaron. Aaron Beutler.'

Aaron shakes first Helene's hand, then Victor's. 'Pleased to meet you, Dr Stern.'

'Oh, it's Victor, please. And Helene.' He nods towards his wife and adds with a smile, 'We're not doctors when we're at home, so I very much hope you won't be asking me to look at a strange rash or anything.'

Esther lets out a laugh that is louder than necessary when Aaron doesn't respond. She practically had to beg him to join her tonight. She has come to know a new and disagreeable side to him – sullen moods that hang over the home for days. Perhaps it would have been better to come without him. But then he surprises her.

'I've brought something,' he says, and takes two bottles of red wine from his bag. 'It's kosher. I got it from a friend at the synagogue.'

Esther looks at him quizzically, but Helene gives him a wide smile.

'Thank you! How thoughtful. Now please, come through.'

They walk through the examination room to a door at the back. The room beyond, the Sterns' living area, is larger than Esther imagined, and tastefully furnished. Two armchairs and a sofa, a bookshelf, several framed photographs on the wall. A dining table, set for five, stands close to the wall. The furniture is scuffed and old, of course, and no one could miss the stains of damp in the corners of the room, but it is cosy and inviting. Best of all is the smell coming from a small room at the back. It is meat, definitely meat.

They take their seats at the table and Helene lights the candles.

'Now. It's nothing too formal.' She shrugs apologetically. 'I hope I've got everything right.'

'Helene is a Christian,' Victor says, pouring them each a glass of wine.

'I didn't know,' Esther says.

Victor nods. 'Not many do. We don't put it about.' He pauses. 'I tried to board the ship without her noticing, but she insisted on coming to Shanghai with me.' He is trying to make light of the difference between them. It isn't quite working.

'You won't get rid of me that easily,' his wife says. They smile at each other across the table, but it is a sad smile. Then Helene gets to her feet and goes into the back room, reappearing a moment later with a large pot.

The smell intensifies, making Esther's mouth water. 'That smells delicious, Helene.'

'What is it?' Anneliese asks suspiciously. She has become exasperatingly picky about food lately.

Esther gives her a sharp look. 'Don't be rude, Anni.'

'Oh, don't worry,' Helene says. 'Look, Anni, I'll just put a thimbleful on your plate for you to taste. If you don't like it, you don't have to eat it. Then it'll be more for the rest of us.'

She ladles out the tiniest amount onto Anneliese's plate. The girl, still frowning, picks up her fork and tries some.

'Well? Is it good?' Helene asks.

Anneliese nods. Her face breaks into a grin. 'More please.'

The adults laugh, and then Helene lets out a gasp. 'Shouldn't we, I don't know, bless the food first? Victor?' She turns to Esther and Aaron. 'Please forgive me if I get something wrong. I just thought ... in times like these, perhaps it's comforting to have some age-old rituals to hold on to. Even if they're not mine.'

Victor chuckles. 'Food this good doesn't need any blessing. Now' – he gestures for his wife to sit down – 'please let us eat before it gets cold.'

'Oh, you needn't worry on our behalf,' Esther says. 'The last time Aaron went to shul was for his bar mitzvah.' She smiles across at him, but he doesn't look up from his plate until it is empty.

'Anneliese starts school soon, doesn't she?' Helene says.

Anni's head jerks up at the sound of her name.

'In September,' Esther says with a smile. 'The Kadoorie School on Kinchow Road. She can't wait.'

'That's a Jewish school, isn't it?' asks Helene.

Esther nods.

'I think it's wonderful, what the community here are doing,' Helene says and gets up to clear the dishes.

'What choice do we have?' Victor says quietly, as though to himself.

Esther gets to her feet to help Helene, but she waves her down. 'Your little one seems awfully tired,' she says with a nod to Anni, who can hardly keep her eyes open.

'It's long past her bedtime,' Esther replies. 'And I can't remember when she last ate so much.'

Helene gently catches hold of her hand. 'Oh, but don't go just yet, please. Perhaps she can rest on the sofa.'

Esther looks at Anneliese. 'Would you like that, *liebling*?' She is enjoying the evening far more than she anticipated.

It would be a shame to leave so early. Anneliese nods and lets her mother bed her down on the sofa. She is asleep within minutes.

Presently, the conversation at the table turns to the Japanese occupation and the resulting hardship for so many of the refugees. The Relief Committee has seen its US funding stopped under the Trading with the Enemy Act, and several thousand refugees, most of them *heim* residents, are now facing starvation. Esther knows that the Sterns treat many of them free of charge but wonders how much longer they will be able to afford to.

'On the positive side,' Helene says, 'now that the Americans have been dragged into the war –'

'Kicking and screaming,' her husband interjects.

'Yes, but now they are part of it, surely it can't be too long before' – her mouth twists – 'before they defeat the Nazis, and we can all go home.'

'Home?' Aaron's voice is hard.

Helene turns to him and smiles. 'We're from Mannheim,' she says. 'My family, of course, are all still there.'

Aaron lets out a sharp breath. 'Nothing would ever make me go back to that place.'

Esther stares at him. She isn't sure what astonishes her more, the statement, or the vehemence with which he made it. It occurs to her that they have never, not once, talked about where they might go – if indeed they will go anywhere together. Helene clears her throat but doesn't speak. For several minutes, they sit in silence.

'Aaron has his own workshop,' Esther says finally, in an attempt to dispel the awkwardness. 'He can repair anything.'

'Yes,' Victor says with a glance towards Aaron. 'His reputation precedes him.'

He has a queer cast in his voice. Aaron must have noticed it too, because he sits up straighter on his chair.

Victor breathes out. 'I was called out to see a fellow last week. He'd just been released from Bridge House.'

'Victor,' says Helene. She shakes her head a fraction. Victor places his hand on hers and squeezes gently. Then he continues.

'You've heard of Bridge House?'

Esther nods. Who hasn't? An eight-storey white apartment building just this side of Garden Bridge. Esther has only heard rumours, but it is said that the Kempetai converted it into hundreds of cells and torture chambers. Those who end up there – suspected spies, businessmen, journalists, criminals, regardless of nationality – are lucky if they are released alive.

Beside her, Aaron mumbles, 'Bridge House, yes.' His lips are stained from the sweet red wine he brought. Kosher wine? Esther thinks. Where did he get it from? No one can afford kosher anymore – apart from the yeshiva students, but they have a whole different source of funds. She will ask him about it later, although he will probably refuse to elaborate. Then she realises Victor is still talking.

'... feet were black.' His hand makes a fist on the table. 'Black. The flesh was peeling off his feet. They'd beaten him, you see. Beaten the soles of his feet with wire and iron piping. For two weeks without a break, in shifts. And all because of his surname, Schmidt. The man they were looking for – he produces illegal liquor, terrible stuff – is called Schmitz. But I don't really think the Japs cared about that.' His voice trembles when he comes to an end. He takes a hasty gulp of wine.

'Will he be all right?' Esther asks.

'No.' Victor's response is tight and hard. 'He won't be all right. I would be surprised if he lasts out the week.'

Helene has been staring at the tablecloth, folding and unfolding her napkin. She raises her eyes and gives Esther an apologetic look. Esther smiles back uncertainly. Now she wants the evening to end before it sours beyond redemption. She opens her mouth, to thank the Sterns for the food and the company, but Aaron speaks first.

'Fair warning, Victor.' He speaks steadily. 'But we choose to be survivors, or not.'

KITTY

———

'Me know you there! Me know!' The knocking on her door quickly turns into banging. 'Me savvy, you hear?'

Kitty stubs out her cigarette and slowly gets off the bed. 'Yes, Madame Ling. I'm in here. You savvy indeed. Just a minute, I'm getting the money.'

She crosses the room, ignoring the banging, which continues despite her response, and kneels in front of the wooden chest where she keeps her belongings. She rummages around in the clothes, takes out the small paper parcel containing the stolen figurine and goes back to the bed, pushing it slightly to one side and lifting the worn rug so she can access a loose floorboard. She has been alternating the hiding place, frantic that someone will find the jade dragon before she has decided what to do with it. She doesn't dare take it to the Del Monte, where it would vanish from the dressing room within the hour. And carrying it around with her would constitute a whole other type of foolishness – Shanghai pickpockets are in a league of their own.

'You no open now, I get key!' the voice behind the door yells. 'Was end of May yesterday. You pay rent!'

'Yes, I'm coming!' Kitty shouts back.

Selling it would, of course, be the sensible option, but her conscience, her *damned* conscience, has got the better of her so far. Once, she even managed to get as far as a pawnbroker on Nanking Road, where she was offered a staggering amount of money for it, but in the end, despite much cajoling and lamenting on the part of the pawnbroker, she just couldn't relinquish the jade dragon.

'Here!' She yanks the door open and thrusts the greasy wad of notes at Madame Ling.

It's been robbing her of sleep – literally: at night she sleeps, or tries to sleep, with the figurine under her pillow. She has always prided herself on her honesty, taking only what she has earned, or what she deserves. She isn't a greedy person, she has just enough for rent and food. But there it was, a blip, a misjudgement, an unthinking act of foolishness, and for ages now she has been thinking of ways to return it. She can't just go to the man's house and say, 'Oh, look what I found in my bag. I haven't a clue as to how it might have got there.' At a pinch, that might have worked the day after she'd stolen it, but that was months ago. Sending it in the post, leaving it on the doorstep, even paying someone to return it anonymously – all these ideas she's considered and discarded. Neither can she quite bring herself to give it away or just dispose of it. She isn't a superstitious person, but at times she feels as if this harmless swirl of jade is a curse.

Madame Ling counts the money and emits a snort of

satisfaction before turning to leave. Kitty makes a point of slamming the door.

Later that afternoon, she heads out to pick up a pair of dance shoes that needed the soles replacing. The cherry trees on Rue Cardinal Mercier have shed their blossoms almost completely, covering the pavement in a pale pink carpet. At the entrance to the Cercle Sportif Français, the French Club, a man sweeps the petals into piles. The grounds of the club are enclosed by a high brick wall to protect the members from the prying eyes of the envious and ill willed, but Kitty pauses at the entrance anyway. She knows Vitali is a member, and it's possible she might run into him. From time to time, she indulges in a very satisfying fantasy, in which she slashes his face with a razor, or claws his eyes out with her vengeful nails.

Through the wrought-iron gate, she can make out a section of the gardens: artificial rockeries, small bamboo pavilions, an ornate fountain with a brass dragon spouting water from its mouth, and the netting of the tennis courts. From where she stands, she can hear the *plock-plock* of the ball being hit from one end of the court to the other, a tranquil contrast to the swirl of fierce traffic behind her. The gates swing open and a black limousine drives out, its tyres crunching on the gravelled driveway. As it passes her, Kitty peers through the window, pretending to brush some dust from her skirt so as not to appear too conspicuous, but it isn't Vitali. She turns to leave.

Then, suddenly, 'Kitty! Miss Blume!'

She freezes, recognising the voice, although it is months since she last heard it. She shoots a glance over her shoulder and sees Timothy Hamilton, dressed in tennis whites, bounding out of the club towards her. She turns back and briefly considers feigning deafness, but he has caught up with her before she can do anything.

'Kitty!' he says in a breathless voice. 'I thought it was you.'

She spins around. 'Timothy! I ... how nice to see you again. I was just ...'

'How are you?' He stands in front of her with an unwavering smile on his face. 'Oh, and please excuse the clothing, I've just been in a tennis tournament. Last place, I'm afraid, but I'm used to it.' He lets out a strange laugh and pushes back a strand of hair that has fallen into his eyes.

'I'm very well, thank you.' She smiles politely, but at the same time considers whether running, running fast, would be possible in these shoes. What's he waiting for? There's probably a gendarme on the next street corner.

'You've ...' He points to her face. 'No damage done, then? I mean, the graze has healed nicely.'

'Yes.' She lifts her hand to her cheek.

The shrill sound of a whistle close by makes her jump, and from nowhere a group of five or six women come running down the pavement on the opposite side of the road. Their faces are rouged and lipsticked, and their dresses are so tight it is a wonder they manage to run in them. They are being chased, at a distance of some ten metres, by two Sikh policemen. The women don't stop to wait for a gap in traffic but run out onto the street and are narrowly missed by an overcrowded bus. The policemen stop and shout something, but they cannot be heard above the roar of the traffic. The women halt on the pavement close to where Kitty and Timothy stand, catching their breath and shouting jeers and taunts back at the policemen.

'What's that all about?' Timothy asks.

Kitty shrugs, although she knows that Rue Cardinal Mercier marks the boundary between the International Settlement and the French Concession, and the women have just successfully crossed over into French jurisdiction, where the stance on prostitution is far more laissez-faire.

For a moment, neither of them speaks, as Kitty frantically tries to come up with an excuse to leave – now.

'I'm late for –' she begins, just as his face takes on an earnest, purposeful expression.

He says, 'Goodness me, where are my manners? Would you care to join me for some tea? Or something stronger?' He gestures towards the entrance of the club.

Is he toying with her? Or does he want her on the club premises, so he can have someone hold her until the police are called?

He pushes his hair back with his hand. It is an unaffected gesture, rather than a vain one. 'I'd rather not sit alone,' he says. The bridge of his nose is pink with sunburn and freckles dance across his cheeks. 'Unless you're terribly busy?'

Her mouth opens but no sound comes out. She gives a little nod, and lets him take her arm and lead her through the gates. In the clubhouse, he signs her in as his guest and they are shown to a table. Timothy orders green tea, and Kitty, still feeling somewhat perplexed and shaky, nods in agreement.

'That's a pretty necklace you have there,' he says. 'What is it, the White Tara?'

'Oh, I'm not sure.' Her hand goes to her throat and she touches the pendant. There is still a tremble to her hand. She's been wearing the pendant ever since she picked it up off the kitchen floor the day after Wing left. 'It's not mine, actually. I'm looking after it for a friend.'

The tea arrives and the waitress, a dainty-looking Chinese girl, pours first her tea and then his. From where they sit, they can see the tennis courts. Gradually, Kitty begins to relax. It occurs to her that he might not even have noticed the figurine missing. Or perhaps, she considers guiltily, one of his servants has had to take the blame.

'I must be the worst player in the whole club,' Timothy says with a grimace. 'It's a wonder they put me on the team at all.'

'They?'

'It's a company thing. The China Printing and Finishing Company. We deal in textiles, dyes and the like. Anyway, they like to ensure I spend at least some of my spare time engaged in these sorts of pursuits.' He nods towards the tennis courts. 'I fear they might be a little concerned I've gone native.'

Kitty laughs. 'I've never heard that expression before.'

'But I'm not complaining,' he adds quickly. 'It's a very familial company. You get the feeling you're being... looked after, you know? Which I suppose is important now more than ever.'

Kitty frowns. She isn't sure what he means.

He misinterprets her look. 'I know,' he says, 'being out here, it's so easy to forget about the war. I mean, just look at us. Back in Europe, we'd be enemies, wouldn't we? And yet here we are, fraternising over green tea.' He gives her a sad smile. 'It just makes it seem so arbitrary, doesn't it?'

He doesn't know I'm Jewish, she thinks. And what would he think if he knew? Perhaps he'd rather believe himself to be sitting – fraternising, as he calls it – with an enemy,

219

rather than a dirty Jew. She takes a hasty sip of tea to stop these noxious thoughts and ends up scalding her tongue.

'Are you all right?' he asks as she places her cup down so hard the bone china threatens to break.

She wipes her mouth on a napkin, ignoring the sting of the scald, and nods. Then something occurs to her. 'Oh, how is your fiancée settling in? When did she arrive? March, was it?'

Timothy ducks his head a fraction and colours. 'Oh. She ... well, Madeleine changed her mind. She wouldn't ... she didn't want ...'

'I'm sorry,' Kitty says, leaning forward. 'I didn't mean to bring up a sore subject.'

He shakes his head. 'No. It's not a sore subject any longer. In fact, I'm glad she was honest with me.'

The turn of conversation renders them both silent. A spatter of applause can be heard from the nearby tennis court, followed by an indistinct announcement through a megaphone.

'Um, there's something, um –' He pauses and takes a nervous sip of tea. 'Kitty, I um –'

Immediately, her pulse quickens. This is it. He's goaded her along, allowed her to let her guard down, sat and talked about his private affairs – and, of course, why else should he have told her these things, if not to disarm her? Her mind races. He must have spoken a few discreet words to the maître d' when he signed her in. The police are probably waiting to come in and arrest her right now. How foolish of her! Why did she come in with him? She should have taken her chance while she was still on the street.

Timothy takes a deep breath and continues. 'Well, what I'm trying to say is, China Printing are holding a dinner tomorrow night at the Cathay, and I was wondering, well, it's a pretty formal affair and with what I told you about the company being tightly knit and such, well, it's just a thought – and please don't hesitate to say no; I realise it's very short notice – but I was wondering if you might like to come as my guest.'

Genuinely bewildered by his words, Kitty can't answer. An icy heat slinks and rises along her spine. She almost cries with relief.

Naturally, he misinterprets her silence. 'Forgive me,' he says, 'it was a ridiculous suggestion. I don't know ...' He lets out a nervous chuckle. 'I don't know what got into me.'

Kitty takes a moment to compose herself. 'No, Timothy,' she says calmly. 'It wasn't ridiculous at all. I would love to come.'

The Cathay Hotel! Situated on the corner of the Bund and Nanking Road, at ten storeys high not the tallest structure on the waterfront, but the most elegant building Kitty has ever seen. Timothy is waiting for her outside the revolving door, smoking a cigarette and looking a little nervous as her taxicab draws up outside. The taxicab – ordered and paid for by Timothy's company – picked her up at the DuPont Apartment Complex, the address she'd given Timothy yesterday. There was no reason he needed to know about her run-down room at Madame Ling's. He gives her an uneven smile as she steps from the car and tosses his cigarette away.

'Thank you for coming,' he says, and adds, 'You look lovely.'

Kitty smiles a thank you. She is wearing the red chiffon

gown she has kept for all this time, and although it sags a little at the hips, doesn't cling as flatteringly to her bosom as it once did, she feels glorious.

'This way,' Timothy says, and lets her step ahead through the revolving door. Inside, it is all Kitty imagined – pink-speckled granite, majestic chandeliers, white marble floors, mahogany furniture, art deco frescoes and, above her, a lead-glass dome. The whole place has a heady smell of cigars and perfume and luxury.

'We're dining in the Dragon Room,' Timothy says and gently takes her elbow. She glides past a glass cabinet displaying items she's almost forgotten existed: Coty lipstick and Max Factor face powder, Vol de Nuit perfume, bath salts in exotic fragrances. She lets her eyes drift across the products, mesmerised for a moment until she feels a soft tug on her arm. Timothy leads her into the Dragon Room, where a long table is impeccably set in silver and crystal. There are fourteen guests, including her and Timothy, and she suddenly understands him not wanting to be the odd number thirteen. Just before they enter, he turns to tell her, a little timidly, that China Printing have booked the entire ninth floor for those guests who would rather sleep at the hotel than suffer the crush and noise of the traffic on their return journey. Timothy has taken the liberty of reserving one of the rooms for Kitty.

'It's no obligation, of course,' he tells her. 'You're welcome to leave whenever you wish.'

Kitty is delighted and gives him what she hopes is a self-possessed smile. 'No, that sounds wonderful.'

At the dinner table, there are brief introductions, but too many names for Kitty to remember. During dinner – she is seated between Timothy and a large, slope-shouldered man who was introduced as one of the senior managers at China Printing – much of the talk is about the war: Rommel in Africa, the Nazis in Greece and, obviously upsetting to most of those present, the relentless air raids on London and Liverpool.

Kitty doesn't pay much attention to the conversation, not only because it revolves around places she will never visit in her lifetime, but also because of the food, which is served on beautiful, hand-painted china. She eats guardedly at first, trying not to appear greedy, but . . . oh, the food! Grilled scallops, foie gras, sautéed crayfish, lemon-and-crémant sorbet, rack of lamb, chocolate and caramel tarts, strawberry-mint mousse: a never-ending, dizzying supply of dishes, each one more mouth-watering than the next.

After dinner, the conversation switches from the war to polite chit-chat: whose horse recently won the Shanghai races, the upcoming wedding of a French business magnate and some American socialite. Kitty is wiping the corners of her mouth with a starched linen napkin when the woman opposite leans across the table. Cupping her mouth with an unsteady hand – the woman has been guzzling champagne all evening – she says: 'We were awfully disappointed to hear of Timothy's fiancée breaking off their engagement.'

'Indeed,' says the man sitting beside Kitty. 'And it's just delightful that he has brought such a charming companion this evening.'

'Yes,' another of the female guests chimes in, nodding as if she's bestowing Kitty with a great honour. 'Indeed. And where did you two meet exactly?' She flashes Kitty a smile.

Kitty isn't prepared for the question and makes a pretence of wiping her mouth some more. Thankfully, Timothy answers for her.

'At the Club,' he says, and she thinks she catches something furtive about his tone. But what else was he supposed to say – that he scraped her off a sordid pavement in the early hours of the morning?

His answer appears to have satisfied the questioner, for they aren't asked any more about their meeting, but Kitty can feel a definite sense of curiosity oozing from the women. They most certainly seem to believe she is Timothy's sweetheart, or something in that vein. She herself has, of course, considered the possibility that he might be courting her. Surely he has other female acquaintances he might have asked to accompany him to the dinner? So why else did he choose to ask her?

She sips her champagne and looks over to where Timothy is now engaged in conversation with a white-haired man opposite. She observes him for several minutes, willing herself to find him attractive. But his nose is too thin, his nostrils unevenly shaped, and his shoulders droop forward, almost as though he is expecting to be punched at any moment. And his hands, long-fingered with oversized knuckles. She tries to imagine those hands stroking her, caressing her. It's no use. She lets out a little puffing noise with her lips, just as Timothy turns to her with a shy smile. She smiles back, feeling the colour rise to her face.

'Are you enjoying yourself?' he asks quietly.

'Yes, very much so.'

She reaches out to touch his hand, ashamed at her earlier thoughts, but at that moment a jazz quartet starts up in the bar opposite, and Timothy's hand slides off the table, out of her reach, as he cranes his head towards the music.

When the plates and glasses have been cleared from the table, a few of the dinner guests decide to take drinks at the bar, but Kitty sees Timothy yawning discreetly and throws him a questioning look. He nods. They stand and take their leave of the others. In the lift on the way up to their rooms, neither of them speaks, but in the hallway, Timothy has gained new wind and begins telling her about the conversation he had with the man seated opposite, about the abysmal working conditions in one of China Printing's factories. He stops talking abruptly when they reach her room.

'We're here,' he says, handing her the key and then placing a hand flat against the wall. He is slightly unsteady on his feet. 'You're here,' he adds. 'Your room. It's one of the smaller rooms, I'm afraid. But the view is lovely. My room is –' He looks around, squinting. 'Yes, 915. Over there.'

But he doesn't move. Kitty inserts the key into the lock and turns it. At least his hair is nice, she thinks. Silky, well kept. And his bashfulness, well, perhaps that's merely hiding a simmering, underlying passion. A German phrase pops into her head: *Schön trinken*. She has drunk him beautiful. She giggles and places her hand on the door handle. Still he makes no move to leave.

'Won't you come in? For a nightcap?' she says.

He stuffs his hands in his pockets, but teeters and pulls them back out for balance. 'I think I'll just –'

'Don't be silly. Just a nightcap. It's only –' She takes his arm and pulls his wrist towards her so she can read the time. 'It's only three o'clock.'

A frown crosses his face but passes. 'Very well, I'll . . . just a small one, then.'

Kitty pushes the door open and they step into the room. 'Oh,' Kitty exclaims, coming to an abrupt stop at the sight in front of her, and then, 'Oh!' again, as Timothy, assuming she was moving forward, bumps into her from behind. They both laugh.

She takes it in at a glance. The room is spectacular – far larger than she was expecting, all mahogany and marble, oriental carpets, a vast four-poster bed made up in crisp linen sheets and a green embroidered silk coverlet. But the best thing is the enormous window, a glass front that covers the entire far side of the room. She forgets all about Timothy for a moment and crosses to the window.

'What a view,' she whispers and places her forehead against the cool pane. Her breath mists up the glass. On the waterfront, the first of the wharf coolies are already at work, stacking rusty drum barrels and heaving huge sacks across the ground. A few of them stand around small fires, warming themselves against the chill. Across the river, on Pootung, she can make out the long line of docks, mills and godowns, studded with factory chimneys that point, almost rudely, towards the sky. And separating Pootung and the Bund is the Whangpoo River, snaking in from the estuary, filled with hundreds of wooden sampans that bob up and down on the swell of the river.

Up here on the ninth floor, the smells and sounds of the city are fantastically remote. In the darkness, it is possible to disregard the cruel, decadent chaos of the city, the ugliness of the ramshackle trawlers, the oily sheen of the water, the stink of raw sewage, the debris being carried into shore, the river rats. Instead, Kitty sees nothing but inky sky and pewter river, punctuated with pricks of light, quivering fires and the smooth undulation of the Whangpoo.

'It's quite something, isn't it?' Timothy comes to stand beside her.

'I think this must be the only nice view of Shanghai.'

He hands her a glass of whisky. 'It sounds very sad, the way you said that.'

'I don't –' she begins, but her voice catches and she starts to cry.

'Oh, Kitty,' Timothy says softly, 'I'm sorry. I didn't mean to upset you.'

She shakes her head and turns, lifting her wet face to his.

'Kitty –' he says, but then she closes her eyes and kisses him. His lips are surprisingly soft; they have a faint taste of caramel and smoke. The kiss is tender and prolonged. She lets her fingers travel down his back, around to the front, slips a finger into his waistband and teases it back and forth, slides it back out. Then lower, her hand cupping his groin, she feels him begin to stiffen, then –

He steps back, away from her. 'I'm sorry, I . . . I can't.'

Kitty's arms drop to her sides. The look on his face sends something fluttering up her throat. Has she really become that repellent? Of course, he was the only man there tonight who didn't gobble her up with his eyes; he snatched his hand away when she reached out to touch him earlier; all evening, he never once looked at her in that leering way she is so accustomed to. And all that time she thought he was being a gentleman. But he wasn't. To him, she's nothing more than a cheap tart in an expensive dress. Her face burns with shame – how could she possibly think he was courting her? The realisation is damning, humiliating. Her legs suddenly can't hold her up and she slumps onto the carpet.

Then Timothy is there, helping her to her feet. He guides her to the bed and sits her down. 'I'm sorry,' he says again. 'I apologise. I must've given you the wrong ... You must think me so ungrateful. But it's ... it's not ... You are an extremely beautiful woman.' He straightens up and turns towards the window. 'I'm afraid –' His fists clench and unclench. 'Damn it!' he shouts. Then his voice drops back down to a whisper. 'I'm sorry, Kitty. I'm sorry for spoiling your evening. I ... I think it's best if I leave now.'

As he crosses towards the door, his footsteps silenced by the thick carpet, Kitty lets out a laugh. It is a soft laugh. She claps her hand onto her mouth, but he hears it all the same. She drops her hand.

'You're a homosexual.' It is a statement, not a question. Deep down, she's known it all along.

He turns. 'I –'

'You are, aren't you? You're a homosexual.'

His cheek twitches. 'I don't –' He pauses and looks at her, deciding something. 'I'd better leave.'

She gets up. 'I didn't mean to laugh, Timothy. I wasn't making fun of you – you're too good and kind for that. It's just –' She reaches out and touches his sleeve. 'It's a relief, that's all.'

He frowns at her.

'I thought it was because you find me unattractive ... too unrefined for you! And to know now, well, that it isn't *me* – it's a relief.'

'Oh, Kitty. I don't know what to say.' His head drops. 'What'll you do now?'

The question hangs in the air, unanswered for a minute. Then Kitty understands. 'I won't tell anyone, if that's what you're afraid of.'

Timothy fumbles in his pocket for his cigarette case, offers her one and leans in to light it.

She takes a long drag on the cigarette before saying, 'I dance with men for money.' She straightens up, feeling a strange lightness inside her. 'And my real name is Käthe,' she adds for good measure. 'Käthe Blumenthal. I'm a Jew.'

She goes to sit back down on the bed. Timothy doesn't respond. After a few moments, he sits down on the bed beside her. They remain in this position for a long time, in a compacted silence, smoking cigarettes, until the diffused dawn light seeps into the room. Timothy is the first to break the silence.

'What a queer couple we make,' he says, leaning gently into her.

August 1942 to
January 1943

周翼

―――

Yì can't tell day from night any longer. He is simply too tired, though he tries to fight his drowsiness and physical exhaustion in the airless hall, because any inattention, the slightest slip or error, could cause severe scalding. The small girl at the vat beside him is testament to that: the skin on her left arm, from the tips of her fingers up to her elbow, is covered in large, red shiny blotches. And from the way she grimaces when her arm comes into contact with the steam rising from the vat she is stirring, the scars are still painful.

The girl is six, perhaps seven years old. Yì doesn't know her name – he has asked, but either she is deaf, or simple, or both, because when he tries to talk to her, she just grins and nods – so in his head, he has given her a name: Zhū. Pearl. He thinks this name suits her because that is what her cheeks look like when she grins – two smooth pearls.

Theirs – and that of a dozen others – is the task of stirring fabric in the boiling dye until it takes on the right colour. The liquid smells acrid, making Yì's lungs tighten if he breathes in the steam too deeply. But he becomes accustomed to the stench after an hour or so of beginning his shift, leaving the remaining thirteen hours with only a biting rasp at the back of his throat. At the other end of the overcrowded, dimly lit hall are the women who sit spinning silk for hours on end. And this is the reason why there is no ventilation here – the slightest draught could damage the precious silk threads.

In the close dampness of the unbreathable air, his thoughts travel to food, always food, and then, inevitably, to Năinai. She has become so thin, it is as though she is disappearing in front of his very eyes. She can no longer stand up, so when he is at home, he carries her to the pot to do her business. She weighs no more than a whisper. Increasingly often, he comes home to find her lying in her own urine. Last week, Huà came and stayed for three days, helping him feed and wash Năinai, before disappearing again without a word. He left no food, not a single grain of rice.

From across the hall, Yì spots one of the overseers coming towards him, a squattish, tight-faced woman who paces up and down the rows of vats, her expression of disgust caused, perhaps, by the stench rising from hundreds of dead cocoons that litter the floor. She carries a short bamboo rod, which she uses to beat the backs of the legs of those children who aren't stirring at the correct pace, or who accidentally let a part of the dyed fabric touch the filthy floor when heaving it out of the boiling liquid. A particularly monstrous punishment – which Yì has witnessed on several occasions – involves thrusting a child's hand into the boiling dye. Their shrieks of pain follow him into his sleep. He lets out a low whistle to warn

Zhū, who has slowed her stirring almost to a standstill, but she doesn't respond. He leans across to tap her shoulder, scalding himself on the vat in the process, and she startles and picks up her pace just as the overseer approaches. But the woman scuttles past; she has spotted a young boy further down the row taking an unpermitted break – probably because his legs can no longer bear his weight after eight solid hours of standing.

The supervisor at the top of his row strikes a gong, indicating that it is time to remove the fabric from the dye. Yì lifts the silk out with his wooden paddle and lets as much liquid drip into the vat as he can, trying to avoid the hot dye splashing up onto his skin. The sopping fabric is heavy, and as he lifts it as high as he can with arms that used to tremble, but which have now become taut and muscular, he notices two figures – a man and a woman – at the far side of the hall talking to the foreman. He notices them because they are *lăowài* – foreigners. The man is tall and thin, his hair the colour of wet sand that flops across his face when he bows, as he is doing now, to the Japanese foreman. Yì has seen him once before. He was here the day after Yì was hired, having a loud argument, in Shanghainese, with one of the supervisors.

The pale-skinned woman beside him also bows to the foreman. Then she turns around to look across the hall, and Yì can't help but exclaim. Her hair is darker, no longer golden, but her eyes are still as round, her skin still as white, her lips still as blush-perfect. She hasn't seen him; a cloud of steam rises up from his vat and by the time it clears, she is making her way out through the door. The muscles in Yì's arms seem to melt, and before he can help himself, the fabric slides from his paddle and drops back into the vat, creating a splash of red that explodes in all directions. Yì calls out in alarm and jumps back. Beside him, Zhū squeals. He thrusts his paddle back into the dye and pulls the fabric out, knowing that it will be spoiled completely if it stays in for too long. But in his panic, he hauls it out too quickly and a corner of the fabric hits the floor with a wet thud. Within seconds, the overseer is beside him. She raises her bamboo rod and strikes him on the arm – short, sharp blows.

'Be. Careful. With. The. Silk!' she spits out as she whips him.

Mechanically, Yì bows, apologising, and then gathers the fabric from the floor. The overseer gives him a last hard look and marches off. Yì rubs his arm and winces. He peels back his sleeve. Ugly red welts have already risen on his skin. But he smiles regardless.

She is still in Shanghai. Mamselle Kitty is alive.

He steps down from the vat and makes his way down the line, his legs propelling him forward as though of their own volition. Ignoring the whispered comments of the other workers, and then the shouts and yells of the overseers, he steers through the hall and runs out through the main doors. The light is thin and hazy – it must be approaching dusk – and as he steps out of the factory onto the road, he sees the shiny black of a car speeding away. He watches until it reaches the end of the street and disappears around the corner.

Behind him, the door to the factory thunders shut.

Days pass. Maybe weeks, he isn't sure. The ache in his belly has become a razor-edged pain. He is always nauseous and dizzy. One day, walking down Nanking Road his legs give way. He slumps down onto the pavement and manages to crawl out of the way of the pedestrians who would think nothing of stepping on him to pass. He sits with his back against the wall of one of the tall, fine buildings that line the road, waiting for the blackness to subside. A coin lands near his feet. He stares at it for a moment, assuming someone has dropped it, and waits for its owner to reclaim it. But the stream of passers-by continues unabated. Yì stretches out his arm, hesitates, and then snatches it up in one sweep. Five fēn. He turns the coin in his dirt-encrusted palm and sees in his hands a bowl of steaming rice, red bean pastries, sweet sesame pork. The vision of food intensifies the pain in his gut. He leans over to vomit, but only dry retches a few times. He knows it won't be long before he is hauled away by police or beaten off by another beggar claiming his territory. He sits cross-legged on the hard ground and waits.

A foot strikes the sole of his shoe, but he doesn't look up. Then, suddenly, he is being grabbed by his shirt and dragged to his feet. Before he can cry out, or raise his hands in defence, a hand strikes him across the face.

A voice hisses. 'No!'

Yì screws up his face as a hand slaps his other cheek. He opens his eyes a little to look at his assailant. It is Huà. He has a bloody gash on his cheek and his left eye has swollen shut.

'You will not beg! Do you hear me? You are not a beggar!' He grabs Yì's collar in his fists and hoists him up, so that Yì is forced to stand on tiptoes.

'Let me go!' Yì shouts. The noise around them is fierce. Horns, whistles, bells, barking, shouting, laughing.

'You shame yourself! You shame me!' Huà shakes him.

'You shame Năinai.' With these last words, he screws up his face, and to Yì's alarm, begins to weep. He lets go of the collar and clasps his brother in an embrace. His sobs are so loud they attract the attention of passers-by, and it costs Yì effort to extract himself from his arms.

'What happened?' he asks, but Huà continues to weep. 'Were you in a fight?'

It takes Huà several long minutes to calm his breathing. 'Năinai,' he says finally. 'Năinai is dead.'

KITTY

The summer heat drops away suddenly, washed out of the air by a series of thunderstorms. There follows a succession of weeks, then months, during which Kitty no longer lives on the edge of malnutrition, instead coming home to carefully prepared meals, freshly laundered sheets and spending a few hours in Timothy's company every day, the 'overlap hours', they call them, after Timothy has returned from work and before she heads out to the Del Monte.

Queer or not – and there are far queerer liaisons in Shanghai – Kitty and Timothy's agreement is straightforward: she has moved out of her rented room at Madame Ling's and taken a room in Timothy's spacious apartment. In return, she pays him a token rent – China Printing pays for the apartment, Timothy told her – and accompanies him to occasional functions at which he requires a female companion. Their cohabitation is an open secret, not even worthy of a raised eyebrow. Indeed, as Kitty soon discovers from Timothy, one of the company's senior executives lives in a huge villa with his wife of forty-something years – and his twenty-five-year-old Chinese mistress permanently accommodated in a bijoux guesthouse at the bottom of the expansive gardens. The façade, Kitty has long since learned, is everything. And ever since the first night she returned here, when she finally got the opportunity to place the jade dragon back among the collection on the chest of drawers, she has slept wonderfully.

'I like that frock,' Timothy says one evening, putting up his feet on the coffee table and watching Kitty, fussing with her hair in front of the mirror.

She looks down at the blue silk dress she is wearing. Ever since Timothy took her on that tour of the factory, the touch of silk against her skin has never quite felt as luxurious. 'Here, would you pass me my lipstick?'

He picks it up off the coffee table and tosses it towards her. 'This is almost like being married,' he says with a chuckle.

She slides a grip into her hair. *Just without the sex*, she thinks and throws him a quick glance. Their eyes meet and a blush creeps up his face, and she knows he's thinking the same thing. She hasn't been with a man for a long time, since Vitali, and at times her body aches for it. But the thought of making herself available to any of her dancing partners makes her shudder, despite their frequent requests and the nightclub manager's less-than-subtle encouragement – he is keen on providing as full a service as possible to his customers.

And what about Timothy? Surely he must ache for it too? She used to know many homosexuals back in Vienna, but these were a different sort of man entirely: flamboyant, sexual, extravagant, melodramatic; men who preened themselves tirelessly and flaunted their otherness to spectacular effect. Like Andreas and Michel, who lived just across the hall from her in Naschmarkt. She and they recognised each other for what they were: misfits existing in the same demi-monde, soft and tough at the same time. And from this mutual recognition grew a friendship rooted in empathy. Towards the end of Kitty's time in Vienna these men, such a distinct species, became an endangered species, of course. Andreas and Michel disappeared overnight one September; others were subjected to public humiliation, forced to walk the streets flanked by SS officers, in women's clothes with make-up crudely applied and their heads shaved.

Kitty licks a finger and uses it to trace her eyebrows in the mirror, then steals another look at Timothy, who has picked up a newspaper and is reading it in his studious, focused way. Timothy will surely be spared anything like that. But from the little he has told her, and that only after too much rice wine one evening, his previous sexual experiences are limited to a few awkward, fumbling – and not particularly satisfying – encounters during his time at university. Watching him in the mirror, the grief for her Viennese friends fresh and acute, she feels an overwhelming tenderness towards him. Yes, they are both outcasts of sorts – perhaps this is why fate has brought them together. She turns to face him.

'Let's go out for dinner,' she says.

Timothy lowers the newspaper and gives her a quizzical look. 'What, tonight?'

Kitty nods.

'But don't you have to go to work?' he asks, still frowning.

Kitty lets out a gentle laugh. Timothy Hamilton, the least spontaneous man on earth.

'I'll take the evening off,' she says. 'They'll hardly sack me. I won't get paid, that's all. And we've never actually been out for dinner together – just the two of us, I mean.'

He sits up and places the folded newspaper beside him. 'Oh. Well, in that case, why not? Yes. That sounds nice. Where would you like to go? I'll make reservations.'

She shakes her head. 'I have a place in mind. Let me surprise you.'

They dine on the fourteenth floor of the Park Hotel. One of the reasons she wanted to come here was to experience the special feature of the dining hall, the retractable roof, but the cold outside has jammed the mechanism. It is a shame, as the night is clear and crisp, and they would have had a wonderful view of the stars, but the food is good and the music pleasant.

'May I ask you something?' Timothy says, placing down his knife and fork.

Kitty dabs at her mouth with a napkin. 'Well, that depends.'

'Please tell me if it's none of my business, but – I happened to notice the scars on your back.' He rearranges the cutlery on his plate. A blush creeps up his collar. 'Did that happen here, in Shanghai?'

Kitty shakes her head. She takes a cigarette and holds it between her lips for him to light.

'I'm sorry,' he says, snapping the lighter open. 'I didn't mean to pry.'

She shakes her head again. 'It's not a secret. Happened years ago. It's just, nobody's asked me before.' She pulls on her cigarette. 'It was my father.'

'Oh.'

Kitty leans back in her chair. 'I'd started bleeding, for the first time, you know, so it caught me unawares.' She ignores Timothy's blushes. He's asked, so she'll tell him. 'I was sitting in my father's armchair, reading. He didn't like anyone else to use his chair, so I jumped up when he came in. And then we both saw it. I'd bled all over his tallit. Bright red it was, all the brighter against the white of his shawl. I laughed out loud – my filthy *niddah* blood on his tallit. I couldn't help myself.' She stops and closes her eyes briefly. 'He grabbed a table lamp and yanked the cord off, and then began whipping me. He whipped me so hard it broke the skin under my blouse. My mother was screaming at him because he'd shattered the lamp. And I just couldn't stop laughing, even though I was crying. He whipped me out of the house.' She pauses. 'I was fourteen. I was drenched in blood.'

Timothy rubs the side of his face. 'I'm so sorry, Kitty. I – I don't know what to say.'

'There's nothing *to* say. I am here, and they . . . are there.'

After dinner, Timothy suggests going to a club for a nightcap, but Kitty feigns tiredness.

'I think I'd like to go home,' she says, pretending to stifle a yawn. 'But I've had a wonderful evening.'

Timothy nods and smiles. 'Yes, so have I. We should come here again.' He looks up at the ceiling. 'Perhaps in spring, when they get this thing to work.'

As they enter the lift to descend, the bellman winks at Kitty. She smiles back. She knows him from the Del Monte, where he used to work clearing tables. In his maroon and gold bellman uniform, this is obviously a step up for him.

'Third, please,' she says to him quietly as he slides the doors shut.

He shoots her a quick surprised look, his eyes flicking towards Timothy and back, and then turns to operate the handle. When the lift purrs to a stop, the bellman pulls open the doors.

'Third floor,' he announces.

Timothy frowns and opens his mouth to speak, but Kitty takes his hand and squeezes it gently.

'It's a . . . a gentleman's club,' she says, her voice wavering a little. She feels excited and nervous at the same time.

He looks at her, confused at first, but then his features relax. 'Oh,' he says quietly.

'You might like it.'

'Oh,' he says again and glances at the bellman, who smiles warmly and says, 'They make an excellent whiskey sour, sir.'

Timothy takes a deep breath. 'Well, in that case . . .'

As he steps out of the lift into a dimly lit foyer, Kitty hopes she hasn't gone too far. But he's a grown man, after all, and if he doesn't like it, he can leave anytime he likes.

When she wakes the next morning, she finds a small gift-wrapped box on her bedside table. Timothy must have put it there during the night. She unwraps it, curious. Inside the box, she finds the jade dragon.

A month later, Timothy comes home earlier than usual. Kitty is wearing a robe and has her hair in curlers.

'I look a fright,' she says, lifting a hand to her hair. 'Don't stare.'

But he just gives her a vacant smile and lays his jacket

over the back of the sofa. He sits down heavily. His skin, which was as red as a lobster during the summer, has faded to a light pink.

'Would you like a drink?' she asks. It's far too early for her; she has only been awake for a couple of hours, but something about Timothy suggests he could do with one.

She fixes his drink, and as she hands it to him, she notices his jacket. 'What's this?' There is a red band stitched onto the left sleeve, embroidered with a large 'B'.

Timothy glances at it. 'Oh. We have to wear those from now on. Japanese orders.'

Kitty continues to stare at the sleeve. 'But what's it for? What does "B" mean?'

He sighs. '"B" for British. The Americans wear an "A", the Canadians a "C" and so on. Simple yet effective, once they decide to round us all up.'

Kitty looks at him blankly.

'I was joking,' he says. 'I didn't mean ... The Japs are just playing power games, that's all.'

Kitty lets the sleeve drop and sits down. Her chin starts to tremble.

'Oh goodness, Kitty,' Timothy says. 'How insensitive of me! I'm sorry, I didn't mean to ...'

Kitty lowers her head. 'It's all falling apart, isn't it? This was a haven for us, but now ...' Her voice is no more than a whisper.

'No, no. I'm sorry. It was a stupid thing to say. Listen, Kitty –' He pauses. 'They're pulling out,' he says quietly.

'Who? What are you talking about?'

'China Printing. The company.' He sips his drink.

'They're closing?'

'Well, they're not closing down completely, just pulling out the "non-essential staff". That includes me.' He pulls down the corners of his mouth as he speaks and places his glass on the coffee table with an angry *thunk*.

For a moment, Kitty thinks it's because his male pride has been dented. What man wants to think of himself as non-essential? But that isn't like him at all.

'Why?' she asks.

'There've been some more worrying noises coming from the Japanese. I don't know how much of it is bravado, but the company's taking it seriously. They've already sent many of the wives and children back. And now the plan is to downscale the company branch here. Apparently' – here his mouth twists into an uncharacteristic sneer – 'there's plenty more lucrative business to be done as part of the war effort back home.'

Kitty sits down on the sofa beside him. 'When will you be leaving?'

'Oh, in a couple of months, presumably. It'll take a while to sort things out. And then –' He sighs, more despondent than she's ever seen him. 'Then it's back to Manchester.' She leans into him, then he looks at her, his eyes suddenly sharp. 'Kitty, I've been thinking.'

She reaches across and picks up his glass. Her hand trembles as she puts it to her lips. She drains it in one go, but it does nothing to stop the curdling of thoughts. It was too good to be true, of course it was. Living like this, it was a façade from the beginning, like everything else in this place; shimmering, hazy. Did she really think her life – that of an outcast, a refugee – could go on like this? She needs another drink. Then she realises Timothy is still talking.

'Sorry,' she says. 'What?'

'I said I'd like you to come with me.'

Before she can stop herself, a bubble of laughter rises up and out of her mouth.

Timothy stiffens. 'I didn't think it was *such* a ridiculous notion.'

'No, I'm sorry. It's just –' She shakes her head, making the curlers wobble and snag painfully at her hair. 'It's such an astonishing idea. Come with you? How is that supposed to work? D'you think I haven't been trying to get out of this place almost since I arrived?' She slams the empty glass down. Now she is working herself into a state of anger, but she can't help it. 'How many times have I gone to the consulates? The Americans, British, French – none of them want Jews! Their quotas are all full, and even if they had a single place left, d'you think they'd want someone like me? Do you? I'm no better than a whore to them.' She gets to her feet. Her outburst has left her feeling flushed and breathy; she feels the alcohol surging in her blood. She is angry – at Timothy, at his stupid company, at the Japanese. At herself.

'Please, sit down,' he says. 'There's more.'

Kitty gives him a hard look but sits back down. She lights a cigarette, hoping it'll take the edge off her fury.

'I'm very fond of you, Kitty. You know that. In fact, you're the best friend I've ever had.'

She grimaces, but he continues.

'I can honestly say that you know me – well, most of me – better than anyone. And I truly think you may have saved my life.'

'Oh, Timothy,' she sneers and grinds her butt into the ashtray. 'That's very melodramatic. I didn't think you were that sort of fag.' She regrets it as soon as it comes out of her mouth. 'Sorry,' she says in the next breath.

He looks away but goes on. 'At the very least, you saved my sanity.'

For a long while, neither speaks.

Timothy breaks the silence. 'The weather is miserable, the food unpalatable and the Germans are blitzing the place to bits. And if you want to stay here, I understand, but frankly, if things heat up, then . . .' He looks down at the table and she sees how red the tips of his ears are. 'Then I don't like to think of you here, on your own.'

Kitty fights a sudden urge to cry. Her tongue feels leathery, but still she goes to light another cigarette to stop the tears. Without speaking, Timothy takes the cigarette from her hand and puts an arm around her shoulder to draw her towards him. He holds her close, even though she knows her curlers must be uncomfortable against his chest. She listens to the thump in his ribcage, slow, then quickening, and in an instant, she knows what his next words are going to be.

'Käthe Blumenthal,' he says and she hears the smile and sincerity in his voice, 'will you be so kind as to marry me?'

ESTHER

———

Esther and Aaron arrive at the music hall on East Seward Road. He is bad-tempered because she has dragged him along to the fundraiser, organised by the Relief Committee to help those hundreds of refugees still living in the *heim*, who would otherwise face a slow and awful starvation.

'For the price they're charging, they can wait until I'm good and ready,' Aaron said earlier when she tried to hurry him into clean clothes.

'Helene and Victor will be waiting for us. We can't be the last ones through the door,' she replied, handing him his jacket and trying to ignore the dirt packed under his fingernails. 'And it's only ten dollars, for goodness' sake.'

'You don't know what we might need that money for in the future.'

'And you don't know what it's like living in a *heim*,' she said bitterly and marched out of the door.

Now, it is already twenty past eight, and they haven't exchanged a word since they left the house. The music hall is packed; there must be over a hundred people here.

There is the dense smell of exhaled breaths and damp wool in the air. A wooden stage has been set up at the far end, and the rest of the space is filled with small round tables and chairs. Esther worries that she won't find Helene and Victor before the event starts but then spots them through the smoke-filled air at a table on the right. Helene waves in her direction.

'I was afraid you might not make it,' Helene says as they reach the table. From across the hall, they hear the discordant tuning of instruments.

'I'm sorry we're late,' Esther says, and adds the lie she prepared on the way here. 'We had a little trouble getting Anneliese settled with the neighbour.'

'Never mind, you're here now. Please, sit down – I think it's about to start.'

As if on cue, a representative from the Committee climbs onto the stage and makes a speech, thanking them for coming, for their generosity, and asking them, in these dark times, not to ever forget the hardship facing so many brothers in faith. He recites a short prayer, the assembled guests tagging their 'Amen' onto the end of his.

'Now,' the man concludes with a broad smile, 'I wish you all a pleasant evening. We have some of the finest musicians in the city playing for you tonight. A mix of klezmer and classical – something for everyone, I hope.'

A moment later the music starts, a hobbling klezmer tune in harmonic minor, played by a group of earnest, bearded men. The clarinet is sad and haunting, but the fiddle adds a hint of humour, something mischievous almost. Esther closes her eyes and lets the music pull her thoughts this way and that. The tune is something Eastern European, possibly Russian, and not the kind of music she grew up with. And yet it plucks at threads in her mind, to finally unravel the memory of some relative's wedding many years ago, when she was still too young and shy to trust herself to dance.

If anyone asked her, she would happily argue that there was no such thing as Jewish music – just as there is no such thing as Catholic or Buddhist music. But here, now, immersed in this flood of sound, she cannot deny its pull, an invisible hook tugging at something deep inside. Something mournful and ecstatic all at once. She hasn't been to synagogue for so long – Aaron has no faith, never has done – and she has, at times, felt her own faith slipping through her fingers. But she should at least give Anneliese the choice. She resolves to take her to synagogue on Saturday.

She is bumped out of her thoughts when the music changes to something livelier – a polka.

Victor gets to his feet. 'Darling?' He holds out his hand to Helene. 'Shall we?'

Helene smiles and lets him lead her onto the floor, where they begin their dance together with an elegance that suggests they spend their time doing nothing else.

To Esther's amazement, Aaron jumps up and takes her hand. 'It's been a while,' he says, 'but let's give it a go.'

She stumbles getting to her feet. She isn't sure if she wants to forgive him just like that, with a mere smile and an offer to dance. But the music rises and dips and swirls around them, and her irritation shrivels. She takes his hand.

They dance on and on – a polka, a foxtrot, a waltz; the recollection of her adolescent dance classes guiding her moves – until the music stops and Aaron excuses himself to go and get a drink. She stands still for a moment, her foot tapping out the rhythm of the previous song, when the music starts up again. Before she knows it, she has been swept up with the other dancers, who have formed a circle and are pulling her around in a dizzying swirl. She is unfamiliar with the steps, if indeed there is any choreography at all, and lets herself be moved along, two steps right, two steps left, a stamp then a clap, until the dancers split into couples and Esther gladly accepts the arm of an elderly man, who smiles and guides her expertly across the floor. A break in rhythm, a turn, and she is spun off, like a spinning top, into the welcoming arms of another dancer. She can hardly catch her breath – she is delighted, giddy, gradually catching on to the tempo of stopping, stamping, clapping, twirling.

She spins around to face her next partner. But no welcome awaits her.

His sneer is immediately recognisable, but so out of context it takes her a few seconds to place him. By then, Franz Hohlbein has his hand around her and is drawing her close.

'I don't –' she begins, but she has no chance against the swing and pull of the dance. Around and around she is spun, Hohlbein's hot, strong fingers pinching at her waist.

'Still not married?' he mumbles into her ear and, when she doesn't respond immediately, turns his head so his nose is almost touching hers – she can smell wine and garlic on his breath – and pushes his moist lips onto hers, forcing them open with his tongue, while cupping her chin with his hand to stop her moving away. She is jostled from behind by another dancing couple, causing her and Hohlbein's teeth to clash. At last, she struggles against him, pulls away and presses through the crowd of dancers, her head down, her whole body disconcerted, back to her table.

'Had enough of dancing, sweetheart?' Aaron asks with a laugh. His eyes are glazed.

She doesn't reply but feels a shameful relief that he didn't see, that she doesn't have to answer his questions. She lifts her sleeve and wipes her mouth, again and again.

Helene, an attractive flush to her cheeks, leans across the table. 'Is everything all right?'

'Yes,' Esther mutters. 'I'm a little out of breath, that's all.'

Aaron gets up. 'Let me get you another drink, sweetheart.'

She doesn't want a drink. What she wants is to get away; away from the heat and crush and noise – there is a roar of applause now, as the band bows and leaves the stage to make room for a string quartet – and she is burning, the sickly sensation of Hohlbein's lips still on her mouth, like a hateful bruise.

'… some fresh air perhaps?'

Beside her, Helene is talking. Esther shakes her head. If she steps outside now, she fears she will run straight home, and she has waited so, so long to see Aaron as cheerful as he is tonight. No. She will stay. Perhaps the music – an achingly beautiful Schubert piece has just started up – will calm her. And it does, a little, though for the rest of the night, she has a ghostly sense of Hohlbein staring at her from somewhere in the room, with his eyes sharp and shiny, his mouth wet and stinking.

It is past midnight by the time Esther picks up a very sleepy Anneliese from the neighbour. When she steps into the flat with her daughter slumped across her shoulder, Aaron is sitting at the table, hunched forward in the low light of the kerosene lamp. Esther knows immediately that something is wrong.

'I have some news,' he says, holding up a letter.

She sits down beside him. 'What is it?' she asks. On her lap, Anneliese shivers and presses into her mother's body.

'When I applied for the architecture project, they said they would give the job to the best man.'

'Oh, Aaron, I'm so sorry.'

He doesn't speak. Then he reaches into his shoulder bag and pulls something out. He places it on the table with a thud. A bottle of sparkling wine.

He says, 'As it turns out, *I* am the best man for the job.'

Esther slides Anneliese from her lap and gets to her feet. 'You got the job? Really?'

He grins and nods. 'I did. I start in a few months' time.' He jumps to his feet and picks up Anneliese, whirling her around in his arms. 'I have a new job, Anni, a wonderful job, the best job in the world.'

Anneliese laughs and squeals as he spins her around, faster and faster. Esther's face actually begins to ache from smiling. She hasn't felt this way for so long. She is dizzy with happiness and hope.

Aaron finally stops spinning and lets a flushed Anneliese back down. She turns to Esther. 'Mama, why are you crying?'

'I don't know, *liebling*. I really don't.'

KITTY

———

The office is located in a small building on Myburgh Road, tucked in among food stalls and trinket shops and laundrettes. The former consulate, a beautiful Renaissance Revival building on the Bund, was commandeered by the Japanese forces several months ago, and now this dingy building serves for the registration of British births, deaths and marriages in Shanghai.

Kitty slows down to bow to the Japanese soldier guarding the entrance and picks up her pace as soon as she enters. She doesn't want to be late, fashionable or not. A cluster of people is sitting on the benches in the corridor, but Timothy isn't among them. The tattered remains of a home-made red-and-green paper chain hang from one of the walls, a reminder of the recent Christmas celebrations.

Kitty smooths down the back of her coat and takes a seat on one of the empty benches. She takes off her gloves and rubs her hands together to warm her frozen fingertips, and wonders lazily where Timothy has got to. He is rarely late for anything. When they get back, afterwards, they will have a light supper and get an early night.

Timothy spent last night at a friend's house. His maid, Huìqín, had insisted he and Kitty spend the night apart before their wedding day.

'But it's not even your custom,' Kitty said, as Huìqín packed Timothy's overnight bag.

'Me not marry,' Huìqín replied. 'You marry. You custom. Bad bad luck if not honour custom.'

But there was no argument over Kitty's choice of dress. Underneath her coat, she wears a bottle-green cotton dress with lace-trimmed butterfly sleeves, bought especially for the occasion and tailored to fit by Huìqín. The maid suggested green, rather than white, which Kitty wouldn't have worn for her own reasons, anyway. Huìqín assured her that green was lucky.

'Symbol of money,' she said. 'White no good. White for funeral. *Our* custom.'

An evacuation ship, the HMS *Ladybird*, leaves for England tomorrow. It is to take the last remaining British families to safety. And this evening, that's what she and Timothy will be – a family, and she will be just as British as him. Her luggage is packed and sitting in the hall in Bubbling Well Road, waiting to be collected and taken to the port tonight. Timothy will have packed his final bits and bobs this morning, while she was at Mr Marcel's getting her hair styled. The thought of England still sits in her gut like an undigested meal, but she tries not to dwell on it. As long as she gets out of this place, she could be going to the moon for all she cares.

She isn't wearing a watch, so she turns to her neighbour to ask the time. He is an elderly gentleman with a bulbous nose and whiskers that are at least twenty years out of fashion. Kitty notes his red armband, the embroidered 'B' beginning to unravel. He barely glances at her when she addresses him but gives her the required information: it is half past two. She thanks the man and puts her gloves back on. She and Timothy agreed to meet here at two. She's starting to feel agitated. Where the hell is he?

She gets up and walks to the door. She is dying for a cigarette, but she ran out yesterday evening. Perhaps Timothy is waiting outside? Out on the street, the fug lies draped across Shanghai like a heavy veil and the familiar reek of sulphur seizes her throat, making her cough. The Japanese guard stands at the entrance in his uniform, shivering slightly, his breath a white cloud on the air. For a snatch of a moment, Kitty feels a little sorry for him to be standing out here in the raw and freezing cold. But he turns to look at her and spits out some choppy words she can't understand, but which don't signify anything pleasant, and her pity dissolves.

She returns to the relative warmth of the corridor. Was there some sort of misunderstanding? Surely they were to meet at two o'clock. She rubs the tops of her arms. And then, for the first time since they cooked up this ridiculous plan, she feels a panicky sweep of doubt. Perhaps he's changed his mind? Perhaps he's decided to leave without her, after all. She takes a deep breath to steady herself, but the sharp chill tickles her throat. She couldn't blame him; in spite of everything, this man owes her nothing.

Then Mr Whiskers is called into the office. His seat is taken by a thin, pale woman with a colicky baby wrapped in a coarse blanket, whom she bounces up and down on her knee. This doesn't help; if anything, it makes the child cry even louder. Perhaps the mother has had to let her amah go, Kitty thinks, and doesn't know how to placate the baby herself. The child's wails seem to make the cold even more oppressive. Kitty tries to stifle her irritation – it isn't the baby's fault, after all – but after another ten minutes she gets up again and knocks on the door to the secretary's office.

The secretary, hunched over a typewriter, looks up as Kitty comes in. She doesn't smile.

'Yes?' Her tone is weary.

'May I use your telephone?' Kitty asks, as sweetly as she can.

The woman pulls the corners of her mouth down. 'It's on the blink, I'm afraid.'

'Pardon?'

'It's on the blink.' The woman sighs. 'It is not working at the moment,' she says, slowly, as if talking to a dim child. 'It is out of order.'

'Oh.' Kitty retreats from the office, ignoring the woman's calls for her to close the door behind her, thank you very much.

At the apartment, the only place she thinks Timothy could be, she finds the front door wide open and Huìqín curled up in a ball on the floor. The place has been devastated. Curtains torn from their rods, silk screens ripped and thrown to the floor, shards of glass and china strewn across all surfaces.

Kitty takes a step towards her. 'Huìqín, what's happened?'

Huìqín doesn't respond. She continues to sob.

'Timothy!' Kitty calls out and rushes into his bedroom. The chaos is just as bad in here. 'Timothy! Where are you?'

She goes back into the hall and tries to pull Huìqín into a sitting position. There are a dozen small round burn marks on her arms. 'Tell me what happened. Where's Timothy?'

Huìqín wails even louder. Kitty gets to her knees and slaps the woman's face – hard. The palm of her hand stings, but it has the desired effect. Huìqín falls silent and looks at Kitty with wide eyes.

'They come for him, they take him. This morning. When he come to pack.'

'Who took him?' she asks, a rising panic in her throat. 'Huìqín!' she shouts, for the woman has gone limp and begun to sob again. 'Huìqín. Tell me, who took him? Was it soldiers?'

Huìqín nods and lets out a final sob. She narrows her eyes. '*Dōngyáng guǐzi*,' she whispers, and then turns to spit on the floor.

Kitty shivers, a shiver of pure horror. *Guǐzi*. Huìqín's word for devils. The Japanese have taken her master, Timothy.

February 1943 to
August 1944

ESTHER

It has been a mild winter so far; even so, the waiting room at the Sterns' surgery is full. Esther sits behind the reception counter in a corner of the waiting room and sorts through the accounts. She has three piles: payments outstanding, invoices paid and invoices never likely to be paid. This third pile grows bigger every week. Victor Stern will discard these invoices when he returns. He is out; once a week, he receives training from Dr Chén, a local doctor with long fingernails who is, according to Victor, a *zhōngyī* – a master of herbalism and acupuncture.

Helene is in the examination room with a patient, a middle-aged woman from Stuttgart who has been a regular since Esther took the job here. Suddenly, from behind the closed door, Helene raises her voice: 'It's a bloody wart!' she shouts.

A couple of the patients sitting in front of Esther turn their heads. One man mutters something under his breath. In the examination room, the woman responds to Helene's outburst, but Esther can't make out what she is saying. A moment later, the door flies open and Helene ushers her out. 'And don't come back unless you have typhoid!'

She throws a glance at Esther, her expression still frozen in anger, but then one of the waiting patients coughs and Helene blinks rapidly. Her features soften and she shakes her head. 'I don't know where some of them think they are,' she murmurs. She calls in the next patient and returns to the examination room.

Esther goes back to the accounts. The remaining patients sit quietly as they wait, one or two of them coughing or sniffling. Until recently, the waiting room was a hotbed for gossip and news – both trivial and substantial. Many of the patients were newly arrived refugees who were having difficulty acclimatising; their already fragile constitutions from near-starvation rations in Germany, or from month-long random internment, unequipped for the exotic temperatures and unfamiliar germs. These were the unsuspecting ones who bought the emerald-green watermelons not knowing they had been injected with dirty water to increase their weight – and boost the vendors' profits. But today, the waiting room is hushed, apart from those occasional coughs and scratches. For months now, there has been very little first-hand news from Europe since the last refugees arrived in the summer, when the Japanese authorities banned any further immigration. The news of the recent German defeat in Stalingrad raised everyone's spirits for a while, but after a few days the cheer dissolved with the realisation that here, on the other side of the world, nothing has changed.

Helene's patient steps out of the examination room just as Victor Stern enters the surgery. Esther greets him and gets to her feet. 'I've put the files on your desk, for this month's accounts, but I need –'

'Excuse me, Esther,' he says abruptly. 'I need to speak to Helene.' He sweeps past her into his wife's office, not stopping to remove his hat or coat.

Startled, Esther sits back down. Then, ignoring the curious looks from the waiting room, she gets up. She taps lightly on Helene's door and opens it. Victor is standing in the middle of the room, reading aloud from a newspaper. Helene stands at the window, a hand gripping the back of her chair.

'Something has happened,' Esther says. Victor looks up and throws her a glance, but then turns his attention back to the paper he is holding. She can see his hand shaking as he reads.

'"… will be restricted to the undermentioned area in the International Settlement: east of the line connecting Chaoufong Road, Muirhead Road and Dent Road; west of Yangtzepoo Creek; north of the line connecting East Seward Road, Muirhead Road and Wayside Road; and south of the boundary of the International Settlement. The stateless refugees at the present residing and/or carrying on business in the districts other than the above areas shall remove their places of residence and/or business into the area designated above by 18 May 1943."'

He stops reading and looks at his wife. 'They've given us three months.'

'They are putting us into a ghetto,' Helene says slowly. Her face is white.

Esther steps forward. 'What's going on? What ghetto?'

Victor turns to face her. 'The Japanese have issued a proclamation,' he says, his voice trembling. 'It's printed in the newspaper.' He holds up the copy of the *Shanghai Herald*. Esther takes it from him and scans the article.

She looks up at Victor. 'But Aaron and I live on Broadway,' she says. 'That's outside this … this area.'

'And so is the surgery,' says Victor. His voice is low.

'But they can't *make* us move, surely!' Helene is incredulous. 'It's, what, only a square mile or so. How are we all going to fit in there?' She steps forward and, wordlessly, puts her arms around her husband. Then she begins to cry.

'Shhh, my love,' Victor says. 'We've managed so much. We will manage this also.'

'But what about Aaron's job?' Esther says. The thought comes as a stab. 'His new job, it's in Frenchtown. What are we going to do?'

There is a soft knock on the door and a patient looks in. 'Dr Stern?' she says tersely, 'I've been waiting for quite some time now.'

Victor, still holding his wife in his arms, turns to her. 'I'm sorry, Frau Löwenstein, but we've had some bad news. We'll have to reschedule your appointment.'

'But –'

Esther goes to the door. She suppresses the tremor in her voice. 'Frau Löwenstein. You need to leave. I'll make sure you're our first patient tomorrow. Just be here at nine.'

The woman hesitates, but then lets Esther guide her out of the room.

Ten minutes later, Esther locks up the surgery and makes her way to the school to pick up Anneliese. Outside, the sun has come out, but its light is pale and cold. She clasps her coat around her throat and sets off.

When she arrives home with Anneliese, Aaron is outside, reattaching some missing nuts and screws to a wheelbarrow.

'Have you heard?' Esther asks as she approaches him.

The sun has already dropped behind the building opposite and the lane is grey and dark.

He doesn't look up. 'Nothing travels faster than bad news.'

'What are we going to do?'

Aaron's spanner slips on the nut and falls to the ground. 'Damn it!' he mutters and bends to retrieve the spanner. A rush of wind funnels down the alley, bringing with it a cloud of paper debris.

Esther leans down to Anneliese. 'Anni,' she says softly, 'go inside and wash your hands. I'll be there in a minute.'

Anneliese dawdles for a moment, sensing the tension, but Esther gives her a gentle shove towards the door and she skips off inside.

'What are we going to do?' Esther repeats, though more quietly now, as if to herself.

'I don't know,' Aaron replies. He kneels on the cold ground and screws on the nut. 'I honestly don't know. We'll have to ... we'll have to find somewhere inside the area. I'll think of something.'

'But how? The place is overcrowded as it is! And a couple of thousand people more? What hope do we have of finding somewhere? Without any money.' She realises she is shaking and tries to swallow her panic. Now the wind rattles the bamboo shutters on the windows. 'Oh God, Aaron, we'll have to go and live in a *heim*, won't we?' A strange sound escapes her mouth, something between a groan and a wail. 'Anni wouldn't survive it! You have no idea what she was like back then, when we were there!'

Aaron calmly slides the spanner back into his toolbelt and straightens up. He lights a cigarette and she notices how red and chapped his hands are. 'We have another three months,' he says, turning towards her. 'We'll sort it out, don't worry. When –'

'But what about your job? It was going to change everything, and now –'

Then she sees it: a gash on his eyebrow, the blood already drying and dark, and a swelling to his jaw, an angry bruise.

'Aaron, what happened to your face?' She goes to raise her hand but he twists his face away.

'Nothing.'

'But your eye! You might need stitches. Have you . . . have you been in a fight?'

Aaron looks at her sharply. 'Calm down, for heaven's sake!' He takes a drag on his cigarette and exhales noisily. 'I was mugged this afternoon, just off Wha Ching Road. Two locals grabbed me and dragged me into an alley before I knew what was happening. When they didn't find anything of value on me, they decided to rough me up a little.'

'You should see a doctor.'

He shakes his head. 'It's nothing. I'll ice it and put some salve on it later.'

Esther takes a step back and looks down at her scuffed, dirty shoes. Her mouth is dry. 'It's never going to get better, is it? We're going to be stuck here, in this awful place, for the rest of our lives, aren't we? It will always be –'

Aaron interrupts her. 'Do you think your snivelling self-pity is going to change anything?' he shouts.

She whips up her head, startled. His expression is dark and hard.

'I'm up to here with all your defeatism and moaning!' He raises his hand to eye level and accidentally touches his cut. He winces. 'Shit.'

'Are you fighting?' a small voice behind them says.

Esther whips around. 'No, *liebling*,' she says. 'We're just talking.'

'Yes, Anni,' Aaron says, his voice smooth and calm again. 'Grown-up things. Now, run along and I'll see if I have a treat for pudding.'

Anneliese hesitates, but then retreats inside.

'Why must you shout at me like that?' Esther asks, fighting a rising urge to cry. 'Am I that unbearable to live with?'

'No! You are my one precious love!' He moves closer and takes her hands in his. 'I'm sorry. We shouldn't argue.'

Esther lets him kiss her hands, but there is something cold, unreadable, behind his eyes. He notices her staring and shifts his gaze away.

KITTY

——————

When Kitty comes to, she is sitting on the pavement, propped up against a building like a beggar, broken and desperate. She doesn't know how she got here, but her head is buzzing, and when she shifts position, she feels a soreness between her legs, between her buttocks. Her skin is sticky and hot. She begins to shake, can't stop it, has no control over her muscles, the chattering of her teeth. She groans. The very sound of it hurts her throat.

The street she sits on is quiet, just the squeal of the occasional rickshaw clattering up a main road somewhere nearby, and sporadic shouts and laughter from far away. Her eyes are swollen and dry, they itch unbearably, but she can't seem to summon the strength to rub them. In the thin light of dawn, she sees a row of low blackish-grey tenements opposite. Further to the right, if she strains her eyes, she can just about make out the huge husk of a godown, or factory. The place looks familiar and alien at once. Her filthy lodgings – the room she shares with three other women who also scrape together the rent any way they can – might be ten metres away, or ten kilometres, she has no idea. She has surrendered. The city has beaten her.

She closes her eyes. From the smell of decaying fish and diesel, she guesses she must be somewhere close to the river. Her bones ache. Her bladder aches too. Then she hears something to her left. Feet, shuffling. A beggar or hawker. She forces her eyelids up as he leans in towards her. His face is sweaty; a goitre grows on his neck. She turns her head away to escape his beseeching eyes and he moves on.

She vaguely recalls music, dull and muffled, and smoke – sweet, sweet smoke. Men. Not just one, like usual; several, a group, a mob. Her stomach heaves at the recollection. She turns her head to the side as the spasms hit her gut, but she only manages a dry retch. The effort leaves her dizzy and exhausted. She lets her head fall back and it hits the wall with a dull thud. She might have passed out again, or just dozed for a short while, for suddenly she becomes aware of activity to her right, a few hundred metres away. A shift at the factory must be over, dozens of people now streaming out and down towards the main road. Her heart flutters – should she call out for help? Or would that be inviting more harm? She screws up her face and her body begins to shake again.

More footsteps, closer, coming in her direction. Brisk, purposeful. Two men, their faces hooded in shadow. They stop in front of her and lean in.

'Leave me ...' Her voice is no more than a hoarse, painful whisper. She swallows and tries again. 'Leave me alone.'

A hand cups her beneath the arm – she feels the warmth

of it in her damp armpit – and tries to pull her up. She puts all her effort into resisting, but she has no strength. She starts to cry. The men exchange a few words in Chinese and finally pull her to her feet.

'Please –' Kitty begins again and looks at the smaller of the two. He smiles at her and she gasps. She must be losing her mind. 'Wing?'

周翼

———

'What's she saying?' Huà says, keeping his voice low.

Yì kneels beside the mat on which Năinai used to sleep and looks down at Mamselle Kitty. 'Wing,' he says. 'That's her name for me.'

Huà sucks his teeth. 'She can't be bothered to learn your real name?'

'Wing is the only name she knows.' He covers her with a scrap of blanket, despite the heat, but her stockings are torn and her dress is filthy, and he feels the need to protect her modesty. As he pulls the blanket up to her chest, he notices deep, ugly bruising on her arms. Then he sees the pendant around her neck. 'The White Tara,' he whispers. 'She kept it.'

'What?'

Yì shakes his head but can't suppress a small grin. 'Nothing.'

Huà crosses the room to light some incense. 'Well, she's alive, but she looks very sick. She might be carrying a disease.'

'She will need a doctor,' says Yì. 'We must fetch Chén *yīshēng*. He treated Năinai when she was sick. With the money Mamselle gave me.' He lays a damp cloth on Mamselle Kitty's forehead. She has stopped mumbling, but her lips still move soundlessly.

Huà kneels down beside her. He sniffs the air. 'Maybe she just has a hangover.'

Yì gives his brother a fierce look. 'I am in her debt,' he says. 'You must go and fetch the doctor. Chén *yīshēng*. He will surely come.'

Huà turns his head and spits on the floor. Then he gets to his feet and leaves.

Yì touches her face. Her skin is hot and clammy, and her eyes dart from side to side beneath the closed lids. 'Mamselle Kitty,' he whispers. 'You safe now.' He reaches out, hesitates briefly, and then lays his hand on hers. With his other hand, he strokes her soft hair. 'You safe now, Mamselle.'

She begins mumbling again, more insistently, and he pulls back, startled. But after a moment, she stops and appears to slide into a shallow sleep. He is so tired; he has to resist the temptation to lie down next to her and nestle his body into hers. So instead, he sits with his back resting against the wall, pinching his cheeks every now and then when he feels his eyelids getting heavy.

Though her skin is pale and dry, and her body as fragile and delicate as rice paper, she is still the most beautiful woman he has ever seen. When he spotted her in the alley, sitting crumpled up against the wall, his heart bounced with joy. He didn't stop to think what might have brought her there, to the street outside the match factory where he works – it was *mìngyùn*, fate. For many months, since he lost sight of her when she sped off with the tall, straw-haired man two winters ago, he has prayed daily to his ancestors to be able to repay his debt to her. He knew the spirits would hear him. He has been given a second chance, and he will not fail her again.

There are shouts from the house next door, and Mamselle Kitty stirs. Through the paper-thin walls, Yì hears the throaty, guttural sounds that make up the language of the foreigners; sounds that are becoming increasingly familiar, even here, in the poorest part of Shanghai. Over the last few months, countless more *lǎowài* have been pouring in. Squeezing into already full houses, sometimes two or three families to a single room. Some of the locals have made good deals, Huà told him, exchanging their squalid, run-down houses for much nicer, cleaner apartments to the south and west of Hongkew. Huà says it has something to do with the Japanese, but then, Huà blames everything on the Japanese or, failing that, on the Kuomintang. All Yì knows is that there are thousands more foreigners here now, living in the same conditions as the most destitute locals.

He hears two of the women talking right outside the front door. Mamselle Kitty coughs weakly. Perhaps he should go and fetch the women in? If they speak English, he could explain that she needs help. But if not, they might think him some sort of kidnapper and call the police. He gets to his feet and stretches his limbs. And where is Huà? What is taking him so long?

The women's voices fade as they move further along the alley. Yì takes the cloth from Mamselle Kitty's forehead. The fabric is damp and hot. He dips it into a bowl of water, squeezes it out and is about to replace it on her forehead when the door opens.

'He won't come,' says Huà, shutting the door behind him. He is out of breath. 'He says it would be trouble for him to treat a white woman.'

Yì lays the cloth on Mamselle Kitty's forehead and turns back to Huà. 'But he must come!' he whispers urgently. 'She is very sick. She will die!'

Huà shrugs and lights a cigarette. He inhales deeply and begins to cough. The tobacco he uses is taken from stubs he finds on the street, and then stuffed into thin papers. Yì only smokes very occasionally, when his hunger is greater than his disgust of the acrid taste of old tobacco in his mouth and lungs.

Huà spits on the floor. 'He wants to know why we have a white woman lying unconscious in our room.'

'Did you tell him I know her? I used to work for her?'

'Yes, though anyone can see she looks more like a prostitute than an employer.'

Yì jumps up. 'Don't say that!'

'Hey, calm down. I didn't tell Chén *yīshēng*. I said she looks as though she might have malaria or something, that she hasn't eaten in a long time. He gave me the name of another doctor. A foreigner, like her.' He pulls a slip of paper from his pocket and hands it to Yì. 'But he only speaks English, so you'll have to go.'

Yì looks at the piece of paper. 'Liaoyang Road, that's not too far. Stay with her, will you?'

Huà scowls. 'I have to meet with some people. This *woman*' – he flicks his head in Kitty's direction – 'is not my friend. Not my responsibility.'

'Please, Huà. I will hurry back.'

'And then what? You think when she recovers, she will marry you in gratitude? You will set up a cosy home

276

together? Ha!' His smirk dies on his face and he narrows his eyes. 'She is trouble. You owe her nothing.'

Yì grabs his brother's hand. 'Huà, I beg you. Sit with her, please. You can rest. You must be tired. And hungry? There is some rice left, up there on the shelf.'

Huà shakes his hand free. 'One hour. Then I leave.'

Yì throws a last look at Mamselle Kitty and rushes out. The sky is overcast, the flat white sky pushing down the air until it feels too close to breathe. Despite his exhaustion, Yì sets off at a run. He reaches Liaoyang Road ten minutes later.

There is a sign at the door of Number 34 with several names written on it. Yì is confused at first, as he tries and fails to read them. But then he remembers the paper his brother gave him and manages to match up one of the names with what is written there. He enters the building and runs up a set of scuffed wooden stairs, leading him to a door on the second floor. This also has a sign with the same name. He knocks, waits, then pushes the door open. The first thing he notices is the smell: it is the slightly sour, curdled odour of foreigners, and a whiff of soap and disinfectant, but beneath that, he detects the smell that is universal among the poor and abandoned. It is the smell of disease. Five people sit on chairs up against the wall, and across the room, half-shielded by a bamboo screen, sits a young dark-haired woman behind a desk. Squashing the strong feeling of being out of place here, Yì steps past the waiting patients towards the woman.

The woman looks up as he approaches. She gives him a puzzled but not unfriendly smile.

'Excuse,' he says. 'I need doctor.'

'Oh,' the woman says. 'Um, they are busy at the

moment. Perhaps you can tell me what is wrong. Are you hurt?'

Yì clears his throat. 'No. I need doctor. For a friend. She hurt. She sick. I am . . . I need doctor for . . .' His brain struggles to find the right words, then his tongue struggles to pronounce them.

The woman frowns. 'Um, well, I think –'

She is interrupted by a door opening on the other side of the room. Yì turns and sees an older woman in a white coat with very pale skin and silver hair step into the waiting area. She must be a nurse. The dark-haired woman calls her over and says something he cannot understand. They both stare at him.

'I need doctor,' he says again. He can feel himself blushing.

The older woman tilts her head to one side. 'How can I help?'

'No,' he says, shaking his head. 'I need doctor.'

'Yes,' the woman says. 'I am a doctor. What is the matter? Are you sick?'

He lets out an exasperated snort. 'No. I need doctor. For friend. White woman, Mamselle. Please.' He looks around the room and then back at the women. 'I need doctor. Hurry. She very sick.'

She again speaks quickly to the younger woman, who then rises from her chair and disappears into another room. Yì tightens his fists in frustration. Why will they not help? Do they care so little about one of their own? He thinks of Mamselle Kitty lying on Năinai's mat, her gaunt face and the bruising on her arms. The feverish heat emanating from her skin. He should go back. Now. He turns to leave.

'Young man?'

A hand touches his shoulder and he spins around to face an elderly man, also wearing a white coat, although it is slightly grubbier than the woman's.

'You doctor?' he asks.

The man smiles. 'Yes. I am a doctor. Just like my wife here.' He nods towards the silver-haired woman.

Yì thrusts the piece of paper at him. 'From Chén *yīshēng*. He say you help. White woman. My friend.' He clears his throat to distract from the blushing, which he feels must be a dark red by now.

The man peers at the piece of paper. 'Ah, Dr Chén.' He looks up at Yì over the rim of his glasses. 'You have a friend who needs help?'

Yì finds himself nodding vigorously. 'Yes yes.'

'And where is she?'

'In my . . . home. Paoting Road. It not far. Please.'

'North or south of Wayside?'

'Excuse me?'

'Do you live to the north or the south of Wayside Road?' The doctor uses his hand to demonstrate 'up' and 'down'.

'North,' Yì says, also raising his hand. 'Please, you come with me.'

The man sighs and turns to the woman he says is his wife and also a doctor. He says something to her that elicits a long pause and then a nod.

'Of course, as long as it's within the boundary,' she says in English. 'I can see to the other patients. But perhaps' – here she turns to the dark-haired woman still sitting behind the desk – 'perhaps you should go with them. This . . . patient might feel more comfortable if there is another woman there.'

The dark-haired woman nods and gets to her feet. Yì wishes they would stop deliberating and has already crossed the room towards the door when he hears the doctor say to him: 'You'd better lead the way, then.'

They hurry through the streets, the doctor carrying a small black bag, which Yì hopes contains some medicines to make Mamselle Kitty better. The young woman trots beside them, struggling to keep up. All the way, the doctor peppers Yì with questions, but Yì cannot understand most of what he says and so keeps repeating, 'She is my friend. She is very sick.'

When they finally reach the narrow alley Yì lives in, lined on either side with one- and two-storey shacks, the young woman pulls out a handkerchief and presses it against her mouth and nose. Yì feels a twinge of shame at the stench coming from the open sewage running along the gutters, but then he remembers that her people also live here. It is the stench of their bodies, their waste, too.

'In here,' he says over his shoulder and pulls open the door to his home. 'Huà? I have brought the doctor.'

In response, there is silence, besides the buzzing of flies that had settled on and around the pot in the corner, and have now been disturbed. 'Huà?' he repeats, more loudly. For a moment, before his eyes become accustomed to the gloom, he fears that Huà might have made Mamselle Kitty leave, or worse, taken her somewhere. But then he sees her lying in the corner. His brother has deserted her. Anger flares up inside him, but the doctor and the woman are already rushing past him to attend to Mamselle Kitty.

The doctor lays the back of his hand on her forehead. 'She's burning up,' he says, adding to Yì, 'Do you have a lamp? Or a candle?'

Yì lights a thick yellowish candle and hands it to the doctor.

The doctor raises his eyebrows. 'A yahrzeit candle.'

'What?'

'This candle, it is called a yahrzeit candle. It is Jewish.'

Yì shrugs. 'It burns long time.'

The doctor lets out a soft chuckle and takes the candle, holding it close to Mamselle Kitty. He lifts her eyelids, one after the other, and gently pulls down her chin to look into her mouth. Mamselle Kitty moans softly.

Yì watches him closely. 'Is it malaria?'

'Perhaps, but from this rash' – the doctor moves the candle lower to indicate a rosy blush on her throat, which stretches down to her chest – 'I would say it is more likely to be breakbone fever.'

This means nothing to Yì. 'But you give her medicine?' he says.

The doctor shakes his head and places the candle down. 'There is no medicine for this. But we will look after her. Put her in a clean bed, make sure she drinks plenty of water. Then all we can do is wait and see if she recovers.' He gives Yì a kind, slow smile. 'Thank you, young man, for coming to fetch me.'

Yì opens his mouth to speak – wants to say that surely, *surely* something more can be done: needles, salves, some herbs that cool the fire in her blood, at least – but then the dark-haired woman lets out a sharp breath. She looks across at the doctor with an expression Yì can't read.

'It's her,' she says. 'I think I know this woman.'

KITTY

———

She doesn't know how long she's slept. The space she's lying in is hardly bigger than a larder, the only daylight coming through a ventilation grid set up high in the wall. The room is hot, cloying, but the heat is coming from the air around her, not from deep inside her body. She no longer feels as though she is burning. There is an odd smell in the air, a mix of onions and something indefinable, but definitely not edible. She tries to sit up, and the effort snatches her breath away. But at least her head feels clear. She wonders if she should call out, but then, from the other side of the curtain that separates the space from the kitchen, she hears whispered voices.

'But how long is she going to stay? That's all I'm asking.'

It's the man's voice. What was his name again? Esther mentioned it yesterday, but she can't bring it to mind.

Esther's voice, barely audible. 'Keep your voice down, please. She'll hear us.'

Kitty shifts position and a foul smell hits her nose. It

takes only a second for her to realise that it is coming from her. Pungent, slightly sweet. She tucks the sheet in around her legs. Her skin itches, and she has never felt so desperate for a bath. The bruises on her arms have faded to yellow and purple splodges. Beyond the curtain, Esther and the man are still talking.

'She's a friend.' Esther's voice comes out as a hiss.

'You knew her for two weeks on the boat. Years ago.'

'It was five weeks. And it isn't up for discussion.'

Aaron – that was the man's name. He looked in once yesterday, when she and Esther were talking. A handsome man, despite his unshaven face and tight-lipped 'hello'. Esther hadn't explained what their relationship was, and Kitty hadn't asked. She was grateful that Esther hadn't wanted to know about how she, Kitty, had ended up here in such a state.

She hears footsteps and a door shutting. Then the curtain is pulled back and Esther stands there, smiling, although the trace of the argument hangs in the corners of her lips. 'Are you awake?'

Kitty nods, conscious of the smell of her body and the bruises patterning her arms.

'How are you feeling today?' Esther asks, setting down a cup of green tea beside the bed.

'Much better than yesterday, actually,' Kitty replies. She takes a long, shaky breath. 'The headaches are gone, at least.' She takes a sip of tea and pulls a face. 'Ooh, bitter.'

'Doctor's orders, I'm afraid,' Esther says and takes a seat on the end of the bed.

She is so thin, Kitty thinks; her collarbones protrude beneath the skin, and her apron string is tied twice around her waist. Looking at her now, Kitty finds it hard to reconcile her with the delicate, soft-skinned woman she met on the ship four years ago.

Esther gestures towards her tea. 'You should drink up. The bitter compounds are what make you feel better.'

'Well, in that case.' Kitty takes another sip. 'The sooner I recover, the sooner I can be on my way.'

Esther's face falls. 'Oh. You heard us.'

'I'm sorry. I didn't mean to eavesdrop.'

Esther waves a hand across her face. 'Don't worry. Everyone's a bit uptight these days.' She attempts a smile. 'I'm just glad you're feeling better.'

Kitty sips her tea, trying to avoid swallowing any of the green leaves.

'You're welcome to stay as long as you need to,' Esther continues. 'I just thought, well, would you like me to have someone fetch your things?' She pauses. 'When you had a fever, you mentioned a name, several times. Timothy. Is he someone I should contact? Let him know where you are?'

Kitty feels her eye twitching. She blinks rapidly and shakes her head. 'No, that's ... that's someone I knew. He's ...' She feels so weak and numb, as though her strength has been sucked from her bones. She rests the cup on her lap for fear of spilling the tea.

Esther reaches across and takes the cup from her. 'Are you all right? Did he –?' She nods towards Kitty's arms.

'No! No, that was –' She stops. It's too much. The numbness disappears abruptly and she finds herself crying – she can't stop – feels the violence of shock swell inside her, the shock of her own capacity for survival. She knows she will never be able to disremember the filth, the degradation, the pain; how her mind slipped out of her passive body when she let the men lie on top of her for the few cents she needed to buy a cup of rice; or the dollar bills she earned from a group of Japanese officers, dollars she spent on opium, rather than food.

'I'm so sorry,' Esther says urgently. 'I didn't mean to upset you.' She lays her hand on Kitty's. 'Is there anything I can do?'

Kitty shakes her head. There is nothing anyone can do. She has been lying here for days now, sick and weak, hoping it might all end, here and now. Trying not to think about the man she fell in love with who wasn't even a real man; the malnutrition-induced hallucinations of a number-one boy who saved her life. And that is all she wants to do – wipe her mind clean of everything.

Esther strokes her hand. 'I didn't think I'd ever see you again.' She smiles, a little wistfully. After a long moment, she says, 'Although . . . the ghetto is so small, we were bound to run into each other sooner or later.'

'The what?' The word shoots straight through the fuzziness in Kitty's head.

'I know, officially it's the Restricted Area, but it's a ghetto all the same, isn't it? Sometimes, I wonder –' She stops and looks at Kitty with a frown.

Kitty swallows. Her head is pounding again now. 'I don't understand,' she says, her voice dry. 'What are you talking about? What ghetto?'

'The proclamation! It was in all the papers. I can't believe you hadn't . . . We've been forced to move – here.' She gestures around her. 'All of us. We've been here for several months.'

'All of us?'

'The Jews.' She pauses again and shakes her head. 'You really didn't know?'

Kitty puts her hand to her head. 'Can we get out? Is it . . . is it a prison?' The room is airless, closing in on her.

Esther shakes her head. 'There's no barbed wire, if that's what you mean. But you need a pass to get out if you don't want to get arrested. And getting a pass, well . . .' She looks towards the door and back again. 'Passes are issued by a Japanese official, Ghoya. He's a real sadist, a nasty piece of work.' Her mouth twists. 'Calls himself the "King of the Jews".'

Kitty lies back, defeated. She doesn't want to hear any more.

'Kitty.' Esther is leaning in close; Kitty can smell her sweat and a hint of disinfectant. 'Kitty, I don't know where you've been for the last few years, but here – well, here we look after each other.' She gets to her feet slowly. 'You should rest. I'll be at work for the next few hours, but if there's anything you need' – she turns her head to look past the curtain – 'just ask Aaron. He'll be here, or working in the yard, if you need him.'

When Kitty next wakes, the air has an even hotter, clammy quality that presses down on her lungs. In the distance, she hears a street vendor shouting, and from closer by, the sound of hammering. Her mouth is dry and foul tasting. She swallows, but this makes her thirst even more urgent.

From behind the curtain, someone clears their throat. 'Excuse me?'

The curtain parts a little and the man – Aaron – pokes his head through. 'Sorry to bother you, but you have a visitor,' he says.

Kitty sits up. 'A visitor?'

'I told him to wait in the kitchen,' Aaron says. Then he turns and leaves.

Kitty pulls back her sheet and slides her legs out of bed. The dress she is wearing – one of Esther's cotton prints – clings to her skin. She smooths it down as best she can and runs her fingers through her hair, thinking that it's probably for the best that there is no mirror in the room.

Kitty's visitor stands at the door, looking down at the floor. She walks quickly towards him, reaches out and touches his arm. To make sure he is real.

'Wing!'

The boy blushes. 'How are you, Mamselle?'

'It really was you. I – I thought I'd imagined it!'

He is smiling from ear to ear. She can see that several of his teeth are missing. His smile drops away. 'Please, Mamselle, sit. You shake.'

He's right. The effort of crossing the room has made her legs tremble. He holds out his arm for support and guides her to a chair. She sits down and stares at him for a long time. He has grown since she last saw him. He is no longer the young boy who scuttled around her apartment, sweeping and tidying. And despite the appalling state of his teeth, his clothes are clean and his skin is smooth and clear.

'You want water?' he asks.

Kitty nods, and the boy looks around, spots a jug of water on the sideboard and fills her a glass. She takes it from him with a small nod of thanks and drains it. The water is tepid but still cooler than her skin. She lifts the empty glass to her cheek and rolls it back and forth across her skin until the glass feels as warm as her blood. She closes her eyes. 'Thank you.'

There is the sound of a door opening and closing. Kitty looks up and sees Aaron, carrying some sort of metal and rubber gadget, which he hands to the boy.

'You can take this back to the doctor, Yì,' he says. 'Tell him it's as good as new.'

The boy takes the item from him and makes a small bow. Aaron heads back outside but pops his head through the door a moment later. 'Yì, before I forget, would you tell my wife I have to go out? I've got *baojia* duty and won't be back until late.'

Kitty waits until Aaron is outside. She is confused. 'Why did he call you that name?' she asks.

'My real name is Yì,' the boy says then, blushing again. 'Wing is name given me by Monsieur Petrov.'

The mention of his name stings; she had banished him from her thoughts long ago. 'Oh,' she says. 'I didn't know. I'm sorry. I thought ... I didn't know this was not your name.'

Yì takes a step forward. 'No, Mamselle. Please. You call me Wing. It is your ... your special name for me. No one else uses it.' Before she can respond, he clears his throat and says, 'I come to see you healthy again. But now I must go. I have new job.' He grins. 'At doctor's.'

'Oh. That's nice,' Kitty says with a frown.

'Stern *yīshēng* give me job. He say I am very useful.' He blushes again. 'For ...' He frowns as he searches for the right word. 'For messenger. In and out of ghetto. I am Chinese so no one stop me.'

'That's wonderful. The job, I mean.'

'Yes.' He pats his belly. 'Doctor pay so much I can eat every day.'

Kitty raises herself up off her chair but the exhaustion

lingers. She sits back down, weary beyond measure. 'Wing.' She says his name self-consciously now, but at the same time cannot imagine calling him anything else. 'Thank you, Wing. For saving me.'

He gives her an awkward smile, making him look five years younger. 'You save me first,' he says. 'Now my turn to save you.'

August to December 1944

周翼

———

The air is dense, filled with grit and fumes and the smell of burning joss paper. All over the city, splashes of blood red and gold startle the grey. Balloon lanterns, paper flowers, banners, paper effigies of the Ghost King and knotted charms hang from every corner in preparation for the Spirit Festival celebrations. Yì stops at a food stall on his way to the temple, orders a bowl of red bean and noodle soup and watches some children release miniature paper boats onto the stinking creek. It is *zhōng yuán jié*, the Hungry Ghost Festival, and Yì is on his way to Xiàhǎi Temple to burn a bundle of incense sticks to pay his respects to the spirit of Nǎinai. It is two years since she died and he still thinks of her every day.

When his food is ready, he lifts the bowl from the counter, inhaling its familiar sour, peppery fragrance, and looks around for somewhere to sit. At the waterfront, the children begin to shout excitedly as their paper boats are carried downstream. Yì takes a seat at a small table set on the pavement and waits for the soup to cool. Despite his good job and his new friends, and the unbelievable fate of meeting Mamselle Kitty again, he carries a quiet sadness of solitude. If only his *nǎinai* were still here – if only she could see him now!

He begins to slurp his soup, reminding himself that it is bad luck to be so discontent when he has no real worries. When was the last time he felt the pain of hunger? In truth, it seems like a lifetime ago. The soup stings the inside of his mouth and the spices warm his gullet on the way down. Only last month, Stern *yīshēng*'s wife saved a loose molar, which was threatening to dislodge itself from his raw and spongy gums, by giving him some ointment to rub on. The ointment burned like fire, bringing tears to his eyes, but within a week, the gums were a healthy pink and the tooth, if he probes it now with his tongue, is firm again. It seems that this white woman, who has the patience and gentleness of a nurse, really is a doctor like her husband.

The ear-splitting spatter of a dozen tiny explosives almost startles him off his chair. One of the children has set off a firecracker and is now being shouted at by his mother, while the others whoop and jump up and down in a cloud of acrid smoke. A boy, in shirt and trousers stiff with dirt, tumbles into Yì's table in his excitement and knocks the bundle of incense sticks to the floor. He looks up at Yì, anticipating a box around the ears.

'*Duìbùqǐ*,' he whispers, apologising.

'*Bù yào jǐn*,' Yì responds, even though he minds very much. It is bad luck to disrespect his ghost offerings.

He makes sure to be home before the ghosts come out after dark and climbs the rickety staircase to his room.

He hangs a knotted charm from a rusty nail in the door frame as an offering for Năinai, should her spirit decide to visit him tonight. Then he unlocks the door, the thrill of owning a key as fresh as the first time he slipped it into the lock eight months ago, when he moved into the house belonging to friends of the Sterns. The rent is twice that of the hovel he shared with Năinai, but as long as he works for the good doctor and his wife, he can afford it. The wooden door frame is old and warped, and it wouldn't require much force to kick the door in, but it has a lock, with a key, and this is Yì's key alone. He pushes the door open and the familiar smell of mildew hits his nostrils. It would be pointless to open the windows though, as the air outside is even more humid, holding the promise of fresh rain during the night. Sliding his shoes off at the door, he steps in and is suddenly shoved from behind. He takes a stumbling step forward, turns with his arms raised, ready to fight, and lets his arms drop again with an astonished outcry.

'Huà!'

The intruder takes a step inside and closes the door behind him. His clothes are rags and the smell emanating from him is overpowering. Sweat, smoke and an underlying foul, meaty stench.

Yì steps back and opens his mouth to breathe without inhaling. 'I thought you were a ghost! What are you doing here?' he asks. 'Where have you been?'

His brother doesn't answer. His eyes slide around the room, taking in the bed on its raised frame, the small charcoal cooking stove, the sack of rice on the shelf, the grimy but intact window, a patchwork bedspread – a gift from Stern *yīshēng*'s wife. His eyes come to rest on Yì, who feels a mix of pride and embarrassment. It is more luxury than either of them have ever known.

Huà sucks his teeth and flicks his chin upward. 'So, you work for the *lǎowài* now?'

Angry that his brother is unimpressed by his new home, and equally angry that it matters to him, Yì crosses the room and begins to light the charcoal stove. He has already eaten, and the room is not cold, but he wants Huà to see that he can afford to light a stove in his room anytime he wants to.

'I work for foreigners all my life,' he grumbles as he crouches down and places a few crumbly lumps of charcoal inside the oven. 'Russians, French, Japanese. Now I work for Germans.'

Huà doesn't respond.

'They are the best foreigners I have ever worked for,' Yì continues, lighting the fire and watching it catch and flourish. He wipes his sooty hands on his trousers and straightens up, feeling somewhat foolish now for wasting precious fuel just to show off to his brother. But when he turns around, Huà is sitting on his bed, hunched forward and picking at a patch of peeling skin on his face. He is trembling. Yì's irritation dissolves.

'Have you eaten?' he asks.

Huà mumbles something he can't catch.

'I'll make some rice, some lentils,' Yì says and without waiting for an answer, sets about boiling some water. As he prepares the meal, neither of them speaks, the silence between them amplifying all other sounds: the clattering of pots and the creak of the floorboards as he walks back and forth; the soft strains of the violin from his downstairs neighbour; the echo of the day dying away on the street below, to be replaced by the furtive buzz and clamour of the night.

Yì knows better than to question his brother, but as he stirs the rice and lifts a steaming spoonful of lentils to his lips to check they are tender, he can't help but glance over at him, in his filthy clothes and mismatched shoes, gauging whether he looked this gaunt and exhausted the last time he saw him, or whether it is just his own relative good health that makes his brother look so wretched.

When the rice and lentils are cooked, he hands his brother the bowl. Huà hesitates and sniffs the food, warily almost, but then attacks it with his chopsticks, shovelling it into his mouth at speed. When he has finished, he places the bowl on the floor. Then he belches and wipes his mouth with the back of his hand.

'Good?' Yì says. He hears eagerness in his own voice and clears his throat in an attempt to cover it.

But Huà just lights a matchstick-thin cigarette and stares at him through narrowed eyes. 'You a taipan, now, little brother?' He nods at Yì's nail.

Yì puts his left hand behind his back. He has been trying to grow the nail on his little finger, to show he is no longer a mere labourer, but twice it has broken off, painfully.

Huà blows smoke out of the corner of his mouth. Then he says, 'Jiàlóng is sick.'

'Jiàlóng?'

'He's ... my comrade. I've known him for many years. He's a brother to me. And he's sick, very sick.' His voice is suddenly low and disconnected.

'*I* am your brother,' Yì says, stung, despite himself, by Huà's statement.

'You are my *dìdi*. Jiàlóng is like my *gēge*.'

297

An older brother. Not some puny seedling who is only good for providing food and a roof over his head, Yì thinks. He snatches up the bowl and makes a show of wiping it clean with a rag, his back to Huà.

'I'm sorry if I've offended you,' Huà says quietly. The unfamiliar gentleness in his voice makes Yì turn around. 'My comrade is very sick. He will die without help.'

'Has he been seen by a doctor?'

Huà grunts. 'You understand *nothing*,' he says, his tone sharp now. He sighs and pinches his cigarette out with his fingers. 'He cannot go to the *yīshēng*, and the white doctors will not treat him. But we know what will help him.' He takes a piece of paper from his pocket. Now it is his turn to sound eager. 'We have comrades, from Russia, who know what medicines he needs. They have written them here.'

He thrusts the paper at Yì.

Yì hesitates but then takes it from Huà, uneasiness spiralling up his spine. He looks down at the list written on the paper in scratchy capital letters. He understands.

'No,' he says, shaking his head. 'I cannot do that. I will not steal from them. They have been good to me, and I owe them –'

'What? What do you owe them? I'll tell you something –' Huà jumps to his feet and stands so close that Yì can smell the garlic his brother has just eaten, and beneath it, the whiff of decay. 'We owe them *nothing*! They come to our country and make us work for a pittance, stealing our resources and labour, breaking men and women's backs like workhorses. They step over the bodies of our dying children on the street. You shame yourself and your people if you refuse to help!'

'No, I can't. I –'

Huà grabs his wrist. 'Change is coming. Soon. And you will be sorry if you stand by doing nothing.'

'I work all day! I have been working all day since I was nine. I can't afford to join your revolution!' Yì shouts back, shaking his brother's hand off. Tears sting his eyes. 'I don't have time.'

Huà snorts. 'You don't have time? *Time*? You think the men and women who are fighting for the revolution do so because they have too much time?' His voice is a bark. 'You think I am lazy? You think I can afford to work without pay? Let me show you something.' He begins to roll up his left sleeve. 'Here! This is my pay!'

The threadbare fabric tears as he rolls it higher, but he doesn't stop until his arm is exposed to above the elbow, and Yì can see the puckered purplish scar tissue of a dozen or so cuts.

'Steel cables,' Huà says. 'And here –' He lets himself fall back onto the bed, the springs groaning at his weight, and takes off his mismatched shoes. 'Cigarette burns.' He touches the sole of his left foot and winces. There are several whitish marks on the calloused skin, with bright red, slightly raised borders. 'These are from last month. Someone betrayed our meeting place.'

Yì wants him to stop but doesn't know how to make him.

'They pulled two of my teeth.' He opens his mouth wide, and Yì can see dark purple cavities in his gum. Huà closes his mouth and presses his lips together. He swallows hard and spits out a short, barking laugh. 'And it's not as if I have many teeth to spare.'

And then he slumps forward, clutching his arms around himself.

Yì cannot bear it. He sits down beside him, whispering, 'I'm sorry, Huà. I'm sorry.' He reaches across and tentatively places his arm around his shoulder. At his touch, his brother leans in and – to Yì's shame and bewilderment – begins to cry. It is a soft, muted sobbing at first, but grows in urgency and wretchedness until he is howling like a wolf, snot and tears and saliva trailing from his mouth and nose, and all Yì can do is hold him fast and cradle him in his arms.

But when he wakes the next morning, his body stiff and aching from the night, Huà is gone.

ESTHER

———

'Esther, is that you? Can you come in here for a moment?'

Esther puts her bag into one of the desk drawers and heads for the examination room. It is five to nine; already people are waiting outside, sitting and fidgeting and scratching in the stairwell. Squeezing through them on her way up to the practice, Esther was faced with quiet grumbling and open complaints about the opening hours. Although summer is finally melting into autumn, the slow drop in temperatures seems to have revived the frayed tempers and short fuses that invariably fizzle out in the heat.

'Good morning,' Esther says as she comes into the examination room. The Sterns stand, talking quietly, next to a cabinet at the far wall and look up as she enters. 'I'll just go and wash my hands –' She stops when she sees the expression on Helene's face.

'There's been a theft,' Victor says slowly.

'Somebody broke in?' Esther asks and scans the room for any signs of damage. But the place looks as clean and orderly as ever.

Helene shakes her head. 'It wasn't a break-in.'

'Some drugs are missing,' Victor says. 'Insulin, aspirin, mepacrine, and some morphine. Also, a couple of bottles of iodine.'

'They didn't break in,' Helene repeats, her voice heavy. 'They picked the lock to the cabinet, or else they had a key.'

Instantly, and to her shame, Esther's first thought is of Yì. She feels herself colour.

Victor must have read her thoughts. 'Yì is never in the office on his own. He doesn't have a key, certainly not to the medicines cabinet, and besides –'

'We trust him,' Helene says, completing her husband's sentence. 'He is honest and loyal, and I can't believe he would jeopardise his job for a few aspirin pills.'

'And you're certain there are medicines missing?' Esther asks with a glance at the glass-paned cabinet. It contains five shelves lined with small and large glass, cork-topped bottles.

Victor nods. 'Yes, we list everything that we prescribe and administer. You know that.'

'Perhaps . . . oh, this is awful. You don't think it was one of the patients, do you?'

Helene shrugs. 'I can't think of any other explanation. We leave the patients in here alone from time to time. For a few minutes at the longest, but . . . I suppose some of them are desperate.'

'Will you report it to the police?'

Helene glances at Victor. 'I don't think so,' she says. 'They probably wouldn't care, anyway. Or they'd arrest someone just for the sake of it. I wouldn't want that on my conscience.'

'No,' Victor agrees. 'But perhaps we should mention it to the *baojia*. Have someone keep an eye out, just in case it's someone sneaking in at night.'

Helene clicks her tongue and looks away. The *baojia*, a self-policing system set up by the Japanese, requires that all male refugees between twenty and forty-five volunteer for several hours of duty each week – mainly as a border patrol, ensuring no one leaves the ghetto without a valid pass. Some *baojia* guards let their fellow refugees sneak in and out unchecked; in others, it has brought out the worst displays of German militarism.

There is the sound of impatient knocking at the front door. Esther turns and sighs. 'That's probably Herr Greiss. He barked at me on my way in, something about his foot.' She turns back to the Sterns. 'Shall I let them in now?'

Victor looks at his wife, then at Esther. 'Yes. I suppose we'll all have to be more vigilant in future. These medicines are more valuable than gold.' He shakes his head. He looks resigned and suddenly very, very old. 'I can't understand how someone would do this to their own people.'

KITTY

———

When the rain comes in October, it brings out the worst in everyone. It concentrates the smell of the city, the foul fermenting stink of sewage and rotting food. Huge river rats, their fur slick and shiny, are washed up from the creek and scuttle along the overflowing gutters.

Kitty sets off for the Café Atlantic. She passes a small park on the corner of Dalny and Ward Road and catches the unlikely fragrance of an osmanthus shrub, which is beginning to shed its small white petals. She knows the name of the shrub because Timothy told her. She finds herself thinking of the endearing, self-conscious way he used to push the hair out of his face and allows the thought to linger for a moment, relishing it the way one relishes the feeling of pressing down on a bruise. She is reminding herself of her ability to feel. She slows and inhales deeply, but the scent is replaced by the stench of fried eel, being cooked by a woman sitting on the side of the road. A passer-by bumps roughly into her shoulder and she moves on.

The streets and side roads are as busy as ever, yet with one noticeable change – among the vendors and coolies and beggars and vagrants, there is hardly a white face to be seen. It is Yom Kippur, and it seems as though even the most secular Jews are observing the occasion. The pavement is heaving; the noise, as always, deafening – people tussling for space to move. Kitty stops again and looks around. She is baffled: where do the thousands of Europeans all fit in when they are not at home or at the synagogue? And will we be missed, she thinks, when – *if* – we ever leave? Will the spaces we existed in simply close over?

She arrives at the café where she works – closed, of course, for this day of fasting and atonement – and lets herself in with her key. The blinds are lowered, the shapes of the tables, stacked with chairs, are indistinct in the darkness. Kitty feels her way in slowly, keeping a hand against the wall for guidance until her eyes become accustomed to the dark. A fat rat comes running through from the kitchen. Kitty hurriedly grabs a broom and chases it out of the open door. A Sisyphean task, if ever there was one. She closes and locks the front door and heads through to the back, hitting the broom off the sides of the doorway to make her presence known to any other creatures that might be lurking. But there is nothing, except for the scraping and scratching of cockroaches beneath the counters.

She goes to wash her hands at the sink and then remembers that there will be no water today; clean water is at a premium and no one will have boiled any for when the café is closed. So instead, she grabs a tea towel, wipes her hands as best she can and sets about gathering the ingredients. She shouldn't be in here, shouldn't be illicitly taking the precious flour or sugar, but it is Anneliese's eighth birthday tomorrow and Kitty wants to surprise her with a cake. It will only be a small cake, and she won't steal any of the eggs. Besides, everyone tweaks off a little something here or there; it's par for the course when there isn't enough to go around.

Gustav, the boss, will never know, and if he ever does find out, then she'll placate him by offering to do a couple of shifts as a waitress. She knows – he has beseeched her often enough – that he would love to have her working up front with the customers. The surplus of men among the refugees in the ghetto makes young women, however worn and brittle their female glamour, a valuable commodity. But Kitty is done with all that. She really has become too worn, too brittle for this game. And she doesn't mind working harder for less pay – on the contrary, she is so exhausted by the time she falls into bed, she finds sleep without the need to numb herself.

She takes out the recipe she got from an elderly neighbour and stares at it. She has never baked a cake in her life. Of course, as a native of Vienna, she knows that baking can be raised to the highest level of art – her mouth waters at the mere thought of Linzer cake and Esterházy torta – but even she should manage a simple sponge cake. It can't be that hard, can it?

In a large bowl, cream the sugar and butter together.

Butter. Fat chance. Should she use margarine? Or perhaps lard? She takes a step back to open one of the cabinets and feels a sudden cramp in her lower belly. She takes a deep breath and waits for the pain to subside. She smiles. It is a sharp, sweet pain that began last night in bed with a wet stickiness between her legs. It is not the first time she has welcomed her bleeding – back in Vienna, it was common among the women she worked with to tick off days in nervous anticipation of either a visit to the man with meaty hands who practised in a filthy, windowless room on Liniengasse, or the delightful relief at the flow of fresh, bright-red blood. The cramp swells and wanes again, and Kitty flinches at the memory of the unfortunate women who required that man's services, many of whom were butchered so savagely they were never the same again.

But now, for her, the relief is always more than sweet; it is the divine severing of the ties to that night, the night she was saved by Wing when she believed there was nothing more to be saved. She squeezes her eyes shut. It is over and she has survived.

When the cramping has receded to no more than a slight tugging in her abdomen, she places a handful of charcoal in a small door of the oven and lights it, then gathers together the things she needs for baking. She works with focus, cursing under her breath when she forgets to halve the quantities given in the recipe and has to spoon out some of the flour. Using her fingertips, she picks out any weevils she finds buried there. Although the cook, Hans, sticks bay leaves in the flour jars to discourage infestation, the insects don't care. They are just as resilient as all the other creatures that creep and crawl around this city.

Soon, the heat from the oven is making her sweat. She wipes her forehead with the back of her hand, folding the batter again and again until it is smooth, feeling the muscles aching in her shoulder, her arm, her wrist as she bakes. She pours the batter into a tin, imagining Anni's face when she surprises her with the cake tomorrow. Such a spirited, uncomplicated child; so different now to the nervy, self-conscious toddler she was on the ship.

Anni will likely whoop and jump about and plaster Kitty with kisses. How the girl has thrived in these conditions is anybody's guess, Kitty thinks, but then, what does she know about children?

She scrapes the bowl with a spatula and an unexpected memory surfaces, of playing dolls in the nursery with her sister Elli, sitting on the polished parquet, hush-hush, don't disturb Father; *Here dolly, eat your gruel like a good baby*, says Elli, *and Auntie Käthe will sing you a lullaby*. Playing out the roles, Kitty thinks now, that came naturally to them: Elli the warm, caring mother, and she the good-natured spinster aunt. The recollection, though poignant, brings a smile to her lips. Even after all these years, she is still quite content to be the spinster aunt. She has never felt the urge to have children, and it is a sweet thought that this will be her final act of rebellion: when she dies, her rotten line will die with her.

The baking time on the recipe is twenty-five minutes. She wonders if she should halve the time, but twelve minutes doesn't seem long enough, somehow. She looks at the grease-covered clock that hangs above the door and decides to check after ten minutes, and then in regular intervals after that. Having gone to all this effort, she doesn't want to end up with a burned cake. The oven door seems stuck in place, but she manages finally to yank it open with a twist and pull, and slides the cake in, slamming the door shut with a childish sense of satisfaction.

She clears up as she waits, keeping a compulsive eye on the time. After nine minutes, she opens the oven and takes a tentative look inside. The cake has risen, which she takes as a good sign, but how to tell if it's done on the inside? As she stands there peering in, the centre of the cake seems to sink into itself and she hurriedly tries to close the oven door again. The door catches, and she presses up against it with the side of her hand, feeling only after a split second the searing heat of the cast-iron against her skin. She recoils, knocking the jar of flour to the floor in the process.

'*Scheiße!*' She rushes to the sink to plunge her hand in the basin that holds the drinking water and remembers that there is no water there. She puts the injured hand up to her mouth, licks the sore skin and blows on it. She inspects the burn. The skin is bright red and throbs painfully, but she shakes her hand out a couple of times and sets about cleaning up the flour. It's too precious to be thrown away, so she scoops what she can back into the jar, plucking out and discarding any remaining weevils.

Then she stops and straightens up. Men's voices, muffled, coming from the alley behind the café. For a panicky moment, she thinks it might be Gustav, and she squeezes her brain to come up with an excuse for being here. She should have thought up something earlier, but then, she has never been one to prepare properly.

She wipes her hands on her dress and creeps to the back door, pulling back the grimy blind a few centimetres. The alley is steeped in shadow, but she spots a group of Chinese children playing some noisy game further up the lane. Then she hears the voices again. They have moved further towards the end of the alley, but she can still make out single words, in German. She stands still for a moment, listening. They appear to be discussing the price of something – a common-enough topic in this thriving black-market economy, where everyone is involved in buying or selling something or other – cigarettes, soap, paper, even buttons. Satisfied that Gustav, whose voice is strikingly high-pitched, is not among them, she steps back and lets the blind drop into place. Then:

'*Sei kein Schwachkopf*, Aaron!'

Thinking she may have misheard, Kitty turns and pulls back the blind again, craning her head to look to the corner where the alley meets the main street. *Don't be an idiot, Aaron.* Three men, standing about ten metres away, at the back of a dusty van. The light is dim, but she has a good view of one of them, a rotund Chinese man with whiskery tufts sprouting from his jowls, but the other two stand with their backs to her. The three of them are silent now, the Chinese man with his head cocked to one side, apparently contemplating something. Then he nods and lets out a raspy: '*Hai.*'

He is not Chinese after all, but Japanese. Which in itself is rather strange, because although Shanghai is full of them, Kitty has never heard of anyone foolhardy enough to make back-alley deals with the Japanese. If caught, a public whipping would be the most lenient punishment one could hope for. After that, a six-month stretch in Ward Road Gaol represents a death sentence – a slow, agonising death.

The two other men begin a whispered conversation; antagonistic, it seems, because the shorter of the two suddenly grabs the other by the lapels and pulls him down to eye level. As he does so, he spins the taller man around, giving Kitty a clear view of his profile. She wasn't mistaken. It is Aaron.

Kitty's skin prickles in the heat of the kitchen. She blinks hard a few times. Didn't Esther tell her just yesterday that she had talked Aaron into going to the synagogue with her and Anni? Outside, Aaron flicks the man's hand roughly from his collar and steps towards the Japanese man, saying something she cannot hear. The man grins, nods and takes some small parcels from the back of the van. Then he makes a small bow and hurries off down the street. The short man closes the back of the van and then gets behind the driver's seat, slamming the door shut. Aaron doesn't move, even as the van's engine starts up and it pulls away. He takes a packet of cigarettes from his pocket, taps one out, lights it and stands there in the encroaching dusk, head down. For a moment, she feels a little guilty for spying on him like this. But something holds her back from stepping out to let him know she has seen him.

Then, out of nowhere, a small, dirt-encrusted face appears right in front of her on the other side of the glass. Kitty lets out a little shriek and takes a step backward. The child grins at her and disappears as quickly as he appeared. She feels her heart racing and chides herself for scaring so easily. She takes a moment to calm herself and reaches for the blind. Surely Aaron would have heard her cry out. But when she looks out again, he is gone.

A scorched smell hits her nostrils. The cake! She rushes to the oven, fumbles with the door and yanks it open. The top of the cake is brown, rather than the golden colour mentioned in the recipe, but she doesn't think it is burned. She takes it out of the oven and places it on the counter to cool, while she goes to open the back door to rid the air of the smell and heat. Outside, the sun has set. The sound of laughing and shouting, in that sing-song language her ears will never quite adapt to, washes down the alley. Then, from the direction of the synagogue, the shofar sounds. A long wailing blast; a nearby, distant lament. Kitty shivers. Soon the Jews will once again fill the streets of Hongkew.

ESTHER

_____

When she has finished the last of her sewing chores that night, Aaron is already asleep in the bedroom. Esther hears his steady breathing and thinks how it is several months since they last made love. And the last few times, their lovemaking had an edge to it, something quick and harsh, but not unexciting. Of course, with Anneliese sleeping close by, it is difficult to surrender to desire. Anni has just turned eight, old enough to be asking questions that are awkward at best, and painfully embarrassing at worst.

Esther picks up the kerosene lamp and enters the bedroom, slipping out of her clothes and pulling on a cotton nightshift. In truth, it is not only the act of lovemaking that she has missed. There has only been the barest of physical contact between her and Aaron recently; an unintentional brush of hands when she passes him a plate; the accidental touching of hips or shoulders when they manoeuvre around the tight space of the kitchen nook. It makes no sense to her. Aaron is a young man, barely thirty. Perhaps his tamped-down desire is the result of malnutrition?

She blows out the lamp and the pale smoke slinks upwards towards the ceiling in a steady, unmoving stream. It is warm; the sudden mid-October heatwave has taken the city by surprise and has been greeted with weary resignation. The electricity in the lane is switched off at night, meaning there is not even a working fan to chop about the air, to give even the pretence of a breeze. She climbs into bed knowing that, in the humidity, sleep will be elusive. The best she can hope for is a shallow, stifling doze, providing barely enough rest to get through the following day. She lies unmoving, listening to Aaron's breath and the monotonous whine of the mosquitoes.

Across the room, Anneliese sleeps soundlessly. As she has done countless times before, Esther throws up a prayer of gratitude for her daughter's robust health. The sharp rise in temperature has led to a spate of dysentery, mostly in the elderly, who waste away at an alarming rate in a rush of liquid bloody shit, but the recent weeks have also seen the deaths of a distressing number of children. She closes her eyes, trying to ignore the thick, scorched smell of paraffin that hangs in the air, and focuses her thoughts away from death and disease and the gnawing in her stomach. Not for the first time, she thinks of the boat journey with Kitty all those years ago – and that kiss, tender and inviting. She touches her fingers to her lips. Then she begins to doze, trying to imagine the cool, dewy freshness of a spring morning in the Grunewald Forest in Berlin.

When the banging starts, she is awake instantly. She extracts herself from the sticky sheets, almost relieved to have an excuse to end the night.

Anneliese stirs. 'Mama?'

The banging continues, shaking the door in its flimsy

frame. Esther pulls a dress over her ragged nightshift and crosses the room in a hurry. 'I'm coming,' she says. 'You'll knock the door down!' Her tongue is thick and dry and she mumbles the words; she must have slept more deeply than she thought.

'Don't let them in,' Aaron says, sitting up. His hair sticks to the side of his face. 'We don't know who it is.'

'Perhaps it's Victor. An emergency.'

Aaron has a brief struggle with the mosquito netting and then pulls his trousers on. Esther tugs the door open and torchlight is shone directly at her face. Behind the torch stand two men, soldiers, Japanese. One is tall, the other short – the height difference must be at least a foot, giving them an appearance so comic Esther lets out a wild little laugh. She covers it with a cough, her heart beating madly.

The taller of the soldiers speaks, the torch wavering. 'You.' He points at Aaron, who is standing behind her. 'You mechanic.'

'Yes.' Aaron's voice is low, and Esther can tell from the way he has curled up his bare toes that he is tense. A bead of sweat trickles down the side of his face. From the corner, Anneliese lets out a fearful cry, and Esther hurries over to her.

'You come. Now.' The soldier steps forward and taps Aaron's bare shoulder with the tip of his rifle. The bayonet flashes in the moonlight.

Esther wraps her arm around Anneliese. 'Aaron?'

He turns to look at her, hesitates, but the soldier taps him again, harder.

'Where your tools?' he says.

'My tools? They're . . .' he trails off.

314

'Give us your tools.'

All of a sudden, Anneliese releases herself from Esther's arms and runs to the door. She slips her hand into Aaron's.

'Anni!' Esther cries, rushing after her. 'Come here.'

The shorter soldier steps forward and stretches his arm out towards Anneliese. He ruffles her hair. She flinches.

'Gold,' he says and smiles.

The other soldier barks something at him, and he bows and takes a step back. As he does so, he steps against the toilet bucket, which Esther keeps close to the front door in case Anneliese needs to use it during the night. The bucket tips, spilling its contents. Immediately, a swarm of flies begins to dance and settle. Esther crouches down to Anneliese and holds her even tighter. The child's skin is clammy and cold.

'Tools. Now!' The tall soldier also steps back, making sure to avoid the stinking mess on the ground, and lifts his rifle so that the bayonet is pointed at Aaron's throat.

'Let them have the tools,' Esther whispers as Anneliese begins to cry.

Aaron fixes the soldier with a cold, hard stare. He points to the shed. 'This way.' He leads them outside.

Esther stands in the doorway, gripping on to Anneliese. 'The key –' she calls weakly, but the short soldier is already bashing at the padlock with the butt of his rifle. There is an unpleasant splintering sound, and the lock falls to the dusty ground with a *thunk*. The tall soldier opens the door and shines his torch into the shed. He grins. Then he turns to the other soldier and says something. The short man takes off a bag he has slung around his shoulder and begins to fill it with Aaron's tools.

'You can't just –' Aaron begins, his voiced laced with

fear or rage, Esther can't tell. The tall soldier doesn't let him finish: he raises his rifle and thumps Aaron hard in the ribs. Aaron stumbles back.

'Just come inside, please!' Esther says. 'They'll kill you.'

Anneliese is sobbing loudly now. Aaron gets to his feet and rubs his chest. His face is dark, and for one terrifying moment, Esther thinks he is going to rush the soldiers, who are cramming tools into their bag. But he turns and sweeps past Esther and Anneliese into the house.

When the soldiers have left, Esther puts Anneliese back to bed. The girl is exhausted and slides into sleep, drawing in occasional shuddery breaths.

Aaron goes to the door and looks out. 'I'd better go and assess the damage,' he says. 'See if the bastards have left anything. You should try to get a few hours' sleep.'

He closes the front door behind him, and Esther cleans up the mess from the spilt toilet bucket as quietly as she can, so as not to wake Anni. Then she takes off her dress and climbs into bed. Even before she lies down, she knows she won't be able to sleep. Her limbs are aching with tiredness, but the weight on her chest makes her feel as though she is suffocating. What if they had hit Aaron hard enough to kill him? What if they'd taken him away? Or, far worse, hurt Anni? A panic takes hold and it paralyses her. Then she becomes aware of a noise in the yard, a scraping and scratching sound from the shed, as though Aaron were dismantling it from the inside.

Slowly, feeling breathless and light-headed, she climbs out of bed and goes out to the yard. Aaron is standing on a box in the shed, stretching up to a wooden beam just beneath the ceiling. There is a dark red mark near his sternum from where the soldier struck him.

'Aaron? What are you doing?' she asks.

He turns to her, startled. But he doesn't speak and climbs down with a small shake of his head. In his hands, he is holding several small glass bottles.

'What's that?' she asks.

No answer.

Esther takes a step forward. 'Aaron, what have you got there?'

'They didn't find them,' is all he says.

'Didn't find what –?' she begins, but then she gets a closer look at what he is holding. Momentarily, words fail her, but then: 'It was you,' she whispers.

Aaron doesn't respond; instead, he sweeps past her and into the house. She follows him.

'You stole medicines from the surgery?' She phrases it as a question, although it isn't one.

He roots around beneath the sink and pulls out a burlap sack. 'How else do you think we can afford to eat?'

'But people need these medicines. They're sick! They might die!' She knows she must keep her voice low so as not to wake Anneliese, but her incredulity is so acute, she isn't sure if she's shouting or whispering.

Aaron stuffs the items into the sack. Then brushes his hand through the air and walks towards the door. 'It's not just Jews who get sick.'

'What?' She hurries after him to the yard and grabs his sleeve, making him turn to face her. 'What did you just say?'

'What kind of world do you think we're living in, Esther? Hmm? It's dog eat dog. It's about survival. This "community" we're living in' – his expression pulls into a sneer – 'it isn't all . . . shalom. It's dirty deals conducted with people you wouldn't want to spit on.'

'So I suppose you'd sell medicines to the Germans, would you?' Esther says. It comes out as a snarl.

He swings round on her and she thinks he might strike her. But he just narrows his eyes and says, 'I sell to whoever is willing to pay the price.'

For a long moment, she is lost for words. Then: 'You put us in danger, Aaron. You put *Anni* in danger.'

He lets out a laugh then, a queer ugly sound. 'You don't understand, do you? You are weak and soft. You wouldn't survive for a day here without me.' His eyes flash, fierce.

'You talk as though you have no stake in this.'

'Stake? What are you talking about?'

'In this! In us!' She spreads her arms out, and when he doesn't respond, studies his face for a trace of understanding of what she means. 'You're not alone in this,' she says quietly.

A look of contempt crosses his face, but almost immediately, his features soften. 'Listen, Esther. *Mein Schatz.* It's best if you forget this. Just . . . let me do what I have to do. For us. For Anni.' His voice is ragged at the edges; she can tell he is trying hard to control himself. 'I'll take the medicines back. In fact, here –' He holds out the sack to her. 'I'll give them to you. You can return them and no one will know.'

Esther takes a step back, aware that she is trembling suddenly, violently. She turns and looks through the open front door into the house, imagines Anneliese lying in her bed, curled up, and she begins to walk, no, to glide towards the door, her only destination Anni's bed, where she will slide in beside her daughter and lay her arm over her and inhale her sweet, innocent smell.

周翼

—

It has taken some getting used to, but with practice Yì has mastered the downward push and upward pull of the pedals, the wobbling of the handlebars and the seemingly impossible task of staying upright, balanced and in forward motion. And only two weeks after Stern *yīshēng* gave him patient, step-by-step instruction of how to ride the bicycle, Yì is threading his way through the traffic at a pace that makes his heart soar and his fingers tingle. The icy November headwind bites his ankles and whips through his collar, but he doesn't care. He has a tufted jacket! Made of stiff cotton, stuffed and quilted, it is cumbersome, but it keeps him as warm as a dumpling on its bed of steam.

He cycles back to Hongkew at speed, his fingers whipped raw by the cold, to deliver his cargo of ampoules, which he collected from a pharmacy on Ferry Road on the other side of the city, to the doctors' office. Stern *yīshēng* is expecting him back in a few hours, but Yì has made good time and will be able to make a stop at the café where Mamselle Kitty works.

And even with a stop there, he will be back at the doctor's office in plenty of time. He wants to impress Stern *yīshēng* and his wife with the speed with which he can carry out his delivery tasks. He has worked hard to make himself indispensable, arriving at the practice well before opening hours, staying on in the late afternoons until scolded home by the doctor's wife, delivering patient files to the Jewish hospital and collecting medicines – like today – from pharmacies across town where the Sterns are not permitted to venture. When he told Stern *yīshēng* of a Chinese herbalist in a lane off Yuan Road who sells a wound-healing salve for a fraction of the price of the zinc-oxide compound he gets from a French apothecary, Stern *yīshēng* shook his hand firmly, like a man, and told him he was the best assistant he'd ever had.

He makes a turn onto Chusan Road, pedalling against the wind and cold, past grey, two-storey tenements whose crumbling chimneys exhale thin wisps of smoke into the leaden sky. The air reeks of the smell of thousands of charcoal fires. The foreigners keep their fires lit all day; Yì has seen them scouring refuse bins for anything that can be used as fuel. It must be much warmer where they come from, he thinks, for them to be so sensitive to the cold. But at the same time, they seem to wilt in the heat of the summer. It is a puzzle. He once asked Mamselle Kitty to tell him more about this place she comes from, so far across the sea, but the corner of her mouth twitched and a sadness clouded her eyes, so he didn't ask her any more. It cannot be a good homeland if it makes a woman like Mamselle Kitty so sad.

And despite what Huà thinks, the foreigners work hard. He has seen foreign men labouring like oxen on construction sites, and foreign women sweating over steaming vats in the Chinese laundries, their pale skin flushed to a blossom pink. And over the past few years, these people have transformed many of the ruins from brick carcasses, that provided little more than shelter from the wind and rain to beggars and vagrants, into homes, with curtains in the windows and small mysterious boxes attached to the door frames. Nothing compared to the grand houses of the rich foreigners in the west of Shanghai, but liveable enough.

Yes, they work hard during the day, but in the evenings the place comes to life with a strange abandon, as though when the sun has set, they are free to pay homage to their place of origin. Bars and nightclubs have always thrived here, but now there are cafés and theatres and music halls – music that is strange to his ears, both melancholy and exquisite. Lying on his rice-straw mattress at night, the memory of these sounds cradles him into sleep, causing strange, exotic dreams of pale and beautiful landscapes.

Up ahead of him, there is some commotion involving two rickshaw coolies and a man leading an obstinate mule, and Yì swerves to avoid them, almost crashing into a beggar on the pavement.

'*Āiyō! Dāng xīn!*' the man cries out, raising a bony, filth-encrusted fist to Yì.

Yì holds up his palm in apology and gets back on the bicycle, only to stop again moments later. The honeyed smell of roasted sweet potatoes fills his nostrils, and instantly, his stomach responds. He looks across the street to the right and sees a woman, with a baby strapped into a wrap on her back, standing beside a steel drum. It might be his imagination, but even from this distance, he can feel the heat radiating from the drum. He shivers, noting the sweat on his skin beneath the thick jacket. He pushes the bicycle across the street. The buckled steel drum is riddled with ventilation holes, like pockmarked skin, and layered on a grate above a charcoal fire lie a dozen or so blackened sweet potatoes. With his mouth watering now, Yì watches as the woman turns the potatoes on the grate with a bamboo stick.

The woman thrusts her chin in his direction, squinting as a curl of smoke drifts up into her eyes. 'You want?'

Before he can stop himself, Yì nods eagerly.

The woman grins, revealing stumps of yellow teeth. 'How many?'

'How much?'

The woman sucks her tooth stumps and adjusts the weight of the baby on her back with her hand. 'For you, twenty yuan.'

'I'll give you thirty for two potatoes.'

She purses her mouth and eyes him up and down, and nods. She picks out two potatoes with fingers that appear to be impervious to the heat, wraps them in paper and waits until he has counted out the money before handing them to him.

Balancing the bicycle against his hip, Yì pauses to relish the warmth the parcels give off in his hands. He unwraps one of them with his teeth and bites into the potato, but it is steaming hot, too hot to eat, so he peels off some flakes of the blackened skin with his teeth and blows ferociously on the flesh. When it is just about cool enough to eat, he takes a bite. In roasting, the flesh of the potato has become a delicious thick yellowy syrup, which he sucks into his mouth, using his tongue to spread the pulp around the inside of his mouth and savour each and every aspect of its flavour – creamy, smoky, and above all sweet, sweet, sweet. When he has gobbled up the first potato and scraped the remaining pulp from the burnt skin with his teeth, he looks at the other parcel in his hand. Should he eat it now, or save it? He hears his *năinai's* voice, *You must keep your strength up, boy – you never know when you might next eat.* He feels a stab in his heart. How he would have loved for Năinai to see him now!

He unwraps the second parcel, and as he raises the sweet potato to his mouth, he sees a man limping down the pavement towards him. It is a foreigner, an old, grey-bearded man dressed in what looks like a rice sack, his thin, liver-spotted arms hanging out through holes cut into the sides. He walks with his head down, with the shameful look of someone who wishes to remain as invisible as possible. His uneven gait is caused by his shoes, where the sole is tied to the upper part with a piece of string. And although the streets are inundated with beggars, this old man's aching humiliation makes Yì take a step forward and thrust out the still-warm potato towards him. The man doesn't look up, just stares at the parcel for a long moment, and then slowly, as if in a waking dream, reaches out and takes it. As he bites into the flesh, a tear drops down his face, and Yì turns away so as not to witness the man's shame.

He cycles on, trying not to brood on the growl in his stomach, as though it is chiding him for giving away precious food, until he reaches the café. He pushes the bicycle into the back alley and peers into the grimy kitchen window. There she is, her hair tied up in a scarf, her long slender arms up to the elbows in soapy water. He watches her for a moment, how the tips of her shoulder blades nudge delicately against the fabric of her blouse as she moves and stretches, neat dancer's steps to the left as she lifts plates out of the water and places them in a rack. He imagines placing his hands on her waist, just above her hips, oh so gently, simply to feel her warmth and grace pulse through his fingers.

Two months ago, he lay with a woman for the first time. She was from the north, like him. When she approached him outside a bar, not too far from his home, his first response was to wave her away. But when she took a step closer and placed her hand on his crotch, murmuring in his ear, he saw in the half-light her powder-white face and soft, circular cheeks. Immediately, he had the biting smell of steaming dye in his nose, the echo of tired, subdued chatter in his ears, and the pain of sore muscles in his arms. The girl wasn't Zhū, of course, but before he knew it, he had let her lead him into the bar, down a stinking passage and into a curtained cubicle with a horsehair mattress, where she lay down and pulled him on top of her and he had pulled his trousers down, his blood hot, boiling, deep dark within his groin. Around the edges: music and drunken laughter; the girl's face illuminated by the glow of the red lantern above the bed. He didn't last long, and as he climaxed, his loneliness was so sharp it was almost intolerable. When the girl saw his tears, she pushed him off and turned away with a bitter smile on her painted lips.

He startles as a stray cat upsets one of the metal waste bins standing near the door; it falls and rolls, leaking its stinking mess. Immediately, several rats appear and begin attacking the waste. Yì taps on the window and Kitty turns. She flashes him a smile and wipes her dripping hands on a towel, then disappears for a moment before returning with her coat.

'Hello, Wing!' she says, stepping out into the lane.

'*Nǐ hǎo*, Mamselle.'

Mamselle Kitty spots the rats rummaging in the waste and claps her hands several times, letting out a 'ksss, ksss' sound. The rats scuttle away into the gutter.

She turns back to him and frowns apologetically. 'No cake today, I'm afraid.'

Usually when he visits, she has a slice of cake for him; delicious, rich, fluffy cake that melts in his mouth and makes his taste buds dance. 'We ran out of briquettes for the oven, so the customers are having to make do with sandwiches.'

'No matter,' he says, careful to keep the edge of disappointment out of his voice. 'I just come to say hello.'

She smiles again and pulls a packet of cigarettes from her coat. 'It's freezing today, isn't it?'

She strikes a match, but the wind blows it out immediately, so Yì cups his hands around hers while she lights another. Her skin is chapped and red, but still warm from the washing-up water. He lets the touch linger for as long as he dares, until she pulls her head back and exhales a cloud of bluish smoke.

'Have you heard from your brother?'

Yì looks down and shakes his head. He kicks at a loose pebble and watches it skitter across the ground.

'You must miss him,' she says, and when he raises his head to look at her, her expression is faraway, the shine in her eyes momentarily gone.

Across the street, two women are haggling over a bag of rice. They both know that the rice will be more valuable tomorrow than it is today, and even more valuable the day after that. The winner in this transaction will be the one who is least desperate.

Mamselle Kitty watches them for a while, and then says, 'Wing, do you know of people who trade with the Japanese?'

The question takes him by surprise. 'The Japanese?'

'On the black market, for example.'

His eyes widen. What is she thinking? 'Oh no, Mamselle. Never with Japanese. They *guǐzi*. Devils!' He bites off the words, hoping to make clear to her how dangerous they are. 'No trade with devils, Mamselle, please.'

'Hm.' She drops her cigarette and wraps her coat around herself more tightly. 'If you had a friend,' she continues after a moment, 'and you knew something, or thought you knew something, that might make that friend sad or even angry, do you think you should tell them?'

He frowns. 'Is this a riddle, Mamselle?'

'No.' She shakes her head and murmurs, just loud enough for him to hear, 'Or perhaps it is, I'm not sure.'

He waits, a little frustrated that he doesn't understand her meaning, but she doesn't elaborate. Instead, she pushes a strand of hair back into her scarf and sighs.

'Back to work. But it was nice to see you, Wing. And I'll have some cake for you next time.' She smiles and gives him a small wink, sending a thrill through his body.

When she has gone back inside he stands watching the door, lit by the glow of her presence, for several minutes, before remembering where he was meaning to go.

ESTHER

_____

In late 1944, the war finally closes in on them. In the ghetto, news of the American landing in Saipan was met with more trepidation than relief – the fear of Japanese retaliation looms large. But for most refugees, the frequent raids on newspapers and warehouses, the roadblocks springing up everywhere, and even the tales of random arrests are just another hurdle to overcome in the daily business of survival.

Then the bombing starts. The war is no longer playing out only on the other side of the world.

On a misty December morning, Esther is walking Anneliese to school when they hear the telltale buzzing of American planes flying overhead. They are flying high; too high, Esther hopes, to indicate an immediate threat. The closest hit so far was the wharf, one night several weeks ago – a loud-enough bang and roar to shake loose flakes of plaster off the ceiling. Since then, every loud noise – a car backfiring, the sputter of fireworks, even a door slamming shut in the draught – sends a jolt through Esther. The ghetto, as confined and crowded as it felt before, seems to have shrunk even more. The siren wails. The planes are closer than she thought.

'Quickly, this way,' she says, pulling Anneliese by the hand towards the nearest building.

They, and a dozen others, make a dash for a nearby shop; there is a jostling for position in the doorway – beneath a lintel, the safest place to be in the absence of air-raid shelters – but Esther holds her ground, clasping Anni close to her body with one hand and grabbing on to the door frame with the other. She is shoved from behind but pushes back and crouches down into a more stable position. The rain falls in large, angry drops just in front of her, and the putrid stench from the gutter near her feet makes her want to gag. She breathes through her mouth and concentrates on keeping her balance.

The deafening wail of the siren, up, up, up, holding in a quivering monotonous pitch, before descending again. There is, from a distance, a thunderous crash. Anneliese squeezes her hand, her fingernails digging into Esther's skin. A few minutes later, the all-clear sounds, and they get up and step out into the rain.

They are twenty minutes late when they arrive at school. Esther gives Anneliese a kiss. Pearls of rain drip from her felt hat.

'Don't forget, Uncle Aaron is picking you up today.'

'Why?'

'I told you. I have to stay a bit longer at work, today.'

'What for?' Anneliese sticks out her bottom lip. She questions everything, these days.

'Accounts,' she says, straightening up. 'Boring grown-up stuff. Now, off you go. You're late as it is.'

★

At the end of the day she is exhausted. Her clothes are still damp and seem to have doubled in weight. Coupled with the rationing and food shortages, which mean only a single meal a day, she has become increasingly unsteady on her feet, clumsy even. Her bones feel as soft as wax. And it is not just her. The patients are growing thinner and weaker every day, and today's waiting room was full of tales of doctors at the hospital having to perform minor surgery without anaesthetic – extracting rotten teeth, lacerating tonsils – instilling yet more fear in everyone.

She places the account books on the desk in Victor's office and checks that everything is locked up. It took her months to replace the drugs Aaron had stolen, surreptitiously, one at a time, by pretending they were part of separate orders. Thankfully, neither Helene nor Victor have much interest in the accounts and signed off on the order sheets without closer inspection. But the ease with which she has been able to deceive them makes the deceit weigh all the more heavily.

She grabs her coat and hat from the small back room in the surgery, avoiding her reflection in the mirror, which surely shows her hair hanging ragged and lifeless onto her shoulders.

On her way home, she stops off at Café Atlantic on Muirhead Road. As usual, the place is packed with Europeans, the design and décor allowing them for one transient moment to imagine that they are not in this far-flung hell, but rather at a street café in Prague or Munich or Vienna. Esther weaves her way through the wicker tables and chairs, gives a nod of greeting to Gustav, the proprietor, and heads in through the café to the kitchen. Kitty is rinsing glasses at the sink, her hair tied up in a scarf and her cheeks flushed. She looks up as Esther slips through the bamboo curtain.

'Esther!'

'I've brought you the sewing kit.' She pulls a small pouch from her bag. It is one of the few of Frau Rosenbaum's belongings she's held on to.

Kitty wipes a wet hand on her apron and takes the pouch, stuffing it into her pocket. 'Thanks.'

Esther looks around. The kitchen is astonishingly clean, by Shanghai standards, with scrubbed floors and barely stained tiling on the walls. 'It's nice and warm in here,' she says.

'I know.' Kitty brushes a damp strand of hair out of her face. 'It's the oven.' She nods towards the large black range against the wall. The air above it seems to shimmer, and the smell it emits is heavenly. 'But I suppose it'll be hell in summer.'

She stops abruptly and their eyes meet. The future is something no one talks about. They only think days ahead, weeks at the most, as if talking about times to come will jinx the future. It is exhausting to live in a state of fragile hope, so instead, they focus on surviving, day by day.

Kitty continues. 'There are three marble cakes in there as we speak. I'll see if I can grab a spare slice or two, for you and Anni.'

'Don't let Gustav catch you.'

Kitty wipes her hands on her apron and shakes her head. 'He won't mind. Come on, I'm due a break.'

She leads Esther through the back door into the alley and pulls a packet of cigarettes out of her apron pocket. 'Like one?' She holds out the packet to Esther.

'Thanks, but no.'

Kitty taps one out, lights and inhales. She tips her head back and blows out the smoke. 'Ah, I needed that.' A moment later, though, she is overcome by a coughing fit.

'Everything all right?' Esther rubs her back until she stops coughing. Kitty is still frightfully underweight, and her skin, though flushed from the heat of the kitchen, has a greyish pallor. 'Shall I get you some water?'

Kitty shakes her head and picks a strand of tobacco from her tongue. 'I'm fine. It's just these God-awful cigarettes,' she says when she has her breath back. 'I have no idea where Gustav gets them from, but at least they're cheap.'

'Either from the black market, or' – Esther shrugs – 'they pick up the butts off the street, unwrap them and take out what's left to make new cigarettes.' She pulls a face.

Kitty laughs. 'You have to take your small pleasures where you find them, don't you?'

The end of her sentence is overlaid by the noise of a plane, buzzing like some grotesque, oversized mosquito. They wait until the sound fades.

'How is Anni?' Kitty asks.

'Fine. Apart from another bout of lice. The school's full of them, it seems.'

Kitty tosses her cigarette down and crushes it with her foot. 'And Aaron? Still managing to make a living fixing and mending?' Her tone is oddly sharp. Esther turns to look at her, but she is pulling at a loose thread on her jacket. She tugs at it and it snaps off. Kitty and Aaron have never quite warmed to each other.

'We're getting by,' she says. She shivers and rubs her arms. 'I'd better be off. He went to pick up Anni from school today, and I'll bet he hasn't thought of making her do her homework.'

'Okay,' Kitty says, patting her pocket containing the sewing kit. 'And thanks.'

'Don't mention it.'

They embrace briefly. Esther can feel her own thinness revealed in Kitty's body, in the touching of hipbones beneath the layers of fabric, and for a fleeting moment, she recalls the warm softness of Kitty's body pressed close to hers so many years ago on the ship.

As she turns into the lane ten minutes later, she knows immediately that something is very, very wrong. Aaron is pacing up and down, his hands clenching and unclenching. When he looks up and sees her, his mouth opens, then closes. Instinctively, she begins running towards him knowing, even before she reaches him, that this has to do with Anneliese.

'Anni?' she says, snatching for breath. 'Where's Anni?'

'What's taken you so long? You should've been back an hour ago!'

'Where's Anni?' she repeats. His breath is sharp and fruity. He's been drinking. 'Aaron, where is she?'

He lifts her hands and holds them in his. His hands are clammy and his breathing is shaky. 'She wasn't there when I went to pick her up.'

'What do you mean, not there?'

He shakes his head. 'I was ... I was late. Five minutes at the most!'

'You were late?' She pulls her hands away.

He screws up his face and lets out a sharp breath. 'Yes, *verdammt*! I waited, then went inside and spoke to her teacher. She said Anni left as soon as the bell rang. I waited there for ages, just in case she was playing some sort of prank on me, and when she didn't come, I thought she might have gone straight home on her own. But she isn't here. I've looked everywhere and I didn't want to go out searching for her in case she came back. I thought it best to wait until you were home.'

'Oh God.' A groan escapes her. She stares at him, wide-eyed. 'Have you called the police?'

He dismisses the question. 'That would be pointless.' He sounds desperate, angry. He grabs her hand again and holds it, tight. 'It was five minutes, five minutes!'

Three hours and forty minutes since school ended. Esther's heart begins to gallop again. *Aaron wasn't outside waiting for her, so Anni tried to make her own way home. She's wandering the streets alone. She's a brave girl, she's trying not to cry, but she's scared. Someone will see her alone and snatch her – a girl like Anni is worth thousands in this place. She'll be kidnapped, and locked away, and . . .* A powerful wave of nausea wells up inside her. She slips her hand from his grip and doubles over to vomit in the dust. Blood roars in her ears.

'I'll find her,' Aaron says. 'I'll set out right away. I'll go down Broadway first – that's where they hang those red paper lanterns that she likes. Perhaps she thought . . . I don't know. If I work my way up through –'

Esther interrupts him. 'Maybe I should go.' The thought of sitting at home waiting, uselessly, is terrifying.

Aaron shakes his head. 'You're in no state. It's best if you –'

He stops suddenly and looks past her down the lane. He squints, and his expression darkens. Esther clasps her hand to her mouth and turns. At the top of the lane, she sees the silhouettes of two *baojia* guards walking towards

333

them. Between them, a smaller shape, struggling to keep up in the grip of one of the men.

It is Anneliese. When she sees Esther, she jerks and twists herself free.

'Mama!'

Esther runs towards her, stumbles on a loose paving stone, scrapes her knee on the ground but continues running until she scoops up Anneliese in her arms, pressing her so tight she can feel Anni's heartbeat thrumming against her own chest. 'Anni, Anni. *Mein liebling.* Oh, Anni. You're safe.'

The guards, one of them young and pimple-faced, the other a generation older, come and stand in front of Esther.

'So this one's yours then?' the older guard asks brusquely.

Esther straightens up and wipes her face with the palm of her hand. She nods. She can't make her tongue work properly.

'We found her up near Broadway, in one of the side streets. She was outside the restricted area.'

Aaron, standing behind her, says: 'It's a ghetto. Just call it what it is.'

The guard gives him a sharp look. 'Either way, she was in violation of the rules. You're lucky we don't report this to the Japanese.'

'We-ll, she is just a child,' the younger guard says.

The older one ignores the comment and looks around. 'You live here?'

'Yes,' Esther says, squeezing Anni's hand tightly in her own. Despite the man's hostile manner, she is so grateful and relieved to have her daughter back, she considers inviting him inside for a drink.

The guard walks around the yard with his hands placed

on the small of his back, his feet crunching on the wet gravel. 'This yours?' He nods towards Aaron's shed.

Aaron nods.

The guard goes to the shed, circles it once and then stands in front of it, tapping the padlock with his baton. 'What's inside?'

'None of your business,' Aaron says in a low voice.

Esther looks from the guard to Aaron. There is a tension she feels but cannot quite understand. 'Tools,' she offers, though it is stretching the truth. The Japanese soldiers left behind only a few rusty spanners and a handful of screws. 'He's a mechanic.'

'A mechanic? And what –'

He's interrupted by the sound of firecrackers going off on the main road, followed by a shrill whistle.

'Come on, Erich,' the younger guard says. 'The girl's back home now. We should really go.'

The older man points a stiff finger at Anneliese. 'Make sure she doesn't leave the restricted area again,' he says. 'If I catch her outside again, I'll report her, child or no child.'

The two men turn and begin walking up the lane, breaking into a trot when the firecrackers start up again.

'They're no better than the Nazis,' Aaron hisses, once they are out of earshot.

'But they brought Anni home,' Esther says. She is dizzy and exhausted. She strokes her daughter's face. 'Why did you run away? Why didn't you wait for Uncle Aaron to pick you up?'

Anneliese sniffs. 'He wasn't there, so I decided to go to our old house and visit Lí Mà.'

Aaron gives Esther an unsteady look. 'She brought the *baojia* here, to our home. It'll be the Japanese next.' He turns to Anneliese. 'What the hell were you thinking?'

Anneliese's chin begins to tremble. 'Everyone at school has a best friend except me. Lí Mà is my best friend so I wanted to go and play with her.'

'So you thought you would just wander off on your own?' His voice is raised. 'Do you not realise what kind of trouble you might have caused?'

Anneliese flinches and presses herself closer to Esther.

'Don't shout at her, Aaron. Please. We're all a little shaken. Let's just go inside and I'll make a start on supper.' Esther cups Anni's face in her hands. 'If you want to visit your friend, *liebling*, we have to get a pass. You must promise me that you will never go wandering off on your own again.'

'But why do we have to live here? Why couldn't we stay living next door to Lí Mà?'

'You know why, *liebling*. Because all the Jews had to move here.'

Tears form in Anneliese's eyes. She stamps the ground. 'Well, I *hate* being a Jew!'

Before Esther can stop her, she turns and runs into the house, sobbing noisily.

'Look what you've done,' Esther says to Aaron. 'You're too hard on her.'

'Me?' He sounds incredulous. 'You're blaming me now?' He runs his hands through his hair. 'It's you. You're too bloody soft.'

'But I'm all she has.' The truth of her words shocks her. She knows she is about to cry, but still she says it. 'I took her father away from her.'

Aaron lets out an angry sigh. 'I thought we put that behind us. It's history.'

'How can you say that? You have no idea how it feels for me – or for her! You're not her father!'

'You don't get it, do you?' He looks away, stung. 'He never loved you. Hell, he wouldn't even fight for you.'

'What are you talking about? You never even met Carl.'

A door opens on the other side of the yard. A woman steps out and sloshes a bucket of water into the gutter. Esther waits for her to retreat back inside. Then she turns to Aaron. 'There's nothing –' She stops abruptly. Aaron is looking down, his eyes sweeping the floor. When he looks up, his expression chills her. 'What is it?'

'I was there,' he says. 'I left him a message, telling him you were coming to meet me. I thought I'd give the man a sporting chance. But d'you know what happened when you left?' He steps forward, quick on his feet. He grabs her shoulders, roughly, and she smells the drink on him. 'I found him skulking outside my apartment, standing there, watching. Too much of a pathetic coward to confront you. He wouldn't fight for you . . . I gave him every chance, but he just swerved and ducked and –' He stares at her with dark eyes. 'If he'd fought me, like a man, he wouldn't have lost his balance. He wouldn't have fallen onto the tracks. So' – his face softens – 'none of it is your fault, sweetheart. I'm the one who loves you – really loves you.'

She feels something twist inside. The past is rushing at her, suffocating her. She tries to fill her lungs but they won't inflate properly.

Aaron suddenly drops to his knees. 'Marry me, Esther,' he says. 'Be my wife. You know we belong together . . .'

He says something more, but she can't hear the words; there is nothing beyond the rushing in her ears. She looks down and sees he has taken her hand. He squeezes it hard, his skin rough against hers.

'You deserve better than him. You, and Anni too. Carl wouldn't have protected you like I have in this stinking place, you know that.' His breathing is ragged, desperate.

She blinks, manages to take a sudden, deep breath that leaves her dizzy. She turns her head, very slowly, to the house.

Anneliese stands in the doorway, her earlier sobbing stuck in her throat. Esther has never before seen such an expression on her daughter's face. It is at once shocked and bereft and tragic. It is utterly wrong. Esther has always led her to believe her father died of pneumonia – the truth being too awful, too shameful to articulate – and what is she to think, now that she has heard from another that her mother is a liar? Esther's heart stumbles, then races, then catches itself in a slow steady beat.

'Come on, Anni my love,' she says calmly. She takes her daughter's hand and leads her away down the lane towards Wayside Road.

April to August 1945

KITTY

———

The dislocated nights are beginning to wear her down. They are all desperate for a few hours of uninterrupted sleep, but just after two in the morning, there it goes again, for the third time tonight – the wail of the air-raid siren, ugly and clawing, like some beast being dragged up from hell.

From the corner of the room, Esther exhales. 'I'm so sick of it,' she says quietly. 'Anni's only just fallen asleep again.'

For a week now, the siren has been relentless – two warnings last night, followed by the all-clear a short time later. Either the Japanese are getting nervous and crank up the siren every time they spot a nuisance raider overhead, or this is just one more way to unravel everyone's last thread of energy. Kitty wouldn't put it past them.

The sound of the siren rises and falls. Outside the door, the neighbours clunk down the stairs, clumsy in their twilight sleep, fumbling for a handhold in the dark. Kitty raises herself onto her elbows, but then slumps back onto the lumpy mattress. What's the point? There are no air-raid shelters anyway, and the dugouts the men have been made to construct on the streets outside are little more than ineffectual foxholes covered with plywood; and, worse, they serve as open latrines during the day. But she climbs out of bed and joins Esther in the familiar drill of pushing two small tables together and heaving the largest of the mattresses on top. Then they wake Anneliese, who lets out a sleepy grunt of annoyance, and crawl under the table and sit, heads bowed, knees touching. They wait.

It has been a squeeze since Esther and Anneliese moved in, the floor of Kitty's small room now taken up entirely by their mattresses; Kitty's few possessions sharing the drawers with Esther's stockings and undergarments and books. Yet at the same time, it has become more of a home, with Anneliese's scratchy charcoal drawings decorating the scuffed walls, and Esther's talent for making even the smallest and most cramped space look neat and tidy. And Esther darns Kitty's stockings, a task Kitty has never quite mastered; in return, Kitty cuts and sets Esther's hair, enjoying the practice of her skills despite having the most rudimentary of means: sugar-water and rusty hair grips.

She doesn't know the circumstances surrounding Esther's decision to leave Aaron – Esther hasn't volunteered much information, and Kitty's sensitivity has so far prevented her from prying. This didn't, however, stop her from surreptitiously checking Esther's body for marks when she stripped down to wash in the days after she arrived. Even an imagined violence against her friend left Kitty feeling sick with fury, but there was nothing, only a deep, bruised sadness.

They hear the long scream of a shell falling from the

342

sky now, the *thump* as it detonates somewhere in the city. Kitty flinches at the sound of the flak guns and reminds herself to stay calm for Anni's sake. It hasn't been easy on the girl, and she is difficult at times, it's true – sullen moods, violent temper tantrums, night terrors that leave her trembling and speechless on waking. But at the same time, Kitty's attachment to Anni, and Anni's to her, has taken on a whole new quality, an intensity that snatches at Kitty's breath when she thinks about it. Is this how it would feel to be a mother? She realises, in a rush so sudden she has to fight not to cry, how happy she has been for the last few months, and understands with a lurch of her heart that if Aaron were to reappear, if he and Esther were to come together again, everything would be even more false and empty than it already is. Without Esther, and Anni, there is nothing.

The sickening thud of another bomb, closer this time, rattles the window glass in its frame. Anneliese whimpers and places her thumb in her mouth. She appears suddenly much younger, like the toddler Kitty first met on the boat. It is the closest any bomb has landed so far, but still they are lucky to have intact panes at all. Kitty shifts her position to alleviate the numbness in her legs and hears a deafening crash – the Americans must be aiming at the radio station two streets away. There is a gentle pattering against the window. For a freak moment, Kitty thinks of rain, but realises it must be a shower of debris and soot. She badly wants a cigarette.

She feels a warmness on her thigh, where it comes into contact with the floor. She places her hand there – it is wet.

'Oh, Anni,' Esther says.

'I needed to go – I couldn't hold it any longer,' Anneliese says and begins to cry.

'Never mind, sweetie,' Kitty whispers, and squeezes Anni's hand. 'We'll clean you up soon.'

After the longest time, the monotonous tone of the all-clear appears, holds for several minutes and then dies away to be replaced by the sound of shouting, coughing, babies screaming, dogs barking, ambulance sirens wailing. Kitty checks the time. It is half past two; the raid lasted for only fifteen minutes, but seemed like an eternity.

Esther undresses Anneliese and sponges her down, the girl squirming against the cold washcloth.

'I want us to sleep together, all three of us,' Anneliese says. 'I don't want Kitty to be on her own.' She looks at Kitty. 'Please? We could push the mattresses together. Like one big bed.'

Esther looks over at Kitty. 'Would you mind?' Her voice is steeped in exhaustion.

'Of course not.'

Anneliese lies in the middle of the mattresses, her form just a bump beneath the wool blanket. It takes her only minutes to fall asleep again, and Kitty envies the ease with which she takes sleep when she needs it.

'They suck you dry, these raids, don't they?' Esther says quietly, sliding in beside Anneliese. She goes to remove the thumb from her daughter's mouth, but holds back, and instead plants a soft kiss on her cheek. 'It's as though each explosion takes a year off your life.'

Kitty pulls the blanket up to her chin and lays her head on the pillow, her hair still damp and tangled from when she washed it earlier. It will be a hopeless mess tomorrow, but she is too tired even to run a comb through it. Next to her, Anneliese lies on her back, breathing soundlessly.

'Let's hope that was it for tonight,' she says, and Esther 'mms' her assent. They lie silently for a while, listening to the sounds of the other residents returning to the building. The flat below them is empty; the Japanese evicted the families living in ground-floor flats in most of the area and are now using the empty spaces to store ammunition and supplies. If the Americans want to destroy the ammunition, they will have to bomb their way through civilians first – it's the Japanese cynically appealing to the Americans' humanity. But Kitty is not too sure there is any humanity left.

In the dark, she turns to Esther. 'You can tell me, if you like.' She blurts it out before she can stop herself.

'Tell you what?'

'Aaron. Why you left.'

A long silence, the sound of Esther turning onto her back, and Kitty is afraid she has overstepped a mark. But then she hears the moist suck of Esther parting her lips.

'I thought it was this place that had changed him, made him so hard. But . . .' She lets out a long breath and her voice dips. 'But he hadn't changed at all. I just didn't see it before. Or perhaps *I* changed. I can't tell any more. He . . . he betrayed us so completely, Anni and me, it makes everything we had together a lie. And I don't know what to say to Anni – I'm not sure how much she understands. Aaron was like a father to her, and I . . . I don't know if the nightmares she's been having are because of the raids, or because –'

From upstairs, there is the loud *thwack* of a door being slammed shut.

'But all this,' Esther continues, 'it's making it impossible to think a straight thought. I just don't know what to believe any more.'

She says this last sentence so softly, Kitty has to strain to hear. 'I'm sorry,' she says, and then they both lie silent again in the darkness.

'Kitty?' Esther says after a while.

'Yes?'

'When the bombs were falling, earlier . . .' She pauses. Then: 'Do you believe in God?'

Kitty reaches out to take Esther's hand, but misjudges its position in the dark and finds Esther's cheek instead.

'Oh, sorry,' she says, pulling away.

But Esther takes her hand and guides it back to her face. 'Your fingers are so cool,' she says. 'It's nice.'

They stay like this, Kitty's fingers drawing the heat from Esther's skin. She is suddenly and unexpectedly resentful of Anneliese's little body lying between them, preventing her from nestling into Esther, pressing her hips and thighs against Esther's warmth, feeling Esther's breath on her face, placing her mouth on Esther's soft lips. She swallows, the strength and immediacy of her feelings taking her by surprise. She feels herself blushing and is thankful of the dark.

'What are you thinking?' Esther asks.

'About how we first met on the boat,' she answers, half-truthfully. She removes her hand from Esther's face, afraid her touch might give something away.

'How naïve we were,' Esther says. 'If I had known, I would've stolen everything from that boat, every linen napkin, every brass ashtray, anything that would've fit in my suitcase. I certainly wouldn't have tossed that cigarette case out of the window.'

346

'How were we to know?' Kitty says, knowing that Esther is smiling in the dark at the memory.

'I suppose we weren't.'

A pause, and then Esther lets out a little rush of air, a hushed laugh. 'Do you remember that you kissed me?'

'Yes.' She can only manage this single, shaky syllable, aware that if she says more, it will all come rushing out, this sudden, frightening understanding.

Esther breathes out. 'You must really miss your sister.'

A stab of shame and intense disappointment constricts Kitty's throat. 'Yes,' she says again.

Esther doesn't say anything more, just lets out a long, tired breath, and soon it becomes the regular breath of sleep.

Kitty stares into the dark, thinking she will never again find the comfort of sleep. Her thoughts are spinning, her body hot and flushed. Something inside has burst, silently but irreversibly, and she can't decide whether the feeling it brings is terrifying or exhilarating. It is both, she decides.

She feels a tickling in her lungs, like trapped moths' wings deep inside, inviting her to cough, and she is glad of the distraction. She takes shallow breaths, resisting the urge to cough for as long as she can, and is eventually carried into sleep.

There is a determined knock at the door. Kitty sits up, her mind webbed with dreams. With the blackout curtain in place it is impossible to guess the time. She climbs out of bed, careful not to disturb Anneliese and Esther, and fumbles her way across to the window. Peeling back the curtain an inch, she can see that the sun has been up for an hour or so. She leaves the curtain open a little to let in

347

a slice of light. Another knock at the door. And another. A thump, as though someone is banging with their fist. Anneliese stirs and opens her eyes.

'Who is it?' Her voice is cracked with sleep.

'I don't know, Anni,' Kitty whispers. 'Best stay where you are. I'll go and see.'

She goes to the door and opens it, but whoever it was has moved on and is now knocking on a door downstairs. She tiptoes across the landing and leans over the banister. A dark-haired woman, barefoot and in a simple white shift, looking like she has just stepped out of Kitty's silken dreams, beams up at her. Her smile is radiant and her eyes more alive with passion than Kitty has seen for the longest time. It is infectious – Kitty can't help but smile in return.

'Hallelujah!' the woman calls, spreading her arms out wide as if to throw Kitty an embrace. 'Hitler is dead!'

ESTHER

It is Esther's first visit to Ohel Moshe Synagogue in months. She isn't sure why she is here, perhaps the promise of the dark interior as she passed, she doesn't know. The service is over; she waits on the street below a low cushion of cloud until the handful of worshipers leave. Then she steps inside. She walks up the steps to the women's gallery and takes a seat on a long wooden bench. The quiet is almost painful. She stares down with vacant, unfocused eyes at the main hall of the synagogue. The ark is set back against the wall on a wooden dais, covered by heavy velvet curtains, like some magician's stage set. The image triggers an odd faraway feeling of tranquillity, but it slips away before she can quite grasp it.

She drops her gaze and notices a tear in the pocket of her dress, at mid-thigh level. But it isn't a tear, it is a cut – a neat slice at the lower edge of the pocket. She slides her hand in and it appears through the hole in the bottom. A razor blade, perhaps. The three dollars she was carrying – she planned to buy Anneliese a small treat – are gone. She has no recollection of any pickpocket, but that is how they are trained. She pulls her hand back up through the hole. Three dollars, three hundred dollars, what does it matter?

It is over two months since the war ended in Europe. A neighbour keeps a tally, cutting a groove in a wooden door beam to mark every day they have spent in this hell since the Nazi surrender. When Esther left the house this morning, she counted seventy grooves.

It's seven months since she walked down that dark lane, away from the man she thought she knew, the man she thought she loved. It seems so long ago, and yet she doubts there will ever be enough time to reconcile the love she once felt for him with what she feels now. But what does she feel? It should be hatred, perhaps, or at least abhorrence, but where there should be a feeling there is merely a dull, hollow ache. She closes her eyes. She doesn't normally allow her thoughts to linger like this, to float towards Aaron... With practised ease, she pushes the thoughts away before they become fully formed.

Perhaps it isn't cool and quiet in here at all. She can't feel anything. But if the coolness and quietness are in her imaginings, then that doesn't matter either. It's gone. Whatever faith she might once have had has gone, washed away in the filthy gutters of her time here. This is what he has taken from her, and she doesn't know if she will ever get it back. She tugs at a thread in the fabric that has already begun to fray around the cut in her pocket.

A woman's voice behind her: 'Don't pull on it, dear. It'll end up unravelling.'

Esther turns her head.

An elderly woman sitting behind her, wearing a dark green scarf to cover her hair, is leaning forward to the row where Esther sits. 'Best to stitch it up as soon as you get home,' she says in a hushed voice.

Esther doesn't respond.

'Goodness me, you're bleeding!' the woman says and comes around the back of the bench to sit beside Esther. 'Let me see.'

Esther can only give the woman a puzzled look as she slides the dress up her leg. Indeed, there is a long, thin cut on her thigh. The bleeding isn't strong; the cut has already begun to congeal, leaving only a smear of reddish-brown on the white skin. Esther stares down at her leg and doesn't recognise it. Surely it is somebody else's skin.

'What happened?' the woman asks, and doesn't wait for an answer to fish a handkerchief from her bag and press it down on Esther's thigh. 'Tell me if it hurts,' she says.

'No,' Esther hears herself whisper, 'it doesn't hurt. Nothing does.'

She steps out onto the street and blinks, startled, as though she has been woken from the deepest sleep; immediately, the smoke and smell make her gag. There is a roar of noise around her, the sound of crashing and screaming and groaning. She must have been so absorbed in the gloom of the synagogue that she didn't hear the siren. She starts running, looking for shelter. The bombers seem to be close, closer than ever before.

She darts from doorway to doorway, pushing against the people crowding up against the buildings. For a moment, she loses her orientation, can't make out any street signs or landmarks through the noise and smoke and floating debris. Then across the street, she spots the sign for Tobias' Wigmaker, which means she is on Kwenming Road, only a hundred metres or so from the market on Chusan Road. The adjacent building is covered in steel scaffolding; the owner must be either hopelessly naïve or impossibly hopeful.

The siren slices the air, elevating her pulse and causing the sweat on her skin to turn to ice. Anneliese is bound to be safe at school, she tells herself, but she has never felt so desperate to hold her. The school is only a fifteen-minute walk away, ten minutes at a run – if she can only get away from the noise and smoke.

Another ear-splitting blast, this time somewhere to her left. The ground shakes; the people crowded in the doorway behind her gasp and groan and scream. She thinks she makes a sound herself, but she isn't sure. The siren is replaced by a loud ringing in her ear.

Then, for a moment, silence. She looks left, right, and makes a dash across the street, her lungs smarting with every breath. She passes an upturned rickshaw, its coolie long since fled, one wheel facing the sky and still spinning. The rickshaw has come to rest on some sacks, of rice perhaps, and she is thinking of the waste of all that food when the sack moves and she sees that it is not a sack, but a man. His leg is trapped beneath the rickshaw and he is bleeding. His face is white with dust, and she doesn't recognise him at first, but he pulls his lips back from his teeth in pain and –

'Get out of the road!' someone shouts. 'They're not done yet!'

There is a strange wailing sound from above, and she lunges towards Franz Hohlbein, tugs at him, pushes against the rickshaw with all her weight and lands heavily, almost comically, on her bottom as she pulls him free,

hen they crawl along the ground towards the nearest
hopfront, across stones and dirt and broken glass, and
omeone steps forward and drags Hohlbein to safety and
omeone else holds out a hand towards her.

A thunderous blast close by and she is thrown forward,
ands with a thud on some straw matting and only then
eels the screeching pain in her left hand as she looks down
o see it crushed beneath a steel girder.

周翼

'That's it for today.' Helene Stern wipes her face with a handkerchief. 'It's just too hot for this sort of work.'

She looks at the dozen large containers with boiled water they have just carried up the stairs to the surgery, a chore they undertake once a week to ensure clean water for drinking, washing and cleaning various cuts and scrapes the patients come in with. It is a two-person job, and Yì would normally do it with Stern *yīshēng*, but the doctor has been suffering with inflamed joints that rule out any heavy lifting.

Frau Stern is surprisingly strong for a woman of her age, he thinks, and yet from her strained expression, he wonders how much of that strength she has left in her.

She lays her head to one side. 'And besides, a little bird told me it's your birthday today.'

Yì smiles, although he doesn't grasp her meaning. His English has improved considerably over the past eighteen months, but he doesn't think he will ever fully understand all the strange expressions. Birds, speaking?

Frau Stern reads his face. 'It's a saying, dear. But never mind that. It's your birthday today – you're nineteen, is that right?'

He nods, still smiling.

'Well, then you shall have the rest of the day off.'

'Many thanks, Frau Stern.' He gives her a little bow.

'Don't mention it, Yì. And if you come with me' – she leads him towards Stern *yīshēng*'s office – 'I think my husband has something for you.'

Yì follows, letting his face relax. He has barely acknowledged his birthday since his *nǎinai* died, and even then, the height of the celebration was a bowl of wheat noodles she would cook him in their dingy room, careful to retain the length of each noodle to ensure him a long life.

'Victor?' Frau Stern says as they enter the doctor's office. 'Here's the birthday boy.' She winks at Yì and leaves the room again.

Stern *yīshēng* gets up slowly from behind his desk and nods, his smile causing the deep creases around his eyes to curve downward around the side of his face. He holds out his hand and takes Yì's, shaking it firmly. Yì catches the faint whiff of antiseptic and leather, two smells he always associates with the doctor.

'Happy birthday,' he says, and moves back to his desk. 'Now, I have a little something here for you.'

Yì follows with his eyes as Stern *yīshēng* reaches into a drawer and pulls out a small blue box. He hands it to Yì and watches eagerly as he opens it. Inside is a metal watch with a leather strap.

Yì's eyes widen in dismay. 'I cannot accept,' he says, his smile beginning to falter.

Stern *yīshēng* shakes his head. 'I insist, my friend. To

be honest, it is not of much value; in fact, I've assembled it from pieces. You see, here?' He points to the hands o the watch. 'They don't match. But my father was a watch maker, and although I've none of his craftsmanship, I do recall the basic mechanics.'

'*Sòng zhōng*,' Yì whispers.

'Pardon?'

Yì shakes his head and forces the smile back to his lips 'I ... no words ...' He trails off. He is horrified. Gifting a timepiece is equivalent to bestowing a curse. But how are they to know? They are *lǎowài*, foreigners, after all.

Misinterpreting Yì's expression, Stern *yīshēng* continues with a smile. 'You must just remember to wind it every day and it should last for a good long time. Here, I'll show you.' He takes the watch out of the box and with his thumb and forefinger, turns the little metal knob on the side. The slim second hand begins to move, tick tick ticking. It is all Yì can do not to cover his ears.

Stern *yīshēng* hands him the cursed watch. 'Now, off you go – enjoy the rest of your day.'

Yì makes his way slowly through the streets, beneath a low, pressing sky. The watch, still in its box, lies heavy in his pocket. It is impossible, but he could swear he hears it ticking, ticking away his life years. Huà would chide him for his superstition; even worse, he would laugh at him. But his beliefs cannot merely be shed like a jacket on this hot, sticky day – and after all, hasn't he seen for himself how a baby is born with a deformity after its pregnant mother kicked a dog on the street? And did he not find Mamselle Kitty that night after seeing the bats – *biānfú* – hanging from a beam in the factory?

And yet – it was not Stern *yīshēng*'s intention to curse him. He was ignorant, yes, but acting out of kindness. Surely this should cancel out the bad omen? Yì is so deep in thought that he doesn't see the Japanese checkpoint until it is too late, and he is being shoved up against the wall and ordered to place his palms flat against the bricks. In addition to the bombs falling from the sky, a number of communist bombs – Huà's bombs, he can't help but think – have exploded across the city in recent days, and the Japanese are increasingly nervous, stopping people at random on the street, raiding teahouses and even temples on suspicion of clandestine meetings. Yì is patted down roughly from behind, feels the coarse brickwork beneath his hands, knowing that if the soldier finds the watch in his pocket, he will likely face a beating, or worse, will be dragged to Bridge House Gaol and left there to rot. His sweat freezes on his skin, but then he hears a sharp sudden cry and a whistle, and the soldier turns and begins running down the pavement to where his fellow soldiers are struggling to arrest a large man with a wheelbarrow.

The tension pours off Yì. He leans back against the building to savour the relief and calm his shaky breath, then looks up to see that he is standing in front of house number eighty-eight. A sign! It is the luckiest of numbers. The watch is not a curse, after all, he tells himself. But just to be safe, he decides he will leave some money on Stern *yīshēng*'s desk tomorrow to counteract any bad luck that remains. If the watch is paid for, rather than given – *sòng* – then it is nothing more than a business transaction. And he will prepare some longevity noodles when Huà comes to eat later. His brother is always there for his birthday. Yì has time to go to the market, buy the noodles and perhaps even find some lucky bamboo. He is feeling reassured, buoyant even, when he turns onto Chusan Road.

Despite the rationing and the scant range of food on offer, Chusan Road is heaving with colour and sound. Foreigners and Chinese stand side by side at their stalls; the locals touting their wares in a mix of loud, tongue-twisting German and sing-song Shanghainese. The foreign vendors are more restrained, engaging potential customers in polite conversation as soon as they show interest in what they are hoping to sell. But what the vendors, Chinese and foreign, have in common is that they are as creative as ever, selling hanging charms made of shells and slivers of metal, padded jackets with rat-fur collars, fans fashioned from old newspaper.

Yì makes his way through the throng, keeping an eye out for any charms that strike him as particularly lucky. Ahead of him on the street, a little girl, no more than five years old, runs behind a wooden cart loaded with six large sacks of rice. The street is, as always, congested, and the girl has no problem keeping up, her small frame well hidden behind the cart. Further ahead, traffic has come to a standstill, where a dead water buffalo covered in thick black flies lies blocking the road. Two men, sweating and grunting, are dragging the bloated carcass to the side. Amid the shouting and cursing and honking of horns, the girl uses the opportunity to creep up to the back of the cart, and with the flash of a knife, cuts a slit in two of the sacks. When the road is clear again, the cart moves on, spilling a trail of hundreds of rice kernels. Quickly and efficiently, the girl sweeps them up with a small besom and scoops them into her pockets. It is a trick Yì has used himself before. At home, the girl's mother will pick the rice clean of dirt, nails, broken glass, before using it to make a meagre soup, or perhaps even sell it on to those who can afford nothing better than stolen, filthy rice.

'Wing!'

The voice rings out over the noise. He turns, recognising the voice, and sees Mamselle Kitty standing on the opposite side of the street. She is wearing a frayed, jade-green dress and carries a basket in the crook of her arm. He raises his hand and waves to her, beaming. Encountering her here, on this day, is surely the best possible omen! She smiles and shouts something to him, but her words are drowned out in a sudden buzzing sound coming from above.

He looks up to the sky, but the thick cushion of clouds blocks the view of the aeroplanes. They are heading west – a dozen of them at least, from the sound of it. But the droning seems closer than usual, and Yì thinks he can see a suck of movement in the clouds. Seconds later, the high-pitched wail of the air-raid siren sounds. Stray dogs begin a chorus of howls, and the familiar noise of anti-aircraft guns peppers the air. A few people in the marketplace glance up nervously, but most others carry on with their business of unloading and weighing and bartering, straining to raise their voices above the din until the entire square is one obliterating mass of noise.

Yì looks back to where Mamselle is standing. She raises her eyes to the sky, shrugs and takes a step towards him.

Then it happens. A flash of light, followed seconds later by an enormous crashing noise, and an invisible sucking force that seems to pull and push him in all directions at once; a force so strong he fears it will rip his limbs from his body. Then a pressure from behind that propels him forward onto the street. He lands on his back, smoke and noise all around. There is a second blast, a little further away, and the ground shudders.

Above him, he sees flares shooting up towards the heavens in red and green, as spectacular as fireworks. Ears ringing, he tries to sit up, but finds he cannot move. And then, the pressure on his back unfolds into a pain so excruciating he cannot breathe. He clutches his chest; his hand comes into contact with something hard, something hot, a piece of hot metal sticking through him. He turns his head – the pain roars through his body – and sees mountains of rubble, shattered glass, wooden market stalls that have been tossed into the air and thrown back to the ground in splinters. He sees the girl who followed the cart lying a short distance away, sees the grains of rice scattered all around her, no longer white, but red, like tiny crimson pearls.

Tiredness washes over him, draws him close. He shuts his eyes and no longer feels the metal in his spine. The ticking of the watch in his pocket fills his ears. Time spills in all directions. He is hot, then cold, painfully cold. He must have drifted off into the tiredness, because he wakes suddenly, with Mamselle Kitty crouching over him, screaming, her voice coming at him in waves:

'Don't you dare die! Don't you dare!'

Her face is blotchy and tear-stained, her hair is caked with soot and there is snot streaming out of her nose, but she still looks pretty – so, so pretty. If only he could speak! Then he would tell her that they didn't know, didn't know about the curse; he would tell her about the number eighty-eight, the longevity noodles, the lucky bamboo; he would tell her how he loves her, how he has never loved anyone as he loves her.

But the words don't come. So instead, he attempts a smile, and the sounds drop away, first Mamselle's voice, then the shouts and sirens and screams and wailing and barking and the ticking of the watch, and he is surrounded by the loudest silence he has ever heard.

His vision goes . . .

replaced by a pure, all-encompassing whiteness . . .

and for a moment, he wonders why the foreigners wear black when they are in mourning . . .

Because surely everyone knows – he himself can see it right now, right here in the place of his ancestors – that death is white.

KITTY

———

They step outside into the white heat of the sun and Kitty bends down to adjust Anneliese's headscarf. Apart from Anni's hair, which is the colour of spun gold, the girl is beginning to resemble her mother more each day: the same soft jawline, the intelligent dark eyes, the strong set of her mouth. In two months' time, she will turn nine years old.

They make their way down Kung Ping Road. Kitty is conscious of the prickle of heat beneath her breasts and on the small of her back, but she has long since stopped being concerned about perspiration marks. The sun-baked streets are cracked and dusty; a few bare-footed children sit in the shade of a bamboo awning on the building opposite, tossing pebbles into a stream of waste that snakes along the ground towards the creek. Kitty grabs Anneliese's hand, just in case she has any ideas about joining them. They may be able to wander the city freely now, but the conditions are as primitive and unhygienic as ever.

For two days after the Japanese left, the silence that

closed over Hongkew was ghostly; the streets swept clean of people, as though nobody quite trusted the news, nobody willing to be the first to test the new freedom for fear of cursing it. But then, when hoarded supplies dwindled and children became restless and the sick and dying desperately needed medical care, a handful of daring refugees came out and began dismantling the signs demarcating the ghetto boundaries. Nothing happened. No soldiers, no police, no *baojia* came to arrest them. It was what everyone had been waiting for, holding their collective breaths, and suddenly, this derelict, rat-infested, stinking ghetto was a party, a mass outpouring of relief and joy; and incredulity, that too – that they had lived through hell and survived.

Though, of course, they hadn't all survived. Wing's face, his smile as he lay dying, haunts Kitty still. A part of her will always feel responsible for his death. If she hadn't attracted his attention in the marketplace, if she hadn't called out, if she hadn't taken that step towards him . . . But it is more than that. She was aware of his quiet, fervent love for her, and in her vanity and selfishness she accepted it without giving anything in return. Her regret at never telling him what he meant to her is as sharp and raw as her grief. She knows it is a silly notion, but she couldn't bear to wear the White Tara after he died. All these years, and she never did discover its origin, or for whom Wing had intended it. She'd just never returned it.

On the day of Wing's burial, she gave the pendant to Anneliese, in the hope the girl would cherish it in her stead.

'Come on,' she says now, gently tugging Anneliese's hand. 'You'll be late for school.'

'Can we go for dumplings later?' Anneliese asks as they head down the lane.

'Of course.'

'And ice cream?'

'I'll have to ask your mama first.'

'That means no.'

'It means, I'll have to ask her first.'

Anni lets go of Kitty's hand and stops short. 'Mama's a liar,' she says calmly.

'Don't say that about your mother!' Kitty says, taken aback. 'Now come on – we have to hurry now.'

Anneliese's dark eyes rest on hers for a moment, her fingers twirling the White Tara around her neck, then she shrugs and continues down the lane.

On every street, they pass mountains of rubble and bombed-out buildings, providing the perfect habitat for rats, and precarious playgrounds for children. Given half a chance, Kitty knows, Anneliese would be among them, playing hide-and-seek in the cracks and crevices. She quickens her pace, tugging a reluctant Anneliese behind her.

They turn onto East Yuhang Road and into the crush and clamour of cars battling rickshaws battling bicycles battling pedestrians. Kitty grips Anneliese's hand in hers, although her palms are sweaty. The city has sprung back to life, carnival-like, and at the heart of it all, the Americans. Tall, young, healthy GIs everywhere, whistling at Chinese girls in tight satin dresses, shouting and whooping as they race rickshaws with bewildered coolies on the back seat, holding on for dear life. Anneliese slips her hand from Kitty's and begins jumping up and down, clapping her hands.

For some, like Anneliese, the men's high spirits are exotic and infectious; for others, they are a reminder that the whole world has been at war, and that nobody knows what is to come. Over the past weeks, information has been seeping in, patchy and uncertain despite the free use once again of shortwave radios and uncensored news articles. Tales of a new, devastating kind of bomb. Of half of Germany reduced to rubble. And whispers of death camps, stories of gas chambers and piles of skeletons and living cadavers, too horrifying to be true.

Esther has gone to check the lists of registered survivors of these camps, which have been posted on Seward Road. Kitty offered to take Anni to school. She doesn't want to know about ghosts from the past.

She steps onto the road, her dress clinging to her body. They have to hurry now, or Anneliese really will be late for school.

'Kitty!'

Anneliese grabs her arm and pulls her backward, hard, as a car speeds past, missing her only by an inch.

'Aunt Kitty! You have to look before you cross the road!' she shouts, sounding suddenly much older than her eight years.

Kitty nods. 'Yes. I'm sorry,' she says, feeling flushed and shaky. They hurry on to school; at the gate, Kitty gives her a hug goodbye.

'Your mama and I will be here to pick you up at four,' she says. 'Then we'll go for ice cream. And that's a promise.'

ESTHER

The lists are fixed to a board on the side of a building; thirty sheets of paper at least, the names typed up in dense black letters. Dozens of people crowd in front of the board, some craning their necks, studying the lists in fervent concentration; others with their eyes down, as though afraid of what they might see. Or not see. It is eerily quiet.

Esther's left hand throbs, the skin itching inside the cast as though covered in thousands of fire ants. Nailed to the blackish brick wall above the lists is a faded billboard, in German, offering repair services for bicycles and sewing machines. Esther drops her gaze. She wonders if Aaron has been to check the lists, but then she remembers that his only relative, Sara, managed to escape to London years ago. She hasn't seen him since the night she left. For months, she feared she would run into him and have to face her sorrow all over again. But she never has. Perhaps he eventually had final dealings with the wrong people; perhaps he got away altogether.

At the front of the crowd, an elderly woman in a patchy cotton dress with damp semicircles under the arms lets out a moan and faints, slumping into the man beside her and almost knocking him down too. Esther pushes forward through the crowd, holding her left arm close to her chest. People make way only reluctantly, anxious of losing their place at the board.

'I work in a doctor's office,' she says with as much authority as she can summon and kneels down beside the woman. She feels for her pulse – it is discernible, though weak – and wonders what to do next, feeling somewhat foolish now under the heavy, expectant gazes of the onlookers.

'It's all right,' a voice says at her shoulder. 'I work in a doctor's office too.'

Esther turns her head. 'Victor!'

'I came to see if . . .' He holds two fingers to the woman's neck and looks up at Esther. 'My brother, he survived.' His voice is clogged with emotion.

The woman lets out another small moan. Victor gently slaps her cheek.

'It's the heat. And perhaps the shock. She needs water, and some air.'

He stands and spreads his arms wide to clear a space. Someone hands him a bottle of water and he pours a little into his hand, moistening the woman's lips with his fingers. The woman opens her eyes, blinks rapidly, and lets Victor and Esther help her up. She is slightly unsteady but manages to stay on her feet. She turns to Esther, her eyes resting briefly on the cast.

'My cousins,' she says in an urgent voice, a white fleck of spittle forming in the corner of her mouth. 'They are alive! Here, look –' She takes Esther's good hand and pulls her towards the board. 'Luzie, Fanny and Helmuth.' She points at their names. 'They are alive.' She breaks down in streams of hot tears.

A man steps out from the crowd and guides her away, still sobbing, but Esther's attention is on the list, now.

Baeck, Leo
Baer, Kurt
Bamberger, Israel
Bamberger, Johanna
Bamberger, Klara
Bardach, Lisbeth

The smudgy letters swim and dance in front of her eyes, her mind struggles to recall the alphabet. But there, there it is –

Barsch, Albert
Barsch, Alice Gertrude
Bernstein, Johanna
Bernstein, Peter

No. She scans the list again. *Barsch, Albert; Barsch, Alice Gertrude.* This should be followed by *Barsch, Leah* and *Barsch, Sigmund.* Her mouth is dry; her eyes burn. She is barely aware of the shoving from behind, the elbows in her back, the trickle of sweat down her temple.

'Esther.'

She blinks and starts from the top.

Adler, Siegfried
Arndt, Julius
Arnheim, Erna
Apt, Ida
Apt, Martin
Asch, . . .

'Esther!'

Victor is standing beside her. He touches her elbow. 'You should sit down,' he says. 'We don't want you fainting as well.'

No, she wants to say, *no, I have to find them – their names must be here somewhere*, but her thoughts can't connect with her words. Her tongue is thick in her mouth; the sounds around her are muffled. Victor stands to face her and puts his hands on her shoulders.

'I don't ... I can't bear it, Victor, I can't bear it!' It comes out in a rush.

'Hush, Esther,' he says. 'They haven't identified all of the survivors yet. It's early days. There will be more lists.' He leans in and touches his brow to hers. His breath is warm and sour. 'Don't give up hope, not yet.'

Anneliese comes running out of the school gate towards Esther and Kitty, beaming. 'We didn't learn *anything* at school today!' she says breathlessly. Her face is pink and shiny. 'We had another party!'

Esther places a kiss on her hair. '*Another* party?'

'Yes, and they gave us these!' She swings her satchel from behind her back and opens it. 'Colouring books, and crayons, and ...' She rummages around in the satchel and pulls out a small red-white-and-blue package. 'Bubblegum!'

'Did they give you any Coca-Cola?' Kitty says. 'I swear, it's so sweet it makes my teeth ache.'

Anneliese wrinkles her nose disappointedly. 'No. They ran out before they got to my class.'

They walk home slowly, the humidity too pressing to warrant quick movement, although it does little to inhibit

Anneliese's non-stop chatter. Esther listens, distracted, to her reports of who said what to whom in the schoolyard, how their teacher Mrs Arndt made Jakob stand with his face to the wall for being cheeky, which books they would be reading this school year.

Anneliese stops talking abruptly, mid-sentence, as a khaki military vehicle drives past, carefully negotiating the rubble that still litters the road. She tugs Esther's waistband.

'Look, Mama! Those are the men I told you about. The men in peeps.'

Esther frowns, but Kitty starts laughing. 'You mean *jeeps*.'

'Yes, jeeps. The men are nice. They give sweets to the children if you wave at them.'

As if on command, another jeep turns the corner, bumping along the cratered street, sending up plumes of dust in its wake.

Anneliese jumps up and down excitedly. 'Can I, Mama? Please?'

Esther sighs, but Kitty elbows her gently in the ribs. 'Go on.'

'Very well.'

Anneliese grins and begins to wave, both arms stretched above her head, at the two men sitting in the jeep as it heads in their direction. The vehicle slows to a crawl and one of the men reaches into the back. He tosses several wrapped bars towards Anneliese, flashing a smile – broad, with white, impossibly straight teeth – and shouts something to her. It is English, as far as Esther can tell, but in such a strange accent she can't make out what. Anneliese whoops in delight and begins to gather up the candy bars that lie on the pavement. The soldier addresses Kitty; holds out nylon stockings, but she shakes her head and turns her back to him.

'Come on,' she says to Anneliese. 'Let's get home quickly, before the chocolate starts to melt.'

They cross the road and head home. Anneliese skips ahead, around the corner and into their lane, her precious candy drawn up in the bundle of her skirt. A moment later, however, she is running back to Esther and Kitty, her brow creased into a frown.

'What it is, *liebling*?' Esther asks.

'Mama, there's a funny-looking man sitting on our step.'

They hurry around the corner, and indeed, there is a man, tall and very thin, sitting on the step to their building, holding his head in his hands. When he hears them approaching, he gets to his feet and stares at them. Even from a distance, Esther can see that his skin is severely sunburned, patches of cracked, shiny red covering his cheeks and nose. Instinctively, she takes Anneliese by the hand and draws her close. Beside her, Kitty lets out a queer mewing sound. Her expression is one of utter horror.

'Kitty?' Esther murmurs, feeling a panic rise inside her. 'Are you all right? Do you know that man?'

But Kitty just lets out a howl and bursts into tears. The man starts to move towards them; he has a limp and walks with slow, jerky movements.

'Anni,' Esther says to her daughter, trying to keep the anxiety out of her voice, 'run up to the main road and see if there are any policemen around. Now. Hurry!'

But just as Anneliese scoots off, Kitty takes a step towards the man.

'It's you,' she whispers. 'Timothy, where have you been?'

July 2014

ANNELIESE

The two suitcases lay, half packed, at the foot of the beds. Hard shell ones with four wheels on the base; so much more practical than the suitcases Anneliese used when she still travelled. The children had just climbed into bed and were busy arranging their sheets and blankets and pillows and stuffed animals. Their two-week visit was nearly over; this time tomorrow, the house would be almost completely silent again.

Anneliese sat in the comfy chair with its wooden arms, sipping a cup of green tea, and waited for them to settle before speaking.

'It must have been October. October 1945.' She smiled. 'That was a very long time ago, long before your mummy was even born. The rainy season came late that year and the stretches of wasteland outside the city were dried and cracked. I think my mother had been concerned about keeping me cooped up in a train carriage for hours – I was like a jumping bean when I was a child, can you imagine? – but she needn't have worried. I was entranced by all that I saw unfolding outside the window as the train sped along – vast expanses that stretched out further than I would have dreamed possible. I kept my face pressed against the glass, mesmerised by the horizon, moving only to rub away the fogginess caused by my breath.'

The door opened and Miriam entered, carrying a neat pile of the children's clothes. She gave her mother an enquiring look.

Anneliese shifted in her chair. 'They asked me,' she said, nodding at Joel and Bekka, who were now lying propped up in their beds.

'The old stories?' Miriam said. 'Again?'

Nine-year-old Bekka frowned. 'Shush, Mummy. Nana's just started.'

'But you've heard them all before!'

Anneliese plucked a tissue from her sleeve and wiped her nose. 'Ah, but still you don't know how it ended.'

Joel sat up. 'See, Mummy? We don't know how the story ends.'

Miriam sighed and kneeled down in front of the open suitcases. 'Well, if you'd rather this than a storybook . . . but then it's lights out, okay? We're leaving first thing.'

'Okay,' Bekka replied. 'Go on, Nana.'

Anneliese waited a moment before continuing. 'We were on our way to the mountain resort of Moganshan, a hundred and fifty kilometres southwest of Shanghai. It was to be my first ever holiday, and I was so excited I felt almost sick. Aunt Kitty and Uncle Timothy were with us – they hadn't been on holiday for many years, either. You remember how I told you about Kitty and Timothy?'

The children nodded, wrapped in their cocoons of blankets.

'Are they our aunt and uncle, too?' Joel asked.

'No, but they weren't my real aunt and uncle either, in truth. And they both died a long time ago now.'

Bekka yawned. 'Don't say that, Nana. I think they sound very nice.'

'Yes, they were. I loved them very much. I think my mother did too.' Anneliese paused for a moment. Then: 'Where was I?'

'You were on your holidays,' Bekka offered. 'Like we've been here.'

'Oh yes. Aunt Kitty, I remember, was wearing a beautiful green dress, and her hair was decorated with small white flowers. That morning, she had styled my hair into two plaited loops – "monkey swings", she called them – with flowers to match hers. She loved hairdressing, always. The grips that kept my plaits in place made my head itch, and my mother had made me wear white gloves to stop me from scratching.'

'That hair sounds weird,' Bekka said. 'But did you look pretty?'

'I think so. Not as pretty as you, though.' She smiled at her granddaughter with her shock of curls and then noticed six-year-old Joel's scowl. 'Or as handsome as you,' she added and was rewarded with a gap-toothed grin.

'Anyway, on the train, my mother sat opposite me. We didn't care how worn out the wooden benches were – they made your bum sore. Still, she looked happy, and like me, spent most of the journey staring out of the window. Her left hand was fresh out of the cast and lay on her lap. It was all pale and wrinkled. She'd recently broken her arm, you see. I don't know if it still hurt her, but if it did, she didn't show it. She was tough, your great-grandma. She'd had the cast on for ages, but even so the fractures didn't heal perfectly. Her fingers were always a little crooked, and her nails, when they grew back, were bumpy and ridged. Just like the shells we found at the beach this morning.'

Joel wrinkled his nose. 'Is that true, Mum?'

Miriam was folding a pair of socks into a ball. 'Yes, my nana's nails were all bumpy,' she said. She stuffed the socks into the suitcase, then sat back to listen too.

'She and Aunt Kitty hardly spoke during the journey,' Anneliese said. 'And Uncle Timothy, who sat beside Aunt Kitty with his bad leg stretched out towards the open carriage door, kept his eyes fixed on his book, dozing off every now and then to wake with a jump when the train rattled on its tracks. He wore a creased linen suit – beige, perhaps, or light grey, I can't remember – and gloves to protect his skin from the sun. He'd been in a . . . in a camp, you see. Even months after his release, the skin on his face was all cracked and shiny. We kept the carriage door open for him because he couldn't bear closed doors, Aunt Kitty had explained, although I didn't really understand at the time. I'll admit that, just sometimes, I was tempted to get him in a room and close the door with a bang, just to see what happened. I never did, though. Thank goodness. I'd still be ashamed of myself if I had –'

'Mum,' Miriam interjected, giving her a stern look. 'They're only little.'

This was met with indignant noises from the children. Miriam threw them a look, too, and they fell into silence.

'Very well,' Anneliese said, and continued. 'As I said, it was a long journey through the wasteland, but at last it gave way to rice fields, then to pine trees dotted here and there, and finally a dense green forest. The journey must have taken only a few hours, but to me, then, it seemed like a lifetime. At the station, we took a taxi to the foot of the mountain, where there was a crowd of sedan carriers. The upward climb took maybe two hours, during which I hopped on and off my sedan several times, until my mother told me off and said I must stay seated.'

'What's a sedan?' Joel asked.

'It's a chair you sit on and servants carry you around,' Bekka said proudly. 'Like you're a queen in the olden days.'

Joel's eyes lit up. 'Can we get a sedan, Mummy?'

'No.'

'Aww, unfair!'

'It's unfair to expect people to carry you around when –'

Anneliese cut them off. 'I thought you wanted to hear the story!' she said. 'I'll never finish if you keep interrupting.'

She waited a few moments. These were her stories of course, weaved from her own memories and the strands she'd picked up from her mother, Kitty, Timothy – and others – over the years. Was it right to pass them on to her grandchildren as bedtime stories, fairy tales almost? She looked over at Bekka, who was curling a springy lock of hair around her finger. Nine years old and headstrong as anything. One day soon, the children would be old enough to hear the darker stories – the ones her mother only ever touched on – of rats and typhoid, dead babies wrapped in straw mats, sunken eyes in gaunt faces, unspeakable sacrifices and betrayals made in order to survive. Horrific stories the children needed to hear – if not from her, then from their mother. But this story would do, for now. She lifted her fingers to her throat in an unconscious gesture and twined them around the small pendant she wore around her neck.

She continued: 'The lodge we were staying in was set among shady bamboo groves, and every so often, when my mother and I went for walks, we would come across a small hut called a pagoda, where we would rest and eat a picnic. The lodge wasn't what you'd be used to on holiday – bamboo-frame beds, no electric light, sliding paper blinds at the windows – but for me, it was pure heaven. The grown-ups spent most of the time talking – Aunt Kitty and my mother in German, and in English when they were with Uncle Timothy. Most of the conversation I didn't understand or was of no interest to me, so I concentrated on perfecting my cartwheeling technique. I remember my record was six cartwheels in a row. Can you beat that?'

She looked at Bekka, who returned her smile.

'The grown-ups talked about the people my mother had been working for in Shanghai, the Sterns. I can't remember much about them now, other than that they seemed very old to me. In truth, they were probably a fair bit younger than I am now. But what I do remember like it was only yesterday is joining my mother to say goodbye to them at the pier. A huge steamer, the *Captain Marcos*, had docked near the Bund to take refugees to Germany. There weren't many who wanted to return there; most, like us, were waiting for entry visas to places where a new beginning seemed possible – America, Australia, England. I'd heard that several hundred people had already left for Palestine.

'We went in a taxi with Herr and Frau Stern to the dock. My mother and Frau Stern were both in tears the whole way there, promising they would write to each other and send photographs. When we arrived, a large group of people had already assembled at the quayside. I thought they were there like us, to wave farewell to their friends, but as it turned out, they were anything but. After a long, tearful goodbye, during which I was squeezed and stroked and petted by Frau Stern until I became quite cross, the passengers were called to board the ship. As the Sterns began to walk up the steps, a commotion broke out among the crowd, and stones were thrown at the passengers. People called out terrible things, curses and shouts of "Traitors" and "Fascist pigs", "Quislings".'

'What's that?' Joel asked.

'Never mind,' Anneliese said, shaking her head. 'Horrid names, nothing the Sterns deserved after all they'd done for everybody. I saw Herr Stern step in front of his wife to protect her and he was hit by a stone. He stumbled back, his face white as a sheet, and a stream of blood trickled down his cheek. His wife took his elbow and they hurried up and into the ship. It upset me beyond measure that I never got a chance to wave goodbye.'

She stopped when she felt a hand on her knee. Miriam was kneeling close to her chair.

'You all right, Mum?'

'Yes, of course. It was all so long ago now.'

'I can read them a story if you like, if you –'

'No. I'd like to finish this one.'

Miriam gave her knee a gentle squeeze and returned to the packing.

'I don't know how long we stayed in Moganshan, two or three days, a week perhaps; my memories have become hazy over time. But the final afternoon is as crisp as a new photo. We took a short walk from the guesthouse – Uncle Timothy couldn't manage long distances – to a ridge, looking out over a valley with a lush pine forest. The sun was pale and large, casting all these soft orange colours onto low-floating clouds. The air was impossibly clean and sharp – I remember noticing that after Shanghai. My mother and Aunt Kitty sat on the grass and chatted about this and that; probably about the visas my mother had applied for. I was desperate to go to America, land of popcorn and bubble gum and Coca-Cola. My mother didn't mind where we went, as long as it was far away.'

She looked over at Bekka and Joel; they were both lying down now, blankets tucked up to their chins. Miriam closed the suitcases. She gave each of the children a kiss on the forehead and switched the main light off. The night-lights on the children's bedside tables gave out a warm orange glow.

'Don't be too long,' she said to Anneliese. 'The taxi will be here at six thirty in the morning.'

Anneliese gave her a small shake of the head. 'I won't tire them out, promise.'

If anything, she thought, their visit had tired *her* out – two weeks of children whooping, running and tumbling about the house. Their visits always left her and David exhausted, and the little house in disarray, but she wouldn't miss them for the world.

A small voice roused her from her thoughts. 'Nana?'

She swallowed. 'Sorry. Yes, yes, the final afternoon in Moganshan. What a lovely day we had! But the grown-ups were busy talking, so I went on the hunt for butterflies, huge velvety creatures that beat their wings so slowly and elegantly and yet managed to evade my sticky hands. I pleaded with Timothy, but he wouldn't join me in my game. I knew his leg was poorly, although I couldn't understand why he didn't just bend it. He still had a knee, didn't he?

'"It's not that simple," Aunt Kitty told me. "But they should be able to fix it in England." And then she gave me a smile that didn't quite reach her eyes. *England*. She said it in German – "eng" means tight, or narrow. Narrow-land. I wasn't sure I liked the sound of it. Even my vivid imagination could hardly fathom a place as tight, or dense, or narrow as Shanghai.'

'I think your holiday sounds exciting,' Bekka said. 'But really different to our holidays here.'

Anneliese breathed out shakily. 'Yes, I suppose it was exciting. For me, at least . . . So I did some more cartwheels until I could cartwheel no more. There were clusters of little star-shaped flowers growing in the grass at my feet and I bent down to smell them. But they had no smell at all, so instead, I plucked a long blade of stiff grass and tried to blow on it between my thumbs.'

She closed her eyes but found she was unable to conjure up the feel of the cool, sweet-smelling air on her face, and was struck by a regret that she had never, in all these years, thought of returning to Moganshan for a visit. The regret was so unexpected, so acute, it almost brought her to tears. She had to take several deep, trembling breaths before she could go on.

'Don't cry, Nana,' said Joel in his sweet, sensitive way. 'It's okay.'

'I know, sweetheart,' Anneliese said. 'Now then . . .' She swallowed. 'A stillness rose around us as the sun began to set. In the valley below was a forest, so dense the pine trees looked almost black. Closer by, there was a copse of trees, but their leaves had dropped away to leave skeletal branches stretched upwards. Birdsong floated our way on a crisp breeze, and ...'

'Mum, they're asleep.'

'What?' Anneliese blinked. A yellow shaft of light from the hallway fell into the room.

'The kids. Out for the count.' Miriam's voice was so low she could barely hear her.

'Oh.' She shifted her weight to the left and felt a disconcerting twinge in her hip. She winced.

Miriam frowned. 'Everything all right?'

'Fine. Where's your dad got to?'

'He took the dog out, but he should be back shortly. I'll put the kettle on, shall I?'

Anneliese nodded and realised she was drooling slightly. She wiped the corner of her mouth with a tissue. God, what an old woman she had become.

'Give me a minute,' she said. 'I'm not so quick to my feet any more.'

Miriam gave her a soft, dry kiss on the cheek and left the room, pulling the door to behind her.

After a long moment, Anneliese continued, a whisper into the darkness:

'And this, in my memory, is how it ended: naked trees clawing the bruised sky; yellow, star-shaped petals at my feet; and my mother and Aunt Kitty watching the pink quivering orb of the sun, suspended for the longest moment before it dropped abruptly behind the mountains.'

AUTHOR'S NOTE

On the eve of the Second World War, Shanghai was one of the world's only free ports, where no entrance visa was necessary. Between 1939 and 1941, an estimated twenty thousand Jews fled there from Nazi Europe. The refugees included doctors, carpenters, midwives, architects, manual labourers, lawyers. They were rich and poor, old and young, devout and secular. At that time, large parts of Shanghai were governed by several foreign powers: the British and Americans, the French, and the Japanese, who had carved up the city into areas forcibly seceded from the Chinese as a result of treaties and war.

Shanghai's reputation as one of the most fascinating and decadent cities in the world was legendary. There, thousands of miles from home, the Jewish refugees encountered an almost unbearable climate, desperate living conditions, shocking crime, a fierce battle for limited resources and an already overpopulated city. Survival was only possible through ingenuity, industriousness, solidarity and – perhaps most importantly – hope. The Jewish community was to face further hardship in 1943, when all so-called 'stateless refugees' were forced to crowd into Hongkew, a small, enclosed area of the city, where they lived until liberated by the Americans in August 1945.

The characters in this novel are fictional, but personal testimonials, interviews, diaries and contemporary reports inspired their stories. The resources I consulted in my writing of the novel are too many to mention, but I would refer the interested reader to the following in particular: Stella Dong's *Shanghai: The Rise and Fall of a Decadent City* (2000), for a concise and evocative history of the city; Ernest G. Heppner's *Shanghai Refuge: A Memoir of the World War II Jewish Ghetto* (1993) and Samuel Iwry's *To Wear the Dust of War* (2004), for fascinating first-hand accounts of life in 1940's Shanghai; Ulrike Ottinger's documentary *Exil Shanghai* (1997); and *Port of Last Resort: The Diaspora Communities of Shanghai* by Marcia Reynders Ristiano (2003), a highly informative and meticulously researched book about the Jewish communities in Shanghai.

In the novel, I have used the old pinyin spelling of place and street names. Any factual errors or inconsistencies are, of course, my own.

Tragically, for many millions of people, forced exile and diaspora continue to this day, and it is to those – past and present – who have fought for survival and against hopelessness, that this novel is dedicated.

ACKNOWLEDGEMENTS

Special thanks to:

Sonja Mühlberger, for her charming company and insightful conversation about life and survival in the Hongkew ghetto;

Professor Zhou Guojian from the Shanghai Center for Jewish Studies, for giving me a tour of the former Jewish Ghetto in the pouring rain;

Mao *laoshī*, for the basics in Mandarin (多谢);

Professor Steve Hochstadt at Illinois College in Jacksonville, for taking time to share his work and research with me; Tsui-Hua Hsu, for her much-needed help on Mandarin phrases (all and any errors remaining are mine);

Super-agent Jenny Brown, for her untiring support, kindness and hospitality; the entire team at Black and White Publishing, especially Emma Hargrave for her judicious and insightful editing; my cheerleaders Eithne Griffiths and Catherine Warburton; and to my family: Jake, Fay, Amy, June, and of course Chrissi – much love.

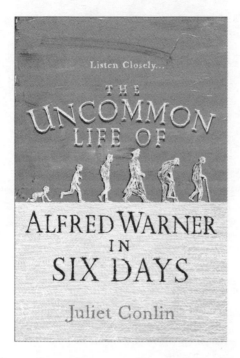

A tour de force of evocative storytelling set against the backdrop of pre-Second World War Germany and post-war Britain.

'Alfred Warner's life is an utterly addictive page-turner.'
Sunshine Radio

'I recommend this book with my heart and soul . . . It's life changing!'
Love Book Groups 5/5

'Unique, gripping and beautifully written . . . I can't recommend it highly enough.'
The Bibliophile Chronicles

www.julietconlin.com